MW00884379

Ivory Obsession

Clarissa Bright

Copyright © 2024 by Clarissa Bright

All rights reserved.

No portion of this book may be reproduced in any form without written permission from
the publisher or author, except as permitted by U.S. copyright law.

Contents

Blurb   1

1. Chapter One: Dante   3

2. Chapter Two: Jade   10

3. Chapter Three: Dante   17

4. Chapter Four: Jade   25

5. Chapter Five: Jade   32

6. Chapter Six: Dante   42

7. Chapter Seven: Dante   55

8. Chapter Eight: Jade   66

9. Chapter Nine: Dante   72

10. Chapter Ten: Jade   80

11. Chapter Eleven: Jade   88

12. Chapter Twelve: Jade   101

13. Chapter Thirteen: Dante   109

14. Chapter Fourteen: Dante   116

15. Chapter Fifteen: Jade   130

16. Chapter Sixteen: Jade   140

17. Chapter Seventeen: Dante 149

18.	Chapter Eighteen: Dante	156
19.	Chapter Nineteen: Dante	162
20.	Chapter Twenty: Jade	168
21.	Chapter Twenty-One: Dante	176
22.	Chapter Twenty-Two: Dante	186
23.	Chapter Twenty-Three: Jade	194
24.	Chapter Twenty-Four: Jade	200
25.	Chapter Twenty-Five: Jade	207
26.	Chapter Twenty-Six: Dante	213
27.	Chapter Twenty-Seven: Jade	219
28.	Chapter Twenty-Eight: Dante	225
29.	Chapter Twenty-Nine: Jade	233
30.	Chapter Thirty: Dante	241
31.	Chapter Thirty-One: Jade	247
32.	Chapter Thirty-Two: Jade	252
33.	Chapter Thirty-Three: Dante	259
34.	Chapter Thirty-Four: Jade	268
35.	Chapter Thirty-Five: Dante	276
36.	Chapter Thirty-Six: Jade	287
37.	Chapter Thirty-Seven: Jade	293
38.	Chapter Thirty-Eight: Dante	300
39.	Chapter Thirty-Nine: Jade	307
40.	Chapter Forty: Jade	313
41.	Chapter Forty-One: Dante	318

Blurb

Obsessed. Powerful. Unmatched. A battle of wills erupts between a city's dark ruler and a brilliant scientist.

Biotech now fuels my business ventures, allowing me to manipulate the city from the shadows...but Dr. Jade Bentley is a variable I never anticipated. Her brilliance is a blinding force that threatens to unravel my plans.

When the opportunity to make Jade's research slip from her grasp pops up, I seize it...but it's not just her work that captivates me.

Jade herself becomes my most intriguing challenge.

Her defiance ignites a fire within me, and her very presence becomes an all-consuming need. I intended to use her, to reign supreme, but my desire for possession has taken a dangerous turn.

In my world, the lines between dominion and desire blur, and Dr. Jade Bentley has become my ultimate prize.

Her resistance fuels my relentless pursuit.

The thought of her escaping my grasp is unacceptable.

Jade Bentley doesn't realize it yet, but she's mine – body, soul, and groundbreaking intellect.

And I am hopelessly, utterly consumed by her.

I just need to make her see it, too.

Fans of Olivia Blair, Zoe Blake and Sam Mariano will love this slow-burn curvy surprise pregnancy mafia romance!

Buy Ivory Obsession to start this spicy mafia prince series today.

Chapter One: Dante

I was about to confront my father.

Confront wasn't exactly the right word; this was more like a pitch. But it still made me feel sick to my stomach. Enzo Moretti didn't love change and I'd already disappointed him enough by not doing exactly what he asked of me. It wasn't that I was unable to find a way and settle down–it was just that there were so many other things to do beyond bribery and money-laundering.

I knew our operation could be so much bigger...if only he would listen to me.

I stood in the heart of power, the Moretti study—a sanctuary of dark woods and history etched into every piece of furniture. The walls were lined with memories, each one whispering tales of dominance and ruthlessness. I felt their eyes on me, the silent witnesses to our family's legacy, as I dared to disturb the stillness with my proposition.

My father's fingers were interlaced in front of his face, his eyes dark behind his reading glasses. "I don't know about this," he mumbled.

"Dad, please. Biotech is the future," I insisted, the leather of the chair beneath my hands groaning as I leaned forward. My fingers danced in the air, tracing the outline of an empire rejuvenated by science. My gaze darted around the room, landing on a dusty DNA helix model tucked away on a shelf behind a stack of ledgers.

I picked it up, turning it over in my hands, trying to ground myself with the feeling of the cold metal on my fingertips.

My dad sighed.

"With this, we can mend bone and flesh in hours, not days. We gain the upper hand, no longer just survivors but reigning sovereigns on a battlefield that's evolving daily. Think about it...We might not even have to pay doctors. We might not have to worry about which hospital to go to. I know it sounds like crazy scifi stuff, but beyond practical applications for our op, what about selling this technology to the highest bidder? Presidents, leaders–we'd be rich beyond measure."

Enzo sat across from me, his figure a shadow against the waning light filtering through the window. His face was stoic, chiseled from the same stone as the men who came before him, unyielding and cold.

"Your head's in the clouds, Dante." His voice was a low rumble, a warning bell tolling in the late afternoon quiet of our Little Italy stronghold. "You speak of playing God, but forget the devil we know best. Our strength lies not in meddling with nature but in the bonds of loyalty and fear we cultivate. People give us money to protect them, Dante. They do that for a reason."

"Father, those bonds break, flesh tears. This...this is control like we've never had." My words spilled out, hot and fast, contrasting his measured tone. "We'd be untouchable."

"Or exposed," he countered, his gaze sharp as a knife's edge. "Every new venture comes with risks. And this miracle healing thing? It puts a spotlight on us when we should be melting into the shadows."

"Then let's be the ones holding the spotlight," I shot back, my heart hammering against my chest in a rhythm I couldn't silence. "Let others cower in our light."

Enzo's eyes, the color of storm clouds over the city, narrowed slightly. He considered me, his eldest son, as if I were a puzzle he'd yet to solve—a piece that didn't quite fit the family portrait.

"Passion blinds you, Dante," he said at last. "It makes you easy prey for those waiting for us to falter."

"Or it's the very thing that will ensure we don't," I replied.

My father leaned back, his hands stilling in front of his face. "I wish you'd drop this," he said. "Stop sleeping around with whichever slut falls in your bed and find a nice Italian girl to marry. Why can't you do that?"

"Suitable brides are not the mortar that will fortify our empire, Father," I said, my voice steady despite the unease brewing within me. Enzo's suggestion had struck a chord, one that resonated with defiance. The room seemed to shrink around us, the air thick with the weight of unspoken truths.

"Family alliances have always been our way, Dante. You would do well to remember that," he replied, his tone suggesting that this was more command than counsel.

My fingers inadvertently traced the spine of an old ledger on his desk, the leather cracked and worn like the traditions he clung to.

"I haven't forgotten," I murmured, almost to myself as much as to him. Then, almost unconsciously, my hand found the DNA helix model that I'd put down just a second ago—a symbol of possibility. I twisted it slowly, feeling each metal rung turn beneath my fingertips.

"Science is not our world," my father's voice broke through my thoughts, a low growl that spoke of a time when might ruled and questions were quelled with force. His eyes flicked to the helix in my hand, and his disapproval was palpable.

"Times change. We have to adapt or be left behind," I countered, setting the helix down with a resolve that mirrored the steel in my voice. "Our empire was built on discretion and brute strength, yes. But we live in an age where intelligence can be just as deadly."

Enzo met my gaze, his skepticism a fortress wall I had yet to breach. There was a chasm between us, widening with every word, every idea that strayed from the path he had trodden for so long.

"Your ideas are dangerous, son," he warned, though I could hear the undercurrent of fear in his voice.

"Only to those who fail to see their potential," I shot back, unwilling to let his doubt become mine.

"Then prove it," Enzo challenged, his voice a gravelly test of my convictions. "Show me how this 'new world' business can strengthen the Morettis without betraying what we stand for."

I inhaled deeply, the weight of legacy pressing down on me. My reply came not as an eager son but as a man ready to lead. "I will. I'll bring us into the future, even if I have to drag us there kicking and screaming."

"And if you don't?" The Don's words hung heavy in the air between us.

"Then I'll do as you say," I conceded with a reluctant nod. "I'm nearly thirty; I'll choose a wife." The prospect loomed over me, yet another chain to bind me to tradition.

Enzo nodded, satisfied with the hedge he'd built around my ambition. But our standoff had only just begun. The old grandfather clock in the corner ticked away the time, each beat a heavy footstep marching toward an uncertain future.

"As you know, my concern is that biotech sounds like a beacon that'll draw unwanted eyes to our operations," Enzo said, his voice carrying the weariness of battles fought in shadows.

"Perhaps," I allowed, standing up to pace slowly before the vast expanse of his desk. "Or perhaps it's a shield that mends our wounds faster than our enemies can inflict them."

My frustration grew, a thorny vine wrapping around my resolve. How could I make him see that standing still was no longer an option?

"I'm serious, Dad. This could change everything."

His silence stretched out, suffocating, his gaze holding mine. His eyes, once the sharp edge of a blade, now looked like they carried the weight of all the years he'd been at war – with other families, with the law, and perhaps with the relentless march of time itself.

"Fine," he said finally, his voice low, "give me the details."

I leaned forward, bracing my hands on the polished mahogany that had borne witness to countless Moretti decisions. "It's simple. We start small, an off-the-books project with minimal investment. If it doesn't pay off, we cut our losses—minimal damage to the family."

Enzo's eyes narrowed, considering. "And if you're wrong?"

"I'm not," I replied, my confidence unwavering. "But if I am, you'll have your scapegoat."

A muscle ticked in his jaw, the only sign of his internal struggle. I pressed on before doubt could poison the ground I'd gained. "Think of the advantages, Father. We're not just talking about patching up after a fight quicker. Biotech might be able to enhance our men, I don't know. I do know that it'll make us rich beyond measure."

The air turned thick as my words settled around us, mingling with the scent of old books that lined the walls. The very essence of power and possibility seemed to seep into the room, wrapping its tendrils around Enzo's old-world caution.

"I don't know," he said. "How can you make sure this op is discreet?"

I had to use the ace up my sleeve.

"Arturo Caruso would love nothing more than to see us falter," I said, my voice steady but edged with urgency. His eyes met mine, a silent battle waged in the space between us. "He's a shark smelling blood in the water. If we don't evolve, he'll tear us apart." The truth of my words hung heavy in the room as I watched my father process the gravity of the situation.

Enzo's features hardened, the lines on his face deepening with the weight of decades spent defending our name. "The Carusos have always been vultures waiting for scraps," he spat, his distaste for our rivals clear as day.

"Then let's not give them the satisfaction," I countered, pressing the advantage. "We can't let our guard down now. Not when there's so much at stake."

I could almost hear the cogs turning in Enzo's head as he mulled over my proposition. His next move was critical; it would shape the future of our family and either cement our legacy or herald its decline.

"Other families are adapting, embracing the new ways," I continued, sensing the moment to drive my point home. "They're pulling ahead while we cling to old methods. We need to innovate, or we'll be left in their dust."

Enzo's gaze remained fixed on me, searching for the conviction behind my words. He seemed to be weighing every possible outcome, every risk and reward. Then, slowly, the edges of his mouth twitched—a reluctant acceptance that change was inevitable.

He was silent for a long time, his expression unreadable. Then, slowly, he nodded. "Proceed with this trial. But Dante," he said, his voice heavy with a warning, "don't forget who we are. Don't forget the blood that runs through your veins."

"Understood," I said, straightening up.

"And son? If you fuck this up, you won't just need to find a new wife," he said. "You'll have to find a new job, a new place to live. I've given you enough chances, Dante. It's time for you to step the fuck up. Now get out of my office before I change my mind."

Chapter Two: Jade

I was on the edge of a breakthrough. I knew it.

I just had to keep working...for a little longer.

The hum of the lab equipment was a steady backdrop as I leaned in, adjusting the focus on the microscope. Ellie was right there with me, peering over my shoulder, her breath warm against my cheek. The slide beneath the lens was our world, tiny and teeming with potential.

"Come on," I muttered under my breath, willing the shapes to make sense, to align with the hypothesis that had kept us chained to this lab for what felt like an eternity.

There it was. A pattern emerged, distinct and undeniable. My heart kicked up a notch, thumping loud in the silence of the lab. "Ellie, look!" My finger jabbed toward the eyepiece, but she was already locked in, her gaze narrowing with concentration.

"Wait...is that—?" Her voice trailed off, anticipation hanging between us.

I couldn't contain the grin that stretched across my face. "It is." I straightened, my spine popping from hours hunched over. "Ellie, I think we've done it! This could change everything!"

"Well, if it is replicable," she said softly. "The unique cell signaling pathway might not be reproducible..."

"Yes, thank you Dr. Spoilsport, I know how science works," I said.

Ellie chuckled, her hazel eyes twinkling with amusement. "I know you do, Jade." Her hand came to rest on my shoulder, a comforting pressure. "I'm just making sure we don't lose ourselves in the excitement. We celebrate the milestone achieved, but remember we have plenty of work ahead."

She was right, of course. My grin eased into a thoughtful smile. The discovery was monumental, but Ellie's words grounded me in reality. There was still much more to do. "Well, I was happy."

She gave me a teasing smile, her brown eyes glinting under the harsh lab lights. "I know. Someone has to keep you grounded, Jade," she replied, her voice filled with camaraderie and just a touch of pride.

Our laughter filled the lab, a welcome interruption to the monotonous drone of the machines. It was these moments – shared success and shared jokes – that made the grueling process not just bearable but meaningful.

We reveled in the breakthrough for a moment, the weight of the discovery momentarily lifting from our shoulders. But the celebratory mood was short-lived. Ellie glanced at her watch, a flicker of frustration crossing her features.

We returned our gazes onto the slide, my heart still pounding with a primal kind of excitement, a mix of fear and anticipation at what this discovery could entail. The world beyond our microscope seemed suddenly insignificant, like the universe had folded in on itself until it was just us and our groundbreaking research in this compact slice of existence.

"We should test it over a larger sample," Ellie said after a while, her tone serious once again as she switched from friend to scientist. She handed me another batch of slides we had prepared earlier. "And then we should go out and celebrate."

I took the slides from her, relishing the sense of purpose they held within their thin glass layers. "Agreed," I replied, the joy of discovery still simmering beneath my practiced professionalism. "Then we take the world by storm."

Hours dissolved into more hours, as we tested slide after slide, our eyes glued to the microscope and hands moving with a practiced ease. The bubbling excitement had settled into a concentrated focus, suspended somewhere between hopeful anticipation and calculated reality.

"Actually, we can't take the world by storm today," Ellie said softly. "The gala."

"Fuck, yes, the gala," I muttered under my breath. "Why do we need to do that again?"

"Because we want to keep our jobs," she replied simply.

I sighed, the frustration apparent in the huff of air that escaped my lips. The thought of suits and gowns and a room full of people who cared more about the bottom line than the scientific breakthrough seemed so distant from our world beneath the microscope. "Right," I muttered, staring at the slide before me, "We need to keep our jobs."

I could imagine Ellie's soft smile behind me, an understanding nod at our shared distaste for the politics of it all. I felt her presence shift as she walked away from the microscope, her steps echoing lightly against the sterile lab floor. "Well, at least we can make it bearable," she called over her shoulder. "Might even be fun if you decide to pull one of your infamous pranks."

"You think I should prank a suit?" I asked.

"I think if you tried, no one would blame you," she said.

I laughed, glancing over my shoulder to toss her a playful smirk. That was Ellie for you - always encouraging me in my mischief, even while keeping me grounded. Her comment sparked an idea in my mind, gears turning with the prospect of bringing some fun into the all-too-serious gala.

"Prank a suit, huh?" I mused aloud, my eyes wandering back to the slide beneath the microscope. "Now that's a thought."

Ellie chuckled from her perch by the lab counter, already organizing our findings into presentable reports. "Don't get too carried away," she cautioned, though there was a twinkle in her eye as she added, "Or at least make sure I've got a good view."

"Didn't you just say we needed to keep our jobs?"

"Yeah," she said. "I meant something harmless. Untraceable."

I snorted, the sound echoing around the otherwise silent lab. "Untraceable, you say? Now where's the fun in that?"

Ellie simply shook her head, an indulgent smile playing on her lips. She flicked through our compiled research, her brow furrowing as she scanned it for errors. "I suppose I have only myself to blame for encouraging you."

"Suppose so," I agreed, turning my attention back to the microscope. The familiar shapes of cells swam into view, their structure almost comforting in its complexity. Yet beneath that conventional facade laid the potential for a revolution, a new world order within the medical field. Our discovery.

The enormity of it suddenly hit me, a wave of realization so profound it took my breath away. We were on the brink of something monumental and nobody knew it yet. Well, almost nobody.

"Do you think he'll be there?" she said wistfully as I busied myself with the upcoming slides. I paused, immediately knowing exactly who she was referring to.

"Our mysterious benefactor?" I asked, keeping my tone as casual as possible. We seldom discussed our elusive funder, the shadowy figurehead of the companies that kept our work afloat. The mere mention of him brought an unwanted chill into our warm lab. "Well, if he is, there's no way for us to know, right?"

"Right. Maybe don't do anything then," she said. "And let's not mention any breakthroughs tonight. I think it might be best if we...I don't know, keep it on the downlow for now."

"I'm not going to talk about unverified research to a man in a suit with a degree in finance," I replied. "What do you think I am?"

"A reckless genius?" Ellie ventured, her voice half-teasing, half-serious. The corners of her lips tugged upward into a gentle smile, the amusement in her eyes softening the sternness of her words.

I laughed at that, shaking my head in mock disapproval. "Reckless? Maybe. But genius? Always." I turned to face her fully, my attention momentarily drawn away from the microscope. "And don't worry about tonight. I may be playful, but I know when to be serious."

"Okay, so don't talk about unverified research with a suit, don't sleep with a suit—"

"—and definitely don't prank a suit," I finished for her, my eyebrows raised in feigned innocence. She let out a laugh that rang through the sterile lab, her amusement evident in the way her eyes crinkled at the corners.

"Right," she retorted sarcastically, her smile still playing across her lips as she shook her head. "I feel like I should add 'don't get arrested' to the list, but I have a feeling that won't deter you either."

"Oh, you know me too well," I said, grinning at the playful accusation. Our banter was familiar, almost comforting amidst the daunting reality of our discovery and its implications.

We then returned to our individual tasks; Ellie meticulously compiling and examining our research data, while I continued analyzing slides under the microscope.

As the hours passed and the room darkened with the setting sun, our conversations began to dwindle, replaced by the hum of high-tech equipment and the scratch of pen against paper as we dedicated ourselves to our respective tasks. It felt like we were in our own little world, lost amongst cells and notes and a future teetering on the brink of our discovery.

Eventually, Ellie broke the silence. "I think we've done enough for today," she said softly, her voice a pleasant interruption to the monotony of my observations. I glanced up from the microscope, blinking away my intense focus.

"Already?" I murmured, looking over at her. Ellie was standing by our cluttered workbench, her hand still resting on a stack of completed reports.

"We need to get ready," she said. "We both need to go home and, you know, wash the science off of us."

"Right, the glamourous world of red wine and black ties awaits," I said with a sigh, tearing myself away from the microscope. I wasn't particularly thrilled about the event, but it was a part of our jobs, one that couldn't be ignored.

Ellie chuckled, her gaze softening as she watched me stand from my seat. "You know," she began in a thoughtful tone, "I always find it amusing when you rumble about these events."

"You do?" I asked.

Ellie nodded, her hands already busy tidying up some of the scattered papers on our shared desk. Her efficiency was a stark contrast to my own haphazard work habits. I watched her for a moment, appreciating her quiet dedication to our cause. "I mean, you look stunning, and you seem to enjoy yourself," she said. "If one of those men wasn't our mysterious benefactor, I would tell you to take one home tonight. After the last few weeks, you deserve to get laid."

I burst out laughing, the sudden sound echoing throughout the lab. It was typical Ellie; under her professional demeanor and composed exterior, she had a knack for throwing curveballs that threw me off guard.

"Really, El?" I choked out between laughs, my eyes watering at her unexpected advice. "You're now my wingwoman?"

"I mean," she said. "You're not doing it for yourself. And what's the harm in a little one-night-stand? You don't call him back, nothing happens. It's just a little fun. You need a fuckbuddy."

"Do you have any suggestions?" I asked.

"What about Dante Moretti? I saw how you were looking at him at that conference," she said.

I shook my head. "The hobbyist? You think he dabbles in scientists too?"

"Hey, you never know until you try," Ellie replied.

I shook my head. "Babe, I don't think I stand a chance with a man that good-looking," I said. "He's probably already sleeping with some sort of model or something."

"Oh my God. Just try it. What's the worst that could happen?" she asked, laughing.

"What if he's *the* benefactor?"

"That guy? That guy is only a benefactor to his own bank account," she said. "I think that one's a safe bet."

"Right," I said. "You're right."

Maybe she was right. But at that moment, I couldn't have known that Dante Moretti would turn out to be far more than I had ever bargained for.

Chapter Three: Dante

Tonight was about proving myself.

The cufflinks clicked into place, their coolness a reminder of the armor I once wore. In my old room's half-light, shadows clung to the corners as if even they knew to keep their distance from a Moretti. I straightened the lines of my suit, the fabric whispering over my skin, an echo of a life I was shackled to by blood and honor.

"Another night, another charade," I murmured, catching my reflection's eye in the mirror. The man staring back had the same hard jaw and calculated gaze that had become my trademark—the mask of Dante Moretti, the dutiful son.

Behind me, Marco's hands were a stark red against the white of the money he counted, his laugh a low rumble that didn't quite reach his eyes. "You clean up well," he said.

He didn't look up from his task, his focus unbreakable—a trait we both inherited from our father, Enzo, The Don.

"Isn't that what we do best?" I shot back, adjusting my tie with a practiced ease.

"I haven't mastered cosplaying yet," he said, looking at the stack of bills in his hand.

Laughter filtered up the stairs, soft and warm like a blanket I couldn't afford to wrap myself in. Ma's cooking—the scent of rich tomato sauce and fresh basil—wafted through the air, tugging at something deep within. Home. It was *supposed* to feel like home, yet here I was, preparing to step out and secure another piece for the empire. The dissonance between the family I loved and the life I led was never more evident than in these moments before the performance began.

"You okay, big man?" Marco asked, his hands stilling.

"Still haven't gotten used to suits," I said.

He nodded. "You said this is all for the family," Marco said, finally glancing up, his gaze sharp despite the red on his hands. It was a reminder, one I didn't need but took all the same.

"Always for the family," I agreed, my voice steady as I left the ghost of my childhood behind, each step down the stairwell heavy with purpose. The laughter grew louder, the scents stronger, but my mind was already on the night ahead. Tonight, I wasn't just Dante Moretti. Tonight, I was the future of the Moretti legacy, and nothing could shake my resolve.

"Right, well, I should be off…"

"Come on, Dante," Marco's voice chased me toward the exit of the bedroom, his words punctuated by the crisp snap of rubber bands as he bundled the money. "You sure you wouldn't rather roll with me tonight? The biotech fundraiser can't be that interesting. This could be for the family too. Mom would flip if you gave her a grandson."

I turned back to look at him, the corners of my mouth twitching despite myself. "Trust me, nothing sounds more appealing than escaping to wherever you're heading, but some of us have responsibilities beyond…what was it? Thongs in yoga pants?"

Marco grinned, unabashed. "Man, I'm telling you, there's nothing like it. It's art, Dante. Pure, unadulterated art."

"Art?" I scoffed. "I prefer a masterpiece of the mind. There's something about a woman who knows her genome from her genomics, if you catch my drift."

"Ah, brains over beauty, huh?" Marco teased, shaking his head. "You always were the deep one."

"Beauty fades, brother. Intelligence is forever sexy." I couldn't help the smirk that danced on my lips. Marco and I might be cut from the same cloth, but our patterns were worlds apart.

"Suit yourself." He shrugged, turning back to his counting. "But when you're bored out of your mind listening to science talk, just remember the offer stands."

"Science talk is exactly my kind of party." I gave him a mock salute before grabbing my keys off the bed closest to me. "And don't forget to clean up before dinner. Ma's spaghetti deserves respect."

"Her wooden spoon demands it," Marco replied, laughing. "Go, show those rich folk how the Morettis charm their way to power."

I shook my head, my keys jingling in my hands. "Well, how did you do it?"

"Baseball bat," he replied, flashing me a toothy smile from the desk we'd use so many times to do our homework on. I looked behind me, at the baseball bat leaning against his childhood bed, decorated by tiny specks of drying blood.

"Baseball bat," I echoed, shaking my head in mock disappointment. "Marco, you're such a simpleton."

"Hey, watch it." He wagged a finger at me. "I've got brains too, just...more practical ones."

"Practical?" My chuckle was sharp, cutting through the thick tension that always seemed to hover around us. "You mean the kind that gets you into trouble with Enzo?"

"You're the one who's going to be in trouble with Dad if you don't deliver whatever it is that you promised. But, hey, at least he can't beat the shit out of you anymore. You're a little old for that."

I chewed the inside of my mouth. "True, but don't forget who we're dealing with here." I paused by the door, letting my eyes roam over the heirlooms of our legacy—the portraits that seemed to judge every move we made. "Enzo hasn't softened with age. Cross him, and he'd cast me out without a second thought."

"Like hell he would," Marco snorted. "Not while I'm around."

"Your loyalty is touching." I meant it, despite the hard shell I'd built around my heart. "Just don't let your guard down."

"Never." His gaze met mine, steady and unflinching. "And hey," he added, softer now, "be careful out there, Dante. We need you back in one piece."

"Always am." With a last look at those silent sentinels on the wall, I stepped into the fading light of dusk. "Love you, brother."

"Love you too, man." Marco's voice was a low murmur, almost lost in the hum of Little Italy waking up for the evening. I gave my mother a kiss good night and waved goodbye at my father as I left my childhood home.

The streets were alive with the pulse of the city as I made my way to my car. The familiar smells of garlic and tomato sauce mingled with the exhaust fumes, a reminder of where I came from—and what I stood to gain tonight.

Tonight wasn't just about power plays and winning over the elite; it was about proving myself, not just as Enzo's son or a Moretti, but as Dante. My own man. A man on a mission to carve his path, even if it was shadowed by the family name.

I was going to prove to my father that investing in biotech was the future. That it was what was best for the family.

I slid into the driver's seat, the cool leather of the car seat hugging me like a silent ally. The engine purred to life with a twist of my wrist, a sound that never failed to send a thrill through me. I maneuvered the sleek vehicle out onto the street, leaving Little Italy's embrace for the wider avenues that led towards the gala.

As I drove, the neighborhoods transitioned from the familiar, worn cobblestones to the polished concrete of the city's affluent heart. It was like watching my own reflection change in the rearview mirror, shifting from the gritty heir of a crime family to the polished exterior I needed to present to the world tonight. The streets were a map of my own evolution, each one leading me further into the role I had to play—sinner and savior, both wrapped up in a tailored suit.

Parking down the street from the gala, I killed the engine and sat for a moment, taking in the scene. The mockingbird's song filled the air, a serene melody that contrasted sharply with the tension coiling in my gut. Funny how a bird could sing so sweetly when it was all about deception, mimicking others to survive. Not so different from me then, I mused, stepping out into the evening air.

The bird's trill followed me as I locked the car and adjusted my jacket, the fabric moving easily over my frame. I was ready for this; I'd been ready for a long time. All those years of being groomed for power, of learning how to hide my true self behind a smile and a handshake—they were all leading to this moment. And yet, there was an edge to it now, a sense of something more personal at stake.

Jade Brantley. She didn't know it yet, but she was the reason tonight mattered more than any other social engagement I'd ever attended. Her work, her mind—it was the future. And I wanted—no, need-ed—to be a part of that. Not just for the family, but for me.

I had followed her research with near fanaticism. If I wanted to take our family business into the future, this was exactly what I had to do.

Taking a deep breath, I started towards the gala. The evening air clung to my skin, whispering secrets of what might unfold if I played my cards right. Tonight wasn't just another night. Tonight was when everything could change.

As I approached the entrance to the gala, the familiar scent of wealth and entitlement filled my nostrils. The doorman nodded, recognizing the signet ring that adorned my finger, a subtle symbol of my status within the city's hidden hierarchy. I couldn't help but smirk; they all played their parts in the grand theater of high society, blissfully unaware of the puppet master walking among them.

I was greeted by the murmur of the gala, a sound that felt like slipping into a well-tailored suit—familiar and contemptuously comfortable. Air kisses landed on cheeks with the precision of a rehearsed play, one I knew all too well. Smiling benefactors clapped me on the back, their eyes hungry for glimpses of the man behind the Moretti name. I indulged them with nods and half-smiles, my gaze never truly meeting theirs.

"Mr. Moretti, always a pleasure," cooed a woman with a practiced smile, her hand lingering just a second too long on my arm.

"Likewise," I replied, my voice smooth like aged whiskey, yet devoid of sincerity.

I moved through the crowd with ease, my every gesture exuding the controlled grace expected from a man of my standing. Yet, internally, I was on the hunt, searching for the unsuspecting key to my ambitious plans—a key dressed in intellect and wrapped in allure.

"Your generosity knows no bounds, Dante," a man said, raising his glass towards me. "To the children's foundation, may your contributions bring hope."

"Here's to hope," I echoed, clinking my glass against his. But my thoughts were elsewhere, calculating, always calculating. Tonight was a chessboard, and I intended to leave with a queen.

My focus was interrupted, not by another empty toast or a veiled business proposition, but by a sight that commanded my full attention. Across the room, framed by the mingling crowd, stood Dr. Jade Brantley. I'd seen her before, of course, at those sterile conferences where she spoke of DNA and genomes with an excitement that was almost palpable. But tonight, away from the fluorescent hum of lab lights, she was different, breathtaking.

Her dark hair cascaded down her shoulders in soft waves, a stark contrast to the severity of her usual lab bun. The dress she wore hugged her curves, a testament to her femininity that left little to the imagination yet remained tasteful, elegant. Her posture radiated confidence, the tilt of her chin like a challenge to any man who dared approach her—and it felt like many did.

I watched, intrigued, as she navigated the advances with polite dismissal, her laughter genuine but reserved. The academic world knew Dr. Brantley as a rising star, but tonight, under the chandeliers' glow, she was more than a keen mind in a sea of intellect; she was a siren amidst the waves, and I found myself inexplicably drawn to her song.

Okay, so I absolutely had a type. But I needed to remind myself that Jade Brantley was a means to an end, not a woman I was dying to sleep with. Though she was...also that.

So when she picked up her head and flashed me a shy smile, her cheeks reddening under the electric light of the grand chandeliers, I took a chance.

And I pounced.

Chapter Four: Jade

I was so out of place here.

I slipped through the grand entrance of the Upper East Side's most opulent event space, the echo of my heels lost amidst a symphony of clinking glasses and cultured laughter. Friday evening had draped New York City in its finest, but the splendor of the charity gala could have been a universe away from the sterile confines of BioHQ lab where I toiled over petri dishes and gene sequences.

"Stick with me, Jade," Ellie murmured, her grip on my arm both comforting and grounding. The weight of our mission settled on my shoulders like a lead cloak—we were here to sell our life's work, to charm the deep pockets into funding our research.

She looked gorgeous; her curls tamed into an intricate updo, her petite form adorned in a glittering black dress that fit her like a second skin. She had a way of holding herself that commanded attention, and I couldn't help but admire her charisma. I was sure I didn't look half as good, though I'd done my best. I was wearing a navy-blue dress that accentuated my curves, the fabric hugging my body with a subtle allure. The plunging neckline was a divergence from my usual high-neck blouses and lab coats, but Ellie had insisted that we blend in with the elite crowd.

I had straightened my hair, letting it fall around my shoulders in a cascade of dark silk, the stark contrast to my ice-blue eyes. As I caught sight of myself in one of the many gilded mirrors adorning the hall, I couldn't shake off the feeling of playing a part - of being a scientist dressed up as a socialite.

Our plan was simple, or at least Ellie made it sound that way. Mingle with the city's influential and convince them of the importance of our biotech research. Only, these were not my people. I would have felt more at home discussing genome sequencing with my lab rat colonies than trying to impress these bejeweled socialites with palatable science chatter.

The room was a carousel of wealth and influence, each face another opportunity, every handshake a potential lifeline to keep our experiments running. I repeated the key points of our project in my head, refining the pitch to perfection as Ellie's eyes flicked across the crowd, identifying the movers and shakers with the precision of a hawk eyeing prey.

"Remember, these people invest in confidence just as much as they do in ideas," Ellie reminded me, her voice a whisper lost in the hum of conversations and orchestral strings playing somewhere in the distance. It was true; we had to be the embodiment of the innovation we promised—poised, persuasive, unyieldingly passionate.

"Why isn't this Dr. White's job?" I said. "Why do we have to be here? We're just lackeys."

"Because we're women," Ellie replied. "Women in STEM. Looks good to investors."

I laughed quietly. "That's gross, El."

"Hey, I didn't make the rules," she replied. "You remember what we talked about?"

"Yes, pretend to be confident," I said, though my stomach twisted into knots at the thought of delivering our spiel to the city's elite, whose interest in biotechnology likely began and ended at the tax deductions it provided.

Ellie gave my hand a quick, reassuring squeeze before releasing it, leaving me to navigate this sea of potential benefactors on my own. I took a deep breath, clutching the stem of my wine glass like a lifeline, and prepared to dive into the depths.

Just as I steadied my nerves to take the plunge, Ellie's path veered off course. Mrs. White, Dr. Stuart White's wife approached her. She looked beautiful with her silver hair coiffed into an intricate updo and diamonds at her throat, catching Ellie by the arm with a gloved hand. "Dr. Harper," she trilled, her voice carrying a melody of old money and practiced charm, "you simply must meet some friends of mine."

Ellie cast a glance back at me, her eyes apologetic but insistent—this was an opportunity we couldn't afford to miss. With a reluctant nod, she allowed Mrs. White to steer her towards a cluster of potential donors, each one more imposing than the last.

Alone now, the gala seemed to swell around me, its opulence suddenly suffocating. The laughter was too loud, the smiles too bright, the clinking of glassware piercing. My life's work, hours upon hours spent in the sterile sanctuary of the lab, felt inconsequential—a mere whisper drowned out by the symphony of self-indulgence that played on around me.

I shifted uncomfortably, aware of the space Ellie's absence left beside me. She was the extrovert, the schmoozer, the one who could charm skeptics into believers with nothing but her wit and a well-placed fact. Without her, I was just a scientist out of her element, adrift in a sea of tailored suits and silk gowns that whispered along the marble floor as their wearers glided past.

"Focus, Jade," I told myself. "Remember why you're here." The mantra was a feeble attempt to anchor me to the mission at hand. I took a sip of wine, its bubbles doing little to lift the weight of isolation pressing against my chest as I watched Ellie mingle, her laughter reaching me from across the room like a lifeline I couldn't quite grasp.

Still, I knew I had to try. For the sake of our research, for the future that hung precariously on the whims of these strangers, I would have to find my footing and step forward into the tide. But oh, how vast the ocean seemed without Ellie by my side.

The wine in my hand was just one more prop in a scene I didn't understand. It's not like the crisp taste could wash away the tension knotted in my stomach. I scanned the crowd again, hoping for someone to latch onto, someone who looked like they believed in more than just the next big investment opportunity.

That's when he caught my eye.

Across the room, surrounded by a pack of well-dressed vultures, stood a man with an aura that commanded attention without begging for it. The soft lighting seemed to wrap around him like a spotlight meant only for him. He was a stark figure against the opulence of the gala, a silent testament to power and restraint.

I'd seen him before, and my breath caught in my throat.

Dante Moretti.

His presence was a gravitational pull, and before I knew it, my body had inched closer, as if on its own accord. My eyes traced the lines of his face, noting the sharp jawline and the way his dark hair fell just so, brushing against his brow with a casual elegance that seemed almost out of place amidst the rest.

I shook my head slightly, trying to dispel the ridiculous thoughts that clouded my mind. Ellie had mentioned him...but I was telling myself that he was completely out of my league.

His eyes met mine, and in that moment, the clamor of the room seemed to mute, the world narrowing down to the silent conversation between us.

I could feel my cheeks burning.

But just as quickly as our connection sparked, it extinguished. Another well-dressed figure approached him, hand extended, and Dante's focus shifted. The intensity that had cocooned us evaporated, leaving me strangely hollow. Who was I kidding? Men like him didn't look twice at women like me—not unless they wanted something. And yet, I hadn't been able to decipher what lay behind his fleeting interest.

I took a small sip of my wine, the effervescence failing to lift the weight that had settled in my chest. It wasn't like me to be so affected by someone—especially someone whose name I barely even knew. This wasn't part of my meticulously planned evening.

"Dr. Bentley," a voice called, jolting me from my thoughts.

"Right here," I answered, turning towards the source—a potential investor I recognized from a recent biotech conference. As we engaged in the necessary pleasantries and discussed my work, I couldn't help but feel the draw of Dante's gravity, my attention split between my words and the place in the crowd where he had stood.

The crowd around me buzzed with a mix of greed and ambition, yet all I could feel was the silent pull toward the man who now monopolized my every thought. Dante Moretti, a name that rolled off the tongue with an exotic and dangerous cadence, was an enigma, his aura thick with unspoken power and secrets.

"Dr. Bentley, are you sure you're alright?" the investor asked, concern lining his face as he caught my distracted gaze.

"Absolutely," I assured him, snapping back to attention. "Forgive me, just... considering the next phase of our project." A lie that tasted bitter on my tongue, but necessary to mask my unruly fascination. "You were saying you're interested in the research?"

I really hoped he was going to mention his own name, but he didn't.

"Yes, indeed," he said, straightening his bowtie. "Your work on genetic sequencing is most impressive, Dr. Bentley. I am curious to know about the potential applications."

I nodded, trying to focus on the conversation and push all thoughts of Dante Moretti away. Now was not the time to fantasize about a man who would barely ever look my way.

"Well, the science behind genetic sequencing has the potential to revolutionize medicine," I began, launching into the rehearsed spiel Ellie and I had practiced when faced with potential investors.

He listened attentively, nodding along and prompting me with thoughtful questions. But as I spoke, my gaze kept wandering back to Dante, magnetically drawn to him. I could see him engaging in hushed conversations with various guests, his charming smile never reaching his eyes.

"The implications are enormous," I continued, "from identifying predisposition to genetic diseases to revolutionizing personalized medicine." The investor seemed interested, nodding along and asking thoughtful questions – a refreshing change from the apathy an unfortunate majority of these high-flyers had shown tonight. Feeling a surge of hope, I found myself warming up to the conversation.

He was listening until someone called him. "Excuse me for a second, Dr. Bentley," he said. "Don't go anywhere. I want to continue this conversation."

"Of course," I said.

And then he turned away, and all the work that I had done seemed to disappear in smoke. I had a horrible headache and it was only getting worse. Ellie was still engaged in conversation with Dr. White's wife and my gaze immediately went to Dante Moretti again, who was speaking to the most beautiful woman I had ever seen in my life.

The night had been a wash. Things weren't going anywhere and I just needed to get away-go home and curl up with a book, leave the fundraising to the person who was good at it, and make use of my vibrator as I thought about the hottest man I'd ever seen in real life.

Maybe I'd just need to go back to being successful in the lab, since clearly, I wasn't going to be successful at this party.

That's why I had to get away.

Chapter Five: Jade

I tried to get away...but I couldn't.

The investor might have abandoned me, but there were other people beckoning me toward them. Swallowing hard, I tightened my grip on the delicate stem of the wine glass, its contents untouched. The thrumming pulse of the party beckoned me to blend in, but every cell in my body screamed for an exit. Instead, I forced one foot in front of the other, slipping between clusters of tailored suits and silk gowns.

"Dr. Bentley," they'd say, their smiles as rehearsed as mine, "tell us about your work."

I did. Over and over, the same pitch, my voice steady even as my hands betrayed a subtle tremble. I squeezed the cool glass, the condensation a welcome distraction from the lukewarm handshakes and vacant gazes. My research was groundbreaking, the future of biotechnology – I believed it with every fiber of my being. But belief doesn't fund labs or buy equipment.

The nods came easy, their eyes glazed with polite disinterest. I could almost hear the doors of opportunity slamming shut with each cordial, "We'll be in touch." It was a dance I knew too well, each step measured, each twirl leaving me slightly more dizzy and disheartened.

"Exciting stuff," one investor murmured before his gaze slid past me, seeking out someone else, something more promising. I smiled, nodded, and moved on. My fingers brushed against the rim of the untouched wine, the temptation momentarily flickering before I shoved it down. Wine wouldn't steady my nerves; it was clarity I needed, not cloudiness.

With each encounter, my smile stretched tighter across my face, a mask that hid the frustration simmering just below the surface. I was a scientist, not a salesman, yet here I was, peddling my life's work like some cheap trinket. I wondered if they could sense the desperation behind my well-rehearsed spiel, if that was what turned them away.

"Your dedication is admirable, Dr. Bentley," another empty suit remarked before drifting off into the crowd.

My glass still full, I resisted the urge to take a sip. Wine wouldn't steady my nerves; it was clarity I needed, not cloudiness. I circulated through the room, my heart sinking a little more with each superficial exchange. But I couldn't afford to show weakness, not here, not in the lion's den where every predator was looking for their next prey. And in this world, vulnerability was the blood in the water that drew them in.

If I had to stay here, I was going to fucking work.

But I needed a minute. I excused myself from the noise and the false smiles, seeking refuge by the balcony. I pushed through a set of double doors leading to a secluded balcony.

Leaning against the cool railing, I inhaled deeply, the night air a soothing balm to my frayed nerves. My eyes traced the city skyline, the twinkling lights like beacons of hope in the darkness. This was why I fought so hard, why I withstood the dismissive glances and veiled condescension. Each illuminated window represented a chance for change, advancement, a better future—all hinging on the success of my research.

As I turned back toward the ballroom, he was there—Dante Moretti. He moved with an assertive stride that parted the throngs of party-goers like he was Moses and they were the Red Sea. His presence was a force field; people either drew near to bask in his confidence or steered clear to avoid his scrutiny.

God, people had always seemed to ignore me. This man had a gravitational pull that was almost too much to even witness.

He was known in our circles for being something of a hobbyist. He attended conferences, spoke to Dr. White and his boss, frequently attended our talks. But beyond that...I didn't know anything about Dante Moretti. I had never even spoken to him one-on-one.

Our eyes met across the crowded room, and a jolt of electricity surged through me. It defied logic. His lips curved into a knowing smile, a silent acknowledgment of the unspoken attraction that crackled between us. It was wrong, so incredibly wrong, to let myself even entertain the thought of him. But the heart rarely listened to reason, and mine was a traitor, thudding wildly against my ribs as he approached.

"Dr. Bentley," he greeted, his voice smooth and velvety, not matching the hardness of his eyes, which seemed to pierce through my defenses with ease. "You look lovely."

I stammered a reply, momentarily thrown by his presence. My voice, usually steady and controlled during events like this, came out as a breathless whisper. "Mr. Moretti," I replied. "Enjoying the evening?"

What I really wanted to ask was where the woman he was with was, but I did no such thing.

"Immensely, now that it's gotten more interesting. But in general, not to be a bore, I do prefer the conferences," There was a hint of mischief in his tone, a playful edge that contrasted sharply with the calculated coldness I'd expected.

I raised my eyebrows. "I didn't expect that."

"Well, I can only hear about people's boats for so long before I get bored," he said. "Please tell me you don't have a boat."

"I don't have a boat."

"Great," he replied. "You just became more interesting than at least half of the attendees."

"Is that right?" I couldn't help the skeptical arch of my brow. "And here I thought these events were all the same to you."

"Normally, yes. But tonight is different." The corner of his mouth twitched upward in a half-smile, and I could swear there was genuine warmth there. Or maybe it was just another trick of the light. With men like Dante, you could never be too sure.

"Because of...?" I trailed off, inviting him to fill in the blanks.

"Let's just say, I've developed a sudden interest in biotechnology." His eyes held mine, dark and unreadable.

"Doesn't seem that sudden."

"No," he replied. "But it's time to finally make a move."

"I'm not surprised you're here," I said. "BioHQ is on the cutting edge of a lot of things."

"Perhaps it's a bit about the company," he said, edging closer. The heat from his body was a tantalizing contrast to the chill of the evening air. He took a subtle step forward, narrowing the space between us. My breath hitched in my throat, and I instinctively took a step back, suddenly acutely aware of the press of his body and the way his cologne filled the air around me. "But I'm particularly intrigued by the brilliant mind behind BioHQ lab's latest breakthroughs."

Jesus, was this man flirting with me?

"Flattery will get you everywhere...or nowhere at all, depending on your intentions," I shot back, my pulse racing.

"Then I'll have to make sure my intentions are crystal clear," he murmured, closing the distance until there was barely a breath between us.

I should have stepped back, put a safe space between temptation and sensibility. Every fiber of my being, honed by years of prioritizing research over relationships, screamed at me to retreat. But something held me rooted to the spot, a strange mix of apprehension and a thrilling anticipation I couldn't explain.

Dante Moretti was a riddle wrapped in a mystery, and I was suddenly desperate to unravel him.

"Look, I—" My words were cut off by the unexpected chaos that erupted from my hand. The wine glass I'd been gesturing with tipped precariously, a fatal tilt that sent red wine cascading onto Dante's pristine white shirt.

"Shit!" I gasped as the dark liquid bloomed across the fabric like a stain on our already complex interaction. Time seemed to stretch, every droplet a tiny betrayal of my usual poise.

"Dr, Bentley, it's fine," he said, his voice still smooth but with an edge that was as sharp as broken glass.

"God, I'm so sorry," I stuttered, grabbing at the napkins from the nearby table and dabbing frantically at the spreading splotch. Each press only smeared the wine deeper into the fibers, my futile attempts making the disaster worse.

"Doctor." Dante's hand enveloped mine, stilling my panicked movements. His grip was firm, his touch sending an involuntary shiver through me despite the mess. "Stop, you're just—"

"Making it worse, I know." I could feel my face burning hotter than the embarrassment coursing through me. "I'm really sorry, Mr. Moretti. Is there anything I can do?"

He released my hand, and for a moment, we both looked down at the ruin of his shirt—a stark reminder that the evening had taken an unexpected turn. It was more than just the spilt wine; it was as if reality had splashed us both with cold water, washing away any pretense of normalcy between us.

"Let's step outside for a moment," Dante suggested, his annoyance cloaked in politeness, but I could tell he was rattled.

"Outside?" I echoed, unsure what good it would do but desperate to make amends.

"Trust me," he said, a phrase that under any other circumstance might have sounded comforting. But coming from Dante Moretti, it felt like stepping into the unknown.

We moved through the throng of oblivious party-goers, our exit barely noticed. Once outside, the cool evening air hit me, a welcome reprieve from the stifling heat of my embarrassment.

"Really, Mr. Moretti, I'll pay for the dry cleaning, or I can—"

"Jade," he interrupted, his tone softer now, almost amused. "It's just a shirt."

But as I looked up into his eyes, I knew it was never just anything with Dante Moretti.

"Look, I have a spare in my car," he said, his voice cutting through the chill of the evening as we stood there, two silhouettes against the backdrop of city lights. "I always carry spare clothes in my car, just in case."

"Good," I stammered, relief washing over me. "That's good."

We walked in silence to where his car was parked, an unassuming black sedan that seemed almost too modest for a man with his magnetism. He clicked the remote, and the car gave a soft chirp before the doors unlocked.

"Here," he said, popping the trunk. Inside was a duffel bag, and from it, he extracted a neatly folded shirt.

"Thank you." The words barely managed to escape my lips. "If you give me the shirt, I might be able to... well, I work with enzymes, and I could probably get the stain out—"

Dante raised an eyebrow, a hint of a smirk playing on his lips. "You're going to science the stain away?"

"Something like that," I replied, realizing how absurd it sounded outside the context of my lab.

"Or I could just launder it," he suggested, his fingers working on the buttons so he could take it off. I watched, my throat dry, my wine long forgotten as he slowly pulled it off his body.

"You're just going to change here?"

"What do you suggest I do?" he asked. "Don't worry about it. This shirt is uncomfortable anyway."

I blinked in surprise as he did just that, removing the shirt with a casual grace that belatedly reminded me we were alone in a dimly lit corner of the parking garage. he movement was deliberate, unhurried, and sent a jolt through me that had nothing to do with the cool night air. The crisp white fabric skimmed his chest before landing discarded on the passenger seat.

My gaze, traitorous and unbidden, swept over the landscape of his practically exposed torso—the cut of his abs, the curve of his muscles under taut skin. I swallowed hard, trying to anchor myself in the reality that this was not a man to get lost in.

"Please, let me at least pay for the cleaning," I insisted, not ready to admit defeat. "I feel terrible about this."

His smile widened, and he shook his head, a silent chuckle escaping him. "Jade, stop. It's fine."

But it wasn't fine; nothing about this felt fine.

"See? No harm done." His voice was light, but there was a steel edge beneath it, a reminder of who he was.

"Right," I managed to say, my voice sounding foreign to my own ears. "But I can't... I mean, I don't have anything to clean it with right now."

"Jade," he drawled, stepping closer, the heat from his body contradicting the cool air around us. "I don't give a damn about the shirt. Seriously."

"It's probably more expensive than my entire wardrobe," I replied. "I mean...I probably shouldn't be spilling wine on the lab's mysterious benefactor."

That was an inside thought that somehow managed to become an outside thought. This fucking wine was going to be the death of me.

His expression didn't falter, but something flickered in his eyes—a shadow of something unreadable. "Well, if it makes you feel better, I can tell you I'm not your mysterious benefactor. But I'm not opposed to investing in science, especially when it's led by someone as passionate as you."

"Your word," I echoed, skepticism lacing my tone. "That's supposed to be enough for me?"

He leaned in, a half-smile playing on his lips. "It has to be, doesn't it? Because right now, that's all I have to give you."

Okay, maybe it wasn't the wine. Maybe this man was going to be the death of me.

I felt the pull of the party's laughter and music beckoning me from beyond the tinted windows of the car park. I was there to do something for my job, not flirt with this tall, gorgeous stranger. "I should go back."

"Or," he said, a new edge to his voice, "we could forget the party for a while." His eyes held mine, unwavering, as if challenging me to deny the chemistry crackling between us.

Before I could protest, his hands found their way to my waist, pulling me against him with a sureness that left no room for doubt. His lips met mine, and I was caught—part of me still fighting to maintain control, the other sinking into the heady sensation of being wanted.

God, he was an incredible kisser–his lips soft and warm and insistent. The taste of him was intoxicating, spicy and bold, like a red wine that was too expensive for my palate yet too delicious to resist. I tried to remind myself that this wasn't a good idea, to pull away, but it was as if my body had forgotten how to function.

His fingers tightened on my waist, a silent plea that made my heart hammer against my chest. I told myself again, pull away but the more insistent part of me begged stay. The heat in his eyes was addictive, a flame that threatened to burn me yet drew me like a moth.

"Come back to my place," he whispered against my mouth when he pulled away. My breath hitched, caught between the wild drumming of my heart and the rational part of my brain shrieking in protest. I had to pull away, I was playing with fire. I didn't have one-night-stands, particularly not with men who had a direct hand in the future of my work.

But he was so sexy.

"I..." My voice was a bare whisper, my eyes locked with his dark gaze that promised sin and salvation in equal measures.

"Say yes, Jade." His voice was rich and tempting, filling me with anticipation that sent shivers coursing through my body.

For a moment, I faltered, hesitant. This wasn't me. I wasn't the type to throw caution to the wind or get involved with a man like Dante Moretti .

And yet... as his thumb traced light circles over my hip bone, sending sparks of heat spiraling into my core, I found myself surrendering to this man's allure.

"Okay," I agreed, almost breathlessly. His smirk widened as he pulled me even closer until there were no spaces left between us.

"Good girl," he murmured against my lips again. "Don't worry. You're going to love it."

I smiled against his mouth, any reservations I had melting away with his touch.

Fuck it, I decided. Ellie was right. I needed to get laid. And this man was beyond out of my league, so...what was the worst that could happen?

Chapter Six: Dante

Jade was nervous, but I was somehow...even more nervous than she was.

It was surprising, I had taken a lot of women back to my place. Not one of them had ever made me doubt myself the way Dr. Jade Brantley had.

But when we got to my apartment building, she didn't hesitate.

"Lead the way," she said.

"The elevator opens to my apartment," I said, sliding my key into the slot. "Top floor."

"Fancy," she replied, her gaze lingering on the sleek, mirrored interior. "I bet you have a doorman."

I smirked. "I mean, who doesn't have a doorman?"

She shook her head. "Right. Fucking plebs."

I laughed. "Hey, that's not what I meant."

"Don't worry, Dante. If I were as rich as you, I would absolutely be a snob."

I bit my lower lip. "I doubt that."

We stepped out of the elevator, and the penthouse door whooshed open silently. The noise of the city faded away. There was a different kind of silence here, thick with anticipation, and my skin tingled with it—Jade's presence charging the air like electricity.

Here, in this silent sanctuary, I wasn't the mob prince; I was just a man, drunk on the nearness of Jade—her floral perfume, the shallow rhythm of her breathing, the undeniable pull of her being.

"Can I offer you a drink?" I asked, voice low and steady, betraying none of my inner turmoil.

"Sure," she replied, her tone laced with a curiosity that made my heart hammer against its cage.

I retrieved two crystal glasses and dropped in ice cubes, relishing the sharp clink that sliced through the thickening tension. As the golden whiskey flowed, so did my thoughts—guilt entwined with lust, obligation clashing with yearning. With every sip we took, the line between right and wrong, between duty and desire, blurred into nothingness.

Glasses in hand, I led Jade through the spacious living area. The cityscape sprawled through the expansive windows, a canvas of twinkling lights that promised a night of indulgence. The air was crisp, the kind of autumn night that sent shivers down your spine, and I felt a raw power thrumming through my veins—a power that softened as I looked at her.

Unable to resist any longer, I strode towards the sliding glass doors that led out to the balcony. The cool night air washed over us as I opened them, carrying the distant sounds of the city and the scent of rain on pavement.

We stepped outside, the city lights sparkling like scattered diamonds against the velvet darkness. The moon hung low in the sky, casting an ethereal glow over the scene.

"Like the view?" I asked, my voice betraying none of the heat coursing through me.

She turned, her gaze traveling from the skyline to settle on me. "Yes," she said, a hint of playfulness in her tone.

That was all the invitation I needed. I put the drinks down. The air crackled with unspoken tension. I reached out, my thumb brushing lightly across her cheek. A shiver danced down her spine, and I knew I couldn't wait any longer.

Cupping her face, I drew her closer. Our lips met in a hungry kiss, a clash of wills that ignited a firestorm within me. Her taste was intoxicating, a mix of sweetness and something wild. I deepened the kiss, exploring the depths of her mouth, my hands finding their way down her back I was hard, so fucking hard for her, and it seemed like my body knew before my mind that she was what I wanted.

Her lips parted, welcoming the invasion of my tongue, her moan vibrating against my mouth. The fire between us was instantaneous, consuming. I could handle heat—I had been baptized by the flames of my family's world—but this was different. This passion held a purity that threatened to undo me.

"Can I take off your dress?" I asked, hands poised at her zipper, ready to unveil the secrets her body held. "I need to see all of you."

She blinked, surprise flickering across her features before she nodded. "I didn't expect this," she admitted, her voice a whisper laced with excitement and something akin to fear—fear of the unknown, of the raw emotion we were about to explore.

"Neither did I," I confessed, pulling the zipper down slowly, deliberately. I didn't remove anything, letting it hang off her for now. "But you're perfect as you are, Jade. I want you—every inch of you."

"No, you don't understand," she said, a blush creeping up her neck. "I'm wearing like...shapewear."

I laughed, my hands stilling and the sound of my laughter rumbling from deep within in my chest. "I don't care about that. I want you. Not some illusion of perfection." I pulled her close, my fingers tracing the curves she had tried to hide beneath the shapewear. The smooth fabric felt cool against my skin. "You are beautiful, Jade," I whispered in her ear.

She pulled away slightly, her ice-blue eyes searching my face for any sign of insincerity. Finding none, she relaxed into my embrace once again, a soft sigh escaping her lips as I caressed her bare back.

"But I don't have to take anything off if you don't want me to."

"I want you to," she said softly.

With her permission granted, I peeled the fabric from her shoulders, revealing the warm skin beneath. My fingertips traced the length of her spine, every touch an unspoken promise, a secret shared without words. Jade shivered, but not from the cold; it was from the magnetic pull that drew us closer, binding us together in a way that went beyond physical attraction.

"Are you sure?" I murmured against her ear, as the last barrier to her nakedness fell to the ground.

"Yes, Dante," she breathed, turning to face me, her eyes alight with a mixture of vulnerability and desire. "I'm sure."

"Good. Because I want you," I said. "Right here. On this balcony."

Her eyes, wide and searching, met mine. "What about your bed? It's right there, perfectly fine."

"Fuck the bed," I growled, the restraint I'd been clinging to disintegrating like smoke. "I can't resist you, Jade. Can't fight how crazy you make me feel. How heady and amazing you smell. I'm so hard I'm practically in pain."

Her blush deepened, coloring her cheeks in the most intoxicating way. She hesitated for a moment, clearly weighing her options, but desire won out.

"Okay," she whispered.

With swift movements, I closed the distance between us and captured her lips with mine. Our kiss was no gentle inquiry—it was a demand, a clash of wills, a battle we were both desperate to lose. My hands roamed over her body, mapping the terrain I was about to claim. I skimmed my fingers over the smooth curves her shapewear had tried to conceal, memorizing every dip and rise.

A gasp escaped her lips as I reached the hem of her dress, bunching it up around her hips. The moonlight cast long, evocative shadows across her body, highlighting the urgency in her eyes.

"Here," I murmured against her lips, guiding her back until her legs hit the chaise lounge. The cool metal sent a jolt through her, a counterpoint to the rising heat within. I bunched her dress up around her hips, exposing her legs to the cool night air.

"Right here under the stars," I finished, my voice hoarse with desire.

With a final, lingering kiss, I broke away, my gaze trailing down her body. The moonlight glinted off the soft sheen of her shapewear, emphasizing the elegant line of her hips and the enticing swell of her curves.

Taking a deep breath, I reached for the clasp at the back, the sound a tiny click in the vast silence of the night. The delicate fabric fell away, revealing the smooth expanse of her skin in the moonlight. Her dress, now just a bunched cloth around her waist, seemed like a distant memory.

But our dance wasn't over yet. Her shapewear, a high-waisted piece that hugged her curves, remained. It was a thin, translucent material, barely a whisper against her skin, but it still held a hint of secrecy.

A slow smile spread across my face. "Let me," I murmured, brushing a stray strand of hair from her cheek.

"I'm not wearing sexy underwear," she said.

"Damn. Here I was hoping you weren't wearing any underwear," I said.

Her cheeks flushed a beautiful crimson under my gaze. A playful swat landed on my arm, more of a nervous flutter than a real hit. "You're impossible," she muttered, but a hint of a smile tugged at the corner of her lips.

The revelation, both unexpected and endearing, only fueled the fire burning within me. "Don't worry about that, Jade," I murmured, my voice husky with desire. "You're beautiful no matter what."

My fingers, which had hovered near the waistband of her shapewear, resumed their task. The delicate fabric was cool against my skin, a stark contrast to the heat radiating from her body. I traced the scalloped edge with my thumb, sending shivers rippling down her spine.

With a slow, deliberate movement, I slipped my fingers beneath the band. The material yielded easily, whispering against her skin as it descended. Inch by inch, I peeled it down, the moonlight catching on the exposed curves of her body. It was a slow tease, a deliberate revelation that left little to the imagination.

Once the shapewear reached her hips, it tangled with her bunched up dress, the lace trim catching for a moment before giving way. With a final, gentle pull, I removed the shapewear completely. It pooled at her feet, a discarded whisper of a barrier that had once separated us.

She sat on the chaise lounge before me, her dress bunched around her waist and revealing simple black boy shorts. A soft sigh escaped her lips, and for a moment, we simply stared, the air thick with unspoken desire. The cool night air sent a shiver down her spine, and she self-consciously reached for the straps of her dress, pulling them down slightly. The dress bunched loosely around her hips, offering a tantalizing glimpse of her legs and the curve of her lower back. She sat on the chaise lounge before me, her gaze locked on mine, a silent invitation hanging in the air.

"I can smell how wet you are," I said. "It's fucking sexy."

Her cheeks flushed a deep shade of scarlet and her lips parted in surprise. "Dante..." she began, but any protest died on her lips as I lowered myself to my knees before her.

"Dante, we're," she swallowed, her eyes wide in the moonlight, "we're outside."

I glanced over my shoulder at the ebony sky, dotted with the winking jewels of stars. A smirk played on my lips as I turned back to her.

"Yes," I replied. "I would eat your pussy anywhere."

Jade's breath hitched at my words, her eyes widening further. A soft blush colored her cheeks as she looked at me, a mix of shock and intrigue in her gaze.

"You're...you're serious?" she stammered.

"Oh, I'm very serious," I murmured back.

"But Dante..." She bit down on her lower lip, glancing nervously around the balcony.

"What if someone sees us?"

"No one will see us up here," I said. "And if they do, so what? They get to see a beautiful woman coming over and over and over again. Sounds terrible for them."

She giggled nervously at my words, her eyes flashing with anticipation, but also a hint of uncertainty. "You're ridiculous," she said, but there was no real conviction in her voice. Instead, it was thick with desire.

"And you're exquisite," I countered, my voice dropping lower as I crawled toward her on the chaise. My hands traced up her legs, feeling the tremors running through her. "Now relax and let me show you just how much."

Without waiting for a response, I wasted no more time. My lips found the sensitive skin of her inner thigh and she gasped. Her hands tangled in my hair, a sigh escaping her lips as I placed tender kisses further up her leg.

Smirking up at her from between her thighs, I could feel the heat emanating from her core and the intoxicating scent of her desire. It was a heady aroma that sent a rush of blood straight to my groin. I barely held back my own groan as I inched closer, nuzzling the soft folds beneath the black boy shorts she wore.

Her fingers found my hair. "Wait, Dante," she said. "I really didn't expect this. I didn't, uh, shave for this or anything."

I glanced up at her, my smirk never wavering. "Does it look like I care?"

Her cheeks flushed again, but she didn't protest any further. With a low growl, I nuzzled my face against the damp fabric of her boy shorts. "You smell so fucking good, Jade."

Jade let out a soft moan at the sound of her name on my lips. Her breath hitched, fingers tightening in my hair as I hooked a finger around the edge of her underwear and slowly slid them down.

She was laid bare before me, exposed under the watchful eyes of the stars. A growl rumbled in my chest at the sight of her spread out on the chaise, panting and blushing under my gaze.

With deliberate slowness, I traced a finger up her inner thigh, drinking in her gasp and the way she shivered under my touch. Her hands found their way back to my hair, gripping it tight as if she was fighting to keep control.

"Stop teasing me," she muttered, her eyes half-lidded and pleading. A soft whimper escaped her lips and her thighs squeezed together.

I chuckled, my breath fanning over her exposed heat. "But I do so enjoy it," I replied, sliding my hands to her hips to hold her in place. "Seeing you squirm under my touch."

She gave a soft gasp as my thumb brushed against her clit, but quickly bit down on her lower lip to stifle any noises. Her entire body shuddered, her grip on my hair tightening.

Leaning down, I pressed a soft kiss to the inside of her thigh, my smirk broadening at the desperate whimper that slipped past her lips. "Tell me what you want, Jade," I murmured against her skin. "Tell me and I'll give it to you."

"I want your mouth on me," she said. "I want your cock inside of me."

Her answer was breathy and raw, filled with a desire that sent a rush of triumph coursing through my veins.

"Your wish is my command," I replied, my voice rough with anticipation. I traced a lazy path with my tongue from the inside of her thigh to the place where she wanted me most.

I teased her with slow, deliberate licks, coaxing soft moans from her lips. The taste of her on my tongue was intoxicating, a heady mix of sweetness and heat that only made me want more.

I didn't realize I could get any harder, but fuck...Hearing her mewl and moan under my touch had every nerve ending in my body on fire, my cock throbbing painfully against my slacks. I was lost in her taste, in the intoxicating scent of her arousal that filled the air. The way she squirmed, writhed, and bucked beneath me only served to add fuel to the raging inferno within me.

I sucked her clit into my mouth and her entire body tensed, a cry of pleasure escaping her lips that seemed to echo through the quiet night. My hands found their way to her hips, holding her down as I continued to explore her with my mouth.

"God, Dante," she gasped, her hands clawing at the fabric of the chaise beneath her. "Don't... don't stop..."

I had no intention of doing so. God, she tasted amazing – sweet and spicy and wholly addictive. I couldn't get enough of her; I could spend eternity between her thighs and still not have enough.

My tongue flicked over her clit again and again, each swipe earning me a cry of pleasure that only spurred me on further. The raw need in her voice was my undoing - I needed to see her unravel beneath me.

Drawing back slightly, I slid two fingers inside of her and watched in awe as her face contorted in pleasure. Her hands fisted in my hair as she arched her back, a broken moan slipping past her lips.

"More," she gasped, her words pushing me further.

Flicking my tongue back to where it belonged, I continued to stroke her from the inside, pushing deeper with each thrust. Her walls clenched around me, coating my fingers in her sweet release.

"Fuck, Dante!" she cried out, her voice echoed across the silence of the night. She was losing herself to the pleasure and I was more than happy to guide her there.

Consumed by the desire to hear more of those sinful sounds escaping her mouth, I increased my pace. My tongue circled her swollen nub as my fingers dove in and out of her in a rhythm that would drive any woman wild. Her body began to shake uncontrollably, a sure sign of the impending climax that I was all too eager to deliver.

"Do you like this?" I asked without pausing. "You're so fucking wet."

Jade's response was caught in a gasp as her body tensed up, legs shaking as her climax built higher and higher. "Dante... please," she stammered out, grasping my hair tight in her fingers.

I smirked against her, flicking my tongue faster over her clit. "Please what, darling?" I asked, my own arousal throbbing painfully at the sight of her writhing in pleasure under me.

"Please... I need..." she moaned, her voice frantic with need.

"Say it," I growled against her sensitive flesh, my fingers curling inside of her to stroke that one spot that made her see stars.

"I need to come!" Jade cried out, the words barely leaving her lips before she was exploding around me.

"So come," I said. "Come on my tongue, beautiful."

Her climax ripped through her like a storm, leaving her shaking and gasping for breath. I didn't let up, not until she was writhing beneath me, her pleas for mercy turning into senseless mumbles.

Ignoring the ache in my own body, I continued to devour her until her orgasm subsided, leaving her panting and glowing beneath the moonlight. I trailed kisses up her body, tasting her sweat on my lips as I finally claimed her mouth in a searing kiss.

"Can you taste yourself on my mouth?" I asked.

She gave a weak nod, her eyes heavy with satisfaction. But there was something else there too. Something raw and unguarded that made my heart pound in my chest. She was looking at me like no one ever had before.

"Good," I murmured against her lips, pressing another soft kiss to them before pulling away. "Because you're delicious."

I stood up and quickly shed my clothes, every nerve ending aching for some form of contact with her. She watched me, her gaze hot and hungry as it roved over my naked body.

"You're ready for me, aren't you?" I asked.

"Yes," she breathed out, her voice shaky but filled with anticipation. Her eyes stayed glued to my hardened length, a blush creeping up her face that was too enflaming for me to ignore.

Grinning at her reaction, I climbed back onto the chaise, positioning myself between her spread legs. My cock twitched at the sight of her flushed and sated beneath me, her sweet centers still glistening from the attention they just received.

With one hand, I guided my hardness to her entrance, slowly pushing inside. The feel of her warmth enveloping me was ecstasy in its purest form. Her body accommodated me like a glove, tight and wet with longing.

Her hands reached up to grip my biceps as she let out a gasp. What I wanted to do was bury my cock to the hilt and set a punishing pace, but I let her get used to me instead.

After several agonizing moments, her fingers dug into my skin and she let out a breathy sigh. "Dante..." she whispered, her voice shaky.

"Move," she pleaded, locking her eyes with mine in a silent plea. Raw need sparked in her icy blue depths, and I lost all self-control.

With a groan of pure pleasure, I began to move inside of her, each thrust drawing a moan from both our lips. Her nails dug into my biceps as she held on, her legs wrapping around my waist to bring me deeper into her.

God, she felt incredible. Tight and wet and so fucking responsive. She moved with me, meeting each of my thrusts with one of her own. The sight of her beneath me, flushed with pleasure and writhing in ecstasy was enough to have me teetering on the edge of release.

"Faster," she gasped out, her hips grinding up to meet mine. Her words stoked the fire inside me, and I quickened my pace, pushing into her with a fierceness that had us both gasping.

Her chest heaved against mine as she clung onto me, the sound of our bodies colliding filling the air.

"You're so tight, Jade," I growled in her ear. My fingers dug into her hips, guiding her movements as I pounded into her relentlessly. The sight of her coming undone was intoxicating; I wanted to capture this moment forever. "Are you going to come for me, bella?"

My thumb found her clit, rubbing it in circles that had her crying out. "I... I can't..." she sobbed, her body convulsing beneath mine.

"Yes, you can," I gritted out, thrusting harder into her. "Come for me, darling."

My words seemed to snap something inside of her and with a loud cry, she came apart beneath me. Her walls clenching around my cock sent me into my own climax, my seed spilling into her as we rode out our orgasms together.

The balcony was filled with the sound of our heavy breathing and the faint ticking of the clock on the wall. Jade's arms went around my neck as I collapsed onto her, spent and satisfied.

I buried my face in the crook of her neck, inhaling the sweet scent of sweat and desire that clung to her skin.

I felt her fingers trace patterns along my back, a feather-light touch that sent shivers down my spine even in my spent state. "Dante," she whispered, her voice as soft as the midnight breeze caressing our bodies.

I lifted myself up to look at her, propping myself on one elbow. Her ice-blue eyes were soft. "Now what?" she asked.

"Well, now," I said. "I can go get you that drink. And maybe after that, we could use the bed."

Chapter Seven: Dante

T he first light of dawn spilled through the curtains, casting a soft glow on her skin. There she was, Jade, curled up on the bed, a serene expression on her face. It messed with my head, how different this morning felt. That bed never held more than cold sheets and the ghosts of last night's sins. But here she was, a quiet storm sleeping next to me, her dark hair spread out on the pillow.

"Jade," I whispered, though not loud enough to wake her. Last night wasn't just skin on skin; there was something else, something that could either be my damnation or salvation.

As the city stirred awake below, so did she. Her eyes, clear and focused, always scanning the horizon for the next discovery, now blinked lazily at me. She hadn't heard me slip out of bed to get breakfast ready and I assumed she was hungry.

"Morning," she murmured, stretching like a cat, unaware of the chaos she could unleash in my world.

"Did you sleep well?" I asked, even though the answer lay in the softness of her smile.

"Better than I have in a long time," she replied, and I wondered if I could say the same.

I ushered her out to the terrace where the New York skyline was a backdrop to our breakfast. She wore nothing but her panties and it was really hard to keep my eyes off her. But I served myself coffee and told myself that this was a great chance for us to talk, though what I really wanted to do was fuck her again.

I should've probably asked if she wanted to borrow some clothes, but I really liked looking at her like this.

The table was set with precision; delicate pastries were arranged alongside fruit, and the coffee smelled like promises and power plays.

"Thank you," she said, her voice a gentle hum over the noise of the city. She reached for a croissant, not bothering with a plate, and bit into it, the flaky crust scattering over her bare thighs. I couldn't help but watch as she brushed off the crumbs, her fingers swift and sure. "Last night was...unexpected."

I smiled at her. "You had fun?"

"Yes," she replied. "A lot of fun."

"So did I. Jade," I started, pouring us both a cup. "We've got a good thing here, you and I." She looked at me, curiosity lighting up her features. "Our connection...it's rare. And I'm not just talking about what happens behind closed doors."

She took a sip of her coffee, her brow furrowing slightly as she waited for me to continue.

"Your brain, your work with biotech—it's groundbreaking. And I've got resources, connections. Together, we could create something untouchable, unbreakable."

"You're talking about work already? I haven't even finished my coffee."

"Please," I replied. "We both know you're just as obsessed as I am. I mean, probably more, since you've dedicated your entire life to studying it."

"True," Jade conceded, setting down her cup with a soft clink against the glass tabletop. "But there's something we need to address before we go any further."

"What's that?" I leaned back in my chair, watching her.

"My NDA with BioHQ," she said, her eyes not leaving mine. "It's ironclad. I can't just share sensitive information, even if...well, even if it's with you."

"Understandable," I replied, my mind already turning over the legalities. "But there are ways around that. We can draft a new NDA, one that covers both of us, tailored for our partnership. It won't conflict with your existing commitments but will ensure our collaboration is protected."

"Can we do that?" The question came out tinged with hope, and it struck me how much she wanted this—how much she believed in what we could achieve together.

"Yes. We'll have it navigate the parameters of your current agreement with BioHQ, keep everything above board. Our partnership will remain as confidential as necessary." I watched as the tension eased from her shoulders, her posture relaxing slightly.

"Right, but you still haven't told me what kind of partnership you want. You didn't just get into bed with me because you wanted to talk business, did you?" she asked, a horrified look crossing over her face. "Wait. You're not like, a science groupie, are you?"

I smiled. "I don't think that's a thing. And no, look, I'm just...entrepreneurial. It's how I've managed to expand my father's fortune. You're here, and I figured you would like to talk more about this than about...I don't know, any awkwardness around last night."

"Ah," she said, not quite meeting my gaze. "That's...much better than being a science groupie."

"Good," I said, inching close to her and putting a hooked finger behind her chin. "But if you prefer, Jade, I can talk about how hot you are. How fucking tight your pussy is."

"I—," she started, then cleared her throat. "That isn't necessary."

"No?" I asked, my grin widening. Her bluster was adorable, and I couldn't help teasing her.

"Absolutely not," she insisted. But her eyes were glinting with intrigue and something else...desire. Her nipples got hard at my words. It took a lot of willpower to continue talking business when I wanted to make her come again and again again.

"Okay," I agreed, pulling my hand away to reach for my coffee.

We sat in silence for a moment longer, the noise of the city below providing a soundtrack to our quiet breakfast. She busied herself with picking at the rest of her meal while I sipped at my drink.

"I guess what I want to know is how this benefits you," she said, tucking a strand of her behind her ear, her breasts bouncing when she did. "BioHQ has contracts with pharmaceutical companies, with giant producers of biological material. But you...you're in real estate, right? I mean, your last name is all over the real estate scene. And when I've seen you at conferences, you said you were a science hobbyist. So I need you to explain this."

I took another sip of my coffee, relishing the bitter taste. It was time to break it down for her, to explain what I saw in this partnership that she was missing. "You're right about my family business," I began. "We've got our hands in real estate, construction, you name it. But we also have a significant investment in pharmaceuticals. And your work, Jade...it has the potential to revolutionize the industry."

"I'm still not following," she said, her brow furrowed.

"Think about it," I pressed on. "Your research could lead to breakthroughs in medicine we haven't even dreamed of yet. And the manufacturing process...well, that requires facilities and infrastructure, doesn't it? And yes, it needs meticulous work at BioHQ, but imagine if you could streamline some of the process."

"Definitely," she admitted, her expression shifting to one of curiosity. "But hiring a team like that takes resources that BioHQ doesn't have."

"Exactly," I said, leaning forward. "That's where I come in. I provide the resources, the facilities...everything you need to bring your research to life. We don't cut any corners or rush anything; we just create an environment where your work can thrive."

"And in return...?" she asked, her voice trailing off as she looked at me for answers.

"In return, my investment pays off when your research leads to new drugs, new treatments...new hope for people who need it." Suddenly everything was out in the open, and I could see her mulling over my words, turning them over in her brilliant mind.

"But what about BioHQ?" Jade asked. "I mean, the work belongs to them. It's their intellectual property."

"Look, I'm not suggesting we steal anything from BioHQ," I said, my voice firm. "We do this the right way. You keep your commitments, and we work around them. That's why we need that complementary NDA. It'll keep both sides safe while we build something monumental together."

Jade hesitated, her lips parting slightly as she considered my words. She reached into her purse, searching for something. "I should show you the email from legal about my current NDA stipulations."

Her hand emerged clutching her phone, but in the process, a slim plastic card edged its way out of her overstuffed bag, teetering precariously on the table's edge. She was so engrossed in her search that she didn't notice it slide out.

I caught a glimpse of the keycard—the one that granted access to the heart of BioHQ's labyrinthine labs. The very labs where her life's work breathed and grew. My eyes flicked to Jade, who was still scrolling through her phone, oblivious.

As if by instinct, I continued talking, maintaining eye contact with her, ensuring she remained absorbed in our conversation. With a casual sweep of my hand, I brushed the keycard off the edge of the table and into my lap, where I expertly palmed it and slipped it into the pocket of my black pajama pants.

"Found it," Jade said, finally looking up from her phone. She seemed none the wiser, her focus solely on the screen as she showed me the email.

"Good," I said, nodding as I glanced at the digital document. "This is good. We'll craft our agreement to complement this perfectly. Your work with BioHQ will remain untouched and protected."

"Okay," Jade said slowly, still reading through the email with me. "If you think it can work without causing any legal issues, then... let's proceed. If I had a team of researchers, I would certainly be able to go faster."

"Trust me," I assured her, my voice smooth as silk. "I have a vested interest in making sure everything goes smoothly—for both of us."

She nodded, seeming to relax a little, and tucked her phone back into her purse. Unaware of the keycard now hidden in my pocket, she took a sip of her coffee and sighed, the weight of responsibilities momentarily lifting from her shoulders. I couldn't help but admire her—the way she dedicated herself to her research, her unwavering ethics, even if they made my life more complicated.

"You can email that to me and I'll set up a meeting with my legal team," I said. "We need to make sure every aspect of our partnership is covered."

She looked at me, her dark hair falling like a curtain around her face. "You're right. I need to understand all the legalities involved." Her eyes, filled with that steely determination I'd come to admire, met mine. "But Dante, I want everything transparent and by the book. No grey areas."

"Transparency and compliance," I echoed firmly, my gaze never wavering from hers. I hoped she couldn't tell I was bullshitting her. "Those are our foundational pillars. You have my word on that, Jade."

As breakfast began to wind down, I noticed Jade's focus drifting back to her work—her true passion. It was time to kindle that fire she had for making a difference. She didn't get into this because she was really into convalescent bonds, I didn't think. I pushed aside the last of my croissant and leaned back in my chair.

"Jade," I said, voice low and compelling. "Imagine the lives we could save, the diseases we could cure with your expertise and...our resources." I gestured broadly, encompassing the world outside the penthouse windows. "We're not just talking local impact here—we're talking global."

Her eyes lit up, and I knew I had her. "The advancements we could pioneer together will be groundbreaking. We could reshape the future of medical technology."

Jade's excitement was palpable as she leaned in, drawn to the vision I painted. "That would be incredible, Dante. To make such a trans-formative change... it's what I've always wanted."

"Then let's make it happen," I said, standing and rounding the table to her side. The promise of what the future held energized me, and I could tell it did the same for her. This venture wasn't just another notch in the belt of the Moretti empire—it was personal. It was hope—a rare commodity in my world.

"Come on," I urged, offering my hand. "Let's get started on making history."

I put my hand on her back and it took everything in me not to slide it lower.

"You have big plans," she said.

"I have a lot of money," I replied. "That helps."

"Yeah?"

I nodded. "Once we've got the legal side buttoned up, nothing will stop us," I told her, conviction steeling my tone. I had to do this. She didn't know it yet, but I would move heaven and earth to make sure this happened.

Walking her to the threshold of my bedroom, I motioned toward the plush space. "You can get dressed in there," I said, doing my best to keep my tone professional despite the intimate undercurrent. "Your blue dress from last night is still hanging up."

"You hung it up?"

"Well, yeah," I replied. "I wasn't just going to let it get wrinkled on the floor."

"Alright," She responded, disappearing into the room without a second glance. As I turned away, I caught sight of her silhouette through the thin fabric of the door. It was tantalizing, yet all I could concentrate on was the weight of the stolen keycard pressing against my leg.

A few minutes later, Jade returned, looking as stunning as she had the previous night. The fitted blue dress clung to her curves in all the right places, and her dark hair cascaded down her back in soft waves. The sight was enough to weaken any man, but I forced my attention back to our partnership.

Reaching the elevator, I pressed the call button, the soft ding echoing in the hushed corridor. The doors slid open with a whisper. But instead of ushering her inside, I pulled her close, my arm snaking around her waist, and claimed her lips with a hunger that betrayed the control I typically wore like armor.

Jade gasped, but she didn't pull away. Instead, she melted against me, her curves pressing into my growing desire. My hand found hers, guiding it down to feel the effect she had on me. The raw need coursing through my veins demanded satisfaction.

"You want this?" I breathed against her lips, seeking confirmation, craving her surrender.

"Yes," she whispered back, her hand gripping me through the fabric of my trousers.

"Good." I kissed her again, harder, sealing the promise of what was to come. "But first, dinner," I said, pulling back just enough to look into her eyes, smirking at the flush spreading across her cheeks. "Even I'm not uncivilized enough to skip wining and dining you first—though believe me, Jade, I really want to fuck you."

Before she left, as the elevator dinged, I grabbed a random business card and scribbled my name and my personal phone number on it. This was a direct line to me, not one my underlings or my father could intercept.

"Use this if you need anything," I said, my voice low. "Day or night."

She took the card, her fingers brushing against mine, sending an electric jolt up my arm. Her eyes locked onto mine for a moment, filled with a mix of emotions—curiosity, excitement, maybe even a hint of fear. Then she tucked the card into her purse without breaking eye contact.

"Thank you, Dante," she replied, her voice steady despite the charged air between us.

"Jade." I paused as the elevator doors began to close. "I'll call you soon."

"Because of work."

"Sure," I replied, smiling at her. "Because of work."

She nodded, and then she was gone, swallowed up by the closing metal doors and the building beyond. I stood there for a second longer, staring at the brushed steel as though I could still see her face reflected there.

Back in my study, the weight of our interaction—and all its implications—settled over me. I poured myself a drink, the amber liquid catching the light as I swirled it in the glass. It was too early to drink but I didn't give a shit.

I sank into the leather chair behind my desk, the one that had seen too many late nights and difficult decisions.

Dr. Jade Bentley. She wasn't just brilliant; she was fucking stunning. And now, she had a direct line to me, to my life, which was something I never gave out lightly. I trusted few people, and for good reason. In my world, trust could be exploited, turned against you in ways you couldn't anticipate. Yet with her, it felt different. Dangerous, but necessary.

"Fuck," I muttered, downing the drink in one go. My father would have my head if he knew what I was getting myself into. Hell, Marco would probably laugh himself hoarse before warning me off. But this wasn't about them. It was about me and Jade, and whatever the hell we were starting.

If I played my cards right, maybe I could prove to my father that this was worth it after all.

The risks were high, but the rewards...

If we *both* played this right, the rewards could be higher than either of us had ever dreamed.

I just had to keep us both alive long enough to reap them.

Chapter Eight: Jade

The sterile smell of the lab clung to us as we squeezed into our usual table at the bistro. The comforting scents of garlic and herbs masked the lingering scent of fluorescent lights, a welcome change from the grueling day spent under them. I sank into the booth's worn leather seat, grateful for the softness against my achy muscles.

"Thank goodness for this place," I sighed.

Ellie let out a similar sigh as she dug into her spaghetti carbonara with gusto. "I needed this break so badly," she said between bites.

"You and me both," I replied, pushing up my glasses and tucking a loose strand of hair behind my ear.

"So spill, what's been on your mind all week? You've been avoiding my texts like the plague," Ellie prodded playfully. "And you keep talking about work."

I hesitated, knowing she wouldn't let me off easily. "I mean, babe, it's work. It's been crazy busy," I finally admitted.

"Don't give me that, Jade. I know you. That's all you talk about. You've been...distracted. You left with Dante Moretti. It's him, isn't it?" Her eyes sparkled mischievously across the table.

I couldn't hide my smile as I nodded. "Yes, it's Dante Moretti."

"I can't believe you didn't tell me. Slut. I mean that in the most encouraging way," Ellie chuckled, shaking her head. "You did say he was out of your league, remember?"

"He is!" I exclaimed, leaning in closer. "I can't believe we slept together. He's so handsome and...you know, rich. And he has a lot of stamina."

Ellie's laughter mixed with the sounds of the bustling bistro around us. But deep down, a small part of me couldn't shake off the feeling that there was more to Dante than met the eye, and I was diving into dangerous waters with him.

"Speaking of well off," Ellie leaned in, her expression turning serious. Her voice dropped to a whisper, the playful spark gone. "Jade, be careful. The Morettis...I'm pretty sure they're not just rich. They're mixed up in some serious stuff. It's not all legitimate."

A chill ran through me despite the warmth surrounding us, the noise of clinking glasses and chatter suddenly distant. My mind raced at the implications of what she was saying—dangerous, unlawful, the kind of trouble you don't walk away from.

I shook my head, forcing a half-smile as I attempted to dispel the cold dread settling over me. "Dante doesn't seem like...He's just been really nice." I wanted to believe that the man I had begun to fall for wasn't tied to the darkness Ellie was hinting at.

Ellie frowned, the lines of concern etching deeper into her face. "Appearances can be deceiving, especially with them. You know how these families operate; they have a facade for everything."

Her words hung in the air, heavy and ominous. She knew I wasn't naive, but this was territory far beyond my expertise in biotechnology. And yet, the idea of Dante being anything other than the charming man I'd come to know seemed impossible.

"Ellie, thanks for looking out for me," I said, trying to reassure both her and myself. "I'll be careful, I promise."

She gave my hand a tight squeeze before standing up. "I'm sorry I have to go," she said. "I promised my roommate I'd feed her dog and she's going away for the..."

"You told me," I said. "We'll go out properly next weekend."

"Thank you! I love you. I'm serious, Jade. Be careful about this."

Then she was gone, the cool night air sweeping in as the door closed behind her, leaving a void where her presence had been.

Alone with my thoughts, the restaurant's buzz morphed into a relentless hum, pressing against my temples. The laughter and conversations around me blurred into a single indistinct noise—a warning siren that I couldn't silence. Ellie's words played on a loop in my head, an eerie soundtrack to my growing unease.

Just as the weight of her warnings began to truly sink in, my phone vibrated against the wooden table. I flinched as I looked at the screen. It was him. Dante. My breath hitched at the sight of his name, the familiar rush of excitement now tainted with a twinge of fear.

Hope you're having a wonderful evening. Thinking of you.

The text read like any other sweet nothing he had sent before–and he had been in touch all week–but now it felt loaded, each word heavy with unspoken meaning.

I stared at the screen, my blue tank top suddenly feeling too tight against my skin, my heart pounding loud enough to rival the cacophony around me. Should I respond? My thumb hovered over the keyboard, indecision paralyzing me.

"Damn it, Dante," I muttered under my breath, the sound lost amidst the din of the restaurant. The charming man who had effortlessly slipped into my life—was he a facade too?

Thank you, Dante. It's been a long day.

I finally typed back, my response as non-committal as I could muster. The moment I hit send, my stomach twisted with a mix of guilt and trepidation. Ellie's words echoed in my mind, casting a long shadow over the warmth that once flooded me at his messages.

I left the restaurant with haste, my ponytail swinging as I darted through the throngs of New York's nightlife. Once home, the silence of my apartment was a stark contrast to the earlier bustle. I needed answers. My fingers itched for my laptop like they did for a pipette when a hypothesis formed in the lab.

I sat down, powered on the device, and let my scientific curiosity drive me into the depths of the internet as I sipped from the foam cup with the lukewarm espresso I'd grabbed before leaving the restaurant.

"Moretti family Little Italy ties" I typed, each keystroke a deliberate probe into the darkness. As the search engine populated results, my heart raced. I leaned forward, glasses perched on the bridge of my nose, peering at the screen.

The shrill ring of my phone sliced through the quiet like a bullet from the dark. I jerked back, nearly knocking over the coffee. It was Dante. I hesitated, staring at the screen as it lit up the dim room.

"Hey, Jade, just wanted to hear your voice," he said when I finally answered, his words smooth and warm like a shot of whiskey on a cold night. But I couldn't shake off the chill that settled in my bones. I held the phone slightly away from my ear, my fingers trembling.

"Hi, Dante," I replied, faking a calm I didn't feel.

"Everything okay?" he probed gently.

"Yeah, just tired," I lied, curling up on the edge of my bed, feeling the weight of my day's discoveries pressing down on me.

"Get some rest then. We'll talk tomorrow," he suggested, but there was something in the way he said it—a hidden question, as if he sensed my tension. "Are we still on for Monday? My lawyer is eager to get started."

"Yes," I said. "I think so."

"Okay. I'll call tomorrow to confirm."

"Sure," I said before ending the call. The room plunged back into silence, leaving me alone with the echoes of our conversation and the hum of New York outside my window.

As darkness wrapped around me, I lay down, pulling the covers up to my chin, my body heavy with exhaustion. But sleep wouldn't come. Instead, images of Dante flickered through my mind—his charming smile, the intensity in his eyes, the allure of danger that seemed to follow him like a shadow.

"Could Ellie be right?" I murmured to the empty room, voicing the fear I'd been pushing away. Ellie's warnings about Dante's world—the violence, the power struggles, the ruthlessness—had seemed so far away until now.

I tossed again, my blue tank top twisting with each turn. My thoughts spiraled, tangling with doubts and the remnants of the safety I once felt with him. The cool fabric of my dark denim jeans offered no comfort as I shifted restlessly, trying to find some semblance of peace.

I had to get dressed for bed, but I knew sleep would be just out of reach for most of the night.

I was right. I'd barely slept.

As the first light of dawn crept through the window, I made my decision. With a sigh, I sat up and reached for my phone on the bedside table. My fingers felt numb as I typed out a text to Dante, a simple message that felt like the heaviest thing I'd ever written:

Need some time to think. Talk soon?

I stared at the words, my heart pounding in my chest. It was one thing to feel them, another to send them into the world where they couldn't be taken back. My finger hovered over the send button, hesitating. Was I ready for whatever his response would be? With a breath that felt more like surrender than resolution, I pressed down.

The day stretched out before me, endless and unforgiving. I spent it in solitude, my apartment a silent witness to the emotional turmoil swirling within me. I curled up on the couch, knees drawn to my chest, and let my mind wander through the labyrinth of my feelings for Dante.

But...there were no feelings for Dante.

There couldn't be.

We were just fucking, and we might become business partners...and it didn't have to become anything else. Right?

Chapter Nine: Dante

The door to the restaurant swung open with a familiar creak, and I stepped inside with Marco on my heels. Little Italy's heart pulsed through this joint—a place where everyone knew your name or at least pretended to if they valued their skin. The scent of garlic and tomatoes wrapped around me like a worn leather jacket as we slipped into a booth tucked away in the back.

"Look at this, Dante. Nona's special is still on the menu," Marco said, flipping open the laminated card. But his light tone didn't match the tightness in his eyes—a look I knew spelled trouble.

I leaned back against the worn leather, my white shirt stretching across my shoulders. "Spill it, Marco."

He put down the menu, his black shirt blending with the shadows. "Dante, we've got issues. The Carusos are pushing into legit businesses faster than we anticipated," he muttered, shooting a glance over his shoulder before locking eyes with me.

"Go on." My voice was even, but inside, my thoughts raced, already calculating moves and countermoves.

"Last week, they got their hands on a tech start-up. Clean money's their new game, but we both know it's just a front." Marco's voice had an edge, the kind that came when our territory was under threat.

"Let's see what they do next. We'll play it smart," I said, my gaze drifting beyond the flickering candle on our table to the rain.

"Smart, huh?" Marco leaned in, his voice low. "You're miles away, brother. What's got you distracted?" His smirk was slight, knowing.

I hesitated, swirling my glass of red wine, watching the ruby liquid cling to the sides like blood on a blade. "It's a woman—Jade."

"Jade Bentley? The doctor?" Marco's question came with a slightly cocked eyebrow.

"Neuroscientist," I corrected him, a small flash of pride lighting up within me at her title. My fingers curled around the stem of the glass tighter. "She's different, Marco. There's something about her..." I trailed off, the image of her dark hair and that determined gaze flashing in my mind.

Marco's eyebrow arched higher, his interest piqued by my rare display of fascination. She was fucking something and goddamn it if I wasn't completely caught up in trying to unravel her.

"Is she now?" Marco murmured, leaning back, the candlelight flickering across his face, throwing half of it into shadow. His grin had faded; replaced with contemplation as he studied me, probably trying to figure out if this was just another fling or something more complicated. Something real.

"Let's eat. We can talk strategy later," I said, closing the subject like a book I wasn't ready to reopen. Not yet. But as we ordered, and the conversation shifted to territories and rivals, Jade's image lingered, stubborn and enticing, promising a challenge like none I'd ever faced before.

The clink of silverware against porcelain filled the silence that stretched between us as we picked at the remaining morsels on our plates. Marco leaned back in his chair, the dim light from the overhead chandelier casting a soft glow on his smirking face.

"A scientist, huh?" He chuckled, shaking his head in amusement. "Never pegged you for falling for the academic type. But I guess if anyone could get you, it'd be someone who challenges you."

"You know I like smart women."

"Yeah, but I thought you meant smart like...'Knows how to shoot a gun without messing up her manicure,' not smart like, 'Can create a new life form in the lab,'" Marco retorted with a raised brow.

I grinned, swirling the last of my wine in the glass. The rich, dark liquid mirrored my thoughts - complex, deep, and slightly intoxicating. "Well maybe I'm growing up."

"Does she know how much you like her?"

I shook my head. "She knows how much I like fucking her."

"Oh?" Marco's interest clearly piqued, his smirk widening. "Details, Dante."

"Nice try," I warned, eyeing him with a smirk of my own. "I'm not going into details."

He drew back, feigning outrage. "What? Rude. C'mon."

"No," I said. "She's great. That's all you need to know."

"Always so protective," Marco mocked, a playful glint in his eyes. His usual cockiness was back, the moment of seriousness having passed. "You're acting like she's your wife or something."

"Watch it," I cautioned him sharply. His laughter filled the restaurant, muffled by the chatter of the other patrons and the clinking of plates.

"You know I'm just kidding around, Dante. But it is interesting seeing you like this. Obsessed over a woman."

"I'm not obsessed. I am serious about her, Marco," I confessed, and the gravity in my voice made him sit up straighter. "But I'm not sure how Father would react."

In the quiet of the restaurant, with the night pressing against the windows and the autumn air turning crisp outside, I felt the weight of our family name bearing down on me, threatening to snuff out this thing with Jade before it even had a chance to ignite fully.

Marco's demeanor stiffened at the mention of our father. "He won't be easy on this, Dante. You know how he views distractions." I could see the concern etched in the furrows of his brow, a testament to the loyalty he felt towards the empire we were born into.

I nodded, my mind already sifting through the labyrinth of Enzo Moretti's stringent views on family and business. "Yeah, I know," I admitted, pushing around a piece of bread on my plate. "But Jade's different."

"Great. She Italian?"

"I don't think so."

"Wants to be a housewife?"

"She's a neuroscientist."

"Cool," Marco said, sipping on his espresso. "Do you need me to say anything else?"

"I'm serious about her being different," I replied.

"Everyone's different until they're not," Marco muttered, his voice laced with a warning that went beyond brotherly advice.

"Let's talk business," I suggested, eager to steer away from personal matters, at least for the moment. The Caruso situation was a thorn in our side, one that needed plucking with precision rather than brute force.

We leaned closer, our heads nearly touching as we poured over the details of our current predicament. Marco's fingers drummed a rapid staccato on the tabletop, suggesting several aggressive moves that had been our father's signature approach.

"Take the docks, cut the supply line, let them bleed until they come begging," Marco listed, each suggestion punctuated by an assertive nod.

"Or," I interjected, "we could play it smarter. Use their own desperation against them. Starve them out slowly, make them think it's their idea to fold."

Marco raised an eyebrow, a slight smirk tugging at the corner of his mouth. "Since when did you become the patient one?"

"Since I realized rash decisions can lead to unnecessary wars," I shot back, my tone firm but not unkind. This was the delicate dance we'd mastered over the years—pushing and pulling in our quest to keep the Moretti name revered and feared.

"Alright then, Mr. Calculated," Marco conceded with a half-grin. "We'll try it your way. But if it backfires, it's on you."

"It won't," I said, the confidence in my voice belying the unease that squirmed in my gut.

"I hope you're sure. Be careful, Dante. Emotions make us vulnerable. Don't let this... affection cloud your judgment." Marco's words cut through the clinking of glasses like a serrated blade.

I met his gaze, steady and unflinching. "Since when did you start spouting philosophy?" I quipped, but his concern gnawed at me. He was right, of course. The Moretti men weren't known for their romantic escapades; we were bred for power, not love.

"Since I saw that look in your eye," Marco returned sharply. "You're too open around her, too...human."

"Jade isn't a threat," I countered, my voice low, almost a whisper.

"Everyone is a threat, Dante. Everyone." His tone was a stark reminder of our upbringing, the lessons drilled into us since we were kids.

A silent nod was all I offered in response, signaling the end of the conversation. We both knew better than to argue further in public.

As we stepped out into the crisp autumn night, the cool breeze of Little Italy brushed against my skin. I pondered Marco's warnings while our father's potential reaction to Jade loomed large in my thoughts.

"Father respects strength, Marco. Maybe he'll see Jade's intelligence as an asset," I mused aloud, trying to sound more convinced than I felt.

"Or maybe he'll see her as a distraction you can't afford," Marco shot back.

"Maybe," I conceded.

"Let's hope you're right. For both our sakes," Marco added, his voice tinged with the weight of our legacy.

"Let's hope," I echoed, my mind racing with possibilities—of a future where duty and desire didn't collide like opposing forces on a battlefield.

We walked in silence, letting the sounds of the city fill the void between us. The occasional laugh from a passerby or the distant hum of traffic were mere background noise to the internal cacophony of my thoughts.

"Remember what we're working towards," Marco finally said, his voice cutting through my thoughts as we neared the sleek black car waiting at the curb. It was more than just a reminder—it was a warning.

I nodded, understanding the unspoken message. The Moretti family didn't get where we were by being careless with our hearts or our business. "I know. I'm not going to do anything stupid," I replied, the lie tasting bitter on my tongue.

"Good." Marco clapped me on the back, a gesture that was both reassuring and a little too hard to be just brotherly affection. "Just remember, big brother, keep your head in the game. Father taught us that."

"And he is known for his wisdom."

Marco laughed, throwing his head back when he did. "Maybe not, but he is a scary motherfucker. I don't want to have to defend you."

"You won't," I said. "I got this."

"You sure?"

"Always," I said, but even as the words left my mouth, I knew that my heart wasn't entirely in it. Jade had already gotten under my skin in ways I hadn't anticipated.

Marco's dark eyes searched mine for a moment longer, as if he could see right through the facade. Then he nodded once, sharply, and slid into the car without another word.

I watched as the vehicle pulled away from the curb, its taillights disappearing into the night. Alone now, I felt the weight of the decisions ahead of me—decisions that held the potential to reshape not just my life, but the lives of everyone connected to the Moretti name.

I took a taxi back to my apartment. The night was cool, the kind of crisp autumn air that makes you feel alive. I shoved my hands into the pockets of my jeans as I walked out of the car toward my building, each step echoing against the concrete. The city around me was quiet, almost peaceful, a stark contrast to the storm raging in my head.

"Family first."

Dad's voice echoed like a mantra I'd heard since childhood. Enzo Moretti didn't just expect obedience; he demanded it. And here I was, thinking about risking it all for a woman who had no idea what she'd walked into. For a woman who believed in making the world better while standing in the middle of a battlefield.

For a woman who had no idea who I was.

Her keycard was still in my apartment–I hadn't used it yet. I was thinking about giving it back to her, telling her she'd just dropped it back at my place. I would do it next time I saw her.

Damn it.

Her name repeated itself in my head like a prayer, or maybe a curse. She was brilliance and beauty wrapped in innocence, and I was neck-deep in a life that could swallow her whole.

I reached my apartment building, the familiar sight offering no comfort tonight. In the elevator, my reflection stared back at me from the polished metal doors–I looked tired, old.

My apartment was dark when I entered, the only light spilling from the cityscape outside. I walked straight to the balcony, pushing the door open to let the city's breath wash over me.

I looked out at the city—the city my family controlled with an iron fist—and felt something inside me shift. For the first time, I wasn't sure if I wanted to be a part of its dark heart. For the first time, I wondered if I could be the one to challenge the empire built on blood and loyalty.

But I hadn't even told her how much I liked her. I couldn't be thinking of throwing my entire empire away for a woman who probably didn't feel the same way I did about her.

No.

First I needed to take over the Moretti operation. Then I could do whatever the fuck I wanted to do.

And that included Dr. Jade Bentley.

Chapter Ten: Jade

The lab had chewed me up and spit me out, leaving my brain tangled in a web of genetic codes and ethical debates. I stood outside the familiar coffee shop, my hand hovering over the door handle like it was an electric fence. Dante's texts were burning a hole in my pocket—polite enough to keep him at arm's length but distant enough to draw a line. Just one coffee, I told myself, you can handle that.

Then I would reach out to him and...figure all this out.

I pushed open the door, the scent of roasted beans wrapping around me like a warm blanket. The barista nodded in recognition as I mouthed my order—a double espresso, no frills. I was running on autopilot, my thoughts still knotted with work until I turned and nearly collided with a wall of muscle and expensive cologne.

Dante Moretti.

"Jade," he said, his voice smooth as the espresso I craved, pulling me back to reality—a reality where Dante Moretti always seemed to be one step behind me, waiting. His dark eyes held mine, and every cell in my body went on high alert. There was no escaping now.

And I was pretty sure I didn't want to escape.

"Jade, what a pleasant surprise," Dante said, his voice rich with warmth that didn't match the cool smirk on his face.

I was caught off guard and could only manage a small smile in response. "Dante, I didn't see you there," I replied, my voice betraying a nervous edge I hadn't intended to reveal.

He stood there, all casual confidence in a tailored suit that probably cost more than my entire wardrobe. Despite my initial reluctance, I found myself being guided toward a small table by the window. We sat across from each other, the city's hustle and bustle a mere backdrop to this unexpected encounter.

"Black coffee for me," Dante told the waitress, never taking his eyes off me. I fidgeted under his gaze, acutely aware of every word that left my lips. My coffee arrived, and I wrapped my hands around the cup, grateful for something to hold onto.

"Thanks for joining me," he said, and I wondered if he heard the pounding of my heart over the clinking of cups and murmured conversations surrounding us. It was just coffee, but with Dante Moretti, nothing was ever just anything.

"Yeah, of course. What were we going to do? Sit in different booths and pretend we didn't know each other?"

He wrinkled his nose. "Like roleplay? Sounds hot."

"Do you ever take anything seriously?" I asked, sounding more harsh than I intended.

"Yes," he said, looking into my eyes. "Plenty of things. Busy day at the lab?"

"Always," I answered, sipping my coffee, careful to reveal little. "We're pushing for some major breakthroughs." My guard was up; there were things about BioHQ that needed to remain unsaid, especially to someone like Dante Moretti. When he had sold me on working together, I had fully believed him. But now that Ellie had warned me off him, I simply couldn't be sure if his intentions were pure.

"Been avoiding me, Jade?" His tone was light, but his eyes searched mine for something more.

"Slammed at work," I said quickly, too quickly maybe, "and I'm sorry about missing that meeting with the lawyer. We'll get to it eventually."

"Sure, when the madness at BioHQ settles down." He shrugged, seemingly unfazed.

"Exactly." I forced a smile, yet my chest tightened.

Dante leaned forward then, his elbows on the table, and his voice dropped to a near-whisper. "It is a nice surprise to run into you like this," he said, and his smile had a way of reaching his eyes that made it difficult to look away.

My heart did a quick dance before I regained control. "You seem to say that every time we meet," I shot back with as much playfulness as I could muster, keeping the conversation buoyant, even though my stomach was in knots.

"It is always nice to see you, yes," he said. "And I do mean it every time."

I opened my mouth to respond, but suddenly, his hand brushed against mine on the table. It was a fleeting touch, probably unintentional, but it sent a jolt through me. My skin tingled where he made contact, and I felt that dangerous warmth creeping up my neck. Instinctively, I pulled back, folding my arms in front of me as if they could shield me from the electricity between us.

"Sorry," he said, though his eyes held a glint that suggested the contact wasn't entirely accidental. "Didn't mean to startle you."

"It's fine," I managed to say, putting a little distance between us. I couldn't afford distractions, not when my work demanded all of me. Not when he was a Moretti.

He tilted his head, observing me with consideration. Then, shifting gears, he said, "Your ambition is something I truly admire." His voice carried sincerity, and his gaze held respect. "You're dedicated to your work, much like I am to my business. Not many can match that level of commitment."

"Thank you," I responded, genuinely surprised by the compliment. This...wasn't the kind of compliment I was expecting from him.

"Of course," he agreed, nodding. "It's the drive that keeps us moving forward. And I see that drive in you, Jade. So if you need to focus on this, then you need to focus on it. But I want you to know, I'm here and waiting."

"Why?" I heard myself ask.

"What do you mean why? You're fucking incredible."

I looked at him then, really looked, and saw something beyond the suave businessman and rumored underworld ties—a reflection of determination akin to my own. It was disarming, and for a moment, I allowed myself to simply appreciate the connection beyond the compliment.

"Drive can take us to places we never imagined," I said quietly, more to myself than to him. But it was true; whether in science or in whatever murky waters Dante navigated, we were both propelled by forces that wouldn't let us rest.

The espresso machine hissed in the background, a stark reminder of the ordinary world bustling around us as I navigated these extraordinary moments with Dante. He was all but an enigma—a man whose life was embroidered with threads of danger and power, threads that could unravel at any moment.

But fuck it. He was already here. There was nothing wrong with just talking to him. I just needed to make sure not to jump into bed with him again.

"Your childhood must've been something else," I said, attempting to steer us back to safer waters. "Growing up in Little Italy, I mean."

Dante's eyes lit up with the mention. "It was...colorful, you could say. Full of life, full of characters." His lips curled into a half-smile as he leaned back in his chair. "You know, there was this bakery just around the corner from where we lived—best cannolis in the city. My old man used to take my brother and me there every Sunday after mass."

"You went to church?"

"Yes, every Sunday," he replied. "We learned early on that we'd be beaten if we didn't."

"Jesus."

"Yes, he was there," Dante said, flashing me a smile. "It wasn't that bad. He's gotten less scary as I've gotten older."

"Sounds charming," I replied, my voice steady despite the fluttering in my chest.

"Charming," he echoed, his smile waning slightly. "Yeah, it had its moments. But not everything is as sweet as pastry cream, Jade."

"Including your dad."

"Yeah," he replied, shrugging. "Oh well."

"Maybe you can show me around some time," I ventured, curious yet cautious.

"Maybe," Dante said, his gaze locking onto mine. "I'd like that."

We sat in silence for a moment, the sounds of the coffee shop wrapping around us like a comforting blanket. It was a reprieve from the intensity of our conversation—a chance for me to collect my thoughts and prepare for the inevitable parting of ways.

"Thankfully, lab work doesn't leave much room for dull moments either," I said, trying to match his earlier ease. "Sometimes it feels like I'm on the verge of something monumental."

"Is that right?" Dante's interest seemed piqued, a flicker of genuine curiosity in his eyes. "And does Dr. Jade Bentley enjoy being on the edge of discovery?"

"Immensely," I said, allowing myself a small smile. It felt good to talk about my work—my passion—with someone who seemed to understand the drive behind it.

"Then here's hoping you find what you're looking for," Dante said, raising his empty coffee cup in a mock toast.

"Here's hoping," I echoed, clinking my cup against his.

The clink of our cups was a soft sound, almost lost amid the hum of conversation and the whirring of espresso machines. Dante's eyes were still fixed on me, his gaze unwavering, intense in a way that suggested he wasn't just talking about my research.

"Jade, I've been thinking a lot about us," he began, his voice dropping to a low murmur. The lighthearted air evaporated as if sucked away by his sudden gravity.

I stiffened, my hand tightening around the ceramic cup. This was not a conversation I'd prepared for, not with him. His world was one of shadows and secrets, a place where my scientific mind could find no foothold. And yet, here he was, unmasking a vulnerability I hadn't known existed within the enigmatic Dante Moretti.

"Us?" The word came out more as a cautious breath than a question, betraying the confusion that knotted inside me.

Just as he leaned forward, perhaps to close the distance between uncertainty and revelation, his phone rang—a sharp, insistent trill that cut through the moment like a warning siren.

"Excuse me," Dante muttered, irritation flashing across his features as he pulled out his phone. He stood up, stepping away from the table with an apologetic tilt of his head. "This is important."

I watched his back as he paced away, the phone pressed to his ear, his body language taut with frustration. My heart raced, thumping against my ribs as if trying to keep pace with the myriad thoughts that tumbled through my head. What had he been about to say? Did 'us' mean what I thought it did?

In the brief solitude his absence afforded, I fought to steady my breathing, to still the tremor that threatened to take hold of my hands. A part of me wanted to flee, to escape before I got caught up in whatever web Dante wove around his life. But another part—a reckless, daring part—wanted to stay, to hear him out.

"Sorry about that," Dante said as he returned, sliding his phone back into his pocket. There was no mistaking the apology in his tone, but also a resolve that had not been there before. "Business never sleeps."

"Seems it doesn't," I replied, finding my voice again, though it sounded far too casual for the storm of emotions brewing inside me.

"Let's have that dinner sometime this week. Just us," he proposed, his eyes searching mine for an answer. "No business talk. We need to catch up, you know, properly."

"When?" I asked, my heart jackhammering in my chest.

"Thursday?" he countered, cocking his head. "I'll pick you up. I did promise to wine and dine you."

I hesitated, caught between the instinct to guard myself and an unbidden curiosity that urged me to leap into the unknown. The thrill of Dante's attention was undeniable—there was something about him that pulled at me, a magnetism that was both exciting and terrifying.

"Jade?" he prompted softly, his voice a low rumble that seemed to resonate within the otherwise quiet space of the coffee shop.

I weighed my choice carefully, aware that dinner wasn't just dinner when it came to someone like Dante Moretti. My life was one of labs and research, of controlled experiments where the variables were known and outcomes predictable. Dante represented an anomaly in my neatly ordered world—one that could either be an astonishing discovery or an uncontrollable reaction. And I remembered Ellie's warning...but it was hard to think about Ellie when Dante was looking at me the way he was.

"Okay," I finally agreed, the word slipping out before my more cautious side could protest. His smile deepened, both triumphant and genuine, and something inside me fluttered in response.

"Great," Dante said. "I'll pick you up at seven on Thursday."

"Thursday," I echoed, locking away my doubts and uncertainties for another time. There was no turning back now—I had stepped into Dante's world, and only time would tell if the risk was worth the enigmatic promise of 'us.'

And if things went wrong...well, fuck it. This was just a bit of fun. It didn't have to spiral.

I wasn't going to let it.

Chapter Eleven: Jade

The crisp autumn air nipped at my skin, a sharp reminder of the city's transition into night. I waited, my breath forming small clouds before me, when the purr of an engine approached. A black car slid to a stop in front of my building, its gleam like a slice of night itself.

Dante Moretti emerged from the vehicle, his suit a shadow against the dimming light of dusk. He strode towards me with a confidence that made my heart do strange things. "Evening, Jade," he greeted, his voice as smooth as the silk lining of his jacket.

"Hey," I managed, feeling suddenly underdressed in my simple blouse and skirt. His smile was disarmingly charming, and when he offered his hand, it felt like a lifeline in a sea of unease. The touch of his palm was warm against mine, and the way he guided me with a hand at my lower back sent an unfamiliar thrill through me.

We slipped into the car, and Dante didn't waste time starting up a conversation as we merged into the traffic. He told me stories about New York – quirky tales of the people and places that made up its heart. It wasn't long before laughter softened the growing tension between our bodies, filling the space with something that felt dangerously close to comfort.

"Did you know Central Park has its own zoo?" he asked, glancing at me with a playful smirk.

"Really? In all my years here, I never stumbled upon it," I said, feigning surprise, though I'd spent countless lunch breaks wandering those paths.

"Maybe one day, I'll have to show you. There's more hidden in this city than you think." He winked, and I rolled my eyes, but my lips betrayed me with a smile.

"Is that a promise or a threat, Mr. Moretti?"

"Depends on how much you enjoy surprises," he shot back, the corner of his mouth lifting in a half-smile that did things to my insides.

Our banter wove through the drive like the city lights streaking past the tinted windows. With every laugh, the walls I had meticulously built around myself seemed to crumble just a little bit more. And though part of me screamed caution, the rest of me was already too far gone, lost in the dark allure of Dante Moretti's world.

The car pulled up to a discrete entrance, the kind of place you wouldn't notice unless you knew it was there. Dante stepped out first, reaching a hand out to help me from the vehicle. His touch sent an unmistakable jolt through me as I accepted it, stepping into the chill of the autumn evening.

"Welcome to Il Nascondiglio," he murmured, his voice low enough that it felt like it was meant for my ears only. The restaurant's name, 'The Hideaway,' seemed more than fitting given its secretive vibe.

We entered through a velvet curtain, and I was immediately enveloped by the warmth of the intimate space. Soft music played in the background, a gentle melody that wrapped around us as we were led to our secluded booth. Dante pulled out the chair for me, and as I sat down, his fingers grazed the small of my back, leaving a trail of heat on my skin.

"Thank you," I managed, trying to ignore how his simple gesture had quickened my heartbeat.

"Anything for you," he replied, and there was something in his tone—a hint of sincerity—that caught me off guard.

A waiter appeared as if summoned by our readiness to begin, presenting us with menus and taking our drink orders. Dante suggested a bottle of red that he promised would "change my life."

"Bold claim," I challenged, arching an eyebrow.

"Trust me, Jade," he said, his eyes locking onto mine. "When it comes to wine—and a few other things—I never disappoint."

Our dinner unfolded with an ease that surprised me. We talked about everything from my latest research breakthroughs, at least as much as I could tell him, to his genuine love for classic literature, a side of him I hadn't expected. With each shared story and laugh, I began to see the man across from me as Dante, just Dante.

"Tell me about your work," he urged, his gaze never straying as he took a thoughtful sip of his wine.

I delved into the complexities of biotechnology, explaining the potential impact of my current project. He listened intently, his interest seeming to go beyond polite dinner conversation. It was disconcerting and flattering all at once.

"Sounds like you're on the verge of changing the world," he noted, admiration lacing his words. "I know I promised not to talk about work, but my offer stands."

"I know. And, about changing it...I don't know. Maybe just a small corner of it," I demurred, feeling the weight of his attention like a physical touch.

"Modesty doesn't suit you," he teased lightly, but his smile told me he meant it. "You should own your brilliance, Jade. It's... captivating."

His compliment, spoken so earnestly, left me momentarily breathless. I realized then that this dangerous, powerful man saw me—not as a pawn in his family's games or a problem to be solved—but as a person of worth. And despite every rational cell in my brain, I couldn't help but feel drawn to the gravity of him, to the possibilities that lay in his dark eyes.

"Thank you, Dante," I said softly, the words barely above a whisper. "For seeing me."

"Seeing you is the easy part," he replied, his voice low. A foot brushed mine under the table, and an involuntary laugh escaped me, a sound I hadn't known was bottled up inside. The contact sparked something, a connection that felt both dangerous and intoxicating.

"Is it?" I teased back, my own foot lingering against his. "You make it sound simple."

"Nothing about this is simple, Jade." There was a heaviness to his words, a hint of the world he came from—a world I knew so little about, yet there I was, sitting across from him, unable to deny the magnetism between us.

"Remember our night together?" he asked, his tone shifting, becoming saturated with a longing that matched my own memories. "I think about it often. About you."

"Only often?" I found myself flirting back, the words slipping out before I could stop them.

"Alright, incessantly," he admitted with a grin that reached his eyes, transforming them into something warm and inviting.

Dessert arrived, decadent and sweet, but it was no match for the hunger that had nothing to do with food. We barely touched it, our focus entirely on each other, the air between us thick with unsaid promises.

"Let's get out of here," Dante said suddenly, his voice rough around the edges as if holding back a torrent of desire.

I nodded, my heart racing at the prospect of being alone with him again. It was reckless, maybe even foolish, but in that moment, with his hand reaching across the table to find mine, I didn't care. I couldn't resist the pull, the magnetic draw that seemed to have a life of its own.

"Okay," I breathed, my decision made. "Let's go."

The black leather of Dante Moretti's luxury car creaked under me as we sliced through the streets of New York, the city a blur of lights outside the tinted windows. My breath hitched with every turn, every stoplight an eternity, every acceleration a promise as I inched closer to the edge of something unknown but irresistible.

"Jade," his voice was a low rumble next to me, "do you want to touch yourself?"

I turned sharply to look at him, his profile etched by the passing streetlights. "What makes you think I would?" I countered, my tone challenging yet laced with the heat that had nothing to do with the climate control of the car.

He chuckled, a sound dark and thrilling. "Because I can smell how turned on you are," he said, each word deliberate, his gaze never leaving the road.

Heat flooded my cheeks, and for a moment, I was grateful for the shadows that cloaked us. The idea that he could sense my arousal, that it filled the space between us like another presence, was both mortifying and wildly exciting.

Before I could muster a response, the car eased to a stop. We had arrived at his apartment, a high-rise building that scraped the evening sky. Dante got out and came around to open my door, his hand extended to help me up. I took it, feeling the roughness of his skin against mine, the contact sending a jolt through me as if his touch was charged with electricity.

"Welcome back," he said.

"Back to..."

"My place," he said, winking at me.

"Right. We weren't far," I said.

"I was hoping you'd want to come back here," he replied, winking at me.

"God. You really were counting on it, huh?"

"What can I say? I'm optimistic."

The elevator chimed, and the doors slid open to reveal a corridor that led to his apartment. Dante's hand found the small of my back, guiding me with an assurance that spoke volumes about who he was—powerful, in control, yet attentive.

Once inside, the door clicking shut behind us, the atmosphere shifted, thick with anticipation. Without a word, he led me to the couch, his hands framing my face as he leaned in. The kiss was immediate, a clash of lips that melded with a hunger that seemed to have been simmering for an eternity. I responded without thought, my body pressing against Dante's as if drawn by some magnetic force.

"Jade," he whispered against my lips, the sound of my name on his breath sending a rush of desire through me.

"More," I managed to say between kisses, surprised at my own boldness but unable to hold back the tidal wave of need crashing over me.

Without hesitation, Dante lifted me, his arms strong and certain as he carried me to the bedroom. The world outside—the lab, my research, all the questions about right and wrong—faded away, leaving only the immediacy of this moment.

He laid me down gently on the bed, and I watched, heart racing, as his hands began their exploration, tracing the outline of my clothes before they fell away, piece by piece. His touch was both revelation and revolution, igniting a fire within me that I hadn't known I possessed.

"God, Jade," Dante murmured, his voice low and laced with the same desire that coursed through my veins.

Our eyes met, and I saw in his gaze something raw and unguarded. It was a look that went beyond lust, hinting at depths and complexities that resonated with my own. And in that instant, I understood that this wasn't just physical. There was something more happening between us, something intense and terrifying in its intensity.

"Stay with me," he said, not a command but a plea, and it shattered the last of my reservations.

He pressed his lips against mine, his hand slowly skimming down toward my blouse as he started to undo my buttons. He leaned close to my ear. "I've been touching myself thinking about you every night," he said, his breath hot against my ear.

"The way your pussy felt around my cock," he admitted, his voice dropping to a husky whisper. "The way you tasted, the sounds you made. All of it. I haven't been able to get you out of my mind."

A blush crept up my cheeks, spreading warmth throughout my body at his words. My mind was spinning, heart pounding like a drum in my chest as his dark eyes held mine with an intensity that left me breathless.

His fingers skillfully undid the last of my buttons, revealing the lace bra I'd worn underneath. His gaze heated as he looked at me, and I felt a surge of confidence under his appreciative stare.

He slid off the rest of my clothes with ease, leaving me bare before him. His hands were everywhere, tracing lines and curves with a hunger that matched my own. Each touch was electric, sparking flares of pleasure that coiled tight in my belly.

"Relax," he cooed, his fingers teasing the waistband of my panties. "Let me take care of you."

His words were a soothing balm, filled with promise and intent. It was in the way he touched me, the way his eyes met mine, that I knew we were on the brink of something life-altering. Suddenly, everything else—my work at BioHQ, the Moretti family's illicit activities—seemed irrelevant compared to Dante.

His hand slipped under the lace fabric, and I let out a gasp as his fingers found my heat. He moved slowly at first, teasing me into a pleasure that sent my senses spiraling. The intensity of his touch only heightened my desire for him, my body responding eagerly to him.

"You're so wet for me, Jade," he murmured, his voice thick with desire. "Do you feel how much I want you?"

I did. The hardness pressing against my thigh was a testament to that, and it sent another thrill of desire coursing through me. I nodded, unable to find the words as he explored me further, his touch coaxing moans from me that echoed around the room.

"Good," he said, his voice a low growl as he slipped a finger inside of me. My body clenched around him, and his other hand moved to cup my breast, his thumb teasing the hard peak through the lace of my bra. "Have you been touching yourself thinking about me too?"

My breath hitched, a sharp intake echoing through the silence of his bedroom. "Yes," I admitted, my voice barely above a whisper. His response was immediate, a low growl that vibrated against my skin as his lips moved down to press heated kisses along the curve of my neck.

"Show me," he commanded, his voice husky with lust.

Confused, I looked at him. "Dante, I-"

With a swift movement, he pulled away from me, leaving only the cold air of his bedroom against my heated skin. He sat down on the edge of the bed, his dark eyes watching me with an intensity that quickened my heart rate.

"Do it for me, Jade," he said softly, leaning back on his elbows. "I want to see you touch yourself."

His eyes were on me, watching with a hungry gaze as I lay back onto the bed. His presence was a raw, pulsing energy in the room, stoking my arousal and emboldening me. The sheets beneath me felt cool against my heated skin as I reached down, following his command.

My fingers hesitated for a moment before they slipped between my folds, exploring the wetness Dante had coaxed out of me. A soft gasp fell from my lips at the touch, the pleasure sparking brightly against the building anticipation.

"That's it," Dante murmured, his gaze dark and approving. His hands moved to unbuckle his belt, his movements slow and deliberate as he watched me touch myself. "Don't stop."

As I continued to stroke myself, Dante slowly undid his pants and kicked them off, revealing the hardness that strained against his boxers. He was breathtaking, the moonlight casting an ethereal glow over his muscular body as he watched me intently.

"You have no idea how much it drives me crazy seeing you like this," he said, a hint of desperation seeping into his voice. His hand moved down to his length, mirroring my movements as our eyes locked together.

"Dante..." I breathed out, my body thrumming with desire. The sight of him touching himself while watching me was intensely erotic, stoking the flames higher and higher until I felt like I was going to combust.

His eyes never left mine as he pushed down his boxers, revealing himself fully to me. "God... Jade...seeing you like this..." he managed to say between heavy breaths.

"Yes?" I prompted, wanting him to finish his thought.

"It's more than I can bear," he finished hoarsely, his grip on his length tightening. His eyes traveled down my body, taking in the sight of me pleasuring myself for him. "You are stunning, Jade."

His words fueled my desire further, and I moaned softly as I continued to touch myself. Dante's gaze was intense, filled with a burning hunger that matched my own. I found myself getting lost in his dark eyes, consumed by the erotic intensity of the moment.

"Are you close?" he asked, his voice barely above a whisper.

I nodded, my breath hitching as the pleasure continued to build up within me. The fire inside was growing hotter, threatening to engulf me completely.

"Wait for me," he instructed firmly.

As if on cue, Dante moved closer, hovering over me while never breaking eye contact. His hand moved from his length to mine, replacing my fingers with his own.

The sudden change elicited a gasp from me, and I arched my back, pleasure coursing through me at the touch of his fingers on my sensitive flesh. My hands moved instinctively, reaching out to clutch at his sturdy shoulders as he continued to stroke me.

"Dante... I can't..." I murmured, the words coming out as a breathless plea. The pressure in my belly was building rapidly now, spiraling upward toward an all-consuming crescendo.

"Hold on," he commanded, leaning in to capture my lips in a searing kiss. Our tongues danced together in rhythm with the movements of his hand, amplifying the pleasure that was threatening to consume me wholly.

Our bodies entwined around each other as we lost ourselves in the moment. His fingers never faltered, drawing out the sweet torture until my body was on fire and my nerves were screaming for release.

"Tell me what you want, Jade," Dante said.

"I need you inside of me," I replied breathlessly.

His eyes darkened at my plea, a rough growl vibrating in his chest. "Fuck. Okay."

He pulled away slightly, only to shed the last piece of clothing that separated our bodies, his shirt. He was stunning in his nakedness, every inch of him exuding raw virility. His dark eyes met mine with an intensity that made me shiver in anticipation.

"Dante..." I murmured, my voice a breathless whisper as he loomed over me, his body casting a shadow that seemed to swallow the room whole.

"Jade," he said softly, his voice laced with a desire that mirrored my own. He moved closer, positioning himself at my entrance. The head of his length brushed against me, eliciting a gasp that was quickly swallowed by his mouth on mine.

Suddenly, he was inside me, filling me in a way that sent shockwaves of pleasure through my body. I gasped against his mouth, my nails digging into his back as he moved slowly, giving me time to adjust to him. I could feel every inch of him, the ridges and veins of his hard length creating an exquisite friction that was driving me insane.

"Fuck, your pussy is so tight," he said into my ear. "Does it feel good, Jade?"

"Yes," I panted, my fingers scraping against his back as he started to move. His thrusts were slow and measured, each one lighting a fire within me that was impossible to ignore.

"Did I tell you you could stop touching your clit while I fucked you?"

I shook my head, a blush spreading across my cheeks as I reached down to follow his command. His dark eyes were heavy with desire as he watched me, the sight of his arousal stoking the fire within me. My fingers moved in sync with his thrusts, creating a symphony of pleasure that was threatening to consume me.

"Good girl," Dante murmured huskily, his hand moving to grip my hip as he continued to move inside of me. His strong, sure movements coupled with the sight of his pleasure filled gaze was intoxicating, pushing me closer and closer to the edge.

Suddenly, his rhythm faltered, his thrusts becoming more erratic as he neared his own climax. His hand left my hip to grasp mine, stilling my movements against my clit.

"Stop," he commanded breathlessly. "I want us to come together."

"Dante..." I pleaded, the knot in my belly growing tighter and tighter with every second that passed. The anticipation was killing me, but the thrill of obeying him was even more intoxicating.

"Stay with me, Jade," he urged, his voice strained as he fought to keep himself composed. His free hand found its way to my breast, thumb rubbing circles around the sensitive bud. "Let me come in your pretty pussy as you tighten around me."

The words sent a jolt of arousal through me, causing me to whimper helplessly beneath him. His fingers were magic, pushing me closer to the brink with each caress. Dante was relentless, his rhythm increasing as he chased his own release. I could feel every inch of him, each thrust bringing me closer to the edge.

"All right," he murmured, his voice barely more than a ragged groan. "Now."

His command triggered something primal within me, pushing me over the edge as I clung to him. A wave of pleasure surged through my body as my climax washed over me. My walls clenched around him in rhythm with my release, drawing a guttural groan from Dante as he followed suit.

His thrusts became more sporadic, each one sending another wave of pleasure coursing through me until I was left gasping and trembling beneath him. He collapsed onto me, his body heavy and sated against mine.

"You're fucking hot," he said. He was out of breath.

I didn't reply. I couldn't. My entire body was still thrumming from the aftermath of our pleasure, every nerve ending ablaze. All I could do was lie there, gasping for breath and trying to process what had just happened.

Slowly, Dante pulled himself out of me, rolling onto his back and pulling me close against his side. His fingers traced lazy circles over my bare skin, the sensation calming and soothing in contrast to our earlier frantic coupling.

"I should probably go..." I started to sit up.

"Stay," he said. "Let's fuck until we physically can't and have breakfast on my balcony tomorrow. What's stopping us, Jade? I'll drive you to work in the morning."

"I don't know..."

"Come on," he said, flashing me that charming smile. "What's the worst that could happen?"

Chapter Twelve: Jade

The fluorescent lights of BioHQ's conference room flickered to life as I made my way through a forest of white lab coats. My notebook was clutched tight under my arm, my brain already whirring with the day's agenda when the room's murmur hushed at the entry of a newcomer. His confident stride and immaculate suit were out of place among our casual scientific chaos.

"Morning, everyone. Let's bring this to order," announced Dr. White, motioning toward the stranger. "This is Edward Rodriguez, your new cybersecurity consultant."

I scanned Edward, his presence a sharp note in our otherwise routine meeting. Why now? Why us? But answers would come later. Now was for observing, for learning what game he played.

"Thank you," Edward began, his voice even, persuasive. "I'm here to reinforce our defenses against prying eyes. Corporate spies are real, and your work on neural regeneration is too valuable to risk."

His words carried weight, the unspoken threat of espionage looming like a shadow over our groundbreaking research. As he detailed his plan, talking firewalls and encryption, I couldn't shake off the feeling that there was more to his story than met the eye. And yet, I found myself nodding along, drawn to the sense of safety his certainty promised.

"Any questions?" Edward finished, locking eyes with each of us in turn.

My colleagues peppered him with technical inquiries, which he fielded with ease. Yet, beneath the surface of every answer, my mind spun with suspicion. Who sent you, Edward Rodriguez? What do you really want from us?

Only time would tell. For now, I had science to attend to.

"Jade, what do you think?" Ellie's voice jolted me back to the present.

"About Edward?" I replied, tucking a stray lock of hair behind my ear. We were outside the meeting room now, in the more casual setting of the lab's break area. The hum of machines and scent of sterile equipment faded into the background as I focused on El, who was fidgeting with the sleeve of her white coat.

"Isn't it odd? Him waltzing in at this stage?" Ellie leaned against the counter, her petite frame dwarfed by the industrial coffee maker she was nonchalantly operating.

I grasped the warmth of my own mug, feeling the heat seep into my palms. "Yeah, it is," I conceded, avoiding her gaze. "I wonder if something happened."

"Like if someone got caught slipping?" Ellie said. "Weird, right?"

I nodded. "I guess."

Ellie gave me a knowing look, her eyes sharp, mirroring my concern. "You're thinking about it too, aren't you? About why now?"

"Can't help it," I admitted, stirring my coffee slowly, watching the vortex I created dissolve. "There's something unsettling about the timing."

"Like he doesn't quite fit the puzzle," Ellie murmured, tapping her finger against her chin. Her intuition was always spot-on, a trait that kept us both grounded amidst the complexities of our work—and lives.

"Exactly." I took a sip, allowing the bitterness to sharpen my senses. "But let's not get carried away with conspiracy theories. We've got a project to complete, and Rodriguez...well, he's just another variable we'll have to account for."

"Let's hope he's one that won't cause an unwanted reaction," Ellie quipped, a wry smile tugging at her lips.

I couldn't help but return the smile. Trust Ellie to find humor in the face of uncertainty. But she was right, as usual. Edward Rodriguez was an unknown, and in the volatile equation that was our lives, one misstep could lead to disaster.

"Let's just keep an eye out," I said, feeling the weight of responsibility settle over me. "For the project's sake."

We made our way to the lab. Once the door was closed behind us, Ellie cleared her throat.

"Enhanced security just as your...I mean, as Dante Moretti shows interest in our research? Seems more than coincidental," Ellie muttered, her skepticism laced with concern.

I glanced around the sterile lab, my gaze lingering on the locked cabinets housing our latest trial samples. "Things are getting more intense with Dante," I said curtly, brushing off her insinuation while feeling the knot in my stomach tighten. "Let's keep our focus on the work."

"Right," Ellie nodded, though her eyes still held a shadow of doubt. She knew the dangers that lurked behind the Moretti name, dangers that were now creeping too close to the world we had built within these walls.

With a deliberate shift, I turned towards our data analysis screen. "We've nearly tripled the efficiency of axonal recovery in our latest trials using targeted protein delivery," I explained with an enthusiasm that felt almost forced. It was crucial to steer clear of personal entanglements, especially when they threatened the sanctity of our scientific haven.

"Wait. Tripled? I thought we were working on a doubling model," Ellie's voice perked up, her natural curiosity piqued.

My smile turned genuine at Ellie's reaction. "We were. But I had a breakthrough last night with the synthesis process," I explained, moving to the terminal to bring up the latest data. "It was a long shot, but the new delivery vector improved uptake efficiency by 150%."

"Why didn't you mention it?"

"During the cybersecurity snoozefest?" I asked. "Nah, I thought it would be better to do it in private. The implications could redefine neural repair strategies."

Ellie leaned closer to the screen, her scientific hunger momentarily overtaking her earlier reservations. "Show me the latest simulations," she urged, already lost in the thrill of discovery.

As I navigated through the graphs and data points, detailing the intricacies of our approach, the rest of the world temporarily faded away.

For now, at least, the lab was our safe harbor, and the science, our shared language of hope.

Over the next several days, that illusion of safety began to erode with each visit from Edward. He really put a damper on our discovery.

"Dr. Bentley," Edward would begin, his tone always respectful but laced with an authority that seemed out of place in the research facility. "I've been reviewing your protocols for data security. Impressive, but there are vulnerabilities."

I watched him, my hands paused mid-gesture over a petri dish, as he laid out his concerns with a precision that caught me off guard. It was disconcerting, this man's knowledge of cybersecurity and the ease with which he dissected our systems.

I really had a lot of other things to worry about. I didn't want to deal with him.

"Your encryption could be stronger here," he'd point at a line of code on the computer screen. "And you should consider two-factor authentication for accessing this database."

"Thank you, Mr. Rodriguez," I replied, the words stiff on my tongue. His dedication was...unsettling. My work was difficult and finicky, and I didn't want to have to pay attention to him.

"Call me Edward when we're alone," he offered with a half-smile that didn't reach his eyes. "Just trying to keep your work safe, Doctor."

"Of course, Edward." I nodded curtly, turning back to my cultures. His visits were becoming more frequent, and while I couldn't deny the usefulness of his insights, it gnawed at me—the way he seemed to weave himself into the fabric of our daily operations.

"Edward," I called out after him one day, a question burning inside me. "Why do you care so much about our research?"

He stopped in his tracks, and for a moment, I saw something flicker behind his stoic facade. "What do you mean? This is my job, Dr. Bentley. I take it seriously. I have a vested interest in protecting your research."

I watched as he walked away, his steps measured and sure. A vested interest. The phrase echoed in my mind, a puzzle piece that refused to fit neatly into the larger picture.

So weird, but not really my business.

I shook my head, trying to dispel the unease that settled over me. It was a feeling I couldn't quite shake, no matter how much data I analyzed or how many results I tallied up at the end of the day. Edward was like a shadow cast across my thoughts, an enigma wrapped in the guise of a protector. A few hours later, it was time to go to the most annoying meeting ever.

"Jade, you coming?" Ellie's voice burst through my reverie, pulling me back to the present. "We gotta go waste a couple of hours."

"Sorry, lost in thought," I admitted as we headed towards the small conference room where Edward had set up for his mini-workshop.

"About Edward's offer?" Ellie queried, her expression unreadable.

"His insights," I corrected, pushing open the door to find a small, attentive crowd gathered. I scanned the room, finding Edward at the front by a projector, exuding that same calm authority that both irked and impressed me.

"Thank you all for joining," he began, his gaze briefly flitting over to me before addressing the group. "Today, we'll discuss phishing, social engineering, and other cyber threats that could compromise not just our personal data but our professional integrity."

His presentation was concise, peppered with real-life examples that made the dangers tangible. He didn't just talk; he showed us how easily our defenses could be breached, how our trust could be exploited. By the end, I couldn't help but feel a grudging respect for the man.

"It's a good reminder of the threats we face," I found myself saying out loud once the workshop concluded, "not just externally but internally."

"Exactly," Edward replied, meeting my eyes with an intensity that suggested he wasn't just referring to cybersecurity. There was a depth to his statement, a subtext that hinted at dangers lurking within these very walls.

"Thanks for the workshop, Edward," I said, forcing a smile. "It's... enlightening."

"Always here to help, Doctor Bentley," he responded, the corner of his mouth lifting ever so slightly.

As I left the room, I couldn't shake the feeling that there was more to Edward than his role as our security consultant. What was it about this place, about our work, that demanded such vigilant protection? And why did it feel like, despite the layers of security, we were still exposed?

"Thorough, isn't he?" Ellie nudged me as we walked back to the lab.

"He's thorough, I'll give him that," I confessed, the words heavy with implications I hadn't yet fully grasped. "But also. So boring."

Ellie laughed. "You can say that again."

The lab was quiet, save for the hum of machines and the occasional bubble from a beaker. I had just finished logging the latest batch of data when Ellie's voice broke through the silence.

"Jade," she called out softly, drawing near with a cautious glance over her shoulder. She grabbed my arm, her grip firm yet gentle—a silent plea for attention.

"Ellie?" I asked, startled by the urgency in her eyes.

"Listen to me," she said, her tone hushed and earnest. "Just be careful, okay? Not just with the tech stuff. People aren't always what they seem."

Her words hung between us, a warning veiled as advice. I could see it in her face—the protective fear that seemed out of place in our world of science and research.

"Is there something I should know?" I pressed, searching her expression for clues.

"Just..." She sighed, her gaze softening. "Keep your eyes open, Jade. Trust your gut. And remember, I've got your back."

"Thanks, El," I murmured, squeezing her hand in gratitude. Her concern warmed me, but at the same time, it reinforced the gnawing unease that had settled in my stomach since Edward's cryptic hints. Was this about Dante? What did Ellie know that I didn't know?

I couldn't ask. I knew she wouldn't tell me.

"Anytime," Ellie replied, flashing a brief but genuine smile before she turned back to her work.

I stood there for a moment, processing her words. The lab suddenly felt colder, the shadows cast by the evening light stretching ominously across the floor. Maybe I had been naive, too wrapped up in my quest for knowledge to notice the undercurrents flowing through BioHQ.

As I resumed my work, Ellie's cautionary advice echoed in my mind. People aren't always what they seem. It was a truth I couldn't ignore any longer, not if I wanted to survive in this place where science and secrecy intertwined like strands of DNA.

I took a deep breath, resolved to heed Ellie's warning. The stakes were higher than I had imagined, and I needed to be ready for whatever lay ahead.

And if that meant getting away from Dante...well, it would hurt, but so be it.

Chapter Thirteen: Dante

I settled my tie, the silk sliding between my fingers with practiced ease. It was a necessary armor for tonight's battlefield—an art gallery opening with a scientific twist. My reflection in the mirror gave nothing away; the Moretti mask was firmly in place. Tonight wasn't just about appreciating art. It was about Jade.

Stepping into the gallery, I let my gaze drift across the room, taking in the artworks that flirted with science and tech—a neural circuit here, a DNA helix there. They were breadcrumbs leading to her, to Dr. Jade Bentley, whose mind spun beauty from the threads of biotechnology. The thought tightened something in my chest.

Jade had been cooler lately, her responses to my texts measured, cautious. A game she didn't know we were playing. It annoyed me, but it also sharpened my focus. I needed her research, and I needed her trust.

"Moretti," someone called out, pulling me from my thoughts. A businessman whose name I barely remembered. I turned, a practiced smile on my lips. "Didn't peg you for an art lover."

"Nor did I peg you for one who enjoys the finer things without lifting them," I retorted, keeping my voice light.

He laughed. "See you around, Moretti. Enjoy your night."

"Thought you'd be here," I said, approaching her. She turned, her gaze locking with mine. Whatever game she thought we were playing, I needed to make sure I won. For both our sakes.

"Do you get recognized a lot?"

"Yes," I replied. "But you just run into people when you live here. I wouldn't say I get recognized."

She raised her eyebrows as someone stopped by and obviously started to listen in on what we were saying. Jade and I weren't public–I mean, I had no idea what we even were–but I didn't want to add any complications to her life.

"Well, Dr. Bentley," I started, aware we were being spied on. My voice carried just the right amount of surprise and pleasure at finding her amongst the throngs of New York's elite. She stood by an installation that looked like a snapshot of a mind at work—the electric pulse of neurons captured in glass and light. "It *is* nice to run into you."

"Mr. Moretti," Jade replied, her words riding the edge of formality and curiosity. Her eyes, dark pools reflecting the neural network before us, searched mine for an instant too long.

"Intriguing, isn't it?" I leaned closer, lowering my voice as if sharing a secret. "Reminds me of the complex workings of the brain."

"Exactly," she said, her lips curving into a smile that told me I'd hit the mark. "It's fascinating to see something so intricate represented this way."

I nodded, watching her with an intensity I reserved for things that mattered—like family business or the woman who stood unknowingly at the center of it all. Her passion was evident, her gestures animated as she explained the parallels between the artwork and her latest research project.

"Your work," I began, steering our conversation back to her field, her comfort zone, "it must be thrilling to be on the cutting edge, shaping the future."

Jade's eyes lit up, and she launched into an explanation about potential breakthroughs and the ethical considerations they entailed. I listened, truly listened, letting her enthusiasm sweep over me. With every word, I wove myself into the fabric of her dialogue, connecting, engaging, ensuring she felt seen and heard.

"Science can have such a profound impact," I added when she paused for breath. "It's not unlike art in that regard."

"Perhaps," she conceded, her gaze flickering back to the installation. "Both can change perspectives, invoke emotions, challenge conventions."

"Exactly," I echoed, smiling at the ease of our exchange. "They both have the power to alter the world around us."

And as we stood there, surrounded by the hum of the gallery, I couldn't shake the feeling that Jade Bentley might just alter my world more than I ever anticipated.

"Speaking of change," I ventured, catching a flicker of unease cross Jade's face as she glanced at her phone, likely a work-related message demanding her attention. "It's not all groundbreaking discoveries and accolades, right? There's a weight to it."

Jade tucked a stray lock of hair behind her ear, her expression sobering. "Of course, the pursuit of knowledge can be a lonely journey." My voice softened intentionally, inviting her to open up.

She hesitated for a moment, then sighed. "Sometimes, it feels like you're up against the world, trying to make a dent in the universe, but the universe isn't always...receptive."

Not really the time to bring up my pitch again, but I knew I almost had her.

"Is that how it is for you?" I probed gently.

"More often than I'd like to admit," she replied, a hint of vulnerability seeping through. "There's so much pressure, so many expectations. It can get overwhelming."

I nodded, feeling a twinge of something—guilt, empathy—tugging at my conscience. "I understand more than you might think. In my line of work, the stakes are high, and the path is never clear-cut."

Jade looked at me, really looked at me, and in that moment, I felt exposed. I was playing a dangerous game, flirting with the truth while keeping her in the dark. But damn if she didn't make every risk feel worth it.

As I stepped closer to Jade, the electric atmosphere of the gallery shifted. Luis "Rami" Rodriguez sidled up beside us with his signature swagger. I should've known he would be here. Rami was intimidating at the best of times, often attending high-profile art shows where the pieces were incredibly expensive. His family was deep in the art business, and the Morettis had helped him with quite a bit of smuggling over the years.

I just wished he hadn't shown up tonight, especially with the air of annoyance that spelled trouble.

"Moretti," he greeted me with a curt nod and lightly accented English, his eyes flicking over to Jade with thinly veiled interest. "Didn't peg you for an art aficionado."

"Rami," I acknowledged him evenly, my tone cool. "I appreciate the finer things in life. You know that." My hand instinctively found its way to Jade's lower back—a subtle move to establish my presence and claim the space around her.

"Is that so?" His gaze lingered on Jade a moment too long. "And who's your lovely company?"

"Dr. Jade Bentley," she introduced herself, extending her hand with a firmness that belied her slight unease.

"Ah, a doctor." The corner of Rami's mouth quirked up in a smirk. "Well, isn't this a treat?"

"She's a neuroscientist," I added.

"Good for you," Rami replied, his gaze boring into Jade's.

I could tell Jade sensed the undercurrents at play, her scientific mind piecing together clues that something wasn't quite right. I needed to assert control over the situation before Rami's veiled threats became more than just insinuations. "Rami was just leaving," I said pointedly, my body angled to shield Jade from any further discomfort.

"Of course," Rami replied, though his eyes narrowed slightly. "But let's not forget—every masterpiece has its price. You know that better than almost anyone, Moretti."

"Well, enjoy the show."

"You too. Nice to meet you, Dr. Bentley," he said.

With one last lingering look, he sauntered off into the crowd. As soon as he was out of earshot, I turned to Jade, searching her face for signs of concern. "Sorry about that," I offered, though I knew it wasn't enough to erase the tension.

"Who is that?" she asked.

"Business associate," I told her. "My family and his are trade partners. He's really not so bad once you get to know him."

"It's fine," she said, though her voice trembled ever so slightly. "Just...unexpected."

"Let's move away from here," I suggested, guiding her to a quieter corner. "Tell me everything. What's been happening at the lab this week?"

She regarded me, her eyes narrowing. "You know," she said. "You ask me a lot about my work, but...you don't seem that interested in me."

Her statement hit me like a freight train. I didn't expect her to confront me so directly, but I welcomed it. It gave me a chance to show her my cards, or at least some of them.

"I apologize if I've given you that impression," I said, meeting her gaze with sincerity etched into my features. "The truth is...I'm interested in you more than you know. Is that why you've been so hot and cold with texting?"

Jade blinked, caught off guard by my candor. She opened her mouth to respond but hesitated, her fingers twirling around the edge of her glass nervously.

"Your work is remarkable," I said. "And it's...common ground. I can talk to you about what interests you all day long, all night long. You're such a fascinating person. I just..."

I trailed off, sighing as I looked at her, struggling to find the words. "I just... I'm not good at this," I finally admitted. "I've never been good at opening up, at... letting people in. You are the most interesting person I've ever met, but I know that if I ask you questions about yourself, you're going to ask me questions about myself. And honestly? I don't want to spook you."

I watched as a range of emotions flickered across her face - surprise, confusion, sympathy and something else. Something that made my heart pound just a bit faster.

"You think you'll scare me off?" she asked, her voice softer now.

"I have a feeling you might not like what you see if you dig too deep," I admitted, my gaze steady on hers.

She took a sip of her drink. "Why?"

"Because it's easier to be charming and make you come than it is to tell you about my ailing father or about all the pressure I have at work," I whispered in her ear. "Because you're stunning, and you deserve someone to sweep you off your feet. You don't have to deal with my shit, Jade. I can deal with it myself."

She stared at me for a long moment, her eyes probing mine as if she was trying to uncover what lay beneath my words. Then she sighed, a heavy sound that seemed to echo through the silent room.

"Dante," she said, her voice almost too quiet to hear. "Everyone has their struggles, their burdens. You don't have to carry yours alone."

I swallowed against the lump in my throat, surprised by her empathy. Was it possible she could see beyond the facade, beyond the son of a mafia kingpin who was expected to take over the family business?

"But..." I started, but Jade cut me off with a soft hand on my arm.

"No buts," she said firmly. "You think you're protecting me by keeping me at a distance...but you're just pushing me away."

"Maybe it's better for you if I keep you away. Did you consider that?"

"I'm a grown-ass woman," she said. "And I get to decide if I want to stay away from you."

And just like that, she pressed her lips against mine—right there, in public—and kissed me.

Chapter Fourteen: Dante

The gallery's chatter and the clinking of glasses faded into the night as I led Jade out onto the New York sidewalk. The autumn air was crisp, a sharp contrast to the warmth we'd left behind. My hand brushed hers as I flagged down a cab, the contact sending an electric jolt up my arm.

"Where to?" the cabbie grunted as we slid into the backseat.

"Drive," I muttered, not yet decided. The lights of the city smeared across the cab windows, a whirl of color against the encroaching darkness. In that moment, with her next to me, the city felt different—charged, like us.

Jade's laughter cut through the hum of the moving taxi, and I turned to face her. "At this rate, you might as well just ask me out, Dante." Her tone was light, playful, but it sliced right through the fog of my thoughts.

I ran a hand through my hair, a smile breaking free despite the storm brewing inside me. It was reckless, all of it, but that's what made it feel so damn right. "You know what? You're absolutely right," I conceded, the words tumbling out before I could stop them.

"Okay then, Dante Moretti. Impromptu date it is. Where are we headed?" Jade's eyes sparkled with anticipation.

I instructed the driver to head to a secluded bar I knew—a place where the shadows clung to the walls and the cocktails were strong enough to dull even the sharpest edges of reality. The cab pulled up to the curb, and I paid the fare before leading her inside, the intimate buzz of conversation greeting us.

The bar was a cocoon of privacy, the perfect place for what I needed now—a moment out of time with someone who could unravel me with just a look. I steered us to a booth tucked away in the corner, its cushions worn from countless confessions.

"Whiskey for me, and..." I glanced at Jade, raising an eyebrow.

"Surprise me," she said, a challenge lacing her words.

"Two of your finest concoctions," I told the bartender with a nod. He understood the assignment—something potent enough to ease the barriers without dulling the senses.

As we settled into our seats, I felt a strange mix of comfort and vulnerability. This wasn't my usual scene—I didn't do vulnerability. But here I was, about to peel back layers of armor for a woman who saw through them anyway.

"Tell me something about you I can't learn from your rap sheet or the company you keep," Jade prompted, her gaze intense yet inviting.

"Rap sheet?" I asked, raising my brows.

"What, you've never been arrested?"

"No, I have," I said, winking at her. "But let me answer your questions. I was thirteen when I learned to drive. Stole my father's car in the dead of night just to feel the engine roar under my fingertips."

Jade laughed, the sound like music in the dimness of the bar. "You're a rebel."

"Was," I corrected her, and took another sip. "I had no choice but to grow up fast, become part of... all this." I gestured vaguely, encompassing a world she'd only glimpsed the edges of.

"Wait, you're no longer a rebel?"

"Maybe in the eyes of the law, but my father would've killed me if the law had found me," I said. "So my brother and I, we had to be smart."

"Sounds lonely," she observed softly, touching a nerve I kept well hidden.

"Maybe," I conceded, and for a fleeting second, I wondered how different things would have been if I'd met Jade under other circumstances.

"Your turn," I said, eager to shift the focus. "Tell me something real about Dr. Jade Bentley. Nothing work related."

She smiled, leaning back against the leather. "When I was seven, I tried to create a new species by cross-pollinating flowers. I was convinced I'd invent a plant that could cure diseases."

"Did it work?" I asked, already knowing the answer.

"No, but I ruined my mom's garden," she replied. "You know the worst part is that she was more devastated than angry. I felt so bad. I never messed with flowers again. Maybe that's why I decided to go to the brain instead of fauna and flora."

We kept talking, exchanging anecdotes about our childhoods for what felt like a very long time.

The bar's rowdy clamor had dwindled to a gentle hum, the hour late enough that only a few night owls lingered over their last rounds. The bartender started stacking chairs on tables, signaling time. I caught Jade's eye, her dark hair falling in soft waves around her face, the dim light casting shadows that only enhanced her features.

"Oh, it looks like they're closing," she said.

"Do you want me to ask the manager if he'll keep it open for us?"

"No," she replied. "You can't...no, it's late. We should probably go."

I leaned in, my voice dropping to a murmur only meant for her. "You're right. Wait. Let me do that again. Do you want to get out of here?"

We both knew what I was implying.

For a moment, I saw hesitation flicker in her eyes, then resolve. "Yes," she said, and the simplicity of her answer made my heart kick against my chest.

We left the bar behind, the chill of the autumn air in New York City biting at our skin. We walked side by side, stealing glances, both aware that tonight was different, that every step took us deeper into uncharted territory.

Because I had slept with her before...but I had never really spoken about myself. I had never really let my defenses down, not even with her.

It was odd...heady. I liked it.

The taxi ride to her apartment passed in silence, but it wasn't uncomfortable—it was electric, charged with the anticipation of what was to come. Our knees brushed occasionally, sending jolts through me, making me wonder if she felt the same.

When we reached her building, she led the way, fumbling slightly with her keys. A nervous giggle escaped her lips as she struggled to find the right one. "Sorry, I'm not usually this clumsy," she said, her smile infectious even as I felt a coil of tension unwind within me.

"Take your time," I reassured her, though patience was a virtue I found hard to come by in that moment. Every second stretched out, filled with the promise of the unknown.

Finally, the key turned, and the door opened to reveal her world—a world so different from mine, yet one I couldn't wait to step into. As I crossed the threshold, following her into the warm glow of her living room, I couldn't shake the feeling that I was crossing more than just a physical boundary. I was stepping into a part of her life, and that felt intimate beyond measure.

"Are you sure?" The question hung in the air as I stood there, taking in Jade's living room – a space that felt leagues away from my own existence. There was an edge to my voice, a hint of the darkness I was bringing with me into her world.

"We've already had sex," she said.

"Yeah, but..." But what? This felt different? "I just want to hear it from you."

"Yes," Jade replied, her voice firm, and it was like a green light igniting something within me. She tugged me closer with a confident smile, and I couldn't resist the pull, the magnetic force of her presence.

I pushed her back against the wall, my lips finding hers with a hunger that had been building since the moment I first laid eyes on her at the gallery. My body pressed into hers, and I could feel her warmth, her curves molding to mine. "Have you been wet since you saw me?" I asked against her lips, needing to know if the heat I saw flickering in her eyes had ignited a fire within her too.

"Since the gallery," she breathed out, and the sound of her affirmation sent a spike of possessive desire through me.

"What about since the last time we saw each other? Have you been touching yourself thinking of me, like I told you to?"

Her whispered "yes" was like fuel to the flame.

We kissed again, and it was desperate, frenzied—the kind of passion that burns too hot and too fast. I was aware of every shudder that ran through her, every gasp that filled the space between us. With each touch, I felt like I was peeling back layers, exposing parts of us that were raw and real.

My fingers found the waistband of her jeans, slipping beneath it with a determination that matched the beating of my heart. As I touched her, feeling the slick warmth of her arousal, I played her body like an instrument.

Jade clung to me, and I to her, as we lost ourselves in the escalation of our passion—a passion that seemed to defy the gravity of our worlds, the weight of my name, and the shadows that I knew would always chase me. But here, now, none of that mattered. There was only Jade, only this feeling, only us.

"Bedroom," I murmured against her lips, the word coming out as a command laced with a need that couldn't be sated standing up.

She nodded, her eyes locked onto mine with an intensity that matched the pounding of my pulse. She took my hand, leading me through the dimly lit space to where her bed waited.

As we stood at the foot of her bed, I reached for the hem of my shirt, pulling it over my head and discarding it without care. Jade's fingers trembled slightly as they worked on the buttons of her blouse, revealing the soft skin I had only begun to know but already craved like a vice.

"Tell me," I said, my voice low, "what you've been using when you're alone, thinking of me."

"Like you want me to touch yourself in front of you?"

"Like I want to know how you've been touching yourself," I whispered against her ear.

A flicker of shyness crossed her face before she turned towards her nightstand. Opening the drawer, she pulled out a big vibrating rabbit dildo, holding it up with a mix of hesitation and defiance.

"Show me," I insisted.

She hesitated for a brief second before sitting on the edge of the bed, parting her legs with a boldness that sent a surge of desire straight to my cock.

"Take your pants off," I said.

She nodded.

And so she did, dropping her jeans to the floor before mirroring the action with her panties. She was bare before me now, and the sight stole my breath away. Her body was a masterpiece painted in curves and softness, and I was the fortunate bastard allowed to admire it.

"Lay back," I instructed, my eyes never leaving hers. I grabbed the vibrator and put it in her hand. "Okay. Show me."

With a deep breath, she reclined back onto the pillows, her legs parting slightly in invitation. As if in slow motion, she turned on the vibrator, the low hum of it vibrating through the room and adding to the tension palpably hanging in the air.

I watched as she moved it slowly down her body, over the soft rise of her breasts and down her stomach. I watched every flicker of emotion that crossed her face—the anticipation, the desire, and then finally, the pleasure.

A soft sigh escaped Jade's lips as she began to tease herself with her toy, the buzz of the vibrator barely audible over the pounding of my heart. My eyes trailed down her body, following the path the rabbit was taking. I could see how her body reacted to each touch, each ripple of pleasure that shot through her - and god, it was a sight that threatened to undo me.

When I couldn't stand the distance any longer, I closed the space between us, taking the toy from her hand and grabbing it. It continued to vibrate in my hand.

"I'm going to fuck you with this," I said.

Without waiting for a response, I pressed the toy against her. Her sharp intake of breath echoed in my ears as she arched her back off the bed, a clear invitation for more.

"Does it rotate?" I asked as I thrust the toy in and out of her.

"Yes," she gasped, her fingers fumbling with the controls before the toy started pulsating in a slow, tantalizing rhythm. The sight of her writhing beneath its touch was mesmerizing, and I couldn't tear my eyes away.

I couldn't take my eyes off of her, the sight of her writhing in pleasure stirring something primal within me. The room was filled with soft sighs and the buzzing thrum of the vibrator, creating an intoxicating symphony that stirred my senses.

"Dante..." she whispered, a plea and a prayer all rolled into one. It was like music to my ears—intoxicating and addictive. I wanted nothing more than to draw such sounds from her, to be the cause of her pleasure.

"Look at me," I demanded, my voice rough with desire as I increased the toy's speed. Jade's eyes fluttered open, finding mine in an intense stare that sent shivers down my spine. The sight of her beneath me, fully exposed and on the precipice of release—it was a sight that could bring any man to his knees. "Don't close your eyes while you come. I want your eyes on me."

Her breath hitched, her body squirming as the vibrations increased. "Fuck," she gasped again, her fingers digging into the sheets. I watched as her eyes filled with a desperate kind of hunger, her gaze never leaving mine even as she trembled on the edge.

"Tell me you want to come," I commanded, my voice thick with arousal. Her responding nod wasn't enough. I needed her to say it.

"Say it. Say you want to come, Jade."

"I... I want to come," she said, her voice a breathy moan that made me ache with desire. Every word, every movement, every gasp of pleasure was driving me closer to the edge, pushing me towards a pinnacle of desire and need I had never known before.

I watched her, every inch of her, as she succumbed to her climax. It was raw and beautiful in its intensity. Her body convulsed around the toy, hips arching off the bed as her orgasm crashed over her. Her eyes remained locked onto mine in a gaze that was both vulnerable and defiant as waves of release swept through her.

"Good girl," I said hoarsely, overwhelmed by the sight unfolding before me. She was stunning—breathtakingly so—and I knew in that moment that there would never be enough of her. Not for me. "Have you ever squirted before?"

"Never," she panted, her eyes wide with something that looked a lot like curiosity.

"Would you like to try?" I asked, my gaze never leaving hers. My hand remained steady on the toy, holding it still within her. Jade bit her lip, hesitating for a moment before she nodded.

"Yes," she whispered.

With her consent, I repositioned the toy, angling it towards a spot inside her that would increase her chances of reaching this new height. I moved slowly, carefully, watching her reaction to each adjustment.

"Do you trust me?" I asked, meeting her gaze as I turned up the vibration once again.

She swallowed hard before nodding. "Yes."

"Good," I responded, pressing the toy deeper within her. Jade's breath hitched, her body trembling as the vibrations began to build up once again inside of her.

"Push down on it," I instructed, then leaned down and sucked her clit between my lips.

Her eyes widened at the sensation, her fingers digging deeper into the sheets beneath her. A soft moan fell from her lips as I worked her with my mouth and the toy. I could feel her body tightening, feel it coiling in anticipation. I fucked her harder with the vibrator as I flicked my tongue over her clit, building up a rhythm that had her writhing beneath me. I reveled in the sounds she made, each gasp, each moan, and every plea urging me on.

"I...I can't," she whispered at one point, her body trembling violently beneath me. But I didn't stop.

Jade began to shake, her thighs quivering as a familiar tension started building up inside her. The sight of her losing control, the taste of her on my tongue, was intoxicating. It was raw, it was primal, and it made me want her even more.

"Do you want to feel my fingers inside of you too while I fuck your g-spot with this vibrator?" I asked.

She looked at me, her eyes heavy with lust, and nodded. It was all the affirmation I needed. I reached down, sliding a finger inside her already quivering core. Jade gasped at the intrusion, her body arching off the bed as she adjusted to the added stimulation.

I kept my movements slow and careful, making sure to hit all the right spots. All the while, I kept my eyes on hers, drinking in the unrestrained pleasure that had her eyes fluttering shut.

"No," I growled, "Eyes open."

I withdrew the toy momentarily, replacing it with two of my fingers while continuing to pleasure her clit with my mouth. A gasp fell from her lips as I curled my fingers inside her, seeking out that sensitive spot that would drive her over the edge. I moved my mouth away and pressed the vibrator, on the highest setting, against her sensitive clit.

She let out a strangled cry, her body arching off the bed as pleasure shot through her. The vibrations were overwhelming, the sensation of my fingers inside of her pushing her closer to the edge.

"Are you ready?" I asked, my fingers never stopping their rhythmic motions. "We're going to make you squirt, Jade."

"I don't know if—" she could hardly speak.

"You can, and you will," I said. My tone was stern, authoritative even, but underneath it all was the desire to see her unravel. "Trust me, Jade."

With a sharp nod, she surrendered herself, her body trembling beneath me as I picked up the pace. The vibrator hummed against her clit, my fingers plunging in and out of her in a rhythm designed to drive her wild. Jade gasped and moaned, her body writhing beneath me as she neared the edge once again.

"Let go," I whispered into her ear, my voice low and rough. "Let go for me, Jade."

And then she did. With a cry that pierced through the silence of the room, Jade came undone. Her orgasm crashed over her like a tidal wave, leaving her gasping for breath and shaking from the intensity. Her eyes were wide and stunned, staring up at me as if seeing me for the first time.

Suddenly, her body tensed in an entirely different way than before - a sharper, more intense reaction.

Then, with an intensity that stole her breath away, warmth gushed from her in an eruption of ecstasy, the liquid splashing against me as she cried out. Her back arched high off the bed, her body trembling uncontrollably as waves of pleasure washed over her. The sight of Jade letting go, surrendering herself completely to the ecstasy, was one of the most stunning things I'd ever seen. Her eyes, wide and filled with awe, connected with mine as a flush of surprise painted her features.

She was trembling, sweat beading on her forehead as the wave of her climax slowly started to roll back.

"Fuck, Dante," she breathed, her voice hoarse and laced with exhaustion. Her body was still shaking from the climax, her chest rising and falling heavily as she tried to catch her breath.

I pressed a slow, tender kiss to her sweat-soaked forehead and then eased away from her. I removed the toy from her trembling body, my fingers tracing over the sensitive flesh there before slowly sliding out as well. The sight of her, spent and panting beneath me, was nothing short of incredible.

"Was that...okay?" she asked softly.

"Shhh," I whispered, ghosting my lips over her cheek in a soft caress. "You were incredible."

She looked up at me with those wide eyes, still glazed with pleasure and disbelief. The blushing hue on her cheeks made her look even more enticing, but I knew she needed a moment to ground herself. Jade had just experienced something completely new and overwhelming.

"Relax," I said gently, wrapping an arm around her waist and pulling her closer.

"You're not going to fuck me?" she asked.

"Later," I said. "There's nothing I want more than putting my cock inside of you, but after watching that, how long do you think I'm going to last? I'm only human. And watching you squirt...I don't think I've ever seen anything more beautiful."

She blushed harder at my compliment, looking every bit the picture of innocence despite what we'd just done. Her bottom lip was swollen from her teeth worrying it, and I couldn't resist leaning down to press a soft kiss there.

"Sleep now," I murmured, carding my fingers through her smooth, dark locks. Jade's eyelids were heavy with exhaustion, and as much as I wanted to continue exploring her body, watching her rest in the aftermath of intense pleasure was its own kind of satisfaction. I pressed my lips against her ear. "I'll wake you up by fingering you. How does that sound?"

She let out a soft, sleepy giggle that felt like a victory. "Sounds perfect," she murmured against my chest.

Her body relaxed against mine, her breathing gradually slowing to the steady rhythm of sleep. I found my own eyes growing heavy as I watched her; the way her lashes laid softly against her cheeks, the slight part of her lips, the steady rise and fall of her chest with each breath she took. She looked peaceful, content.

I brushed a loose strand of hair from her face, tucking it behind her ear before leaning down to press a soft kiss to her forehead. "Sweet dreams, Jade," I whispered against her skin.

This...was not supposed to get serious.

I was meant to keep her at arm's length, use her for my own pleasure and nothing more. That was the plan. The rule. No attachments, no commitments. It wasn't long before I realized how impossible that task would be.

Jade was too special to be swept up in my dark world, yet here she was, wrapped around my arms, spent from the pleasure I had given her, and all I could see in my mind was the way she'd looked at me with those wide eyes filled with trust and...something more.

I ran my fingers along her arm, tracing soft patterns onto her skin. My mind whispered against reason, reminding me of what we had just shared. It was intimate, more so than anything I'd ever experienced before.

She wasn't supposed to get under my skin like this.

But being with me...that was dangerous. And being someone I loved just put a target on her back.

So maybe what I needed to do was get away from her. But for now...for now, I would just enjoy her. For as long as I could.

Chapter Fifteen: Jade

I woke to the soft intrusion of morning light weaving through the curtains, stirring the shadows in my bedroom. Dante's arm was a reassuring weight across my waist, his breath steady against the nape of my neck.

"Can I use your shower?" Dante's voice, rough with sleep, broke the quiet.

"Sure," I murmured, sitting up and stretching. As I shuffled to grab clothes, the crisp scent of my lavender body wash clung to him, a reminder of our closeness that seemed out of place in the daylight.

"Wait. Let me rephrase that. Can we use your shower?"

"What?"

"Come on," Dante's voice suddenly broke through the charged atmosphere, his hand slipping from my hip to grasp mine. "Let's wash away the lab for a while."

He led me toward the bathroom, and I followed, my mind still reeling from the intensity of our exchange the night before. The steam from the hot water filled the room, fogging up the mirror and creating an intimate cocoon that enveloped us as we stepped into the shower together.

"Can you do it again?" he asked, his voice low and husky as the water cascaded down over us, turning my skin sensitive to every touch.

"Squirt? I don't know if I–"

"Shh, just relax," he murmured before pushing me gently against the cool tile wall. His mouth found mine with a hunger that left no room for doubt or insecurity, and then he was descending, his lips trailing fire down my body until they reached the core of my desire.

The world outside the steamy enclosure faded to insignificance as Dante's skilled tongue worked its magic, coaxing pleasure from me in waves that crashed over and over, leaving me breathless and clinging to him for support.

"God, I fucking love the way you taste," he said. "I could eat you out for hours."

"Are you always this forward?" I asked breathlessly, my fingers lacing through his wet hair.

"Only with you, sweetheart," he murmured, his lips curving in a wicked grin before he was on me again, his tongue flicking and lapping around my clit, the sensation raw and overwhelming. I clung to him as the pressure built and the knot in my stomach tightened to an unbearable tension.

Just as I was about to unravel, Dante pulled away, standing up to his full height and positioning himself between my thighs. The sensation of him entering me was so electric that I gasped aloud, my fingers digging into his shoulders.

"Do you think I can make you squirt with just my cock?" he asked, his breath hot in my ear.

"Damn it, Dante," I breathed out, my body responding fervently to his provocations. "You're...superbly confident."

"Only when it comes to making you feel good," he countered, adjusting his pace and angling deeper into me. The intensity of every thrust sent shockwaves of pleasure through me. "Because making you come is my favorite thing."

As Dante began to thrust in time with the pulsating water, he slid his hands up my chest and grasped my breasts, pinching the sensitive nipples through my wet clothes, causing me to moan as he did so. He took one nipple into his mouth and sucked gently, rolling it between his teeth before releasing it to replace it with the other. Meanwhile, his hips kept moving in a rhythm that was both slow and steady, making me feel every inch of him inside me. The way he worked his cock against my G-spot sent shivers down my spine; it almost felt like he could read my mind.

The sensation of Dante's mouth on my breasts combined with his relentless thrusting sent me spiraling into sensory overload. He continued to stroke my G-spot with his cock, the rhythm unyielding, until I was shaking with the intensity of it.

"Fuck, Jade," he groaned as he drove into me. "You feel so good wrapped around me."

His words echoed in the steam-filled room, punctuated by the rhythmic slapping of our bodies coming together. The sensual assault of his words, his touch, and his unwavering gaze sent me teetering on the brink of ecstasy.

"Dante," I whimpered unsteadily, my legs beginning to quiver as the pressure built impossibly within me.

"Hold on for me, Jade," he encouraged, his voice raw with need. "I want to feel you come around me."

The feeling was too much—the pleasure too intense—as a wave of desire roared through me. With a final thrust from Dante, I surrendered to the building crescendo inside me. The world ceased to exist beyond the pulsating pleasure that consumed me. Dante's name ripped from my throat as I came hard around him.

"Fuck, Jade!" Dante growled, his movements becoming erratic as he succumbed to his own climax. His body shuddered against mine as he rode out the waves of his orgasm. His fingers dug into my hips, anchoring himself to me as he succumbed to the overwhelming pleasure coursing through him.

"God, you're so beautiful," he rasped, his breath hot against the crook of my neck as he slowly pulled out of me. We stood there for a moment, catching our breaths, the steaming water washing away the remnants of our passion.

As Dante wrapped his arms around me and held me close against his chest, I felt something akin to peace settle over me. It was unfamiliar territory—raw and vulnerable—but not entirely unwelcome. I let myself relax into his embrace, my head resting on his broad shoulder.

"But you are hungry, right? Let's go get that breakfast. I can't just leave off eating your pussy, no matter how much I want to."

"Dante," I admonished lightly, shaking my head at his audacity. But beneath the reprimand, there was no hiding the soft smile that curved at the corner of my mouth. Dante's forthrightness was as refreshing as it was intimidating.

"Come on, Doc," he teased, a twinkle in his eyes as he released me from his embrace and turned off the water. "Let's get dressed."

"Yeah, let's do that."

Some time later, we emerged from the shower, wrapped in towels and silent in the aftermath of our shared surrender. Dante suggested coffee, and I agreed, eager to hold onto the normalcy of the gesture.

The café was nice and not too far from my house. As we walked into the café, the scent of fresh coffee mingling with the subtle hint of baking pastries hit me, instantly making me feel warm and comfortable. Dante held the door open for me, his hand lightly touching the small of my back as he ushered me inside.

I scanned the cozy space, taking in the rustic wooden tables and the chalkboard menu behind the counter that offered a variety of breakfast options. Dante guided me towards a corner booth that offered some privacy from the rest of the patrons. I slipped onto the plush seat, looking across at Dante who was now shedding off his jacket and rolling up his sleeves.

We settled into a booth, the warmth of the coffee mug seeping into my hands as I took a sip. It was peaceful, comfortable—until I noticed Dante's gaze shift to a man entering the café.

The air around us seemed to thicken, charged with an invisible current that set my nerves on edge. Their exchange was brief, their words too low for me to catch, but the tension between them was unmistakable. Dante's posture was relaxed, but there was a hardness in his eyes that I hadn't seen before.

"Friend of yours?" I ventured when the man left, trying to keep my tone light despite the unease coiling in my gut.

"Something like that," Dante replied, his attention returning to me. He offered a smile, but it didn't quite reach his eyes. "Don't worry about it, Jade. Old business."

I wanted to believe him, to take comfort in his reassurance, but the encounter had peeled back another layer of the life Dante led—a life that was now inching its way into mine, whether I was ready for it or not.

"Old business that comes with threats?" I pressed, unable to ignore the flicker of danger that had passed between them. "Dante, what aren't you telling me?"

He reached across the table, his hand covering mine in a gesture meant to soothe. "Jade, look at me," he said firmly, and I met his intense gaze. "Whatever happens, I've got it under control. You have my word."

His assurance should have eased my mind, but instead, it was like a patch over a dam about to burst. I could sense the floodwaters rising behind his calm facade. And though I wanted to trust him, to lean into the safety he offered, doubt gnawed at me.

"Okay," I whispered, tucking away my questions for now.

The remainder of our coffee was spent in an uneasy silence. Dante, a brooding statue beside me, seemed lost in thought, his gaze occasionally flicking to the café's entrance. I felt it then—the protective warmth radiating from him—as he shifted in his seat, angling his body ever so slightly in front of mine, forming a subtle barrier between me and any potential threats that might walk through the door.

It was...weird to think about threats. I didn't want to, but he was clearly on edge.

"Everything okay?" I asked quietly, tracing the rim of my now cold coffee cup.

"Always," he replied, but the tightness in his jaw betrayed his words.

I wanted to push, to pry open the vault of secrets I knew he carried with him, but fear held me back. Fear of what lay hidden there, fear of how it might change us—change me.

We left the café, stepping out into the crisp air that did nothing to clear the fog in my head. Dante's world, a world I had only glimpsed the edges of, was creeping slowly into mine, bringing shadows I hadn't anticipated when I fell into his bed—or his arms.

As we walked, his presence was as commanding as ever, yet I couldn't ignore the growing doubts swirling within me. With each step, I felt the tug-of-war between the affection I had for Dante and the fear of the unknown elements he was involved with. How could I reconcile the man whose touch set my skin ablaze with the man who dealt in whispered threats and concealed weapons?

"Jade," he said, breaking through my thoughts as we stopped at the curb waiting for the light to change. "You're quiet. Talk to me."

I looked up at him, at the concern etched in the lines around his eyes, and wondered how deep I was willing to dive into the tumultuous waters of Dante Moretti. How much of myself was I prepared to risk on a man bound by blood to a life that was worlds away from my own safe, structured reality?

"Nothing," I lied. "Just thinking about work." But even as the words left my lips, I knew that sooner or later, I would have to face the truth—and Dante would have to face me.

I just needed to gather my courage...because I wasn't going to accuse him of something I wasn't sure of.

We didn't really talk until we got back to my place. He pressed a soft kiss against my forehead as we stood outside my apartment.

"Stay safe," Dante's voice was a low rumble, the warmth of his breath brushing my cheek as we stood outside the door to my apartment. He pulled me into him, his arms wrapping around my frame with a possessiveness that both comforted and alarmed me.

I leaned into the safety of his hold, but the tremor in my heart wasn't just from the cold. "I will," I murmured, feeling the weight of our separate worlds on my shoulders.

He drew back just enough to look at me, his eyes searching mine for something I wasn't sure I could give. "I'll check in later." His thumb grazed my jawline, and I wondered if he felt the quake of my resolve.

"Okay," was all I managed, caught in the intensity of his gaze.

Dante leaned down, his lips claiming mine in a kiss that spoke of promises and goodbyes. It lingered, deep and thorough, leaving me breathless when he finally stepped back. With a final nod, he turned and walked away, his figure blending seamlessly into the city's heartbeat.

I watched him go until the distance swallowed him whole, then turned to face the solitude of my apartment. Inside, the quiet was deafening. I shed my coat and sunk onto the couch, replaying the morning's revelations and the unsettling encounter that had preceded this farewell.

The memory of how his touch unraveled me the night before washed over me in waves of heat and confusion. How he made me lose control, surrender to sensations I didn't know I craved, left me yearning for more despite the fear gnawing at my mind.

I needed answers. I needed to understand what being with Dante truly meant—for me, for my future. Resolute, I decided our next meeting wouldn't be shrouded in uncertainty or lost in the haze of desire. No, I would confront him, demand transparency about his life, his loyalties, and where I fit amidst the chaos he embodied.

But as I paced the confines of my apartment, my thoughts were a tangled dance of logic and emotion. The safe, predictable parameters of my scientific world seemed galaxies away from Dante's turbulent realm, yet here I was, straddling the line between order and chaos. There was something about him, an inexplicable pull that defied my rational mind and whispered promises of passion and depth.

"Focus on what you can control," I murmured to myself, the scientist in me trying to formulate a hypothesis for a future with a man whose life was a constant variable. Maybe it was possible to find equilibrium within the disarray, to be part of his universe without losing myself in its darkness.

My hands found their way to the drawer of my bedside table, fingers wrapping around the silicone form that had become a tangible memory of Dante's touch. It was as if every nerve ending remembered him, craved his presence. With a deep breath, I let go of my reservations and allowed my body to sink into the bed, the cool sheets contrasting with the heat building within me.

I unbuttoned my jeans, sliding them down my legs along with the fabric of my underwear. Lying there, exposed and alone, I closed my eyes, letting the fantasy of Dante wash over me. His touch was a ghostly sensation against my skin, his breath a phantom whisper in my ear. I shivered at the thought of him - no, the memory of him – of us entwined in the throes of passion.

I brought the silicone form close to me, its cold, lifeless touch a stark contrast to Dante's warmth, to his living, breathing reality. But as I let it explore my body's landscape, it began to mimic his touch - tentative at first, then confident, insistent. My breath hitched as a wave of pleasure rolled through me.

I closed my eyes, surrendering to the sensations as I guided the dildo with a steady hand, each movement a reflection of last night's ecstasy. In my mind's eye, it was Dante's hands exploring me, his body pressed against mine. My breath quickened as I lost myself in the fantasy, in the connection that bound us together despite the messiness of our worlds colliding. I pressed the dildo inside of me as I turned the vibration on bringing me closer to the edge.

With each thrust, my thoughts were consumed by him. His scent filled my nostrils; his voice echoed in my ears, whispering sweet words of longing and lust. It was as if Dante was here with me - guiding the movements, coaxing pleasure from every inch of my body. The mere thought was enough to drive me over the edge.

"God, Dante," I gasped out, the intensity of my longing pushing me closer to the edge.

I rode the wave of pleasure, letting it sweep me under until my body went limp with satisfaction. It wasn't real; it was a pale imitation of what I had experienced in Dante's arms, but it was enough to soothe the edge of my longing.

As the last echo of my climax washed over me, I lay there panting, hand still gripping the silicone as if it was my lifeline to sanity. Strands of hair stuck to my forehead, plastered by sweat and spent passion. But even in the post-coital haze, I was aware of his absence—aware that despite the orgasmic release, I felt hollow.

And then I knew that no matter what the fuck the rest of his life was like, I was definitely going to reach out.

Chapter Sixteen: Jade

What the fuck did my boss need me for?

I had barely gotten into the lab when Dr. White called me in to see him. I plopped down in a leather chair across from Dr. Stuart White, his office a fortress of knowledge with books stacked like sentinels watching over us. The patter of rain against the window provided a steady rhythm to the weighty silence between us.

"Jade," Dr. White began, his voice coated with concern, "your research...it's groundbreaking, but it's also vulnerable." His fingers drummed on the mahogany desk, the sound oddly menacing. "You have to tighten up your digital security."

He only addressed me by my first name when he was being condescending, so I already didn't love this.

I nodded, my throat tight. I knew the stakes; my work wasn't just petri dishes and microscopes—it was power, the kind that could tempt the greediest of souls.

Edward Rodriguez stepped forward, his presence commanding despite the lack of any physical intimidation. He laid out a blueprint of our digital defenses—or lack thereof—on the desk. "Let me be blunt," he said, his eyes locking onto mine. "Your data could be snatched up before you even realize it's gone."

I leaned in, absorbing every word as he detailed firewalls and encryption protocols with the kind of urgency that told me this was no hypothetical threat. Edward wasn't just talking about hackers; he was talking about predators lurking in the shadows of the cyber world, waiting to pounce.

But...why target me?

Everyone at work had difficult research that was groundbreaking. I forced my focus away from the mounting fear, shoving it to the back of my mind. Calmly, I asked, "If my research is safe in the lab, why should we worry about digital threats?"

"Because it's important," Dr. White replied.

"I understand that I need to be careful about my digital trail, but haven't we had workshops about this already? Wait, did I do something wrong?"

"No, Jade, you haven't done anything wrong," Rodriguez replied, his voice steady. "But your work...it's more than just groundbreaking. It's revolutionary." He leaned back in his chair, looking at me with an intensity that made my breath hitch. "And revolutionary work can inspire...immoral reactions."

A chill ran down my spine. 'Immoral reactions' sounded a lot like euphemisms for threats and danger, neither of which I was prepared to deal with. Science was supposed to be a field for innovation and exploration, not a battlefield.

"But bioinformatics is a standard tool in most labs," I countered. "What makes my research so different?"

And also, what the fuck do you know about this, you tech monkey?

I didn't say that, though. I wasn't crazy, and my boss was right there.

Edward chuckled, evidently amused by my cluelessness. "Jade, it's not about the tool, it's about what you're using it for." He glanced at Dr. White significantly, and the older man nodded in agreement. "Your project on genetic modification... let's just say there are those who would kill to get their hands on it."

"Dr. Bentley," I replied.

"Right," Edward said. "Dr. Bentley. My point stands."

"Okay," I managed to squeak out. "So... what do we do then?"

"We tighten security," Edward said with finality. "We make sure your work, and you," he added with a pointed look, "are safe."

"Understood," I replied, my voice steadier than I felt. Dr. Stuart White gave me a sharp nod, his eyes reflecting the weight of his words as he concluded the meeting.

"Jade, remember, we're not just talking about data here," he said, emphasizing each word with gravity. "We're talking about lives—potentially millions. The security measures are not just protocol; they're essential."

"Of course," I murmured, folding my notebook closed and rising from the table. I felt both honored and overwhelmed by the responsibility laid upon my shoulders. I hadn't taken any notes, but the meeting had left a sour taste in my mouth.

The success of my project hinged on more than just scientific prowess; it required vigilance against unseen threats.

Later, in the BioHQ cafeteria, I found a secluded corner to enjoy a much-needed coffee break. Ellie was already there, stirring her tea with a furrowed brow. She looked up as I approached, her warm brown eyes clouded with concern. "What was that about?" she asked. "Are you in trouble with the principal?"

I laughed. "Kind of feels like it," I said. "What's wrong with you?"

She straightened up. "I didn't want to bring this up today, but I think I'm going to have to."

"Is something wrong with the duplicating–"

"No. Dante Moretti," she said.

I took a slow sip of my coffee, buying time. Dante Moretti—a man whose very name sent a shiver of something dangerous down my spine. Smart, seductive, and connected to the city's underbelly in ways I didn't want to contemplate.

"El, you worry too much," I tried to reassure her, my tone light. "Dante is just... a distraction. A minor one at that." I forced a smile, hoping to convey confidence I wasn't entirely sure I felt.

"Are you sure about that?" Ellie pressed, her gaze sharp and probing. "Because when you talk about him, it doesn't seem like a minor thing."

"Trust me," I insisted, though the image of Dante's alluring smile and the sound of his velvety voice lingered unbidden in my mind. "He's got no influence over me or my work. He's just...it's complicated."

"Complicated can be dangerous," Ellie warned, but I shook my head, refusing to let her fears taint the thrill of Dante's attention.

"Let's focus on what we can control, like the research," I suggested, eager to steer the conversation away from territory I was still navigating myself. I needed Ellie to believe that Dante Moretti was nothing more than a passing fancy—an entanglement I could easily untwist myself from.

"You can control Dante Moretti, Jade," she said.

"El," I replied, my tone a whisper. "Weren't you the one to say I needed to get laid? Now I'm getting laid and you have a problem with it."

"No, I have a problem with him," she replied. "Not with it. I absolutely think you should be getting laid."

"He's really good in bed, Ellie," I said. "Like...really good, okay? So just back off."

"Fine," Ellie conceded reluctantly. "But if things get... messier, promise you'll tell me?"

"Promise," I lied smoothly, because in truth, I had no idea what I'd do if—or when—things with Dante Moretti escalated beyond a minor diversion.

"I know you're gorgeous," Ellie said. "But with a man like that, don't you ever worry he's going to have an ulterior motive?"

I opened my mouth to answer when she looked down at her vibrating watch. "Shit," she said. "I'm doing a guest lecture today, and they just told me it's going to be in person instead of online. I need to go get ready for that. Don't forget what I said, okay?"

I nodded, watching as she stood up. "You think they'd tell you this kind of shit well in advance," she said. "Idiots."

I nodded. "Couldn't agree more."

The moment Ellie left, I exhaled a sigh I didn't realize I'd been holding. Alone with my thoughts, the seed of doubt Ellie planted began to sprout. Could Dante's presence in my life ripple out further than I anticipated? The man had resources and connections that ran deep—too deep for someone like me to fathom fully.

But maybe he could be the key in helping me protect all this research. I made my way back to the lab after I was done with my breakfast and paused by my desk, my fingers drumming against the cool metal surface as I reconsidered every interaction with him. Each smile, each touch, each word exchanged—was there a hidden meaning I'd missed? I knew how to analyze data, to look beyond the obvious for patterns and anomalies, but deciphering Dante Moretti required a different kind of scrutiny.

"Damn it, Ellie," I groaned under my breath. Her intuition was annoyingly on point at times, and now the possibility that Dante could somehow influence my career, or worse, my personal safety, loomed over me like a dark cloud.

Was he using me for something? It didn't seem like he was but...he was out of my league. He could've had an actress–a smart one, like one who went to an Ivy and was the most gorgeous woman in the world–with him, rather than me.

But he didn't. At least I didn't think so. He seemed to want me, and only me, as far as I knew. Though we hadn't really discussed being exclusive yet.

"Focus on the work, Jade," I reminded myself, trying to push away the growing unease. Dante was just a man—a complicated, dangerous, irresistibly charming man—but still, just a man. How much power could he truly wield over my life?

...More than I wanted to admit.

Fuck.

"Distraction or not, we're going to have to set some boundaries," I heard myself say, steeling myself for whatever confrontation lay ahead. It was time to make it clear to Dante—and perhaps more importantly, to myself—that my work came first, and no one, not even a man as enigmatic as Dante Moretti, could compromise that.

But I needed to think on it for a bit, so I dove back into the work I needed to do that day. After Dr. White had called me to his office, my entire day had been less productive than I wanted it to be.

It didn't take long before I was working. I adjusted the microscope, my gaze locked on the slide beneath the lens. Cells danced across my field of vision, each a tiny universe unto itself. It was here, in the complexities of biological life, where I found solace from the chaos that seemed to have erupted in my life.

My phone buzzed again. I glanced at it, irritation pricking at my focus. Dante's name flashed on the screen once more—a siren call I was determined to ignore. My thumb hovered over the 'silent' button before pressing it decisively. Silence enveloped the lab, broken only by the familiar hum of machines and the sound of one of my colleagues chattering in a different lab.

"Back to work," I muttered to myself, feeling the gratifying sense of control as I pipetted a reagent into a series of wells. The task demanded precision, and I welcomed its requirement for my undivided attention. Each droplet fell in a rhythmic sequence—my counter-melody to the chaos trying to seep into the sanctity of my lab.

The experiments laid out before me were my world, my battleground. As much as Dante's presence loomed large, he had no dominion here. This was my realm, where I called the shots, dictated the pace, and sought answers to questions he probably never even pondered.

"Dr. Bentley, the results won't change if you glare at them harder," I chastised myself, smiling wryly at the intensity of my own focus. It wasn't just about proving Ellie wrong or putting Dante in his place—it was about the thrill of discovery, the passion for knowledge, and the unrelenting drive to push the boundaries of science.

Let him wait, I thought, a smirk playing on my lips. If Dante Moretti wanted to play a game of patience, he was up against a master. After all, good science took time, and so did unraveling the enigma of a man who thought he could unsettle me with a few persistent texts.

As the day wore on, focusing got more difficult. I took a break after a while, leaning against the cool glass of the lab window, staring at the rain pelting down on the sidewalks. It was a gray wash of a day, the kind that made everything else seem sharper—even my thoughts.

"Ellie thinks you're playing with fire, Jade," I murmured to myself, my voice barely audible above the drumming rain. It was true; part of me was drawn to Dante Moretti like a moth to a flame. That allure, that danger—it shouldn't have been enticing, not for someone like me.

I shook my head, trying to shake off the image of him—immaculate suit, smug smile. But it wasn't just the danger, was it? There was something about him that I couldn't quite figure out, something that piqued my scientific curiosity. And damn it, Ellie had seen right through me when I pretended otherwise.

"Focus, Bentley," I chided, turning away from the window. My experiments were waiting, but the pull of personal life was getting harder to ignore.

By late afternoon, as the last of the daylight surrendered to evening, I knew what I had to do. The boundary between work and whatever was happening with Dante needed to be crystal clear. I had too much at stake—my research was my life's work, and I couldn't afford any distractions or compromises.

But if Dante and I were going to get into business together, then I needed to cover my bases. Dr. White and the board members couldn't see him as scary, but rather a legitimate person that was interested in my research without trying to take over.

And when that happened, if we ever got serious, it would be easier to soft launch our relationship.

I sat down at my desk, the glow of the computer screen casting a soft light across the papers strewn about. My fingers hovered over the keyboard for a moment, hesitating. Drafting an email to Dante Moretti wasn't something I could do impulsively; every word had to be chosen with care, considering that Dr. White and a lot of other people in the org could just see my correspondence.

"Dr. Bentley invites you to dinner," I began, but backspaced quickly. Too formal. He'd see right through it. I needed to be professional, yes, but not cold. We were well past formalities anyway–he was the only to have ever made me squirt.

"Moretti," I typed, and then paused, considering. Just his last name felt too impersonal considering how close we'd been. "Dante," I amended, letting the familiarity of his first name settle in the address line. It was a risk, using his first name like this, but risks were part of the game now.

"I'm sorry for putting this off for so long" I continued, my fingers moving steadily now. "How about dinner? I know a place. It's neutral ground, good food, no surprises." The words were a careful blend of invitation and challenge. I needed him to know that this was on my terms.

"Let's talk business," I said aloud as I read the words. "I think the bar is open until eleven."

Perfect.

I read the email over once, twice, making sure there was no hint of vulnerability in the lines. When I was satisfied, I hit send. The message whisked away into the digital ether, carrying with it the potential for alliances or perhaps the spark that would ignite a war.

Now all I could do was wait for his response, prepare myself for whatever came next. Whether it was the calm before the storm or the beginning of an uneasy truce, only time would tell. But one thing was certain: Dante Moretti was dangerous—dangerous to my career, to my well-being, and most of all, to my heart. Yet here I was, inviting the lion to dinner, and wondering who would end up being devoured.

Chapter Seventeen: Dante

I slipped through the shadows, the ID card hot in my grip. It was Jade's. The irony wasn't lost on me—using her own key to unravel her life's work. My heart hammered against my ribs, but I couldn't afford to let nerves get the better of me. Not tonight.

The building loomed ahead, its façade barely touched by the weak glow of street lamps. It was late, the kind of hour where decent folks were tucked away in bed, not skulking around labs playing goddamn spy games. With each step closer, the weight of what I was about to do pressed down on me like a lead vest.

Clad in an unassuming ensemble of dark jeans and a black coat, I blended with the shadows. My attire was nondescript, calculated—chosen with the intention to render me invisible in the dimly lit streets. The cool night air bit through the fabric, gnawing at my skin. But it was a small price to pay for the anonymity it afforded me.

I was doing this on my own.

I could have asked my brother for help...but I didn't want to get him involved. I didn't want to have that conversation with Marco yet, when he asked me what she meant to me, since I wasn't sure.

I didn't know how to begin to untangle that.

A cold knot of anxiety twisted in my stomach as I approached the entrance. Jade's ID card felt like a betrayal in my hand. She trusted me...and here I was, about to dismantle it all. Shoving the guilt aside, I focused on what needed to be done. Consequences would be dealt with later; for now, I had a mission to see through.

A quick swipe and the door clicked open, betraying no hint of my illicit entrance. Inside, the halls were silent except for the low hum of machines—sleepless sentinels of science. I could almost feel their electric breath on the back of my neck as I passed by.

Then there it was: the lab's door, standing like a gatekeeper to all of Jade's secrets. Dr. Bentley's name glared at me from the plaque, her photo with Ellie beside it—a stark reminder of the personal cost of this heist.

Fuck.

"Sorry, ladies," I muttered under my breath, my fingertips grazing over the cold metal of the handle. "This is business."

I stepped into the sanctuary of intellect and ambition, every inch of the room charged with the power of human potential—and the danger of its misuse. My mission was clear; get the information and get out.

With one last glance over my shoulder, I closed the door behind me, sealing myself inside with the ghosts of tomorrow's science.

I spotted Jade's desk by the far window, bathed in the faint moonlight filtering through the blinds. Papers were scattered in her controlled chaos, the ink-stained evidence of countless hours of work and dedication. The sight gave me pause, a momentary flicker of regret. But I pushed it down, forced my feet to carry me forward.

Jade's workstation was a mad scientist's playground, scattered with neural diagrams and genomic sequences that glowed on the large monitors like constellations. I wondered if she just didn't turn these off. I could almost hear her voice, low and precise, explaining each one, but there wasn't time for imagination—the clock was ticking.

The system accepted her credentials without a hitch. How many times had I watched Jade, from the corner of my eye, typing in her password after we'd fucked? She didn't know I was watching her then.

She'd been so engrossed in her thoughts, oblivious to the world around her, let alone my careful observation. Even in my betrayal, I couldn't deny the admiration I felt for her dedication.

The admiration I felt for her.

The surge of adrenaline made my hands tremble, or maybe it was the gravity of betrayal—hard to tell when your heart's a traitor too.

The desktop came alive with icons and folders, an unassuming façade for the treasure trove beneath. It didn't take long to find what I was looking for. Dr. Jade Bentley was methodical in her record keeping, and her system wasn't hard to crack.

The folder's name stared back at me: "Neurogenetic Projects - Confidential." My gaze lingered on the label, the words alone enough to raise the hairs on the back of my neck.

"Here goes nothing," I whispered to no one, clicking open the file. Rows upon rows of documents lined the screen, each one a Pandora's Box begging to be left alone. But I was past the point of no return.

I plugged in my USB—a lifeline back to my world of shadowed alleys and silent promises. Dragging and dropping, I copied the files, watching as the progress bar filled up. Each percentage was a step closer to unlocking the future—or damning it.

"Come on, come on," I urged the machine, my impatience a pulsing beat in my veins. The seconds stretched out, infinite as space, until finally, the transfer completed. A digital heartbeat echoed through the silence—the potential for pioneering brain regeneration now at my fingertips, nestled among the mundane on a piece of plastic and metal.

My father might've been a real estate mogul–among other things–but he had no idea what kind of riches awaited the Moretti family, if I could just sell this to the highest bidder.

"Gotcha," I breathed out, relief washing over me in an unsanctified baptism. With the data secured, I pulled the USB free, its weight now immeasurable in my pocket.

I turned back to the workstation, the embers of victory cooling into the hard, cold reality of what needed to be done next. My fingers danced over the keyboard as I navigated through the system's history. The login records stared back at me, evidence of my ghostly passage through their digital world.

"Nothing personal," I murmured, and with a few keystrokes, I wiped the logs clean, eradicating my digital footprint. It was like I'd never been there—a specter in the wires, unseen and unheard.

Satisfied, I stood up, pulling on my gloves with deliberate care to avoid leaving any lingering trace of myself behind. I scanned the workstation one last time, ensuring not a single fingerprint or stray piece of DNA remained. The Moretti name was built on being untouchable, and I intended to keep it that way.

The exit greeted me with a rush of crisp night air, a sharp contrast to the sterile hum of conditioned air inside. I filled my lungs with it, letting it clear my head for a moment. But as I descended the steps into the deserted street, that brief solace was ripped away by the gravity of what I carried with me—the potential to change lives or destroy them. The data was a beast in my pocket, whispering sweet promises one minute and growling dark threats the next.

I slipped into my car, the leather seat familiar beneath me. As I drove through the streets, the city seemed to hold its breath, waiting to see which path I would tread. My mind raced, each thought a ricochet bullet, bouncing between the miracles and menaces nestled within Jade's research.

"Careful, Dante," I told myself. "This is bigger than you can imagine."

I took a turn, my hands steady on the wheel despite the storm brewing inside me. Street lights flickered overhead, casting long shadows that played across the dashboard, reminding me that no matter how far I drove, I could never outrun the choices I had to make.

Once I reached the familiar confines of my place, the door shut with a weighty thud behind me. The silence was a stark canvas to the chaos of my thoughts. I shrugged off my jacket and made straight for the laptop sitting on the dark wood desk, an unassuming witness to the nights spent unraveling secrets best left in the shadows.

I booted up the machine, its screen cutting through the darkness, illuminating my face in its blue glow. I didn't bother with lights; they'd only serve as a beacon for prying eyes. Instead, I let the moon spill its silver judgment through the windows, casting slanted bars across the room like a jail cell.

The files opened with a click, their contents spilling out before me—charts, graphs, emails, all pieces of Jade's life's work. I scanned the data, my heart hammering at the implications of each document. Groundbreaking didn't even begin to cover it. Neuroplasticity, the brain's ability to rewire itself, to heal—she'd cracked it wide open.

I dived deeper, my brows furrowing as I consumed her complex explanations and calculations, the technical jargon swimming before my eyes. It was like trying to read a foreign language, one riddled with complex equations and biological terms that transcended my understanding. Yet the implications were clear—this was monumental, unprecedented even.

With each scroll, I felt more of Jade's passion bleeding into me. The enormity of the impact this could have on humanity was staggering—treatments for brain injuries, cures for neurodegenerative diseases, the possibilities were endless. And dangerous. The power to manipulate the very fabric of human cognition could easily become a tool for control in the wrong hands.

This was some sci-fi shit.

Forget making the Moretti family wealthy for as long as we were around. Owning this research meant controlling the fucking world.

Suddenly, the grim reality of my actions hit me hard. I was holding something that could rewrite the laws of nature, something Jade had created out of pure altruism and passion for her research. And here I was, ready to sell it to the highest bidder—ready to betray Jade in the most profound way.

"God damn it." I scrubbed at my face, feeling the rough stubble beneath my fingertips. My reflection stared back at me from the glossy laptop screen, distorted by codes and graphs—the traitor in the mirror, wearing a look of regret.

Regret...it was a bitter pill to swallow, but there it was, irrefutable and heavy in my chest.

I retrieved my cell phone from my pocket, my thumb hovering over Jade's contact. For a moment, I hesitated. There was still time to undo this—to warn her. But then would come questions—questions laden with suspicion and doubt. Questions I wasn't ready to answer. Not yet.

My thumb wavered, but then I shoved the phone back into my pocket. The die was cast, for better or worse.

I sat back in my chair, staring at the screen until the words blurred together. The hum of the city seemed to grow quiet as if holding its breath in anticipation of what was to come. An eerie silence filled the room, amplifying the rapid beat of my heart. This wasn't just about money or power anymore. It was about the future, about lives that could be changed—or ruined.

And it was better that it was in my hands instead of someone like Lorenzo Caruso's.

Right?

Chapter Eighteen: Dante

I'd spent all day chewing on what I needed to do next...and this was a meeting I definitely didn't want to have.

I pushed open the door, the hinges silent as secrets. The room was all shadows and whispers of power, with men who knew how to keep their mouths shut. My father, Enzo, sat at the head of the table, his presence like a fortress. Marco was there too, his eyes sharp and calculating.

My uncles Tony and Leo flanked my father, and my cousins Rob and Jago chatted amongst themselves. They were useless, I had no idea why they were there. But this was a family business after all, and I needed to do whatever to keep my father happy. They all looked up, waiting for me to break the silence.

"Thanks for coming so quickly, gentlemen. Alright, let's cut to the chase," I began, my voice steady as I laid out the cards. "Jade—smart as they come, she's on to something big. Neurogenetic research." I watched their faces, saw interest flicker in the dim light. "This isn't just about playing doctor. It's a game-changer for us, especially with the Carusos always breathing down our necks."

The old oak table gleamed under the low lights, reflecting back the serious lines etched into each man's face. Every one of them knew what was at stake. We weren't just running numbers and pushing product; we were fighting for the throne of Little Italy, night by bloody night.

"Enhancing loyalty, boosting cognitive abilities," I pressed on, watching as the shadows seemed to lean closer. "Imagine our guys, sharper, more dedicated. Unbreakable."

Enzo's eyes narrowed, and I knew he was seeing the same vision—a battalion of soldiers with minds like steel traps. But then his gaze shifted, a slight hardening at the corners that told me he was about to shift gears.

"Sounds like sci-fi," my cousin Jago said helpfully.

"I'll admit it's far off," I replied. "For now, let's think of the profit."

"And this neuroscientist you've been seeing," Enzo said, his voice smooth as aged whiskey, "what's her role in all this?"

I stiffened. Jade. Her name was a bullet in the chamber, ready to fire off into dangerous territory. "She's not part of this," I shot back. The thought of her getting tangled in our web had my heart slamming against my chest. She was a civilian, innocent in a way none of us could claim. "She's just... research. An easy in," I added, hoping to God he'd buy it.

Enzo leaned back in his chair, a thoughtful frown settling on his face as he took in my response. "Just research," he echoed, before his gaze turned towards Marco. "And what do you think of this, son?"

Marco pursed his lips, the wheels turning behind those sharp eyes. "Why not?" he said calmly, with an indifferent shrug. "Every war needs its weapons, and if science can give us an edge, then we should use it."

But I could see the calculating glint in his eyes—Marco wasn't interested in the hypothetical super abilities. No, he was thinking about the goldmine that genome data could represent. Healthcare companies, pharmaceutical giants, Silicon Valley—they'd all kill for that kind of information.

"However," Marco continued, his slick tone a stark contrast to the menacing implication of his words. "The question isn't whether we can use it, Dante. The question is how long it will take us to get our hands on it."

Enzo turned back to me, his piercing gaze demanding an answer. The room was thick with tension, the stakes were high and each second ticking away was a reminder of the war that raged outside these walls.

"I have it," I said. "Almost all of it. And if things keep going my way, I can make Dr. Bentley work for me outside of her official BioHQ capacity, which means the data I stole will have more legitimacy."

Enzo's lips twitched in slight approval, a small victory for me. "Make sure you keep things under control, Dante. Don't let your feelings for this woman cloud your judgement." His words were measured, but his tone was a clear warning.

I nodded, swallowing the lump in my throat. The whole thing threatened to spill over the edge - Jade, BioHQ, the Carusos... It all hung in a delicate balance. But I was Dante Moretti, and I wasn't about to let it shatter.

"Do we need to dispose of her once you're done with getting the data?" My father asked, ever practical.

I felt the blood drain from my face, my heart pounding a brutal rhythm against my ribs. "No," I said quickly, too quickly, and I knew they'd picked up on it. The room seemed to darken, the air becoming tight. A coil of fear spiraled in my gut.

There was a silence that fell over us like a shroud - heavy and foreboding. Marco was staring at me, his sharp gaze boring into mine, analyzing, calculating. Enzo was watching me too, his eyes hard and unyielding.

"Listen," I started again, forcing my voice to remain steady. "Jade has no idea about our operations. She thinks she's helping out with an independent research study. We keep it that way."

The silence was like a loaded gun, each of us waiting to see who would pull the trigger first. I cleared my throat and leaned forward, hands clasped on the polished oak table that had seen more bloodshed discussed than a battlefield.

"Let's cut through the crap," I said, desperate to shift the topic away from Jade. My voice was steady, but inside I was tightrope walking over a pit of vipers. "We have a chance here to pioneer something the streets haven't even dreamed of. We need to do this quickly. We shouldn't worry about ethical considerations beyond what we have to show to look legitimate," I scoffed lightly, a wry smile touching my lips as I met my father's steely gaze. "We've never played by those rules."

Enzo's eyes narrowed just a fraction, but it was enough to tell me I was treading on thin ice. I quickly forged ahead before the old man could call me out.

"We've got covert medical facilities already set up," I continued, speaking with a confidence I was far from feeling. "They're disguised as public health R&D—perfect fronts for us. We can run our tests without anyone getting wise to it. And the best part? The money we put into this? It gets cleaned through legitimate channels."

"Legitimate?" Marco snorted, his tone laced with irony. But there was interest there now, just beneath the surface. I could work with that.

"Legit enough to keep the feds off our scent." I leaned back, mirroring Marco's earlier posture, and watched him closely. "And if we play our cards right, nobody connects it to the Moretti family. It's all under the radar, untouchable."

Enzo finally spoke, his voice low and gravelly with the weight of command. "You're talking about a lot of moving parts. A lot of risks."

"Risks we can manage," I replied, annoyed. "We've always been about adapting, staying one step ahead. This is how we do it in this new world. You told me to pull this off, Dad. I'm pulling it off. I just need your help."

My father pondered this, his fingers tapping a slow, deliberate rhythm on the tabletop. "Proceed with your tests," he said at last, giving me a nod so slight it could have been missed. "But remember, Dante, we are Morettis. We don't just adapt; we control."

"Understood," I said. I felt the weight of what we were embarking upon settle around me like a cloak. Tonight, I had convinced the most powerful men in the room to walk a razor's edge. Tomorrow, I'd have to deliver on the promise of revolution.

"Are you sure you know what you're doing?" my uncle, who rarely spoke, asked. Tony was a terrifying man—I didn't like him at all, and my dad liked him even less, but he had to be there.

"Yes, Tony. The projections," I started. "They're more than promising. We're talking about an expansion of revenue streams that makes our traditional rackets look like chump change."

I laid out the charts and graphs across the mahogany table, each line and curve a testament to the potential that lay within our grasp. They all studied them, his eyes sharp as razors, missing nothing.

"Biotechnology," Tony mused, his finger tracing the upward trend on the graph. "You're certain this isn't a house of cards?"

"Solid as concrete," I assured him. The figures didn't lie. "We dominate this niche, we don't just survive, we thrive—eclipsing the Carusos in ways they can't even imagine."

My dad's nod was slow, cautious. A seasoned predator giving respect to a new weapon, but wary of its bite.

"I don't know about this," Jago said.

"Well, good thing he didn't ask you," my father replied. "A preliminary trial, then. Quiet as the grave, Dante. If there's even a hint of a leak, or if security doesn't hold up..."

"Then we pull the plug," I finished for him. "But it won't come to that. I've got people on this who are ghosts; they make sounds vanish."

"Good." Enzo leaned back, the leather chair creaking under his weight. "But remember, we tread softly until we're sure. The last thing we need is the Carusos sniffing around before we're ready to move."

"Understood," I replied, feeling the weight of his trust like a mantle on my shoulders. This was it—the moment where I steered us into new territory, away from the bloody streets and into the silent war of technology and information.

The old man stood, signaling the end of the discussion. His movements were deliberate, every inch the Don who'd navigated a lifetime of threats. "Stay sharp," he said. "And Dante? Make me proud."

Chapter Nineteen: Dante

I stood by the window of my office, high above the city that never sleeps, feeling like a damn traitor. The guilt was a heavy load, pressing down on my chest with each thought of Jade's ID card, now in my possession, and the research I had accessed - her life's work, handed over to the Moretti family like it was nothing more than a bargaining chip.

My reflection stared back at me, a troubled man trapped between the world he was born into and the one he yearned for. In the stillness of my office, I could almost hear the whispers of betrayal echoing off the walls, mingling with the distant hum of New York below.

Enough. Shifting gears, I reached for my phone with a resolve that masked the storm inside. Dialing the number of an exclusive seaside restaurant, I pictured Jade's face, imagined the way her eyes would light up under the soft glow of candlelight. For a moment, the tension that had carved itself into my features eased at the thought of her smile.

"Reservation for two," I said into the receiver, my voice steady despite the anticipation drumming through my veins. Tonight, I'd see her smile, bask in the light of her presence, and try to forget the darkness of my own deeds. Tonight, it was about her.

"Do you want your usual table, Mr. Moretti?"

"No, I want the whole venue," I replied.

"We normally take venue reservations well in advance—"

"I don't care," I said. "I'll pay you triple your asking price, and half again if you manage to get it ready within the hour. Just the chef and your best server."

The line went silent for a moment before the voice returned, a note of surprise apparent even over the phone. "Of course, Mr. Moretti. Consider it done." I hung up right away and ran my fingers through my hair, taking a deep breath as I tried to swallow the tight knot of anxiety lodged in my throat.

"Good," I said. "Thank you."

I hung up, sinking back into the plush leather of my office chair. There was a bitter irony coloring my actions; here I was, securing entire restaurants for Jade while behind her back, endangering her life's work. Forcing down a sigh with a swig of my bourbon, I was reminded once again of the life I was neck-deep in – one where duplicity was a currency more valuable than the greenbacks itself.

I opened my laptop, the glow of the screen illuminating the dark room. I clicked through Jade's research files, each page a testament to her intellect. She was making strides in biotechnology that could change the game for many, and here I was, stuck in a world where power plays overshadowed human progress.

"Damn it," I muttered under my breath, feeling the weight of my actions. I'd promised myself I wouldn't let her get caught up in this life, yet here we were. The thought of her becoming collateral damage was something I couldn't stomach. With every click, I admired her more and despised myself for betraying her trust.

"Get a hold of yourself, Dante," I scolded. This wasn't about me or the shadows I inhabited; it was about doing right by Jade. I owed her that much.

But...how could I tell her? She needed to get away from me, get away from all this.

I slouched in the leather chair, my head tipped back, eyes closed. The silence of the room was a cruel joke—it did nothing to quiet the war raging inside me. I pinched the bridge of my nose, a useless attempt to stave off my growing headache.

"Jade," I whispered her name like a prayer, or maybe a curse.

The taste of betrayal soured my mouth, and I couldn't shake the image of Jade's face when she'd learn the truth—that every tender moment shared was laced with deception. My gut churned at the thought.

"Tonight, everything changes," I murmured, steeling myself for the confession that would either set us free or tear us apart. I pictured her sitting across from me, the soft glow of candlelight making her dark hair shine like obsidian. How could I break the heart of someone who saw the world with such clarity and hope?

"Jade, there's something about me you don't know," I practiced under my breath, each word heavier than the last. I ditched the charm, the easy smiles—none of that had a place here. This was raw, unvarnished truth I was dealing with.

"I need you to leave. Get out of New York. You're in danger here."

Yeah, I didn't think she was going to listen to me. I let out a long breath, bracing for the fallout. My heart hammered, but somewhere underneath the fear, there was a flicker of hope. Maybe, just maybe, she'd see the man I was trying to be, not the one I had been.

I didn't know what exactly I had to tell her–but I could tell her something. A little bit.

Just enough to keep her safe.

And then, maybe, she would forgive me. If I was lucky.

If she was a better person than me. I sure as fuck wouldn't forgive me if I were her.

I locked the file with a final click, the sound echoing in the silence of my office. The research data, Jade's life's work, sat encrypted on my laptop—a symbol of betrayal that weighed heavy on my conscience. I had spilled her secrets to the Moretti family, and regret gnawed at me like a hungry rat.

"Keep your friends close, and your files closer," I muttered to myself.

The evening air was crisp as I flicked off the lights and headed to my room. Tonight's attire required more thought than usual—a suit that had to speak of remorse and hope in equal measure. I slid open the closet, hands brushing over fabric until they paused on the dark blue suit. Perfect. It matched the depth of Jade's eyes—the ones I'd have to look into as I laid bare my sins.

Dressing was methodical, each button fastened with precision, each crease smoothed out meticulously. The man staring back from the mirror was one I barely recognized.

Tired, old, scruffy.

"Tonight you're just a man, Dante, not a damned capo," I told my reflection, straightening my tie.

"Let's do this," I said, slipping on my jacket. My heart thudded against my ribs, a reminder of what was at stake—everything.

With a deep breath, I grabbed the keys from the dresser. It was time to face the music, and whatever tune it played, I was ready to dance.

The engine's hum was a steady backdrop to my restless thoughts as I navigated the streets of New York, autumn painting the city in hues of fire and gold. Inside the car, I rehearsed my confession, my voice low and earnest against the silence.

"Jade, there's something I need to tell you," I started, gripping the steering wheel until my knuckles whitened. The words felt clumsy, too coarse for the delicate truth they had to convey. "What we have...it's real to me. And I've done something that might wreck it."

With each run-through, my heart raced like I was closing in on a deal with life itself as the wager. Jade meant more than a fling, more than a strategic move. She was the unexpected calm, a serenity I hadn't known I craved.

Parking outside her place, I took a moment to gather myself, my breath fogging up the windshield. In my hands lay a bouquet of deep red roses, lush and vibrant—a stark contrast to the knot of dread in my gut. They were a symbol, an olive branch extended before the battle of confessions began.

I stepped out into the crisp evening air, straightening my jacket as I approached the door of her building. I called the elevator and tried to take deep breaths. My palms were sweating, betraying the cool exterior I fought to maintain. This wasn't just about spilling secrets; it was about laying my heart at the feet of a woman who could either embrace it or crush it beneath her heel.

I approached her apartment. I rang the bell, the sound echoing through the quiet hallway. There was no turning back now. I braced myself, ready for the door to swing open, ready for the light in her eyes that always seemed to pierce right through my armor. It was time to face whatever came next—be it absolution or ruin.

The click of the lock echoed a welcome, and the door swung open. There she stood, Jade, with that smile that could throw the darkest shadows off kilter. "Hi," she said, her voice a soft melody against the hum of the city night.

"Hey," I managed, my throat tight as I handed her the roses. Her eyes lit up, like the first break of dawn over a restless sea, and for a second, all my fears drowned in the depth of her gaze.

"Thank you, Dante, they're beautiful." She stepped aside, ushering me into the warmth of her place.

"You look beautiful," I said as I looked at her.

She blushed at the compliment, casting her eyes down before she looked back up at me. "Thank you," she said, her voice soft.

The drive to the restaurant was quiet. The city lights played against the shadows inside the car, twisting and flickering as I clenched the steering wheel. My mind raced with thoughts of the confession ahead. What would she say? Would she understand? Or would it be too much for her to bear?

As I pulled up in front of the restaurant, a sigh escaped my lips. This was it. The night of truths. I turned to look at Jade and saw her gazing out of the window, her face illuminated by the city lights.

"Are you alright?" she asked, turning away from the view to look at me.

I nodded, forcing a smile onto my face as I reached out and took her hand. "I am now," I said, squeezing her hand gently. "Thank you for setting this up, by the way. I was so glad to get your email. I have a surprise for you."

"You do?"

I nodded. I did have a surprise for her. I just...wasn't sure it was a good one.

Chapter Twenty: Jade

I never imagined science could lead me to a moment like this, where the soft glow of candles danced upon fine china and crystal glasses. Dante Moretti had just ushered me into a private dining area that seemed to have been plucked from a scene in one of those old romantic films I'd only half watch while scribbling notes on genetic sequences.

"Wow," I murmured, taking in the exclusive setup that felt surreal compared to my usual evenings hunched over lab reports. "This is... incredible, Dante."

He offered a smile, but it didn't quite reach his eyes—a look I was beginning to recognize all too well. His voice was smooth as always, though. "Only the best for you, Jade."

We settled into our seats, the menus between us rich with options. I couldn't help but notice how Dante fidgeted, his fingers tapping a silent rhythm against the linen tablecloth. It was subtle, but to a woman who spent her days observing reactions under the microscope, it was glaringly obvious.

"Are you alright?" I asked, trying not to let my curiosity morph into concern. "You seem... somewhere else tonight."

"Ah, just thinking about some work stuff," he replied, waving off my question with a practiced ease.

I knew dismissal when I heard it, so I didn't press him on it. The lines around his eyes tightened when he thought I wasn't looking, and I fought the urge to question him further. Instead, I focused on the elegance before us, the clink of our glasses serving as a temporary reprieve from the tension that simmered beneath the surface.

"Did you try the veal?" I ventured, aiming to steer us toward safer waters. "It's supposed to be exceptional here."

"Yeah, I've been here a lot," he replied.

"Do you always take your dates here?"

"Sometimes," he said softly. "But it's rare that I rent out a whole venue for them. I mean, it's never happened before."

I blinked, surprised. His confession swam through my mind, but before I could respond, he was pouring us each a glass of red wine. The rich aroma filled the air around us as he set the bottle back on its metal stand. Dante raised his glass and looked at me with those sea storm eyes.

"To new beginnings," he toasted, and I clinked my glass gently against his. His eyes never left mine as we each took a long sip of our wines.

His gaze slipped from my face down to the table. "There's something I need to tell you, Jade," he muttered, his voice low and heavy.

I swallowed hard, bracing myself for what was to come. "Okay," I managed to respond.

He reached across the table and held my hand gently. His eyes searched mine as if seeking reassurance or maybe forgiveness. "I..." He released a shaky breath. "I'm not exactly who you think I am."

The world seemed to tilt beneath me, his words eroding whatever foundation of understanding I had of him. "What do you mean?" My heart pounded against my chest with a terrible urgency.

"I...I'm involved in some things that..."

His phone buzzed on the table between us.

His gaze snapped to the device, and the expression that crossed his face was pure torment. "I have to take this," he muttered before he picked up the phone, turning away from me as he spoke in hushed, fraught tones.

He excused himself with a curt nod and strode to a quiet corner of the room, his back to me.

"Family business" was the term he'd toss around, a shield that kept his world neatly separated from mine. I wasn't stupid. Maybe I'd wanted to think the best of him. But he was about to tell me about his father's illegal dealings and that meant he trusted me.

He liked me.

I couldn't push him on it, which made this more difficult than I wanted it to be. I just had to wait for him to tell me himself.

Yet, as I watched his silhouette framed against the soft glow of wall sconces, his shoulders tense, the air around him seemed charged with something more than familial obligation.

His voice was too low for specifics, but the way his free hand clenched and unclenched spoke volumes. The murmur of his voice ebbed and flowed, a current I couldn't ride but felt all the same. Words like "immediate" and "handle it" slipped through the cracks in the ambient noise, and they stuck to me, cold and foreboding. This was no ordinary call about business or a family squabble over Sunday dinner.

When he returned, his face was a mask of composure, but his eyes betrayed the storm just passed. They flicked to my face, searching for signs of suspicion or fear. Perhaps he found neither, or maybe he saw both.

"Everything okay?" I asked, unable to temper the worry edging my words. My heart thundered in my chest, not from the wine or the rich food, but from the gnawing thought that Dante's world was bleeding into mine, dark and unbidden.

"Family business," he replied, the phrase rolling off his tongue with practiced ease. His lips curved into a semblance of a smile, but it didn't reach those piercing eyes, windows to a soul caught in a vice. "Nothing to worry about."

His answer did little to quell the unease that had taken root inside me. The man before me was an enigma, cloaked in charm and danger, and every instinct screamed that there was so much more beneath the surface—more than I might be ready to face.

But fuck. I needed to try.

"Sometimes sharing what's weighing on you can help lighten the load," I offered softly, hoping to coax him into opening up. My own experiences had taught me that much.

Dante's laugh was short, devoid of humor. "In my world, sharing can get you killed." His words hung heavy between us. He snapped his head up to look at me. "I mean, uh, figuratively, of course."

"Of course. Was that your father?"

"Yeah, that was my old man. I don't know, Jade. It's just that Enzo has high expectations," he admitted, his jaw tensing. "And the stakes are...let's just say they're higher than in most families."

"High expectations...I know them well," I began, taking a deep breath. "My parents pushed me toward academia. Becoming a neuroscientist wasn't just an aspiration; it was a mandate. The pressure was suffocating at times."

"Are your parents academics?" he asked, obviously eager to stop talking about his own father.

"My mom was a teacher before she had me and my siblings," I shared, hoping my openness would encourage Dante. "She gave up her career so that we'd have the best upbringing possible. My dad was a scientist, worked at one of the top research facilities in the country. He was--is--very prestigious. They both expected us to follow in his footsteps."

"He's a neuroscientist too?"

I laughed. "No, his job is harder," I replied. "He's a theoretical physicist. He worked on projects I can't even begin to understand. But his brilliance...it was both inspiring and daunting. I never wanted to disappoint them."

Dante waved me off after taking a sip of his wine. "Wait. I understand familial pressure, I get that. But how is his job harder than yours?"

I chuckled lightly at his question, shaking my head slightly. "Theoretical physics deals with concepts and dimensions that bend the fabric of reality. They attempt to understand the universe, its origins and structure, it's a task of cosmic proportions." I paused, looking into his curious eyes. "But what we do in biotechnology is more...here and now, I guess."

"Your job is hard too!"

"Well, no, my job is specialized," I replied. "That doesn't make it hard. With the brain, you can map it, study it, predict its responses to stimuli. But the universe? It's constantly expanding, constantly changing. The rules aren't as clear-cut. My father's work, it's poetic in its complexity." I paused, swirling my wine in my glass. "Not that biotechnology isn't fascinating in its own right."

He cocked his head. "I don't understand a lot about physics. I do agree that the brain is fascinating. Did you ever think about going into that instead of neuroscience?"

"I did," I admitted, "But my passion leaned towards something more tangible, more immediate. Neuroscience felt...right. It's like understanding the hidden language of our minds, our very essence. And it's in being able to decode that language where I find the most satisfaction."

His eyes displayed an intense curiosity as they held mine. "And what about your siblings? Did they follow the path laid out by your parents?"

"Somewhat," I mused, a hint of a smile playing on my lips. "My sister Emily is a research chemist and my brother Tom...he rebelled." I laughed lightly at that. "Well, he went to law school first. Then he moved to Nashville and became a professional musician."

"Is he any good?"

"He's so good," I told him. "I don't think he would have gone to Nashville if he wasn't. He said being there was humbling."

Dante's eyes softened with amusement. "I mean, that makes sense." He took another sip of his wine, his attention never wavering from me. "A family of overachievers. No pressure, huh?"

I let out a short, mirthless laugh. "You could say that," I replied. "But I mean, you feel it too, right?"

"Yeah, my dad can be hard to please," Dante said. "He's very traditional. I'm the eldest son and I made a lot of mistakes when I was younger. I didn't always listen to him when I should have, which put me...behind."

"In terms of his expectations?" I asked, my tone gentle.

"Yeah, exactly," Dante replied, leaning back in his chair. His eyes left mine, focusing instead on the table between us. "And it's been a... challenge catching up. I tried to worry about what my mother wanted for me instead."

"What did she want?"

"Well, what she really wanted was for me to marry a nice Italian girl," he replied. "She had to settle for college."

A soft chuckle escapes my lips at his confession. "I take it you didn't give her the nice Italian girl?"

Dante's eyes snap back to mine, a mischievous glint sparkling within their depths. "Not exactly," he replies with a smug grin, "But I did give her a college degree."

"Where did you go?"

"Where do you think I went?"

"That's not fair. Just tell me."

"Cornell," he replied.

"Cornell? Impressive," I said, trying to hide my surprise. In spite of his rough exterior and intimidating aura, Dante was a man of intellect - Cornell's business school was one of the best in the country. "That's prestigious."

"Yeah. My mom was very happy. My dad was not as happy. He thought I'd be better off at home, learning the ropes of the family business." He paused, his gaze drifting off into the distance, clearly lost in some distant memory. "I wanted to make my own path, away from what he had planned for me."

"Yet here you are," I observed, my tone softer now.

"Turns out having a business administration degree from an Ivy League school is super useful when it comes to running a legacy family business," he said, bitterness creeping into his mocking tone. "Who would have guessed?"

His words hung heavy in the air, a bitter humor cloaked in self-deprecation. I couldn't help but watch him; the bravado fading as a hint of vulnerability seeped through. It was an odd sight, Dante Moretti showing a side of himself that seemed so far removed from his confident exterior.

"Legacy family business?" I echoed, partly to break the silence and partly because curiosity pricked me. "So you're running it now?"

Dante looked at me, his expression unreadable. "It's...complicated," he finally muttered, his gaze dropping to the wine glass cradled in his hand. "I'm trying to. My dad still doesn't trust me. Says my ideas are too out there."

"And...are they too out there?" I asked. The look on Dante's face had me quickly adding, "I mean, not that your father is the only one who can judge that, but... well, you get my point."

He grinned, some of his earlier confidence returning. "Well, let's just say I've got a few ideas that would rock the boat. But change isn't always a bad thing."

The waiter finally brought our food and Dante's eyes lit up at the sight of his favorite dish. "Here we go, linguini with clams. The best in the city," he announced proudly.

I couldn't help but grin at his enthusiasm. "That does look amazing," I said, my gaze affectionately lingering on him before shifting to my own dish, a plate of creamy fettuccine alfredo.

"You said you had something to tell me," I said after I took a bite of my delicious meal.

"Yeah," he replied, looking into my eyes. "But it can wait."

"Wait for what?"

He smirked, winking at me. "Wait for me to be done with my dessert."

Chapter
Twenty-One: Dante

I straightened my tie, a black silk noose that marked my allegiance to a world of shadows and whispered oaths. The venue, usually buzzing with the kind of energy that clung to your skin like a second layer, fell silent as I stood at its heart. My voice cut through the dimness. "Everyone out."

The staff was gone after only a few seconds. Now it was just the two of us, alone.

"Come with me, Jade. Let me show you the view."

I gave her my hand and pulled her toward the window.

Jade stood by it, the city's glow painting her in strokes of gold and amber. Fear and fascination flickered across her face, a living canvas of contradiction.

"Come here," I commanded, not unkindly. Authority laced my words, an invisible thread pulling her towards me.

She hesitated for a moment, then walked to me, each step measured. When she was close enough, I reached out, encircling her waist with an arm that had both protected and punished. Her body tensed then yielded, fitting against mine like it belonged there all along.

"Relax," I murmured, feeling the rapid rise and fall of her chest against me. It was moments like these—raw, charged with the promise of what lay ahead—that reminded me why this life, with all its darkness, could sometimes feel worth it.

"Is this what you meant when you were talking about dessert?" she asked softly.

"Yes," I replied, a smirk on my lips. I was going to have to tell her everything—I knew it. But right now, the plan was to just enjoy her for as long as I could. "I was talking about your pretty pussy."

"Jesus," she said softly.

"Jade," I began, my voice steady as the weight of our reality pressed down on us. We were a mess of contradictions, her innocence entangled with my sins.

Her gaze flicked to the window, eyes widening as she took in the vast expanse of glass, the only barrier between us and the world. "What if anyone sees?" Jade's question was barely audible, laced with the kind of vulnerability that did strange things to my chest, things I wasn't used to feeling.

I couldn't help but smile at her concern, the tenderness she evoked in me as unexpected as it was unwelcome. "Let them look," I said, brushing a stray lock of hair away from her face, my fingers lingering against her skin longer than necessary. "They should count themselves lucky."

Jade's breath hitched, and I felt her body relax incrementally against mine, surrendering to the inevitability of our connection. In this city of millions, in the heart of my family's empire, she was mine, and I would have her—completely.

I kneeled before her, taking in the sight of Jade clad in simple black leggings and a pristine white dress that contrasted with the shadows around us. My hands traced the contours of her hips, sliding down her sides as I felt every dip and curve beneath my fingertips. Her skin was soft, warm.

Inviting.

"Relax," I murmured, my voice low and controlled, a stark contrast to the racing of my own heart. The dim lighting of the room seemed to wrap around us, as if it too recognized the gravity of this moment.

My gaze drifted to the cityscape outside the window; New York never slept, its lights relentless and vibrant against the coming night. But inside this room, it was just us—Jade's breath quickening, my resolve hardening. The reflection of the outside world in the glass only made the intimacy we shared that much more acute.

"Look at me," I commanded gently, and when her eyes met mine again, something primal ignited between us. It was raw and undeniable, a connection that seemed to stretch beyond the confines of time and place. "I'm going to strip you bare now and I'm going to pleasure you until you're literally unable to walk. Got it?"

"Yes."

"Good girl," I said.

With that, my fingers found the hem of her leggings and began to slide them down, taking my time while savoring the moment. There was a certain thrill in stripping her bare, in revealing her to myself in all her raw essence. She was beautiful, breathtakingly so, and I couldn't help but marvel at how she could be so unaware of the effect she had on me.

Jade shifted slightly under my touch, her breath hitching when my hand brushed against the sensitive skin on the inside of her thigh. I could feel heat radiating off her, a silent testament to the desire coursing through both of us.

I dropped her leggings to the floor and pushed the white dress up slowly, revealing inch by enticing inch of her body. My fingers traced along the contours of her curves, stoking a fire that threatened to consume us both. I brushed against the lace edge of her panties before pulling them down and discarding them with the rest of her clothes.

I kissed the inside of her legs then, tasting the sweet warmth of her skin as my hands roamed upwards. Jade's breath hitched and she arched against me, her body taut with anticipation. I glanced up, locking eyes with her as my fingers brushed against her. A shiver ran through her, drawing a gasp from her parted lips.

"Jade," I whispered, my voice rough with want. "You're beautiful. You're going to look even better when you're crying from all the orgasms I'm about to give you."

I didn't wait for her response. I flicked my tongue against her, relishing the sharp intake of breath that echoed through the room. Her fingers tangled in my hair, pulling me closer as I set about making good on my promise.

I didn't wait for her response. I flicked my tongue against her, relishing the sharp intake of breath that echoed through the room. Her fingers tangled in my hair, pulling me closer as I set about making good on my promise.

"Wait," I said, pulling away from her. I intended to grab the wine I'd left on the table, intending to make this experience as intoxicating as possible. I found her eyes already on me as I returned.

"What's the wine for?" Jade asked, a hint of uncertainty in her voice.

"Consider it...an enhancement," I said with a smirk, uncorking the new bottle the waiter had recently left there with a soft pop.

I poured a small amount on my hand and then trailed it down her abdomen, the liquid cool against her heated skin. Jade sucked in a sharp breath. "Dante," she protested, but the argument died on her lips when my mouth followed the same path, licking up the wine and tasting the intoxicating combination of Jade and rich red grapes.

"Here," I said, handing her the bottle. "You don't need a glass. Drink."

Jade took the bottle from me, her fingers brushing against mine in a silent exchange of electricity. She brought the rim to her lips and took a hesitant sip, her eyes never leaving mine. The sight stirred something raw within me—something dark and hungry.

"Good," I murmured, watching the flush of pleasure color her cheeks, the way her eyes shone with an intoxicating mix of fear and desire. I took the bottle back from her and placed it back on the table next to us.

"Now, lie back," I instructed softly, guiding her down onto the plush carpet beneath us that was as rich and decadent as everything else in this highrise restaurant. Her hair splayed out around her like a dark halo, framing her face in an image that was pure sin against the white purity of her dress.

"Hold onto your legs for me," I said.

She complied, her fingers curling around the back of her thighs. The position left her further exposed to me—a sight almost breathtaking in its raw vulnerability, the view making my blood thrum with anticipation.

"Perfect," I whispered, eyes never leaving her as I placed myself between her knees. My mouth descended on her once more, and this time there was no hesitation. Jade made a soft sound from deep in her throat, and I felt satisfaction crackle through my veins. "How many orgasms do you think you can have in one night?"

"Wha-what?" The question clearly startled her, a blush creeping up her neck and spreading across her cheeks.

"Just a number, Jade," I said, my fingers tracing over her exposed skin. I wanted to pace myself.

"I don't know," she said.

"Okay. Well, let's find out," I said, my voice low and husky with desire.

I didn't give her time to respond before I pressed my mouth back against her, my tongue flicking against her in a rhythmic dance that pulled a mewl of pleasure from her lips. She tried to squirm away, lost in the sensations I was causing, but I held her firmly in place.

"Dante," she gasped, her hands clutching at my hair as I continued to tease and torment her. Jade writhed beneath me, completely at my mercy, and it was a view I could get used to. "I...I can't..."

"Yes, you can," I countered, pulling back just enough to look at her. The sight was breathtaking - Jade Bentley, brilliant scientist and the woman who held my dark heart in her hands, coming undone because of me. "Look at me. You're doing so good. You're being such a good girl for me."

The whimper that escaped her was music to my ears. I licked her clit again, pressing a finger into her tight pussy.

She gasped, the sound sharp and breathless in the quiet room. I couldn't help the smug grin that spread across my face at the reaction, the satisfaction of knowing I was making her feel this way.

Her hands tightened in my hair, her body arching off the carpet as she strained against me. Her breaths came in short gasps, her cries growing louder with each pass of my tongue.

"Dante," she moaned, her voice trembling with desire. "I...I can't ...I'm..."

"I didn't say you could come yet," I said.

Her eyes widened as she whimpered, her body trembling on the brink of release.

"Oh... oh God..." she moaned, her grip in my hair tightening as she bit her lip.

"No," I growled, pulling back to look at her. "Just Dante. No gods here.

"Dante..." she breathed, a plea in her voice that made me smile.

"That's right," I said, pressing a kiss to her inner thigh. "You belong to me tonight."

Without wasting a moment, I dove back into her warmth, my tongue swirling against her clit with practiced ease. She writhed beneath me, her fingers digging into my scalp as she tried to keep from falling over the edge.

"You can come now," I said, pressing a finger into her pussy to find her g-spot. "You can let go, beautiful. Are you going to squirt for me?"

Jade's eyes widened at my words, but she didn't reply. She didn't need to. Her response echoed in the tight grip of her hands in my hair, the arch of her back, and the beautiful flush staining her cheeks.

I didn't hold back this time. I licked her with vigor, pushed my finger deeper and curled it just right. Jade let out a scandalized moan, her thighs trembling around my head as her climax overtook her.

There she was, coming undone beneath me, just like I'd promised. The sight was intoxicating—better than any wine could ever be.

Hot liquid seeped from her and pooled onto my hand, and I couldn't help but groan in satisfaction. I took in the sight of Jade, flushed and panting heavily beneath me.

Swiping a thumb against her slick thigh, I brought it to my lips, tasting her release. Jade watched through half-lidded eyes, the blush deepening on her cheeks.

"Again," I commanded, voice soft but firm.

"But Dante..." she protested weakly.

I interrupted her with a devilish smirk, "I did promise you multiple orgasms, didn't I?"

"No more surprises," she pleaded softly.

"None at all," I agreed absently, my mind already planning the next wave of pleasure. Seizing the bottle of wine once more, I poured another small amount on her stomach, watching as it pooled in her navel before dribbling down towards her still-sensitive clit. "But by my count, that's just one, right? And so far, we know you can have one orgasm."

Her eyes widened, her breath hitching as I lowered my mouth to her navel, tongue flicking out to taste the mixture of wine and her arousal. She shivered underneath me, her thighs tightening around my shoulders in anticipation.

"Dante..." she moaned, her voice barely a whisper as I continued my ministrations. I hummed against her skin, sending vibrations through her core that had her writhing beneath me.

I raked my teeth down her stomach, finally capturing her clit between my lips. She tasted so good. Her hands found their way back into my hair, tugging gently with each flick of my tongue. There was a note of desperation in her movements now, a needy quality that sent a thrill of satisfaction coursing through me.

"God...Dante," she gasped. The sound of my name on her lips was intoxicating, driving me to continue my assault on her senses.

"Again," I commanded, the word a husky whisper against her sensitive flesh.

"Dante... I can't," she protested. Her voice was weak, breathy with the strain of holding back.

"Yes, you can," I countered, looking up to meet her gaze. Her eyes were glazed with desire, partly obscured by heavy eyelids that fluttered closed every few seconds. "You're doing so good for me, Jade."

A whimper escaped her as I continued to taste her, my tongue delving deeper into the folds of her pussy. I watched as she clenched her fists in the plush carpet beneath us, the tension in her body evident as she pushed herself closer to the edge.

"Let go for me, Jade," I said softly, giving her clit a final flick with my tongue before pulling away just enough to watch her. She tried to squirm closer, a whine escaping her at the loss of contact.

"Do it, Jade," I growled, my eyes locked onto hers. "Come for me."

Her breath hitched, her grip on my hair tightening as she let out a guttural cry of pleasure. Her body clenched and released rhythmically, waves of her orgasm washing over her. The sight of her in the thrall of ecstasy was something out of this world.

I watched with hunger-filled eyes as Jade writhed beneath me, lost in the throes of passion. Every gasp, every shuddering breath, every little whimper was a symphony to my ears. Each time she said my name like a prayer – a desperate plea – sent a thrill down my spine.

She began to come down from her high slowly, her body loosening its taut hold gradually.

She tried to catch her breath. "Wait," she said between gasps, her hair sticking to her face. "What about you? Don't you want me to take care of you?"

I smirked at her. "That's adorable, beautiful," I chuckled softly, brushing a loose strand of hair out of her face. "But tonight is about you. You come first."

"But Dante..." she started to protest, only for me to silence her with a deep kiss. As our lips moved together, I trailed my fingers over the curves of her body, reigniting the sparks that had only just begun to fade.

"I meant that literally," I said, pulling away from her. "I'm going to wait until you're at the very peak of your pleasure. And I will fuck you tonight, but only then. I'm going to train you to associate mind-blowing orgasms with having my cock inside of you. Every time you're about to come, you'll think of me. My face, my hands, my tongue, my cock."

Her eyes were wide and her breath had hitched at my words. "And how are you planning to do that?" she asked breathlessly.

"Well, babe," I replied, smiling at her. "I'm just getting started."

Chapter Twenty-Two: Dante

I could barely keep my hands on the wheel, the black leather slipping under my sweaty palms as I navigated through New York's deserted streets. The city was our private labyrinth, and the hum of the engine played background to the heat that simmered between us. Jade sat there, her curves hugged by the dress she wore, a smirk dancing on her lips.

She wasn't wearing her leggings or her underwear anymore, and the sight of her legs was driving me crazy.

"Bet you thought about taking me right on the floor of the restaurant," she teased, breaking the silence.

"Christ, Jade," I exhaled, my grip tightening. "You have no idea. But I've got this trick, see? Learned it way back in college." I shot her a half-grin. "Flexing the thigh muscles diverts the...excitement."

"Really now?" Her eyes glinted with mischief. "And why would you want to stop yourself?"

"Because when I finally take you," I said, voice low, "I plan on making it count. Give you the kind of release that's worth waiting for."

Her cheeks flushed a deeper shade of red, and I didn't need a mirror to know I was hard again. Damn her blushes.

"Every time you turn that color, I swear..." I let the words hang, the air thick with unsaid promises.

In one fluid motion, I steered us into the parking space outside her building. The glow from the streetlights painted her face in soft amber tones, revealing an eagerness that mirrored my own. I killed the engine and stepped out, reaching over to open her door. She slid out like a dream, and I couldn't peel my eyes away.

"Can still smell you," I murmured, leaning in close enough for my breath to brush her neck. "How wet you are."

Jade shivered, and I knew it wasn't from the autumn chill. "The wine," I nodded toward her feet where the bottle lay uncorked, a souvenir from the night's earlier indulgence.

"Right," she said, bending to pick it up, giving me a view that made my throat dry.

I grabbed the bottle from her. "Open your mouth," I said.

Jade complied, biting her lower lip in anticipation. I tilted the bottle, letting a few drops of the midnight red wine slip onto her tongue. Her eyes fluttered closed, savoring the taste before looking up at me with a smoldering gaze.

The sight was almost enough to unravel me right there, but I maintained control. "Good," I complimented, my voice rougher than I intended.

She twisted a lock of hair around her finger, a blush creeping into her cheeks as she looked away. "Let's go inside."

The elevator ride up to her floor was a silent battle of restraint. The confined space magnified everything—her breath hitching slightly, the way she leaned into me without realizing it, the faintest brush of her body against mine. It was an unspoken dance of anticipation, each small movement charged with meaning.

"Could've been at my penthouse by now," I remarked casually, though there was nothing casual about the way my body reacted to her proximity.

"BioHQ is closer from here," Jade countered, her eyes locked on the ascending numbers above the elevator door. "Efficiency for the morning."

"Efficiency," I echoed, suppressing a chuckle. "Right."

When we reached her apartment, the key barely had time to turn in the lock before the door swung open and we stumbled inside. Without a moment's hesitation, my lips crashed down onto hers, devouring any pretense of patience I might have feigned. She responded with equal fervor, her fingers clawing at my shirt as if it were a barrier to be conquered.

Clothes were shed without care, our movements hurried and rough. Her dress landed somewhere near the couch, my jacket following suit. There was no time for neatness, no room for second thoughts. All that mattered was the heat of her skin against mine as we navigated through the sparse light of her living room.

"Bedroom," she gasped between kisses, her hands fumbling with the button of my pants.

"Lead the way," I managed, voice strained with desire.

She pulled away just enough to guide me, walking backward with lips parted and eyes dark with longing. I followed like a man possessed, every rational thought drowned out by the need to claim her, to lose myself in the sweet obliviousness of her embrace.

The moonlight spilled through her bedroom curtains, casting an ethereal glow over the scene as I laid Jade down on the bed. Each touch was calculated, every movement a testament to the hunger that raged within me. My hands roamed her body, mapping out the terrain of her curves and valleys with a possessive intent.

"Remember how you touched yourself, thinking of me?" I murmured, my voice rough with arousal.

A soft "Yes" escaped her lips, barely audible, but laced with anticipation.

"Where's the toy you used?" I asked, my need to see her unravel under my command growing stronger by the second.

"Nightstand," she breathed out, her chest heaving.

I reached over, snatching the vibrator from where it lay. The silent promise of what was to come hung heavy in the air as I turned my attention back to her.

Her response was immediate—a symphony of gasps and moans that drove me wild. With deliberate care, I parted her thighs and descended upon her with my tongue, tasting her, savoring the sweetness of her pleasure. My fingers joined the dance, one coated with the slickness of my own making before pressing into her, eliciting another sharp cry from her lips.

"Fuck, Dante," she whimpered, her body tensing and releasing in rapid succession.

"Let go for me, Jade," I coaxed, my movements unrelenting.

The vibrator hummed to life against her clit, and she bucked beneath me. Riding the wave of intense pleasure I was orchestrating, Jade's body began to convulse. The sight of her lost in ecstasy was more intoxicating than any high I'd ever experienced. I increased the speed of the toy and my tongue, pushing her towards the precipice.

And then she came, her release a wild cry that echoed through the silent room. Her body arched off the bed, back arching as her fingers dug into my shoulders. I continued my ministrations, drawing out her orgasm as I pressed a crooked finger against her g-spot.

"Can you squirt again for me, beautiful?"

Her eyes widened in surprise, but I kept up the pace, relentless in my pursuit of her pleasure. My fingers sunk deeper inside her, hitting that magic spot that had her gasping and writhing beneath me.

"I don't know if I can…" she said, her legs moving. "I'm so sensitive, I…"

"I told you I would make you come until you cried," I said. "I didn't say you could come, but I didn't say you could stop."

Her protest was lost in a moan as I increased the pressure, the toy vibrating against her swollen bud even as my fingers moved relentlessly within her. She was trembling, her hands gripping my hair as if I were her only anchor in the storm of pleasure threatening to consume her.

"Dante," she gasped, her voice a desperate plea. "I… I can't…"

"Yes, you can," I said, voice firm but surprisingly gentle. "For me."

She shuddered beneath me, a soft whimper escaping her lips. With a final thrust and flick of my fingers and the relentless hum of the toy, she let out a scream that ricocheted off the walls. A rush of warmth wet my hand and soaked the sheets beneath us. Jade's body tensed before collapsing back onto the bed, panting and shivering from the intensity of her release.

But I didn't give her time to recover. "Ride this wave," I said. "Because I'm about to fuck your pretty pussy with my cock and I want you to remember every inch of me."

"Dante, I…" she began, but her words were cut off by a moan as I slid into her, the wetness from her previous orgasms making it easy for me to be buried to the hilt.

She was still twitching, the aftershocks of pleasure making her tight around me. My breath hitched, the sensation almost too much to bear. But there was a promise to keep – one of pure carnal pleasure, and I was not one to break my promises.

The rhythm started slow, each thrust dragging along her sensitive walls. Her nails dug into my back, imprints that would surely leave marks in the morning. But the pain was nothing compared to the sweet torture of feeling her around me.

With each thrust, her moans grew louder, more desperate, a sweet symphony to my ears. The sight of her beneath me, her body writhing in pleasure, was enough to drive any man insane with desire. And I was no exception.

"Fuck," she said. "You're so big."

"And you're so tight, beautiful," I shot back, my rhythm picking up speed. Her words, her moans, they were all egging me on, fueling the fire in my veins.

With each thrust I could feel her body respond, her walls clenching around me in a way that had my own body shuddering in response. My own pleasure was building, a crescendo of desire that threatened to consume us both.

"But you can take it, can't you?" I asked, leaning down to nip at her sensitive nipples. "You can take every inch of me."

Her response was a choked-out moan, her body arching into mine, her fingers gripping my shoulders like vices. Her body was ablaze beneath me, each touch sparking another wave of pleasure that coiled within her.

"God...Dante," she gasped, surrendering to the unrelenting rhythm of our bodies. "Don't...don't stop."

A grin broke across my face at her desperate pleas. The sight of her underneath me, flushed and writhing in pleasure, was enough to set my blood on fire. And I had no intention of stopping.

I increased the pace, my thrusts becoming more relentless as I sought to drive us both off the edge. My fingers dug into her hip bones for leverage, pulling her closer with each thrust. Her moans got louder, turning into a high pitched wail, the sound of pure ecstasy echoing through the room.

"Are you close?" I growled in her ear. I felt her nod against me, her nails digging painfully into my back as her body tensed beneath me. She was on the cusp, teetering on the edge of oblivion, and it was my job to push her off.

"Then come with me," I commanded, my voice a hoarse whisper against her ear. "Let go and let me feel you."

Her response was a wordless cry, lost in the cacophony of our combined moans and panting breaths. But I didn't need words to know she was there with me, ready to tumble into the abyss of pleasure.

With one final, powerful thrust, we both went over the edge. Her body bucked beneath me, her walls clenching around me in a vice-like grip that sent me spiraling into my own release. My hips jerked erratically as I buried myself deep within her, riding the waves of ecstasy that washed over us both.

As the world spun into a haze of pleasure, I collapsed on top of her, our bodies slick with sweat and tangled together. Her chest heaved beneath mine, each gasp in sync with my own ragged breathing. Her fingers traced lazy circles across my back, the touch soothing against my heated skin.

"Fuck...Dante," she gasped out, her voice shaky from exertion. "I...that was..."

"Four?" I asked. "That was at least four orgasms, right?"

She laughed. The sound, so warm and joyously exhausted, made my heart flutter in a strange, unfamiliar way. "I lost count after the first two," Jade admitted with a light chuckle, her fingers continuing to gently dance across the expanse of my back.

"I didn't," I said. "We'll make you come more next time."

Chapter Twenty-Three: Jade

P ain hammered inside my skull, a relentless drumbeat that dragged me from the depths of sleep. The darkness of the room offered no comfort, the faint glow of moonlight barely revealing the contours of the unfamiliar space around me. I reached out, my hand fumbling for the solid warmth of the man beside me.

"Dante," I murmured, my voice raspy with the remnants of dreams and discomfort. "Can you hand me some Aleve? This headache's killing me. It should be on the side of the bed."

A soft groan answered me, the bed shifting as Dante turned his body toward mine. His movements were sluggish, weighed down by sleep, but he managed to find the bottle and placed it in my outstretched palm. His fingers brushed against mine, sending a current of concern through the touch.

"Do you need water?"

"No," I replied. "I'm okay."

"Is this happening a lot?" His words were thick with drowsiness, yet edged with something sharper.

"More often than I'd like." I popped the cap off the bottle, the sound echoing too loudly in the stillness.

Dante propped himself up on one elbow, the sheets slipping to reveal the muscular expanse of his chest, the ink of the crucifix on his pecs catching in the moonlight streaming in from outside.

His gaze was heavy upon me, searching. "You should get that checked out," he said, and I could hear the worry threading through the gravel of his voice.

"Yeah, once there's time," I replied, trying to brush off his concern with a half-hearted smile that felt more like a wince. The room seemed to close in on me, the air too thick to breathe, and yet the nearness of Dante provided an anchor in the storm of pain that refused to abate.

"Jade," he started, but I shook my head slightly, not wanting to delve into the possibilities of what these headaches might mean—not now, not when I had his arms around me, grounding me in the present. For a fleeting moment, I allowed myself the illusion of safety, the belief that nothing could touch me here, in the quiet embrace of night. But the ache in my head persisted, a cruel reminder that even in the darkness, you can't outrun your fears.

"Come on. Let's get back to sleep. I'm tired."

He nodded, pressing a soft kiss against my forehead and wrapping his arms around me, holding me close. "Okay. Hopefully you'll feel better soon."

It took a little while, but I did end up falling asleep again.

But my sleep was short, and it didn't feel restorative.

The first light of dawn was already bleeding into the night sky as I pulled up to BioHQ, the sprawling complex where science and ambition converged in a dance of innovation. My head was still pounding, each throb a cruel metronome counting down the seconds until I had to mask my pain and be the brilliant Dr. Jade Bentley once more.

I stepped through the sliding doors, greeted by the sterile familiarity of white halls and the distant hum of machinery. The scent of antiseptics was undercut by the unmistakable aroma of coffee—a lifeline for many of my sleep-deprived colleagues. I made a mental note to grab a cup but doubted it would do much for the ache that seemed to have taken permanent residence behind my eyes.

"Security audit again, Jade," Dr. Stuart White called out, his voice slicing through my fragmented focus as he strode towards me, clipboard clutched like a shield.

"Morning to you too, Stuart," I murmured, fighting back a wince as I forced my gaze to meet his. "Didn't we just do this?"

His expression was unreadable, but the slight furrow of his brow told me this wasn't a courtesy visit.

"Someone logged in last night," he continued, his words clipped and efficient. "It's in the IT logs, but the details are gone—erased. That's what Edward told me."

"Where is he?"

"Working," Stuart replied.

I shook my head. "Erased?" I echoed, the word sitting heavy on my tongue. It hinted at something deliberate, calculated. I didn't have time to chase shadows—not with my project deadlines looming and this relentless headache.

"Completely." Stuart's eyes were sharp, analytical, as if he could unravel this mystery with sheer willpower. "I'll need your access logs, just to check."

"Of course," I replied automatically. "Everyone's logs, right?"

"Yes," he replied. "We're just going alphabetically. From the As to the Ds first."

"Got it," I told him.

"Thanks. I know you've got a lot on your plate," he said, offering a curt nod before moving away, his lab coat billowing slightly with the briskness of his departure.

I watched him go, the sense of disquiet growing. But there was no time to dwell on security breaches or vague threats lurking within lines of code. I had work to do, breakthroughs to chase, and a headache that showed no mercy. Pushing through the pain, I set off toward the lab, ready to lose myself in a world of data and discovery, where every answer led to more questions and the truth was often hidden in plain sight.

The sterile hum of the lab welcomed me, a familiar sanctuary against the chaos of the unknown. I slid into my routine, the motions grounding me until Ellie's voice sliced through the focus I had fought so hard to maintain. I hadn't even noticed or greeted her when she had come in.

"Jade, are you alright?" she asked, her brows knitting together in concern.

I paused, test tube in hand, and forced a smile. "Yeah, just a rough night," I replied, trying to shake off the throb in my skull that seemed intent on crippling my thoughts.

"Oh, a date?"

"Yes," I said. "El, he took me to this restaurant downtown in this high-rise and he'd rented the whole place out."

Ellie's eyebrows shot upwards, a mix of surprise and amusement in her warm brown eyes. "Well, someone's gone all out," she said, her tone teasing yet gentle.

I nodded, my lips curling into a small smile at the memory. "It was...incredible," I admitted, before quickly adding, "But it was also overwhelming. I didn't get much sleep."

"Incredibly overwhelming as in good or bad?" Ellie asked the question carefully, her gaze now filled with concern rather than amusement.

"He made me come so many times," I said in a whisper.

Her eyes widened in understanding, a hint of a smirk tugging at the corners of her mouth. "And that's why you're on edge," she said, her tone shifting to one of gentle teasing. "No rest for the wicked, huh?"

I let out a soft chuckle, despite the ever-present ache in my head; leave it to Ellie to make light of such situations. I had always admired her ability to balance seriousness with levity.

"Well, that, the headache, and Edward Rodriguez. Dr. White said something about someone accessing the data in the middle of the night?"

Ellie set her pipettor down with a soft click and leaned against the bench, her eyes searching mine. "I heard about that."

"Any idea who might want access to our data?" I asked, tracing the edge of the lab bench with my fingertips.

Ellie shrugged, her expression thoughtful. "Well, it could be an internal mistake, or perhaps a competitor trying to sneak a peek at our breakthroughs," she offered.

The thought sent shivers down my spine. My work was more than just research; it was a piece of me. The thought of our discoveries being exploited...

"Or it could be something more sinister," Ellie added, breaking into my thoughts as she studied my face.

"Oh, yeah. Someone broke here and heisted some data," I said with a smirk. "That sounds totally plausible."

One corner of Ellie's mouth kicked up in a wry smile. "Well, you never know. We're doing some groundbreaking stuff here," she countered gently, her gaze never leaving mine. I could tell she was trying to lighten the mood, but her words stoked the unease that had been nagging at me all day.

I rubbed my temple, the headache suddenly getting worse.

"You okay, babe?" Ellie asked.

"Just a headache."

"Again?" Ellie's concern visibly deepened, her playful demeanor evaporating instantly. She reached out, placing a soft hand on my shoulder. "You had one like, last week. Thought it was a period thing."

"Yeah, actually...I think I'm late," I said. "I don't know. I just haven't been paid attention to it."

Ellie's eyebrows shot up, a mixture of surprise and concern washing over her features. She quickly removed her gloves and disposed of them into the biohazard bin before turning back to me. "Let's take a minute, okay? Come, sit down."

I didn't argue. Folding myself into the chair she pointed to, I leaned forward, resting my elbows on my knees. The headache still hammered in time with my heart, and anxiety gnawed at my nerves. Ellie rolled another chair over and sat next to me, her warm hand finding mine.

"The stress could be messing with your cycle," she suggested gently. "There's no chance you're pregnant, right?"

"Right," I said. "No chance."

The words rolled off my tongue like a well-rehearsed line, but there was an odd hollowness to them—a dissonance between what I said and what I felt.

"You're sure?" Ellie pressed gently, her warm brown eyes studying me with an intensity only she could manage.

"Yeah, El. Absolutely."

But as soon as I said it, it sounded like a lie.

Chapter
Twenty-Four: Jade

My head was still pounding when I woke up.

A strange weight knotted in my stomach, an unwelcome guest making itself at home. Tiptoeing out of bed, the world felt a little off-kilter, like I was walking a tightrope above the chaos of my own life.

I checked my phone, and there it was — Dante's message from last night, his words a digital caress against the mess in my head. "Goodnight, Jade. How's your headache now?" I read it aloud, ignoring the pang in my heart. I let the phone fall back onto the nightstand, the soft thud grounding me for a moment.

The first rays of sunlight were sneaking through the curtains, casting long, slanted shadows across the room as I shuffled towards the bathroom. The tiles were cold underfoot, a stark reminder of reality biting at my heels.

My hands, usually so steady and precise, betrayed a slight tremor as I reached into the cabinet. The pregnancy test lay there, inconspicuous among bottles and boxes — a sleek white stick that could tilt my world on its axis. I wrapped my fingers around it; it was cool to the touch, like holding a piece of ice that wouldn't melt.

Resolve steeled my spine as I followed the instructions printed on the box with clinical precision. Then came the wait, every tick of the clock stretching seconds into eternities. My breath hitched, chest tight with anticipation as I watched, willing the test to reveal its secrets.

Time froze, the air thick with the weight of unspoken possibilities until, finally, the result flashed before my eyes.

Positive.

That single word echoed in the cramped space, bouncing off the tiles and drilling into my skull. I blinked, once, twice, refusing to accept the truth staring back at me from the digital display. The ground beneath my feet felt like it was shifting, trying to throw me off balance. My mind raced with the implications, each one more daunting than the last.

The bathroom mirror caught my gaze, reflecting a woman who looked like a stranger. Dark hair fell haphazardly around a face pale with shock, eyes wide and disbelieving. This can't be happening, not to me, not now. I'm Dr. Jade Bentley, for God's sake, with a career that doesn't have room for... this.

"Okay, think, Jade," I murmured to myself, my voice sounding hollow against the tiled walls. The reflection didn't respond, just continued to stare back with that same look of utter disbelief. But doubt gnawed at me, relentless as the headaches that had become my uninvited morning companions. What if the test is wrong? It happens, right?

With a surge of desperate hope, I tore open another package. Repeating the process felt like a twisted déjà vu, each step heavier with dread and silent prayers for a different outcome. I clutched the second test like a lifeline, heart pounding against my ribs so hard I could almost hear it echoing in the silence.

I watched, breath held tight in my chest, as the minutes crawled by until the result locked into place. There it was again, those bold lines forming a plus sign that seemed to brand itself into my consciousness.

Unmistakable.

Undeniable.

Positive.

A bitter laugh escaped me, void of any real humor. "Twice confirmed, then," I said aloud to no one, the sound of my voice an attempt to anchor myself to reality. My life, meticulously planned and controlled, suddenly felt like a house of cards caught in a tempest, ready to collapse under the weight of a secret two pink lines thick.

I'd never called in sick before—not when I had the flu last winter, nor when I sprained my wrist a couple of years back. But today, my fingers trembled as I typed out a message to my supervisor. The lie tasted like ash on my tongue; I claimed a sudden fever, a sore throat, the usual suspects for a day spent curled under the covers instead of beneath the sterile hum of lab fluorescents.

"Sent," I whispered, dropping the phone on the counter as if it burned. The room spun slightly, and I gripped the edge of the bathtub, willing myself to stay grounded. My head throbbed—a cruel reminder that no matter how much I wished this morning away, reality wasn't going to change.

"Get up, Jade. Focus," I muttered, forcing myself to stand. I needed answers, something concrete to hold onto. Dressing quickly, I chose jeans and a black tank top, clothes that wouldn't draw attention or raise questions. Clothes that said 'normal' even though nothing about today was.

The walk to the clinic was mechanical, each step a bitter march toward an unknown future. I ignored the passersby, the shop windows, the vibrant life of New York City waking up around me. Their normality was a world away from the chaos churning inside me.

My phone buzzed, derailing my train of thought. It was Ellie.

You okay? the text read, simple and direct.

Ellie always knew when something was off.

Headache's turned into maybe the flu, I lied again, thumb hovering over the send button before committing to the deception. I couldn't face her worry, not now, not with my own fears still clawing their way through my mind.

K. Take care, babe, came her immediate reply, followed by a little heart emoji. Guilt pinched at my heart.

Will do, El, I typed back, pocketing my phone with an exhale that felt more like surrender than relief. Onward to the clinic, to confirmation, to decisions I wasn't ready to make. But ready or not, the truth waited for no one—not even Dr. Jade Bentley, who thought she had control over every aspect of her life.

The clinic was a nondescript building sandwiched between a run-down laundromat and a bodega with neon signs that had seen better days. The bell above the door chimed softly as I entered, not quite ready to face the reality I suspected waited for me.

"Can I help you?" a nurse at the front desk asked, her voice professional but not unkind.

"Jade Bentley," I murmured, the name feeling foreign on my lips.

"Please fill out these forms," she instructed, sliding paperwork across the counter. I took a seat in the waiting area, its sterile neutrality oddly soothing compared to the storm inside me.

The walls were adorned with bland, abstract art—splotches of color that meant nothing and everything all at once. Other patients sat around me, lost in their own worlds of private concerns. I scribbled answers mechanically, ticking boxes without truly reading the questions.

"Jade Bentley?" A nurse's voice cut through the soft hum of activity, the sound making my heart leap into my throat.

"Here," I answered, standing up too quickly, my legs a little wobbly.

"Follow me, please." Her scrubs rustled as she led me down a hallway that smelled faintly of antiseptic.

The examination room was small, functional. A man with a name tag that said Dr. Alvarez and looked about five years younger than me entered soon after, his eyes scanning the chart in his hands before they met mine.

"Miss Bentley, I'm Dr. Alvarez. What brings you in today?" His tone was kind, his gaze steady—a rock amidst my swirling sea of doubt.

I rubbed my temple. "Doctor."

"Yes, I'm–"

I held my hand up. "I'm Dr. Bentley."

He nodded. "Right. A physician?"

I shook my head. "No, and look, it doesn't matter," I said, wishing I hadn't corrected him.

"So, what does bring you in today, Dr. Bentley?"

I hesitated, the words catching like hooks in my throat. "I've been having persistent headaches...and there are two positive tests." My voice was barely a whisper.

He took a second to process this. "Oh, right," he said. "I understand. We'll take good care of you. Let's start with some basics and go from there."

"Thank you," I managed to say, tucking away my fears. There would be time enough for those later. For now, I was just another patient in Dr. Alvarez's capable hands, clinging to the hope that maybe, just maybe, things would be okay.

A few minutes later, I was sitting at the examination table.

"Take a deep breath for me, Dr. Bentley," Dr. Alvarez had instructed as he pressed the stethoscope against my back. I complied, feeling the cool metal through the fabric of my tank top, inhaling the sterile scent of the clinic that had become too familiar in the last hour. The crisp paper beneath me crinkled with every shift of my body, each sound echoing my unease.

"Any discomfort here?" His touch was clinical as he palpated my abdomen, eyes focused, searching for signs I couldn't begin to understand.

"None," I replied, staring at the ceiling, willing myself to be anywhere but on this examination table.

"Alright, we're going to run a few tests. It won't take long." Dr. Alvarez's reassurance was meant to comfort, but the wait churned my insides more viciously than any centrifuge. "We could do another urine test for hCG, but I have a feeling you're going to want a blood test."

"Is it more accurate?" I asked, grasping at the hope of certainty.

"Both tests are accurate," he said with a gentle smile. "However, a blood test can provide quantitative results, telling us how much hCG is in your system. This might give you some peace of mind."

The mention of peace of mind sent a hollow laugh rising up my throat, but I swallowed it back, nodding instead. "Yes, let's do the blood test. Will you be able to tell how far along I am?"

Dr. Alvarez nodded, a thoughtful frown playing on his lips. "We can estimate based on the hCG levels, yes. But keep in mind that it's just an estimation. An ultrasound would be more accurate."

I took a steadying breath, decision made. "Let's do both."

He gave my shoulder a reassuring pat, pulling his sterile gloves off with a snap. "Alright, I'll have the nurse order your tests and we'll get started. Get comfortable, Dr. Bentley. I have a feeling you're going to be here for a good while."

Dr. Alvarez's prediction proved correct. The tests were time-consuming, the waiting heavy, pressing down on me with an intensity that seemed to consume all else. A technician rolled in with an ultrasound machine, positioning it next to my examination bed with the precision of years of practice. Her name tag read 'Nancy', and she smiled at me gently, aware of the tenseness that clung to me like a second skin.

"Hi, honey. Just breathe, okay? This is going to be a little cold on your skin."

The cold gel sliding over my stomach sending tremors up my spine. I watched her eyes flicker over the monitor, her silence amplified by the steady hum of the machine.

The room shrank with every passing second, until there was only Nancy and me and the dull grey images flashing across the ultrasound screen. Numbers and data points blurred into a confusing jumble, my scientific mind scrambling to find answers where there were none.

Then, a sound cut through the discord - a tiny rhythm pulsing with life. A heartbeat. So fast, I almost couldn't compute it.

The impact was immediate. It was a jolt of electricity, a free-fall, a seismic shift beneath my foundation. The world seemed to tilt on its axis, everything suddenly off-kilter.

"Is that...?" My voice tapered off into nothingness as Nancy nodded, her smile gentle, her eyes filled with a kindness that made the room feel less cold.

"Yes, honey. That's your baby's heartbeat."

Chapter Twenty-Five: Jade

I was so fucking nervous.

I lingered outside Rothko's, a Chinese fusion bistro-style restaurant Dante had recommended, my fingers threading through my dark hair in a futile attempt at calm. The city buzzed, its nightly symphony of horns and chatter wrapping around me. With a steadying breath that did little to ease the tightness in my chest, I pushed open the mahogany doors.

The place was a swath of lowlights and soft murmurs. A cocktail of charred meat and aged wine hit me as I scanned the room. There, in a shadowed corner, sat Dante, waving me over. Unruffled, he raised his bourbon to me, an unspoken welcome from across the room.

"Hey, you," I managed, my voice betraying none of the chaos brewing beneath the surface. His smile didn't reach those guarded eyes as I settled into the chair opposite him, the leather cool against my back.

He greeted me warmly, getting up to slide a chair away from the table for me. Soon, the waiter came to take our orders, which was the perfect distraction, since I needed to steel myself for what was about to come next.

The waiter had barely left our table when Dante leaned back, swirling the liquid amber in his glass. "You alright? You've been distant," he said, the furrow of his brow betraying concern beneath the sheen of confidence.

"Just slammed at the lab," I murmured, my voice steadier than I felt. It wasn't entirely a lie; the lab was my life, after all. But tonight, it was a convenient shield.

I had to tell him, but...he was a complicated man, and if he wasn't committed, then maybe I didn't have to drag him into this at all. "Yeah," I said. "I'm starving. Let's eat."

We talked about the food and our days as we ate. It was nice. This, I could get used to. If only I could figure out everything else.

But soon we were done...and it was clear that the thing I had been so nervous about had to happen, whether I wanted it to or not.

"Is everything to your satisfaction?" the waiter asked as he slipped our check onto the table alongside two fortune cookies.

"Perfect, thank you," Dante replied with a nod, his attention never leaving me.

I cracked open my fortune cookie.

The slip inside said 'Fortune favors the bold.' How fitting. I tossed it aside, my gaze returning to Dante.

"Something wrong?" He asked, studying me with those piercing eyes that seemed to see every lie I'd ever told.

I took a shaky breath. "Dante...we need to talk."

He raised his eyebrows.

My breath came out in a shaky exhale. I should have probably told him I was pregnant right then and there, but he wasn't even my boyfriend. I needed to firm up some details before sharing. I looked into his eyes when I spoke. "When am I going to meet your family?"

Dante's face hardened, the joviality that had danced in his eyes moments ago replaced by a cold edge. His jaw tightened as his fingers began to drum on the table, a rhythmic tap that was more a threat than a tune. "Why would you want to meet my family? I thought you wanted to keep things casual."

I had never fucking said that. But it was not the time to call him out on it.

My heart clenched, the weight of the secret I harbored felt like an anchor pulling me down. I willed myself to maintain eye contact, to not look away and show weakness. "Maybe we need to define what 'casual' means," my voice wavered despite my effort.

His annoyance was a tangible thing, a shadow that passed over his face like a cloud obscuring the sun. "Why the sudden need to meet them? Are you not happy with what we have?" he prodded, his tone sharp.

I bit the inside of my cheek, fighting back the emotions threatening to spill over. My mind screamed to just come out with it, tell him about the baby, but fear rooted me to silence. "Because...things change," I murmured instead, my eyes pleading for him to understand without having to spell it out loud.

Dante leaned back in his chair, the lines of his suit stretching across broad shoulders. There was a battle playing out behind his eyes, one I wasn't sure which side he favored. He studied me, as if looking for an answer written on my face, but whatever he sought remained hidden beneath my carefully constructed facade.

"Jade," he started, his voice a low rumble that filled the space between us. "I don't know if you know this, but my life is extremely complicated."

"I do," I managed to get out, feeling the walls close in around us. The bistro with its soft lighting and hushed conversations seemed suddenly suffocating.

"Then you should understand why this isn't simple," he said, his gaze finally breaking away from mine to stare at something only he could see.

I sat there, unsure of how to navigate through the minefield of our conversation. The connection between us, once electric, now felt like a frayed wire, dangerous and unpredictable. Dante reached for his suit jacket draped over the chair, his movements slow and deliberate.

"Let's get out of here," he said, standing up and throwing a couple of bills onto the table. "We'll talk about this...somewhere more private."

"Talk about it somewhere more private?" I threw the words back at him, my voice rising despite my attempt to keep it steady. "No, Dante. We do this now, here." My hand slammed onto the table, causing the silverware to clatter and a few heads to turn in our direction.

Now I had no idea where that had come from...and I wasn't sure I liked it. I put my hands on my lap, telling myself to calm down.

Dante's eyes narrowed as he sat back down, the authority he normally wielded seemed momentarily shaken. "I don't want to drag you into my family mess. It's not because I don't like you, Jade. Believe me, I really like you."

The honesty in his voice was almost enough to derail me, but the ache in my chest demanded answers. I looked away, blinking rapidly against the sting of tears. When I finally spoke, my voice was thick with emotion. "Then what am I supposed to be to you?"

There was a pause where the world seemed to hold its breath. His face softened, but the vulnerability vanished as quickly as it had appeared, leaving a cold mask in its place.

"Maybe we shouldn't even do this," I found myself saying, the words spilling out before I could stop them. "Maybe we shouldn't even fuck anymore."

The silence that followed was deafening. The clinking of a wine glass from a nearby table sliced through the tension, a stark reminder of the ordinary life that buzzed around us, oblivious to the storm brewing in our little corner.

Dante ran a hand through his hair, a gesture of frustration that was so uncharacteristically him. He opened his mouth to speak, but no words came out. Instead, he just looked at me, and in his gaze, I saw something that resembled fear.

He reached across the table, his hand enveloping mine, warm and insistent. "That's not what I want. I need time, Jade. My family is...complicated." His thumb brushed against my skin, a silent plea etched in the motion.

I stared at our joined hands, feeling the steady thrum of his pulse against my fingers. The gesture was meant to comfort, but it gnawed at me instead—how could such a simple touch speak of both solace and sorrow?

"And what about us? What about how I feel?" The words tumbled out, a turbulent rush of confusion and longing. I needed him to understand that this wasn't just about stolen moments and muffled moans in the dark. This was about more than that.

This was about another fucking human being.

His eyes held mine. But he offered no answers, no solutions—just the quiet acknowledgment of a truth too heavy to bear alone. And in that silence, the reality of our situation settled like dust upon the wreckage of my resolve.

I withdrew my hand, the absence of his touch like a sudden chill. "I can't keep playing this game, Dante. I need more." My voice wavered, betraying the turmoil that writhed inside me—a knot of fear, hope, and a desperate craving for something more than whispered secrets and shadows.

Dante's face hardened, the softness in his eyes vanishing. The air between us grew thick with tension, a tangible force that seemed to push us further apart even as we sat mere inches from each other.

I opened my mouth, the words teetering on the brink of revelation. I wanted to tell him about the life growing inside me, our unintended creation that had already begun to anchor me to this world in a way I never thought possible. But the confession lodged in my throat, a silent scream that refused to break free.

His gaze searched mine, looking for an answer or perhaps an escape. But there was none to be found—not in the dim warmth of the restaurant, nor in the cold streets that awaited outside.

"Jade, I'm serious about how I...feel about you," he said. "I just need a second to think."

I watched him, his face a mask of conflict as he wrestled with his words. It was disarming to see Dante Moretti—suave, articulate, intimidating—struggling to express himself.

"How much time do you need, Dante?" It was a question meant to be rhetorical, but spoken aloud it seemed to hang in the air between us like a challenge.

He looked at me, not with his usual confidence but something else, something bordering on desperation. "I wish I knew," he admitted softly, reaching for my hand again.

"Well," I said, standing up and trying to fight the tears in my eyes. "Now you have all the time in the world."

Chapter Twenty-Six: Dante

She was gone.

Jade had left, her parting words slicing through the din like a blade. My mind was a scrambled mess of thoughts, all tangled up with images of her walking away. Desperation clawed at my insides, disbelief nipping at its heels.

"Check, please," I muttered to no one in particular, tossing down a wad of cash without counting. It could have been hundreds or just ones – didn't matter. Nothing did, not without Jade.

The cold night air slapped me as I shoved through the restaurant doors. The city was alive around me, uncaring, while my world crumbled. I spotted her, a retreating figure on the sidewalk, her shoes clicking out a rhythm of escape.

"Jade, wait! Let me drive you home," I shouted, my voice slicing through the cacophony of honking cars and chattering pedestrians. The raw edge of my plea hung between us, desperate enough for both our sakes.

She didn't stop, didn't turn, but I'd be damned if I let her walk away into the night. Not like this. Not when every fiber of my being screamed to pull her back into my arms.

I caught up to her, my hand closing around her arm, more gently than I had intended. She spun around, a flash of anger igniting in those steel eyes. "I'll take the subway, or a cab. I don't need a ride," she spat out, an icy barrier forming with each word.

"Absolutely not." My words cut through the chill, laced with a menace I didn't bother to hide. "Let me at least do the gentlemanly thing."

Defiance etched her features as she crossed her arms, but she followed me, silent and seething, to where my car waited. The sleek, black sedan stood like a shadow against the concrete and the dim glow of the streetlights.

Unlocking the doors with a beep that sounded too loud in the night, I held one open for her. She slid into the passenger seat, her movements stiff, as if every inch of her protested the act. I got in beside her, and the tension swelled, filling the confined space like a malevolent ghost.

My hand found her thigh, a move once welcomed, now fraught with a desperate need to ignite what we'd lost. She flinched away from my touch, her body language screaming louder than any words could.

"This is over, Dante," she said, her voice so stern it might as well have been a slap.

"No, it isn't," I said. "I can smell how wet you are, Jade."

"Stop it," Jade insisted, her voice strained with an emotion she was trying too hard to mask. Her eyes darted away from mine, but I could see the pulse quicken at the base of her throat.

I ignored her plea, my fingers inching up the fabric of her skirt, determined to reclaim the connection between us—forcefully if necessary. Her scientific mind might be a fortress of logic, but her body...her body never lied to me.

"Jade," I growled low, pulling her face closer, "you can't deny this part of us."

"Let go of me, Dante," she demanded, but even as she spoke, her lips parted slightly, a telltale sign of her ambivalence.

The patrons in the parking lot were lost in their own worlds, oblivious to the tempest brewing within the confines of my car. Our breaths mingled, her resistance faltering as I found the warmth between her legs, my fingers moving with a familiarity that belied the chaos of our situation.

She bucked against me, caught between protest and surrender, and I knew I had her. The fight left her eyes for a fraction of a second, and I seized it, pressing my advantage with a relentless pursuit of her pleasure.

I pulled the fabric of her panties to the side. "See, I know exactly what you want," I said. "And you're going to sit here and let me pleasure you until you're screaming my name." I shoved two fingers inside her, her body arching under the violation, under the pleasure.

"Dante..." she gasped, and there it was, the surrender I'd been chasing. Her eyes fluttered shut as she sank into the sensation, her hands clutching the sides of her seat while I worked her into a frenzy. "Please stop."

"No," I said. "If you didn't want me, you wouldn't be sitting here in my car."

Each stroke of my fingers sent a jolt through her, the sheen of sweat on her skin catching the faint glow from the city lights outside.

"I want to memorize what the inside of you feels like," I said as I continued fucking her with my fingers. "I want you to remember what it feels like to be taken apart by me."

Her protests fell silent as waves of pleasure coursed through her, her senses overtaken by the relentless rhythm of my touch.

The taste of victory was sweet on my tongue as I delved deeper, matching the rhythm of her body with my strokes. Her breath hitched, her eyes fluttering open to meet mine. There was a spark in them I hadn't seen in weeks. It was resistance, yes, but also a flicker of the desire she'd been trying so desperately to bury.

"Stop... Dante," she managed through gritted teeth, but it was a plea without conviction. Her gaze held mine, the fierce determination that was so uniquely Jade slowly giving way to a raw need.

"No," I said again. "This isn't over until you come for me."

"Enough," she gasped, trying to pull away. But my grip tightened, and I pressed my fingers deeper, setting a rhythm designed to tip her over the edge. The car filled with her soft moans and my low growls, punctuated by the sound of fabric rustling against skin.

"You're so fucking wet," I said. "Does that feel good?"

"That's not the point—"

"You know, anyone could stop to watch you," I cut her off. "They could see that you're getting fingered in a parking lot like a cheap whore. But you know what?" I leaned closer, my lips brushing her earlobe as I whispered the next words. "I think that turns you on."

She gasped, a blush creeping up her neck and coloring her cheeks. Whether it was from embarrassment or arousal, I didn't know – and frankly, I didn't care. I had her where I wanted her: teetering on the edge, caught between her stubborn mind and traitorous body.

"I'm not...I don't—" she stammered out, only to be interrupted by my thumb grazing her clit.

"That's it, Jade," I encouraged, smirking at her sharp intake of breath. "Admit it, you like being watched. You like being taken like this. You're a scientist, a fucking genius. That doesn't stop you from being a whore for me."

Jade gave a half-sob, half-moan, her eyes welling up with tears. But beneath the hurt, beneath the betrayal, there was something more. Something wild. Something untamed.

"God damn it, Dante..." she gasped out, her words ending in a breathless moan as my fingers picked up the pace inside of her.

"That's it, that's my good girl," I coaxed, determined to wring every last ounce of pleasure out of her.

My fingers continued their ruthless assault, matched by the rhythm of her breathy moans and gasps.

Clinging to the last vestiges of her resistance, Jade twisted away from me. But with my free hand, I caught her chin and turned her back. My gaze burrowed into hers, unyielding and heavy with unspoken promises.

"You don't turn away. You look at me when you come."

"And what if I don't want to?" she shot back, defiance lighting up her eyes. But even as she spoke, her body betrayed her. Her hips jerked against my hand, seeking me out despite the words that hung in the air between us.

"I said look at me," I demanded, my tone hardening. "Or do you want me to stop?"

Her gaze met mine, her eyes a tumultuous mix of desire, pride, and resignation. "Don't... don't stop," she whispered, swallowing hard as she conceded.

"That's my girl," I murmured, satisfied. My movements became relentless, pushing her further into the pleasure she was so desperately trying to deny.

As I felt her walls clenching around my fingers, I knew she was close. "That's it Jade," I purred into her ear, "Come for me."

"No," she whimpered in protest, but even as she tried to fight it off, her body was betraying her. Her release was imminent, ready to break its hold over her and reclaim her body with an intensity that would leave her breathless.

"Come for me, Jade," I repeated, my voice a low growl in the near silence of the car. My finger found her clit again, applying just the right amount of pressure to push her over the edge.

"No...I..." She gripped my arm tighter as she fought for control, her resolve wavering under the onslaught of pleasure. But I was relentless, thrusting again and again until with a gasp, she went rigid beneath me.

"That's it," I whispered into her ear as her orgasm washed over her. I didn't let up, kept moving within her until the spasms subsided and she dropped against me, panting and spent. Each twitch of pleasure that pulsed through her sent a triumphant thrill down my spine.

I cradled her against me, my fingers stilling inside her as she rode out the aftershocks. Her body was warm and lax, the tension that had wound her so tight now dissipated. But despite her surrender, I could see the battle raging within her. The fight between morality and desire, between fear and yearning. She was a creature caught between two worlds: one of cold logic and sterile laboratories, the other of darkness and forbidden pleasures.

"You're mine," I said softly into her hair, my fingers gently stroking through the damp strands. She flinched at the words, but there was no denying the truth in them. Jade Bentley belonged to me, in a way I hadn't imagined possible. In a way, perhaps, that neither of us was prepared for. She looked up at me, her eyes glassy with tears. "And this is only over when I say it's over."

Chapter Twenty-Seven: Jade

I stood there in the quiet sanctuary of the BioHQ lab, my fingers tight around a pipette as if it were my anchor to sanity.

The steady hum and whirr of machines played background to the chaos unspooling in my head. I couldn't shake the images from the car—the way Dante's hands had moved without permission but awakened something dark and wild within me.

"Focus, Jade," I muttered to myself, trying to drown out the memory of how his eyes had locked onto mine, demanding and fierce as he brought me to the brink. It was a twisted mix of fear and desire, and I hated that part of me craved the intensity of his gaze again. But no, I wouldn't let Dante Moretti, with his dangerous allure, pull me any deeper into his world of shadows.

I wasn't going to tell him shit. He had made it clear that sharing my pregnancy with him was not safe.

The sterile lab seemed to glow eerily under the fluorescent lights, highlighting the rows upon rows of samples like soldiers at attention. Data sheets lay scattered, their numbers a comforting puzzle waiting to be solved. I threw myself into the work, each measurement and calculation a lifeline pulling me away from the edge.

"Replicate and confirm," I muttered to myself as Ellie hummed along with the music coming through the bluetooth speaker, allowing the progress of the experiment to cocoon me from the storm of emotions. The results, neatly plotted on the graph, were a solid proof of my dedication, a temporary shelter from the turmoil Dante had stirred within me.

"Shit," I breathed out, feeling the nausea rise unexpectedly. Was it the smell of antiseptic or something else? I took a deep breath, moving away from the pipettes.

"You okay, babe?" Ellie said, turning her head to look back at me.

"Still getting over that flu," I lied. I hated lying to my best friend, but how could I begin to explain all of this when I was pregnant with the child of a man she had literally warned me about?

"I don't know. You seem distant," Ellie's voice cut through the hum of the lab as she turned around, leaning on a bench behind her.

I turned to face her, forcing a smile that felt foreign on my lips. "It's nothing, Ellie. Just tired, I guess." The words came out flat, a poor attempt to deflect her probing gaze.

Ellie's eyes narrowed as she leaned against the bench, studying me with that analytical mind of hers. "You've been absent which isn't like you and your mood swings are noticeable. Something's definitely wrong," she pressed, her voice soft but carrying a weight that demanded honesty.

I willed myself not to look away, to give nothing more away. "I'm fine," I insisted, but my voice lacked conviction. I could tell she didn't buy it for a second, and a part of me was grateful for her persistence. "I just haven't been sick in like, years, and it really took it out of me."

"Headache again?" Ellie asked, tilting her head to the side with a knowing look.

"Must be all this groundbreaking research frying my brain," I joked weakly, hoping humor would throw her off the scent.

She let out a small chuckle, but her eyes remained latched onto mine.

"Let's just get back to the experiment, El," I said, turning my attention back to the pipettes now that the nausea had subsided a little.

Ellie hesitated for a moment, then shrugged and joined me. We worked in silence, the familiar rhythm of our tasks providing a welcome distraction.

But as I pipetted the final sample into place, I couldn't shake the dread pooling in my stomach. The fear that Dante's world—the darkness, the violence, the power plays—had infiltrated mine, and there was no going back. Not even the clean lines and precise calculations of my work could offer true sanctuary now.

"Hey, Jade, any word from Rodriguez about his tech integrity investigation?" Ellie's question pulled me out of my spiraling thoughts.

I shook my head, trying to appear nonchalant. "No idea. You know how tight-lipped they can be about these things."

"Right," she agreed, her focus returning to the lab results. "Hey, would you fuck him?"

"Who? Rodriguez?"

"God, no! He's not my type," I said with a laugh, shaking my head. The question was innocent enough, a splash of levity to ease the tension that had been steadily building within me. "Wait. Are you saying..."

"I'm just saying this dry spell is rough," Ellie said. "Last night I had a date with a guy I met online and it went so poorly."

"Really? I thought you were excited about this one," I said, momentarily distracted from my own problems. Ellie dates were always full of unexpected twists; they were a welcome break from the usual patterns of work and research.

"Oh, well, you see, he read I was a scientist, and he really wanted to talk about CRISPR."

"Aw, he was interested in your job," I said.

She held a hand up. "No, he wasn't," she said. "No, he wanted to talk me out of doing my job. Because it turns out his understanding of CRISPR was based solely on some conspiracy video he saw on YouTube. The whole date turned into a lecture about how we're all going to become genetically modified super humans," Ellie rolled her eyes dramatically, her hands waving for emphasis.

"Wait, we're not? Then why do we even do this shit?" I said with a laugh.

Ellie chuckled along, her head shaking in a mix of disbelief and amusement. "Yeah, I certainly spent all those years studying molecular biology just to secretly create a new race of superhumans."

"I knew it was Youtube that would eventually come for us."

Our laughter filled the lab, a welcome reprieve from my haunting thoughts. But even amid the waves of levity, I felt a deep sense of foreboding. One I couldn't shake off, no matter how hard I tried.

Ellie, still basking in our moment of camaraderie, began cleaning up. "I hope the next one isn't as crazy," she said, her back turned to me as she started washing the pipettes.

"I hope so too," I murmured absently, my mind already wandering back to Dante. "Didn't your last date bring his pet iguana along with him?"

"Okay, in his defense, I told him I liked iguanas," Ellie defended, triggering another wave of laughter between us. That was the Ellie I loved - the one who could find humor in even the most bizarre situations.

"So why did you ask about Rodriguez?"

"Because he's weirdly muscular for a tech geek, wouldn't you agree?"

I shook my head, smiling. "Honestly, I haven't noticed."

"Maybe when he's done being a nuisance, I can ask him if he's single. You haven't seen a ring, have you?"

"No," I replied. I didn't want to tell her it wasn't like I had been looking. "But I'll try to find out if you want."

"I wouldn't hate that. In the meantime, I guess it's back to the grind," Ellie quipped with a half-hearted chuckle, signaling our return to the hum of machines and the scent of progress that was our daily soundtrack.

But as we approached the incubators housing our latest experiment, a pungent odor snaked through the air. It wasn't the usual sanitized tang of disinfectants or the sterile nothingness of filtered air; this was different—organic and intrusive. My stomach lurched in protest.

"Ugh, do you smell that?" I frowned, pressing a hand against my abdomen as if to quell the sudden nausea.

"Smell what?" Ellie's brow furrowed, her nose scrunching as she sniffed the air like a bloodhound on the scent. "I don't catch anything off."

"Never mind." I waved her off, my voice steadier than I felt. Maybe it was just me. But as I stood there, surrounded by beeping equipment and petri dishes lined up like soldiers, a thought slithered into my consciousness, cold and unwelcome.

Could this place, this temple of science and sterility, be a danger to the new life slowly taking root inside me? A shiver ran across my skin—a traitor to my resolve. The idea was absurd, surely. I lived for this work, sacrificed so much for it. But the unease clung to me, a silent question mark etched into the back of my mind.

"Jade?" Ellie's voice cut through my spiraling thoughts. "You're looking a bit pale. Everything okay?"

"Fine." The word tasted of steel, but I forced a smile. "Just a long day. Let's wrap this up."

And with that, I turned back to my screen, to the numbers that made sense, the variables I could control. Because in this world of mine, uncertainty was not an option, and fear had no place. Not even the faint shadows of doubt cast by the underbelly of Dante's world could reach me here.

Or so I desperately wanted to believe.

Chapter Twenty-Eight: Dante

I reached for my phone, and then practically threw it across the room. I wanted to call Jade. I just knew I shouldn't.

The morning sun had a way of sneaking past the heavy drapes, casting slivers of light that cut through the darkness of my office. I sat there, engulfed by the scent of aged leather and the sheen of polished wood, papers strewn before me like fallen soldiers on a battlefield. Each sheet was a fragment of a larger scheme, line graphs and pie charts depicting the infancy of our legitimate investments—our future, unchained from the family's dark legacy.

I sighed, trying to ignore my pounding headache, and went back to work.

I sifted through the numbers, the potential profits from businesses untouched by blood money. The BioHQ data lay amongst them, its implications as potent as the power it promised. It was a game-changer, sure to pivot the Moretti name towards something resembling honor—if such a thing wasn't too far gone for us.

I was working—I was *only* working—because I desperately didn't want to think about Jade. In the background, a news report droned on. One of Caruso's capos had been indicted, which meant Caruso would be angry.

Fuck.

Without hesitation, I grabbed my phone, feeling its cool surface against my palm. This time, it wasn't to call Jade. I scrolled to Marco's contact card and pressed the call button. "Meet me at the new property site. We need to discuss the next steps," I ordered, my tone leaving no room for argument. There was a brief acknowledgement on the other end before the line went dead.

I hung up and leaned back in my chair, the leather creaking under my weight. My gaze drifted to the hidden compartment in my desk. Inside, the original stolen BioHQ data was tucked away, a constant reminder of the lengths I'd go to protect what was mine—and the power I wielded to sway fortunes in our favor. This was bigger than just us now; it was about carving out a life where the shadows we cast didn't stretch quite so long or dark.

"Marco, this is the backbone of our future," I said later that day, standing with him amidst the iron bones of what would soon be not just a building, but a beacon of our new direction. Steel beams rose around us like ribs of some giant beast, the air thick with dust and the clamor of progress.

Marco, clad in his usual sharp attire that seemed oddly out of place against the backdrop of hard hats and concrete, gave me a nod of understanding. "As long as we keep our hands clean, Dante. That's what you're aiming for, right?" His skepticism was a thin veil over genuine curiosity.

"Cleaner than they've ever been," I affirmed, feeling the weight of the responsibility settle on my shoulders.

He stuck his hands in his pockets. "I mean, worse comes to worst, we can at least charge tenants exorbitant rates. It's all about location."

I looked at the workers walking around the construction site. "Yep," I said. "You're not wrong. Can you stick around here? I have a feeling Caruso might want to fuck our construction sites over. I can send a couple of guys here, but..."

"No, it's all good," he said, smirking at me. "I get a day rate?"

"You don't need a day rate."

"And yet..."

I rolled my eyes, smiling. "Yes, you get a day rate," I said. "And a per diem."

Marco smiled. "Great," he said. "I'll just borrow a hard hat."

"Right. You don't need any more brain damage."

He flipped me off. "Hey, fuck you," he said with a smile. "That shit's genetic, so don't think you're getting off scot free."

"Yeah, trust me, I know," I said, clapping him in the back. "Don't do anything I wouldn't do. See you later."

I had a lot of errands to run, but the evening brought me back to my darkened office—a stark contrast to the bright chaos of the construction site. There was comfort in the solitude, in the familiar scent of ink and leather that filled the room. I keyed open the hidden drawer and pulled out the file marked with the BioHQ insignia, its contents as potent as any weapon in our arsenal.

Every document within it was a step towards legitimacy, towards a life where Jade could exist without the taint of my family's sins. With each report, each piece of paper that bore our name, I was rewriting our story—one where the Moretti legacy meant more than fear and whispered curses.

If I legitimized everything, then...then she could meet my family. Then she wouldn't be in danger of getting hurt when I introduced her to my dad or my brother.

This is for you, Jade, I thought, allowing myself a moment to imagine her safe, untouched by the darkness that had cradled me since birth. Her brilliance deserved a world free from the shadows that clung to my every move. It was a world I'd build for her, brick by brick, lie by lie, truth by hard-won truth.

I stowed the file away and locked the drawer, its soft click a punctuation in the silent room. Tomorrow, I'd walk into another boardroom, shake hands smeared neither with blood nor grime, and speak of futures bright with promise. But tonight, it was just me, the quiet, and the singular resolve to reshape the destiny of the Moretti name—for profit, for power, and for Jade.

My mom had invited Marco and I over for dinner, but I could tell it was just an excuse for Enzo to check up on us. Though when my mother invited us for dinner, we didn't say no.

We valued our lives too much for that.

When I got there, she was in the kitchen finishing up the food. I made my way to Enzo's study, the door creaking open like a confession. The old man sat behind a mahogany desk that had seen more secrets than a confessional. His eyes flicked up, sharp as ever.

"How's it progressing?" he asked, his voice betraying nothing but a hint of curiosity.

"Better than expected," I replied, handing over the financial reports. My fingers brushed against the leather-bound ledgers, thick with the scent of ink and power. "The legitimate fronts are booming, and BioHQ's little gifts are paying off. We're on track to eclipse our old income from the rackets within a year."

Enzo studied the figures, his expression unreadable as he turned each page. Finally, he looked up, and for a moment, I saw something like pride flash in his eyes. "Good work," he grunted, and that was all the praise I was going to get.

"Thanks, Dad," I said.

Everything after that happened so quickly. Jade wouldn't text me, she wouldn't answer my tests. I didn't call her. I understood she needed space, even though the desire to reach out to her clawed at me.

A few weeks later, I swapped the dimly lit streets for the sterile glare of corporate America. The boardroom of the pharmaceutical company we now controlled—through a corporation that had been pursuing a merger for four years, but with a nudge in the right direction with some strategic...contributions—was a world away from Little Italy. Here, the sharks wore Armani, not leather jackets, but the glint in their eyes was every bit as cold and calculating as the glint of a gun barrel.

As I took my seat at the head of the table, I felt the shift in me. The transition from mafia prince to corporate mogul was seamless; it was a game of power, just played on a different board. The executives eyed me warily, sensing the predator beneath the polished exterior.

"Our focus will be on neurogenetic research," I announced, my voice calm and decisive. It wasn't a suggestion—it was an order, and they all knew it. The BioHQ data had given us an edge, and I intended to use it. Every nod around the table was another piece moving into place, another silent victory.

"Are there any objections?" I asked, already knowing the answer.

Silence greeted me, confirming my control was as absolute here as it was on the streets. I allowed myself a small, satisfied smile. This was the future—a future where the Moretti name didn't echo with the sound of gunshots and whispered threats.

It was a future I could offer to Jade, if only she'd take it.

The city never really slept, but as night cloaked it in a deceptive calm, I found myself alone in the penthouse that scraped the heavens. The view stretched out like a canvas of flickering lights and dreams just out of reach. In that moment, with a glass of scotch in hand, I was both master and servant to the life I had carved out.

I savored the taste, the warmth spilling down my throat, a fleeting comfort against the cold reality. Each sip was a reminder of the duality I juggled—mafia don by night, entrepreneur by day. Jade was the linchpin to it all, the reason for this double-edged existence. I did it all so that the shadows would only ever kiss her edges, never swallow her whole.

I imagined as she stood among her test tubes and microscopes, her sanctuary of science and progress. She would note the new equipment, the accounts flush with funds that seemed too good to be true. She wouldn't know it was me.

But there was still work to do. The next day, I had to meet with my uncles to make sure everything was in order.

The next day, I made my way back to my childhood home. "Uncle Tony, Uncle Leo," I greeted them with a nod as we settled in the fortress of tradition that was the Moretti home's study. My father, Enzo, sat in with us, but he didn't say a fucking thing. Marco was there too, leaning against the bookshelf, playing absentmindedly on his phone.

Tony, all sharp angles and scrutiny, leaned forward, his fingers steepling like the spires of an old cathedral. "We need to ensure there are no gaps," he insisted, the skepticism in his voice slicing through the thick air of cigar smoke and aged leather.

I laid out the spreadsheets before them, a tapestry of numbers and projections that spoke of clean profits and cleaner consciences. "Look at the margins here and here," I pointed out, tapping on the paper for emphasis.

"BioHQ's data is gold, and our experts are turning it into something even more valuable—legitimacy." My voice was steady, my gaze unflinching. "We're clean, Tony."

Leo, ever the silent observer, gave a slow nod of approval, his eyes reflecting the firelight like polished onyx.

"Alright, Dante," Tony conceded, but his tone suggested he still held reservations only time could erode. "Enzo?"

"The boy's numbers are solid," my father said.

I wonder how old I'd have to be before he stopped calling me the boy.

With their nods of reluctant agreement, we wrapped up the meeting, and I stepped out into the crisp autumn evening, the crunch of fallen leaves underfoot marking my passage.

The community clinic we now owned stood like a beacon, its sterile walls and the hum of efficient activity a stark departure from the world I knew too well. I watched as patients were ushered in, each one a testament to a future where the Moretti name meant healing, not harm.

"This is for you, Jade," I whispered to myself, a mantra that had woven itself into my very being. But the words fell flat in the empty air, unanswered just like my calls to her.

Jade's silence was a verdict I couldn't appeal—a guilty sentence I had to serve. It didn't matter that the clinic's existence was because of her, that every life it saved was a tribute to her brilliance. She wouldn't see it, couldn't see it, because of what I had done.

Still, I allowed myself a moment to watch, to hope. For Jade, for us, for a chance at redemption I wasn't sure I deserved but was determined to fight for. Even if I had to do it alone.

But I wouldn't do it alone.

Because I was going to get her back.

Chapter
Twenty-Nine: Jade

S unlight snuck in, throwing a harsh glare on the chaos of my apartment. I sat on the edge of the bed, one hand absentmindedly resting on my stomach.

I couldn't shake the knot in my gut—the thought of walking away from BioHQ was like a vice around my heart. This child growing inside me, it needed safety, a shield from all this shit. But the lab...it was my life's blood. To leave it all behind felt like tearing away a piece of my soul.

My phone buzzed against the nightstand, and I knew without looking it was Ellie. Her text popped up.

Just double-checked your notes for the conference. It's all great, loved the jokes. Broke up some paragraphs. It's a big day, but you got this!

"Damn," I murmured, feeling the weight of apprehension mixed with a stubborn will to push through. I shuffled through the papers scattered across the bed—notes, slides, years of research condensed into bullet points and graphs. Sliding them into a slim folder, I tucked it into my bag alongside a bottle of prenatal vitamins. The morning sickness crept up on me like a thief, always poised to steal any semblance of comfort.

"Ellie's right," I told my reflection as I stood to smooth out my blouse, professional but forgiving around my changing figure. "It's just another hurdle." I steeled myself for the day, knowing that no matter what, the safety of this baby trumped every other fear. It was a new kind of resolve, unfamiliar and fierce. But it was mine, and I'd cling to it through whatever storm was coming our way.

I went to work and as I stepped out into the crisp morning air from the taxi, the buzz of the city was a familiar backdrop to the chaos that was my life. Ellie was already there waiting for me, her energy almost tangible even from across the street. She waved, a beacon of encouragement in the midst of my storm.

"Ready for the conference, Jade? Your keynote speech will be amazing!" Her voice danced with excitement, and for a brief moment, her confidence became mine.

"Let's hope so," I managed to reply, mustering a smile as we slid into the backseat of a waiting taxi. "I told the cabbie to wait. You didn't bring a car, did you?"

She shook her head. "Fuck no," she said. "Come on. Let's go."

We walked back to the taxi. The driver pulled away from the curb, merging into the river of yellow cabs and honking horns that flooded the avenues. The city was alive, pulsing with a rhythm that felt both exhilarating and overwhelming.

"Look at you, all calm and collected. I'd be a wreck," Ellie said, giving my hand a quick squeeze. I appreciated the lie; she knew just how frayed my nerves were.

"Years of pretending," I joked weakly, but the humor fell flat, crushed by the weight of the day ahead.

The conference center loomed before us, a modern fortress of glass and steel teeming with the brightest minds in technology. We wove through the crowd, a sea of eager faces and name badges fluttering like leaves in an autumn breeze. But then it hit me—a wave of dizziness so strong it nearly buckled my knees.

"Whoa," I muttered under my breath, gripping Ellie's arm for support.

"Jade?" Concern flickered in her eyes, but I was quick to plaster on a confident smile.

"Fine, just...excited," I lied, masking the unease that clawed at my insides. It wasn't just nerves or nausea; it was fear, raw and relentless, haunting me with every step I took. But I couldn't let it show. Not today. Not when I had so much to lose.

I shook off Ellie's concern with a forced smile, knowing I couldn't let my guard down, not even for a moment. The auditorium swallowed me whole as I made my way to the stage, the sea of faces blurring into one intimidating mass. My notes, once a crutch, now seemed trivial as I set them aside.

"Good morning," I began, my voice steady despite the turmoil churning inside me. "Today, we'll be delving into the intricacies of neurogenetic research and its potential to revolutionize medicine." The words flowed from me, practiced and precise, a veil of professionalism I clung to like a lifeline.

But something was off. The empty seat where Dante should have been gnawed at me—a silent accusation, a missing piece in the elaborate facade of my life. I pushed the thought away, focusing on the science, the data, the truth that I could wield with confidence.

The room faded as I dove deeper into my presentation, until a figure at the back snapped me back to reality. Edward Rodriguez. His stern gaze locked on me, sharp enough to slice through the distance between us. A shiver ran through me, though I was careful not to let it show.

Why is he here? The question echoed in my mind, insistent and unnerving. What is his interest in this?

Why does he seem to follow me around like a bad smell?

I stepped down, my heart racing, and the world rushed back in—a kaleidoscope of sound and color that did nothing to ease the dread coiling in my stomach.

"Great job," Ellie whispered as I rejoined her in the crowd. Her praise was a balm, but the shadow of Rodriguez's presence lingered, a dark cloud over the bright promise of the day.

"Thanks," I muttered, my gaze darting around the room, searching for that unwelcome specter. Rodriguez's eyes found mine again, a silent challenge that sent a ripple of unease through me.

"Jade, you're doing that thing where you overthink. It's probably nothing," Ellie said, reading my tension like a book she'd written herself. "Maybe he's just here for the tech talks."

"Maybe," I agreed, but her words did little to quell the storm inside me.

The afternoon unfolded like a deck of cards, each panel and demo another layer of complexity to absorb. My mind should have been captivated by the innovations being unveiled—the potential of our research was limitless. Yet, there was always a 'but'. But with every turn of a corner, every shift in the crowd, I felt his presence. Rodriguez, a hawk circling silently above its prey.

I clung to the excitement bubbling around me, let it buoy me through the sea of faces, past booths boasting advancements that could change the world. All the while, my thoughts tangled in a net of worry. How could I protect what was mine—what was growing inside me—when every instinct screamed that danger had entered the fray?

"Jade?" Ellie nudged me, her voice pulling me back from the edge of panic.

"Sorry, just...thinking about the next steps for the project," I lied smoothly, or as smoothly as I could manage with my heart pounding a frantic rhythm against my ribs.

"Let's grab some coffee; you need a break." Ellie steered us toward a less crowded part of the venue, her small frame surprisingly effective at parting the sea of people.

I allowed myself to be led away, grateful for the momentary escape. Yet even as we stood in line for our drinks, I couldn't shake the feeling of Rodriguez's eyes boring into me, branding me with suspicion. Every glance over my shoulder confirmed it—he was still there, still watching.

"Jade, you're doing that thing again where you zone out," Ellie said, her voice a lifeline in the sea of my worries.

"Sorry, I'm just..." My words trailed off as I saw Rodriguez once again. This time he was huddled with another so-called IT expert, their heads close together, deep in conversation. He caught my gaze and offered a smile that didn't reach his eyes, an apology without words for a crime I couldn't quite grasp. "Isn't it weird that he's here?"

"I mean, he works with us, so I don't see how it's so weird?"

"Maybe I'm just being paranoid," I replied, taking another sip of my coffee.

I tried to shake off my unease and concentrate on the moment. We were supposed to be celebrating our work, not fearing every shadow. But shadows have a way of growing long at the worst possible times.

Later, during the panel Q&A, the lights flickered briefly, and the screens glitched. Murmurs rippled through the room like the first signs of an unwelcome storm. Onstage, I felt exposed, vulnerable.

"Must be some technical difficulties," Ellie said into the microphone, her composure unshaken.

The snafu was brief, but in those seconds, my mind raced with possibilities. Was this a sign? A hack into BioHQ's systems? My heart hammered with the realization that my research—my life's work—could be splayed open for all the wrong eyes to see.

Had pregnancy made me weirdly paranoid? Probably. No, definitely.

Ellie leaned in, whispering, "Jade, stay calm. We've got this."

But I could barely hear her over the blood rushing in my ears, my gaze fixed on Rodriguez, who stood off to the side. His smile was gone now, replaced by an apologetic shrug that did nothing to ease my annoyance. How could someone so useless be tasked with protecting us? Wasn't he supposed to be some sort of IT expert?

"Sorry folks, just a little hiccup," I managed to say, forcing a smile for the audience. The rest of the session passed in a blur, my responses automatic, my mind elsewhere. Protecting my baby, my work, myself—that was all that mattered now.

As the final question hung in the air, I felt Ellie's eyes on me. Her concern was a tangible thing, and it took all my will to not let the fear show on my face. When the last round of applause echoed through the hall, signaling the end of the panel, I let out a deep, shuddering breath.

"You need to relax, Jade. You've done great today. Let's just focus on the positive," Ellie suggested with a reassuring smile.

"Easy for you to say," I muttered, but I nodded at her, attempting to push aside the doubts and anxieties clawing at my insides. The room was bathed in the late afternoon sun, its warm glow a stark reminder that life outside this conference was waiting for me—life with its dark corners and uncertainties.

The hall slowly emptied, leaving behind scattered chairs and the faint smell of industrial cleaner. As we gathered our things, I couldn't shake the sense of exposure that clung to me. I was pregnant, vulnerable in ways I'd never been before. The weight of impending motherhood was like an anchor, dragging me into depths of worry I fought to ignore.

"Let's head out," Ellie said, handing me my coat. "We can talk strategy over dinner, maybe unwind a bit."

"Thanks, El," I replied, feeling undeserving of her steadfast loyalty. The questions about Rodriguez's presence spun around in my mind, each one a potential threat to the life growing inside me.

As Ellie led the way out of the conference room, I followed closely, the exhaustion of the day seeping into my bones. This pregnancy wasn't just another challenge; it was a paradigm shift, forcing me to confront the risks I'd blithely ignored before.

I missed Dante then, his absence more pronounced amidst the crowd's dispersal. He would've known what to do, would've shielded me from this cold dread with his easy confidence.

...or he would have held me down and fingered me until I came while I stared into his eyes. Right.

Probably that one.

The conference center's sliding doors sighed shut behind us, releasing Ellie and me into the evening's embrace. Fresh air licked at my cheeks, a respite from the day's sweltering debates and dense crowds. I drew in a breath, letting it out slow, trying to shake the weight of being watched.

"Feels good, doesn't it? To be out of there," Ellie remarked, her eyes squinting against the dying light. "But you crushed it."

I didn't say anything, shielding my eyes from the sun with the palm of my hand. "Jade?"

I blinked, forcing a smile for Ellie. "Just tired."

Ellie cocked her head. "Are you sure? Because..."

I turned my head to look at her. Maybe she couldn't help, but maybe I'd feel lighter if I'd told someone. Anyone.

And I knew that Ellie would keep my secret no matter what. "Actually," I said, biting on my lower lip. "Let's go grab that bite. There's something I want to talk to you about."

Chapter Thirty: Dante

The steady tap-tap-tap of my fingers on the desk always helped me think. That was until the sound was cut by a knock, sharp and urgent. I looked up as Luca slipped through the door, his face etched with lines of worry that didn't belong there. I'd gone to the office for the first time in what felt like months because I couldn't keep working from home just to think about Jade, which meant that I saw my men a lot more often than when I had first started seeing her.

"Boss," he said, voice tight, thrusting a stack of papers at me.

I took them, feeling the shift in the air. "What's this?"

"Trouble. Lorenzo Caruso's not sitting pretty anymore."

Luca's news hit hard, a punch to the gut. My hands, steady as stone till now, faltered as I flipped through the report. The bastard had made moves in Little Italy, our Little Italy. His men were burrowed into the businesses like rats, claiming turf we'd bled for.

"Christ," I muttered, rage simmering in my veins as I read on. Each word on the page was another move in his power play, a silent battle cry. This wasn't just a scuffle over streets; it was war, plain and simple. "Did you put this together?"

"Yeah, boss," he said. "You told me to keep an eye on Lorenzo, right?"

"Sit," I told him. Luca did as he was told, cocking his head and waiting for me to say something.

"Bastard's playing chess while we're playing checkers," I muttered, the sound of my own voice like gravel tossed onto a silent street. My gaze lifted from the report, meeting the expectant eyes of the men gathered around me.

Marco slipped quietly into the room, his presence like a shadow that fell over all of us. He caught my eye, reading the situation as easily as one might read the headlines of a morning paper. "What's the move, Dante?" he asked, his eyes sharp and vigilant.

"Were you just waiting outside?"

Marco tilted his head toward Luca. "He'd already said something about the report," he said.

"Right."

I paused, feeling the weight of every life in my hands, the gears in my mind working overtime as I sifted through options, discarding them as quickly as they came. This was more than a territorial piss; this was Caruso clawing at the foundation of our empire, a challenge to the Moretti throne.

Just as I was about to lay out the beginnings of a plan, the door burst open again. Salvatore staggered in, his breath coming in hurried gasps, eyes wide with an urgency that sent a cold stab through my chest.

"Lorenzo sent a message," he panted, clutching the doorframe for support. "He's threatening 'Dante's little whore.'"

"A message like..."

"A Milwall brick," Sal said.

"The fuck is a Milwall brick?" Luca asked, turning to look at him.

"It's a weapon, made from a newspaper rolled up tight," Sal explained, his face pale under the office light. "Used to be popular among hooligans at football matches."

"And the connection with Jade?" Marco asked, his brow furrowed in confusion.

Sal extended a shaky hand, opening his palm to reveal a crumpled piece of newspaper - the obituary section. It wasn't wet, so it had to be wrapped around the Milwall brick. My heart stopped as I saw a single name circled in red: Jade Bentley.

"She's not...dead," I said, my heart dropping to my stomach.

"No, but they did call up to get this placed in the paper," Sal replied, his voice heavy with concern. The room filled with a silence so complete it felt like a suffocating shroud, punctuated only by the rustle of newspaper as I touched the circled name. "Do you want me to read it or..."

"Do I want you to read it?" I echoed incredulously.

"No, I mean if you can't..." Sal trailed off, his cheeks flushed with embarrassment.

I picked up the newspaper, my hands trembling as they held the fragile pages. The words blurred together, forming a sea of black ink that drowned my rational thoughts. Jade. My Jade. The thought of losing her was unbearable. Yet, here it was, her name circled in a death notice she didn't deserve.

There it was. Her credentials, her age, her neighborhood, her families' names.

"Holy shit," I breathed, the words caught in my throat like a snare. This was a warning, a sick and twisted promise of what was to come.

The words I was reading seared through the room, crude and venomous, an insult meant to provoke. My vision tunneled, the edges tinged with a red haze. The implication of those words, the sheer audacity—it made my blood boil hot enough to scorch the earth beneath my feet. But despite the wildfire raging inside me, I clamped down on my rage, locking it away behind a mask of composure.

"Keep talking, Sal," I said, my voice steady despite the storm inside, putting the newspaper down in front of me. "Every damn word."

"Caruso's men were seen near Jade's lab," Salvatore continued, his voice strained as if he could feel the tension strangling the air. "Lorenzo's saying they can reach her whenever they please."

"That son of a bitch," I growled, my knuckles blanching as I gripped the edge of the mahogany desk—a gift from my father, its surface now bearing witness to the fury that threatened to splinter it. Violence was a beast writhing under my skin, eager for release, but I couldn't let it dictate my moves. A rash decision now could crumble the empire we had built brick by bloody brick.

Marco stepped closer, a mirror of my own tightly coiled anger. "We can't just sit on this, Dante. Caruso's closing in, and he just made it personal," he warned, his gaze locked onto mine, fierce and unyielding.

I nodded, the image of Jade—her dark hair, her determined eyes—flashing in my mind. Protecting her wasn't just about safeguarding an asset; it was about shielding something far more precious.

"Personal is right," I spat out. "But we're not going to play this game on his terms. We'll be silent. Deadly. He won't see us coming until it's too late."

"So what's the plan, boss?" Luca asked.

"We tighten our own net. Increase our surveillance on Caruso's movements. Find every weak link in his operation and exploit it."

"Already on it," Salvatore muttered, his fingers drumming on the table as he mentally sifted through the intricacies of Caruso's empire.

I turned to Luca. "Double the men around businesses Caruso has targeted. I want eyes everywhere, no corner left unchecked."

"Salvatore," I called out, making sure my authority resonated with each syllable. "Start pulling the strings. We need everyone on high alert, but not a word to anyone outside this room."

"Got it," Salvatore confirmed.

"Caruso made it personal," I murmured into the silence, a vow hanging in the air, poised between the shadows and the light. "He'll regret it." With every fiber of my being, I committed to the path laid out before me.

"What about your girlfriend?" Marco asked.

The capos shifted uneasily, their eyes locked on mine as I made my next declaration. I didn't want to correct him. I didn't want to tell him that Jade had never been my girlfriend, and if she had been, she certainly wasn't anymore.

"Jade needs to be protected round the clock. Increase her surveillance, but keep it invisible. Caruso can't know we're onto him," I ordered, feeling the weight of each word as they left my lips. Jade's image flashed through my mind—her dark hair, her focused gaze—a reminder of why this was more than just business.

"Got it, Dante," Marco said, his nod resolute. He understood what I didn't say; keeping Jade safe was a task that went beyond loyalty—it was about protecting someone who could change everything for us, for me.

"Make sure it's done discreetly. No mistakes," I added, locking eyes with each one of them in turn. The gravity of the situation settled heavily in the room, an unspoken acknowledgment that our actions now could mean life or death.

"Anything happens to her, it's on us," Luca muttered, his usual stoicism giving way to the seriousness of the matter at hand. Protecting Jade wasn't just a strategic move in a war against Caruso; it was personal, and each man in the room knew the stakes.

"Let's get to work then," I concluded, watching as they filed out of the room, each man carrying a part of the burden that now rested on all our shoulders. Alone now, I allowed myself a moment to consider the depth of my feelings for Jade, the intensity of which both surprised and concerned me. But there was no time for hesitation; actions were needed, not emotions.

And with that, I set into motion the gears of a machine designed to protect, to serve, and to avenge. For Jade, for the family, and for the future I dared to envision—one where threats like Caruso were nothing more than a distant memory.

I had been so good lately.

But if I had to kill him to make sure that nothing happened to Jade, well, fuck it. That was exactly what I was going to do.

I just needed to make sure he suffered first.

Chapter Thirty-One: Jade

The tang of bile stung the back of my throat, and I swallowed hard.

Across from me, Ellie's brows knitted with concern as she watched me push around the untouched food on my plate.

I was supposed to be telling her, but I was chickening out. The nausea wasn't making it easy for me to focus.

"Jade, you sure you're okay?" Ellie asked, her voice a mix of worry and suspicion.

I mustered a weak smile, feeling the lie slip out easier than I expected. "Yeah, just this flu bug that's been going around. It's really got a hold on me."

"You might need to go to the doctor," she said.

"Yeah, I know," I replied. "I got a...I should probably go home. I need to rest."

Ellie wasn't convinced, but she nodded, reaching across to squeeze my hand. "Text me when you get home, alright?"

"Will do," I promised, though my thoughts were already racing ahead. I needed space, time alone to digest the news that had upended my life—news I couldn't yet share, not even with Ellie.

Even though I really wanted to.

I hailed a taxi outside the restaurant, grateful for the anonymity it provided. The cabbie glanced at me in the rearview mirror, but I paid him no mind, my fingers scrolling aimlessly over my phone's screen. It was a futile attempt at distraction; my mind was a whirlwind of what-ifs and how-abouts.

Home came too soon, or perhaps not soon enough. I stumbled into the sanctuary of my bedroom, letting the door click shut behind me. The bed called out to me—a soft, inviting expanse where I could lay out all my tangled thoughts.

"List," I murmured to myself. A list would make sense of the chaos. Pros and cons, simple and clear. It was the scientist in me craving order amidst the emotional storm.

My phone buzzed, a jarring sound against the silence of the room. Dante. His name lit up the screen, and a surge of something—fear, excitement, longing—fluttered through me. But I ignored the call, let it fade to voicemail. There were more pressing matters at hand, like figuring out the logistics of a life growing inside me, tied to a man whose very existence threatened to unravel mine.

I would have to face him. But first, I would have to face this.

"Okay, Jade," I whispered, steeling myself. "Time to face this head-on."

I settled on the edge of the bed, the organic cotton sheets rustling beneath me. The pen felt heavy in my hand, like it was more than just ink—it was a lifeline to clarity. I drew two columns on a fresh page of my notebook, labeling one "Pro" and the other "Con." Through the cracked window, the city's breath sent a hum that mingled with the cacophony in my head.

"Pro," I started, pressing the tip of the pen against the paper as if it were a sacred act. "This might be the right time to have a baby." I wrote it down, my fingers tightening around the pen. Thirty-two years old and the ticking of my biological clock was not something even I, with all my scientific knowledge, could silence.

There were other pros. Surely, there were other pros. But my hand hovered above the paper and I couldn't will it to move.

"Con," I scrawled under the word on the opposite page, my eyes narrowing as I focused on the word that felt like a judgment. The skyline outside my window blurred into a sea of sparkling lights as my mind wandered to the sterile environment of my lab. "Research demands my full attention." The truth of the statement settled in my chest, heavy and undeniable.

No, I needed more pros. I was sure there were more.

"Pro: Could actually be fun," I added, allowing myself this one concession to levity amidst the gravity of my situation. The pen danced across the paper now, less burdened by the weight of practicality.

"Con: The danger," I whispered, the word slicing through the quiet of my apartment. My hand trembled as I wrote, not wanting to acknowledge how deep into Dante's world I might be pulled. How could I reconcile the life growing inside me with a life entwined with...whatever the fuck Dante was entwined with? I wasn't stupid, nor naive. I had just not wanted to take it into account. I had been having too much fun with him.

But now there was someone else's life to consider.

Someone who needed me to protect them no matter what.

"Con: Potential for...chaos." That was an understatement. The unpredictability of being connected to someone like Dante, it was all-consuming. I swallowed hard, considering how my child's life would be shadowed by threats and secrecy.

A soft snort escaped me as I remembered Dante's sculpted jawline, the way his dark hair fell effortlessly across his forehead. With a wry smile tugging at my lips, I scribbled on the 'Pro' side, "Dante's genes might create a very good-looking child." I shook my head slightly at the absurdity of such a superficial thought, but it was an undeniable fact; the man was attractive, painfully so.

Fuck. I really had to tell him.

If I chose to keep the baby, Dante needed to know the truth.

I set the pen down, my list far from complete. But in that moment, I realized no amount of pros and cons could make this decision for me. It was about more than science or safety—it was about what I wanted my life to mean, what legacy I wanted to leave behind.

The sounds of the city rose up, the distant clamor somehow soothing. I wasn't alone in my indecision; the world outside was full of people making tough calls every day. I just had to decide which call was right for me.

I stared at the list, my stomach tightening into a knot. The list of cons could have filled this entire notebook, and yet I knew my decision had already been made.

"Pro," I said, though I didn't write it. "I'm already attached. Wait, is that a con?"

I leaned back against the headboard, my hand gravitating to my abdomen. It was still flat, practically unchanged to the eye, but it harbored a secret—a burgeoning new existence. The air around me stilled, thickened by the gravity of what I was about to acknowledge.

Eyes closed, I took a deep breath, steadying myself against the swell of emotions. A faint smile, one that scarcely dared to manifest, played across my lips. "Okay. Fuck the list. I choose to keep you," I whispered into the silence. The words, tentative yet resolute, filled the room and encased my heart in a vow.

This decision, born out of chaos, injected me with an unforeseen vigor. Pushing up from my bed, I made my way to my office—a fancy name for a desk I kept in the corner of my bedroom.

I approached the desk that bore the weight of countless hours of research. Papers strewn about, notes scrawled in my meticulous hand, books with dog-eared pages marking breakthroughs and ideas—all of it now secondary to the strategy I needed to devise for my unexpected future. One by one, I shuffled through the documents, reordering my life's priorities. The crisp rustle of paper punctuated my movements as I sectioned off areas of focus: prenatal care nestled beside gene therapy, childcare books propped up against molecular biology texts.

"Okay, Jade," I muttered to myself, plotting out the practical steps for both the pregnancy and my ongoing projects. "You're a damn good scientist. You can figure this out."

And just like that, plans began to take shape. Time lines, budgets, contingency protocols—my mind buzzed with the logistics of combining motherhood with my career's demands. But beneath the surge of efficiency, a tender undercurrent hummed—the realization that my life was no longer solely my own.

The evening sky darkened outside, the early signs of nightfall casting shadows across my workspace. I glanced at the clock, noting how the hours had slipped by unnoticed. For the first time in years, my research didn't consume every waking thought.

"Okay," I said as I flipped through the pages of one of my textbooks. "Okay. Guess I'm having a baby."

Chapter Thirty-Two: Jade

My entire life was about to change...I was sure of it.

But before I had finished organizing my thoughts, a knock—sharp and unexpected—pierced through my muddled thoughts. Curiosity peaked, laced with annoyance at the disruption. I glanced up at the clock on my nightstand.

It was nearly midnight.

Who could it be at this hour?

I hoped everything was okay. I was already wearing my pajamas and slippers, my hair a messy tumble of curls against my neck. I stood up, crossing the room to see through the peephole. My heart stuttered in my chest when I recognized the figure standing there. Dante.

All the oxygen seemed to be sucked out of the room. I could feel my pulse quicken and a wave of dizziness threatening as his silhouette blurred then sharpened once more in my view. The edges of my vision danced with the threat of panic, but I took slow, deep breaths, reminding myself that this was Dante. He was complicated, yes, and dangerous in ways I was still discovering, but he was not a threat to me.

"Dante?" I asked, opening the door a crack. He looked out of place in my apartment corridor, his tailored suit gleaming under the dim lights, his chiseled features hardened by a taut expression.

His jaw clenched at the sight of me, his pained expression a stark contrast to his usual confident demeanor. He looked even more handsome under the low light, if that was even possible.

His face was drained of color; the jovial mischief I'd grown accustomed to was nowhere in sight. Dante's eyes were clouded with urgency. His chest rose and fell heavily, as if he'd been running.

"Jade," he began, but his voice caught in his throat as if the words were too painful to form. He fumbled for composure, raking his fingers through his hair.

"I need..." he started again, swallowing hard. I watched, my heart pounding against my ribcage like a wild animal defending its territory.

I knew I should tell him to go away. There was no reason for him to be here. And yet he looked so upset...

"Dante, are you okay?" I asked tentatively, opening the door wider. The concern in my voice was genuine, this was nothing like him.

Dante glanced behind him before stepping inside, his movements shaky. His usually confident demeanor replaced by a palpable unease. "I need...to tell you something," he finally managed to say, fixing me with a look that sent a chill down my spine.

"Alright." My throat tightened as I closed the door behind him and led him to the living room. Our relationship was anything but ordinary, yet this felt different, it felt loaded and potentially life-altering. My heart pounded in my chest as we both took a seat.

Dante's fingers drummed restlessly against his knee, his gaze darting around my apartment. "I'm going to show you a picture on my phone," he said. "It's not going to make a lot of sense, but I'm going to explain it. You can ask me any questions you want, but all I ask is that you let me finish explaining before you ask me any questions. Is that okay?"

I nodded, swallowing the lump in my throat, my curiosity piqued by his strange behavior and cryptic words. His hand slipped into his pocket, pulling out a sleek, black phone. What could possibly be on that phone that was causing him so much distress?

He showed me a picture of a newspaper clipping. My name was on it. My picture was on it. I read it a couple of times, unable to make sense of it. It seemed to be an obituary for me. But I was alive.

Very much alive, and very much pregnant.

My heart throbbed in my chest. My hands felt like ice blocks. My mind spun with impossible thoughts.

"I... What is this, Dante?" I asked, voice trembling. "What's going on?"

He took a deep breath, his knuckles turning white as he gripped the phone a little tighter. "Jade...it's a long story, but the short version is, I have a lot of powerful enemies and one of them found out we were seeing each other. Don't worry. I'm going to take care of him. You won't have to worry about this. But in case someone sends this to you on social media or something, you should know so you can play it off as a prank."

"A prank," I said, my voice a whisper.

Dante nodded, the tension in his face easing slightly. "Yes, Jade. A prank," he reiterated. "My family's criminal empire extends far beyond what you see at face value, and unfortunately... you're caught in the middle."

A soft sigh escaped my lips as I handed his phone back to him. I didn't speak for several moments, letting the silence stretch between us.

He cleared his throat. "Do you have any questions for me?" he asked.

My mind was a whirlwind of confusion and fear, with questions echoing like a broken record in my consciousness. There were the obvious ones, like 'How could you let this happen?' or 'Why didn't you tell me sooner?' But those weren't the questions that scared me. The ones that truly terrified me were along the lines of 'Who wants to kill me?' and 'Am I going to die?'

"Are they going to kill me?" I finally asked.

Dante's expression darkened. "No. I would never let anything happen to you."

"How can you know that?"

"What do you mean?" he asked. "I'll kill them first."

My breath hitched at the cold determination in his voice. His words were chilling, but they resonated with an uneasy comfort. Framed by the soft glow of my living room lamp, Dante seemed more like a protective avenger than anything else.

But I definitely couldn't tell him about being pregnant. Not until I managed to untangle all this.

"I wanted to warn you, tell you I have this handled and, uh, apologize," Dante said. "I have a...hang on a second, I'll be right back."

He stepped out of my apartment for a brief moment, and he came back with a gorgeous bouquet of flowers in his hand. "I put this just out of view," he said. "In case you decided not to let me in. So thank you for letting me in."

"Well, it seemed important," I said as he closed the door behind him.

"It was. I was tending to this all day. I'm sorry I missed your talk."

I shook my head. "I didn't expect you to be there. You're a hobbyist, not a pro. It would have been boring for you."

He smiled. "I doubt that. Watching you talk about what you care about is my favorite thing. It was genome sequencing, right?"

I sighed, rubbing my temple as I gestured for him to sit down on my sofa. "Honestly, it was hard to let you in. I don't trust you after what happened last time," I said, the words sharp like broken glass underfoot.

He exhaled, a look of regret washing over his features. "I'm sorry, Jade. I got carried away. I just... I wanted to show you how much I needed you. That's why I missed your conference."

"Needed or wanted?" I corrected, unable to stop the scientist in me from seeking clarity. "And it was about biotechnological applications in neuroscience, not genome sequencing."

Dante's lips curled into a smile, a soft chuckle escaping him. His reaction was like a spark in dry underbrush, threatening to reignite something dangerous between us.

"What's so funny?" I asked, struggling to keep my voice steady.

"Nothing," he said, his smile lingering. "I just love hearing you talk about your work. You light up, you know? It's captivating."

My defenses wavered as he spoke, the genuine admiration in his tone disarming me. "The conference didn't go great," I said. "Well, the talk was fine, but the vibes were weird."

"I'm sure it's better than you think. And if it isn't, hey, you'll knock them dead next time," he said, then looked at the flowers. "Do you want me to keep holding these on my lap or..."

I smiled, taking the flowers off him. I navigated the small kitchen, its familiarity bringing a sense of order to my thoughts. Plucking an empty vase from the shelf, I filled it with water before arranging Dante's flowers within it. The petals were vibrant against the dull steel of the sink, a slash of color in the otherwise drab space.

"So what exactly were you doing today? You weren't actually killing anybody, right?"

He shook his head. He scratched at the back of his neck—an awkward gesture that seemed out of place on someone who usually exuded such confidence. "That's just a figure of speech."

"But real estate?"

"Look, Jade, it's just business stuff," he said finally, his voice low. The apartment was tiny, so he remained on the couch as we had this conversation. "You know how it is."

Did I, though? His vagueness gnawed at me, the unanswered questions piling up like the unread journals on my desk. But there was something in his tone, a hint of something deeper, that made me pause.

"Sure, Dante," I replied, not quite ready to let him off the hook, but also aware that pushing might only drive him further away. "Just 'business stuff.'"

He looked at me then, really looked at me, and for a moment, I thought I saw a crack in the façade—the weight of worlds unspoken pressing against it.

"Jade..." he started, but the words trailed off, leaving an unfinished thought hanging between us like the steam from the tea kettle I'd forgotten on the stove. I watched Dante's struggle, the play of his Adam's apple as he swallowed whatever half-truth he had prepared. "Contracts, property negotiations, you know the drill."

"Right," I said, my voice flat. My arms folded over my chest as I leaned back against the counter, my gaze not wavering from his face. His answers were like breadcrumbs, leading me away from what I really wanted to know. And I could tell there was so much more he wasn't saying.

"Why the rush to apologize?" I pressed, watching him closely. His eyes, dark and fathomless, flickered with something I couldn't quite read. The silence stretched out, becoming another presence in the room, demanding an answer. "To be clear, what I want to know is why you're apologizing about missing the conference and not about forcing me to come in a parking lot."

He smirked. "Well, you loved that."

"I didn't--" I stammered, feeling the familiar heated flush creep into my cheeks. But I couldn't deny a certain undercurrent of truth in his words. And beneath that, a long-buried desire began to stir, the memory of his hands on me quickening my breath.

"Jade," his voice was gentle now, and he rose from the couch, closing the gap between us. His glance darted briefly to my stomach before finding my eyes again. For a moment, I was sure he knew about the baby. Then he shook his head slightly, as if to clear it, and held out his hand to me - palm up - like an offering.

"I'm sorry," he said again, more earnestly this time. "For everything. For all of it."

I could see the sincerity in his eyes and it made my heart twinge. I put my hand in his, feeling the warmth spread from his fingers to mine.

"I appreciate that," I managed to say, meeting his gaze with a hesitant smile.

He pulled me close to him. "Now," he said into my ear. "How many times have you touched yourself thinking about me fucking you in that parking lot?"

Chapter Thirty-Three: Dante

G od, I loved making her blush.

I leaned in, my voice rough like gravel as I hovered over her. "Show me how much," I demanded, watching Jade closely. She turned her head, the soft glow of lamplight washing over us and throwing our tangled silhouettes against the walls.

Her fingers twisted together, a nervous dance betraying her composure. The air felt thick with something unspoken, a storm gathering force behind her eyes.

"It's—all I think about," she confessed, her voice so faint I had to strain to catch the words. My gaze fixed on her, the darkness in them sparked by the raw honesty in her admission. I could almost taste the tension that filled the room, heavy like the air before a thunderstorm.

"Go get your vibrator," I ordered, the command rolling off my tongue with practiced ease. My hand lifted her chin, compelling those wide, expressive eyes to meet mine.

Jade's gaze faltered, a slight shake of her head conveying her reluctance. For a moment, neither of us spoke, the silence stretching out like a challenge. The weight of her confession hung in the air between us, thick and undeniable.

"You do what I tell you," I said. "Go get it."

"It's... out of battery. I've been using it so much. I, uh, forgot to charge," she stammered, her voice barely above a whisper, but it cut through the quiet with the sharpness of broken glass.

My smirk grew as I leaned closer, close enough to feel the warmth of her skin against mine. "Then we'll just have to make do without it," I murmured, my breath mingling with hers. "But should I buy you another one? So you can always keep one charged?"

Before she could answer, I claimed her mouth, swallowing the soft sound that escaped from her lips. My hands explored the curves of her body, tracing the lines of her figure through the thin fabric of her pajamas.

"I should get one of those I can control from my phone," I said. "Have you wear it when you go to work and make you come when you're at the lab."

She gasped, the words catching in her throat. Her body shivered beneath my touch, her hands clutching at the lapels of my tailored suit.

"Would you like that, Jade?" I pressed on, my voice a low, husky whisper against her ear. "Let me be in control while you're trapped behind a microscope? You'd have to bite your lip and try not to scream."

Her breath hitched as I slowly traced a finger down her spine, feeling her shiver against me. She didn't reply, but the flush creeping up her neck told me all I needed to know.

"I think you'd enjoy it. Just like you enjoyed the parking lot," I added with a smirk.

Her eyes widened, and she swallowed hard. It was a struggle for her to meet my gaze, but she did it anyway. Brave Jade.

"Maybe," she said finally with barely a murmur, her cheeks burning a deep pink now under the soft glow of the lamplight.

I chuckled softly, my heart thumping wildly in my chest at her unexpected concession. The thought of her squirming in her lab coat, biting her lower lip to stop from moaning out loud as I took the reins...Adrenaline surged through me, the blood going straight to my cock.

"But for now," I whispered huskily, unbuttoning my suit jacket and letting it drop to the floor. "We're gonna do this old school."

Her hand slid down to my belt, her movements hesitant at first but growing bolder by the second. "You're such a fucking tease, Dante. Why don't you ever just fuck me?"

"Are you making demands?"

"Yes. Use your cock. Now," she demanded, her voice finding strength from somewhere deep within.

With a swift movement, I lifted Jade, my arms wrapping around her with ease that spoke of strength honed through years of strict physical discipline. Her body was a contrast to mine—curvy where I was hard, soft where I was rough. And it was fucking lovely.

I pressed her body against the kitchen counter, sliding her pajama shirt up. She wasn't wearing pants, but I was.

I quickly unzipped my trousers, freeing my already hard length, as Jade watched with wide eyes. Her breath hitched when I pulled her closer, positioning her just right against me.

"You asked for it," I murmured into her ear, mustering all the self-control I had left not to simply plunge into her. "Pull your panties to the side."

Her movements were slow, tantalizing, a slight tremble in her hands as she fixed her gaze on mine. The anticipation was palpable, a delicious tension that had my heart pounding in my chest. Her fingers hooked around the thin fabric of her underwear, pulling it aside to expose her to me. A soft gasp left her lips as I ran a finger along her slick folds.

"You're already so wet," I murmured approvingly, my voice dropping an octave at the sensation of her wetness against my skin. She shivered at my words, a blush spreading across her cheeks. "I love how wet you get when you think about me."

"Dante," she moaned, her eyes fluttering closed as I slipped two fingers inside her. "I want you."

"I know." I drew my fingers out slowly, making her whimper with need. "And I'm going to fuck you. But first, you're going to beg for it. Tell me how much you liked it when I made you come in public."

Her eyelashes fluttered open to meet my gaze, a look of defiance flashing within them. "I'm not going to beg you, Dante." Her voice wavered, the tremble in it telling me I was close to breaking her.

I smiled at her challenge, one that excited me as much as it intrigued me. "Really?" I said thoughtfully, brushing my thumb over her swollen clit. Her hips bucked slightly and she bit her lip, restraining a moan. She was playing a dangerous game, testing my patience.

I smiled at her challenge, one that excited me as much as it intrigued me. "Really?" I said thoughtfully, brushing my thumb over her swollen clit. Her hips bucked slightly and she bit her lip, restraining a moan. She was playing a dangerous game, testing my patience.

"Then maybe I should leave you here," I suggested, withdrawing my fingers from her. Her back straightened against the counter, clearly taken aback by my words. The surprise in her eyes was priceless.

"Wait..." she panted out, her eyes pleading with me not to follow through on my threat. "No...Dante don't..."

"And why is that?" I asked teasingly, the pulsing erection straining against the fabric of my boxers.

"Because I need you to fuck me. Because I loved it," she said.

"Good girl," I murmured, my fingers absentmindedly sliding through her hair, causing her to shudder.

I spread her legs apart with my own, then reached down and guided myself to her entrance. She was so wet and desperate for me, and it felt so damn good. My resolve crumbled at the first touch of her heated core against my cock, the explosion of sensation taking me by surprise.

"Are you ready?" I asked.

She nodded rapidly, her breaths shallow and quick. "Yes," she managed to pant, her hands clutching at the edges of the counter. "God, yes."

My thumb, wet with her arousal, teased her clit as I slowly pushed into her. She hissed through gritted teeth, trying in vain to suppress the mewls and whimpers that spilled from her lips. Her walls clenched around me so deliciously tight I had to fight the overwhelming urge to bury myself in her at once.

"Relax," I whispered soothingly, my voice a low growl that vibrated through her. "Let your body adjust. You're doing so good for me."

She let out a low moan at my words, her nails biting into my forearms. But I didn't mind the sting. It was a reminder of the pleasure I was giving her - and a promise of what was yet to come.

Her body gradually relaxed around me, adjusting to my size. As her tension eased, I started moving in earnest, each thrust making her gasp and whimper with pleasure. The sound of our bodies coming together filled the room, mingling with Jade's soft cries.

"We should make this a tradition," I said. "Whenever I come over to your place with flowers, you should get on the counter, pull your panties aside and wait for me to fuck you."

Her eyes shot wide open, incredulous amusement gleaming within them. "Every time?" she echoed between ragged breaths, her fingers clawing at my skin as I continued my slow, deliberate rhythm.

"Every time," I said. "Unless of course, you'd rather do it closer to the door so that we wouldn't waste time getting to the counter."

A soft laugh escaped her lips, almost drowned out by a moan as I hit a particularly sensitive spot. "On the—ah!—counter is...fine..."

"Good," I drawled, a slow smirk playing on my lips as I angled my hips to dig deeper into her, making her cry out. Her body bucked against mine, her hands gripping my arms hard enough to leave marks. "I'll be edging you all day with a toy and then when I come over, you'll be dripping and ready for me."

"Good," I drawled, a slow smirk playing on my lips as I angled my hips to dig deeper into her, making her cry out. Her body bucked against mine, her hands gripping my arms hard enough to leave marks. "I'll be edging you all day with a toy and then when I come over, you'll be dripping and ready for me."

Her eyes widened at my words, a blush rising on her cheeks. "You wouldn't..." she breathed, her voice a ragged whisper. But I knew by the glint in her eye that she found the idea equally terrifying and exhilarating.

"Oh, I definitely would," I told her, punctuating my words with a particularly hard thrust that had her crying out. Her guttural moan echoed off the cold tiles of the kitchen, a stark contrast to the warm flesh pressing against me. "I'm going to train you to be so desperate for me, you'll be begging for my cock every time I walk through the door. You'll be watching your genomes on petri dishes or whatever it is that you do all while you can't help but think about how my cock would feel inside of you."

The thought of that, of her so wet and wanting for me, had my control slipping.

"That's not really how it—fuck!"

Her words were cut off by another moan as I plunged deep into her, the sound echoing in the small kitchen. I kept up my steady rhythm, savoring each gasp and whimper she tried to stifle.

"That's not how what works?" I asked after a moment, my voice rough with effort. The sight of her so undone beneath me, struggling to form coherent sentences while I took her on the counter of her own kitchen, was driving me to the edge.

Her breath hitched and she bit her lip as if trying to gather her thoughts. "That's not...how...genomics...works..."

I traced my fingertips across her lower lip, sticking a thumb into her mouth as I quickened my pace. "Okay, doctor," I said, fucking her hard as I looked into her eyes. "Tell me how it works."

Her eyes widened, a combination of disbelief and lust flickering within them. "Right...right now?" she stammered, a shaky hand sliding down my arm and gripping my wrist.

She paused for a moment, her brow furrowing as if she were actually considering my challenge.

"Genomics is...the study of...fuck...Dante...genome sequences..." she panted out, her eyes rolling as I hit that sweet spot inside of her.

"And what do you do with these sequences?" I pressed on, slowing my pace to give her a chance to catch her breath.

"I..." she began, her words trailing off into breathless moans as I twisted my fingers around her sensitive bud. "I analyze them...for genetic variations...implications on health...and....oh God! Dante!"

"All while you think about my cock, right?"

She nodded, her eyes fluttering closed at my touch. "Yes," she gasped, her legs wrapping tightly around me. "Always about your... your cock..."

"Now, that's a good girl," I purred, my hand sliding into her hair to tug her head back, giving me better access to her neck. I peppered kisses down her exposed throat, making her giggle and squirm beneath me. "Can't get enough of you."

I felt her body start to tense up again, the telltale signs of her impending climax beginning to show. Her breathing became more ragged and uneven, and she clung onto me as if I was her only lifeline.

"Dante..." she moaned out, her nails digging into my back while she grinded herself against me, chasing the waves building inside of her.

"I'm going to come inside of you now," I told her.

She nodded, her nails digging into my back, her body taut as a bowstring. "Yes," she gasped out, her voice barely more than a whisper. "Please... Dante..."

Her plea was all the encouragement I needed. With a final thrust, I buried myself deep inside her, my body shuddering as I spilled myself into her warm depths. Jade's body quivered beneath me, her cries echoing around us as she came undone.

I could feel the tremors of her orgasm around me, milking me for everything I had. The sensation was too much - too intense. I lost myself to it, the world blurring around me as pleasure consumed every inch of my being.

When the last shudder rolled through me, I cradled her gently to my chest, resting my forehead against her head. Still buried inside her, I felt every aftershock that rippled through her body.

"We should... definitely make this a... tradition," she said, her breath hot and shaky against my lips when she picked her up. She gave me a dazed smile, her cheeks flushed and eyes shining brightly.

"That's my girl," I whispered, brushing a stray lock of hair from her sweaty forehead and pressing a soft kiss to her lips. "You're so perfect for me."

We stayed like that for a while. Me inside her, slowly softening but unwilling to pull away just yet. Her in my arms, head tucked under my chin, fingers tracing lazy circles on the back of my hand.

"Dante?"

"Mmm?"

"I'm glad you came over. There's something I need to tell you."

"Okay..."

She looked into my eyes for a second. "But later," she said. "Will you stay over tonight?"

Chapter
Thirty-Four: Jade

We had fallen asleep cuddling.

I woke up with another headache, something my doctor had reassured me was a symptom that would go away as I got further into my pregnancy.

I threw off the covers, the chill of the night air striking against my skin, contrasting with the warmth still lingering from where we had lain together. My feet met the cold floorboards, sending a shiver up my legs that had nothing to do with the temperature. I needed Dante. The need pulsed through me, urgent and demanding.

Padding quietly across the bedroom, I approached the bathroom, my sanctuary turned ominous by shadows that played upon the walls. The apartment felt like it was holding its breath, waiting for something to happen. I paused, my hand hovering over the door handle, the soft hum of electricity from the lightbulbs the only sound in the silence.

I heard quiet talking coming from inside. That made sense, the bed was still warm and Dante couldn't have gone too far.

Then Dante's voice, muffled but distinct, sliced through the stillness. Low and tinged with annoyance, it crawled under my skin, raising hairs on the back of my neck. I stood there, hand frozen mid-air, heart pounding against my ribs. Should I go in? Or should I wait?

"Just handle it," he ordered, a simple command that carried more weight than I could fathom. My breath caught as I pressed my ear closer to the door, trying to decipher the tension woven into his every syllable. The 'Caruso problem' he mentioned—a name that meant nothing to me, yet seemed to mean everything to him.

I strained to hear more.

"You heard me, Luca. Clip one of Caruso's men. Can you get a capo?" Dante's voice was strained, the frustration clear even through the barrier between us. I didn't move, didn't breathe, as I waited for the response I couldn't hear.

There was a silence from his end—likely the person on the line was answering him—and then Dante spoke again, his tone sharp like shards of glass. "Well, then get another henchman. Just make it clear — tell him to back off Jade."

That's when my world tilted. The words crashed into me, every syllable a dagger aimed straight at my heart. He was talking about violence, about retribution. All because of me. That had been no figure of speech earlier.

Fear and confusion spun in my mind, creating a sickening cocktail that threatened to overwhelm me. This was a side of Dante I hadn't known, a side that perhaps I had refused to see.

The click of the phone ending the call was brutal in its finality. It echoed in the room, bouncing off the walls and inside my skull. I stepped back, a shaky exhale escaping my lips as I tried to process what I'd just heard.

Dante, the man who could be gentle and caring—the man I'd fallen for—was cloaked in shadows so dark I could no longer pretend they weren't there. My chest tightened, my stomach knotted with cold dread. There was a world he belonged to, a world of power plays and threats, and I knew so little about it.

I was faced with the stark reality of who Dante was, or at least part of who he was, and it left me standing in the hallway of my apartment, feeling more alone than ever.

I glanced down, my hand instinctively resting on my abdomen. Beneath the thin fabric of my pajama shirt, my fingers traced the secret I carried—our child, a life we created together. The weight of this knowledge was immense, pressing down on me, stealing my breath with its gravity.

I had always dreamed of having a family, but this... this was a twisted mockery of every hopeful picture I had painted in my mind. How could I bring an innocent soul into this chaos? How could I tie a child to a legacy of brutality and bloodshed?

Dante emerged from the shadows of the bathroom, clad only in his boxers, an odd juxtaposition to the violence that clung to him like a second skin. He looked at me, his gaze searching, a trace of vulnerability flickering behind the storm brewing in his eyes. He didn't have to say anything; the silent questions hung in the air between us.

"Jade," he said softly, his voice a velvet caress that belied the harshness of his earlier words. "What's wrong?"

I wanted to scream, to unleash the torrent of emotions that threatened to suffocate me. Instead, I swallowed hard, forcing back the tide of words that fought for release. Now wasn't the time for confessions or ultimatums. Now was a moment suspended—a precarious balance between what was known and the unspoken truth that lay heavy in my heart.

I needed to keep this quiet, for my unborn child's sake.

"Nothing," I lied, the word tasting bitter on my tongue. It was a feeble attempt to shield both of us from a confrontation neither was ready for. "Just woke up and noticed you weren't there. Thought I'd come check up on you."

Dante closed the distance between us, his presence enveloping me. I could feel the heat radiating from his skin, the barely restrained power of him. He reached out, his hand gently cupping my face, thumb caressing my cheek in a tender gesture that contrasted sharply with the man who had just been issuing threats over the phone.

"Talk to me, Jade," he urged, his voice low and earnest.

But how could I? How could I reveal the storm raging inside me—the fear, the love, the desperate desire to protect something so fragile from the very man before me?

"Later," I whispered, knowing that sooner or later, this conversation would have to happen. But not now. "I think I just woke up during a bad dream or something."

"Later then," Dante agreed, though the concern never left his eyes. He pulled me into an embrace, his arms a refuge that offered comfort despite the turmoil surrounding us. For now, I allowed myself to sink into his arms.

As I rested my head against his chest, listening to the steady beat of his heart, I made a silent promise to myself and to the life growing inside of me. Whatever it took, I would find a way through this labyrinth of secrets and lies. Love and fear might be entwined within me, but my resolve was solidifying. I would fight for our future—even if it meant going up against the shadows that clung to Dante Moretti.

He pulled away from me. "Jade, are you sure you're okay?"

"Yes," I answered too quickly, the lie stinging my tongue. His eyes bore into mine and for a moment, I was sure he could see through the façade. But he merely nodded, wrapping a protective arm around me as we made our way back to bed.

"If the dream was bad, I can eat you out until you fall asleep with my tongue inside of you," he said.

A soft gasp escaped my lips at his brazen words, the immediate physical response coursing through me, momentarily banishing my sorrow. His offer was enticing - a distracting contrast to the dark world he inhabited. It was this Dante, the sensual and passionate lover, who made it so hard to reconcile with the violent reality I had glimpsed earlier.

"I..." I stuttered, my mind racing, the weight of our situation pressing on me from all sides. The ticking time bomb of secrets between us seemed to pause in this intimate moment. The carnal promise in his eyes held a tantalizing escape from the harsh truth we were both avoiding.

I searched his face, the lines of worry etching a new pattern around his eyes. He was waiting for my answer yet his gaze held an unspoken request - let's forget, if only for tonight.

Mustering a weak smile, I nodded.

And as soon as I did, he dropped gracefully to his knees.

He looked up at me, his dark eyes intense and full of desire. The sight of him, half naked and on his knees for me, was a powerful one. I watched as his hands trailed up my legs.

"Jade," he murmured, his voice muffled against my skin as he pressed a soft kiss to the inside of my thigh. The sound of my name on his lips sent a shiver down my spine.

His hands slipped beneath my panties, his fingers dancing lightly over my skin as he pulled them down with excruciating slowness. The way he was looking at me - it was like I was the only thing that mattered in that moment.

He swirled his tongue around my sensitive clit, eliciting a gasp from my lips. He opened his mouth and dipped his tongue inside, his movements firm yet deliberate. The pleasure was immediate and overwhelming, like electricity arcing through my body. The tensions and fears of the day started to dissipate as he worked me with expert precision.

His hand rose to rest on my lower abdomen, and I sucked in a breath–the secret there a silent echo between us. His touch was gentle, protective even, as he continued to stroke me rhythmically with his tongue.

He pulled away from me for a second, picking up his head to smile at me. "Fuck, you taste so good," he said. "You taste like my come and your arousal."

He plunged his tongue back in, fucking me with it. The sensation was intense - bordering on unbearable. As he flicked his tongue over my clit, a sharp jolt of pleasure raced through me.

"D-Dante," I whimpered, my fingers tangling in his hair, anchoring myself to him. He moaned against me and the vibration sent another shockwave of pleasure through my body.

Suddenly, his fingers found their way into my pussy. He pumped them in and out of me while still making love to my clit with his mouth.

I let out a choked moan as his fingers curled within me, finding that sweet spot that made my vision blur with pleasure. My body responded instinctively, hips moving in time with his rhythm. His mouth continued to drive me wild, his tongue flicking over my throbbing clit over and over.

"Can you squirt for me again, beautiful?"

His words were a catalyst, and I felt the pressure building deep within me. My mind was filled with Dante and nothing else. The rest of the world fell away, my vision narrowing to just this moment, just this man.

I clung to him tightly, my body shaking as the pleasure built. I could feel his smile against my clit as he worked me into a frenzy. The knowledge that he was enjoying this—enjoying me—just as much as I was made it all the more intense.

"I want you to squirt all over my face," he growled out, his voice low and raspy, sending shivers cascading down my spine. "Give it to me, Jade."

His words were like a spark to dry kindling, setting my body alight with an unfathomable pleasure. His pace quickened, the rhythm of his fingers matching the desperate need that coursed through my veins.

"Dante," I moaned again, my voice barely a whisper as I surrendered to the onslaught of sensations he was eliciting within me. His name spilled from my lips over and over, each utterance pushing me closer to the precipice.

Tension coiled tightly within me, spiraling outwards from where Dante's mouth met my body with fervor. A gasp tore through me.

Suddenly, the world shattered into a million pieces of white-hot fire. An intense surge of pleasure radiated from my core and washed over me in waves. My knees practically buckled, the strength of the orgasm leaving me breathless. Dante didn't pull away, his mouth still locked onto my quivering clit as he milked me for everything I had to give.

I could feel myself squirting, drenching his face as he had desired. A low groan rumbled from deep within him, his satisfaction palpable as he continued to lap at me. The aftershocks coursed through me, my body quivering uncontrollably under his touch.

He finally pulled back, his face flushed with satisfaction. He rose up, his fingers tracing a teasing trail up my trembling body until he was level with me. His lips met mine in a lingering kiss, the taste of myself on his tongue a reminder of what had just happened.

"Okay," he said, slinging an arm around my waist. "Now let's do that again, but in bed."

Chapter
Thirty-Five: Dante

I pulled the sheets tight beneath her, an excuse to touch the smoothness of her skin one more time. The lamplight threw shadows over Jade's body in a way that made her look like she was still moving, still writhing under my touch. Sweat shimmered on her curves, her pajama shirt clinging to her skin.

"Jesus," I muttered as I knelt there, taking in the sight and smell of her laid out before me. "You smell fucking amazing. Holy shit, I could come just from the way you smell."

Her chest rose and fell with rapid breaths, eyes locked on mine with something like wonder—or maybe it was just raw desire. It was difficult to tell with Jade; she always had that look about her, like she was seeing things for the first time.

As I leaned in toward her, her legs gave a little shake. It was a small thing but telling—it said she was ready for whatever I had planned next. My lips found the inside of her thigh, and Jade let out a soft sound that might have been a whimper if it had any weight behind it.

"Like that?" I asked without looking up, feeling the affirmative tremor run through her as my mouth moved higher.

"More," she breathed out, and that was all the permission I needed.

My tongue followed a slow path upward, tasting her anticipation. Each flicker against her skin was calculated and precise, meant to stoke the fire that was already burning low in her belly. She gasped and moaned, each sound spurring me on, feeding the heat that coiled in my own gut. With every shudder that ran through her, my resolve to push her right to the brink—and then some—only grew.

"Jade, look at me," I commanded, my voice rough with need. "Do you want me to stop?"

Her response was immediate, her hands gripping the sheets, knuckles turning white. "No," she said, the word filling the room with a fervor that matched the pulse I could feel against my lips.

I smiled against her skin, a predator basking in the transparency of her desire. Rewarding her for her honesty, I intensified my efforts, feeling the rhythm of her body against my tongue.

The taste of Jade's climax hit me like a shot of the finest whiskey—sharp, heady, and damn intoxicating. She came apart beneath me, her cries echoing off the walls as her body arched off the bed.

Heat suffused my body, my satisfaction primal and complete in drawing out her ecstasy.

"Fuck," she said, locking her legs around my head. Even then, I refused to relent. I continued my assault, teasing and torturing her in the wake of her climax. Her body jerked with each flicker of my tongue, a delicious response that spurred me on further. My name fell from her lips, half-choked and strangled by the waves of pleasure washing over her.

I paused to catch my breath as Jade's hip bucked. I pressed a finger inside her wet pussy as her hips rose off the bed, her body begging for more even though her voice couldn't find the words. I grazed her clit with my thumb, coaxing and urging her as she almost tumbled over the edge once again.

I curled my finger inside of her, finding her g-spot and pressing another finger down on her clit with a rhythmic precision that matched her panting breaths. "Again," she whimpered, her hands clawing at the sheets as her body tensed beneath my skilled touch. I could feel her walls clenching around me in anticipation, and I couldn't help but smirk.

"Patience," I murmured against her skin, pulling back just enough to draw out yet another needy whimper from her lips. The sight of Jade sprawled out, wanting and waiting for me, was a vision I would never tire of.

I wasn't gentle—I don't think either of us wanted me to be—but I was controlled. My fingers moved with purpose, my thumb torturing her clit with a relentless focus that had Jade gasping for air and pleading for more.

I kissed between her legs until my mouth found her clit, licking, sucking, and nipping at the sensitive bud. Jade's body convulsed beneath me, her moans turning into high-pitched whimpers as she once again neared her climax.

"Fuck, don't stop," she gasped out, the desperate sound of her voice spurring me on. I plunged my fingers deeper into her, alternating between steady thrusts and gentle circular motions—an onslaught that soon had her legs shaking around me.

"Damn," I breathed against her, my voice husky with arousal. The sensation of Jade writhing underneath me was as intoxicating as her taste, and I reveled in every minute of it. I gave her no respite, my tongue tracing intricate patterns over her clit while my fingers continued to stroke her insides.

"Oh God!" she cried out as her body clenched around me. With a satisfied smirk on my face, I savored the echo of her cries bouncing off the walls of the room. Her body thrashed beneath me; her breath frantic and ragged as she rode out the waves of her climax.

Her chest heaved as I slowed my movements, fingers still buried deep within her. I released my hold on her clit, replacing it will soft licks that made her jerk and twitch beneath me. The sweet taste of her release lingered on my tongue, a flavor I would never tire of.

Her fingers knotted in my hair. "Wait," she said. "I'm...fuck, it's really sensitive."

"You stop coming when I say you stop coming."

Her eyes flickered open, a whimper escaping her lips at the intensity of my gaze. I felt a surge of power course through me at the sight of her so vulnerable, so bare before me.

"Dante..."

"And you don't stop coming until you're crying from the pleasure."

I watched her swallow hard, her hands gripping my hair tighter.

"Too much," she breathed out, but the tremble in her voice told me she was not entirely against the idea.

"I'll be the judge of that," I retorted, my words washing over her like a command.

"No...too much..." Jade repeated, but this time there was a pleading note in her voice, a desperate sound that only ignited my desire further. Her protests were weak, and even as she said them, her body answered differently. The way she arched against me was an invitation too tempting to pass up.

Ignoring her weak protests, I dove back in, pressing another kiss against her swollen clit. She gasped audibly, hips bucking up off the bed again.

"Relax, Jade," my voice was raspy, a stark contrast to the practiced smoothness of my touch. "Let me take care of you."

Her response was a moan, loud and unashamed, echoing around the room and winding its way around my senses. Her legs twitched, her body coiling tight as she teetered on the edge of another release. I could feel the tremors racking her frame as I slid a third finger inside her, feeling her walls clench around me.

"Dante!" Jade gasped out, back arching off the bed as a resounding orgasm shattered through her. She clung to me, her nails digging into my scalp while her body shook with the force of her climax.

I didn't slow down. Instead, I intensified my movements, relentless in my pursuit to bring her as much pleasure as she could handle.

Her body convulsed beneath me, her toes curling as wave after wave of pleasure ripped through her. I didn't let up, didn't slow down. Instead, I drank in every moan, every gasp, every plea that spilled from her lips.

"Dante! Dante, please...I can't!" Her breathy sobs filled the room, her words broken and desperate. It was music to my ears—a symphony of sweet surrender.

"You can," I reassured her without halting my rhythmic assault. "And you will."

Her body was bathed in sweat, her skin flushed and glistening. I could feel her trembling beneath my hands, the desperate writhing of a woman on the brink of pleasure so intense it was almost painful. Every flick of my tongue, every thrust of my fingers sent her spiraling further into ecstasy, her cries growing louder with each passing second.

And then she screamed.

Jade's body arched off the bed, her fingers dug deep into my hair as she came undone. Her release washed over me as if it were mine—the taste of her climax on my tongue, the sound of her ragged breaths in my ear, the sight of her flushed skin beneath me—it was an intoxicating blend that only increased my growing desire.

"Dante..." she whimpered, collapsing back onto the bed as her climax subsided. Her chest heaved with exertion, her body slick with sweat and trembling from the aftershocks. I could still feel her pulsing around my fingers, the tremors a testament to the intensity of her orgasm.

"Goddamn," I muttered, pulling my fingers out slowly, relishing in the whimper that elicited from her. I wiped my hand on the sheet, my gaze never leaving her as she gasped for air. Her body was a beautiful sight—limbs sprawled out on the bed, hair clinging to her damp forehead and eyes closed tightly shut as if to shut out the rest of the world.

"Fuck," she said. "I don't think I can do that again."

"I beg to differ," I replied, my voice laced with unmasked desire. The sight of her all spent and flushed from the pleasure I had given her only made me want her more. There was a wicked satisfaction in knowing I had been the one to unravel her so thoroughly.

The way her cheeks blushed at my words was nothing short of adorable. But I wasn't going to let her off the hook just yet. I had plans for Jade Bentley, and they didn't involve her getting much sleep tonight.

She was staring at me, eyes wide and pupils dilated. Her chest heaved with each shallow breath, the rise and fall mesmerizing.

"What are you--" she started, but her words were cut off by a low groan as I trailed my fingers down her body, slipping them between her thighs.

I could feel the heat radiating from her, the slick wetness coating my fingers. Her hips twitched involuntarily at the contact, a soft gasp escaping her lips.

"Dante..." she whispered, her voice barely there. It was an intoxicating sound—her voice strained from pleasure, her body a quivering mess under my touch.

"I told you," I murmured against her skin, pressing a kiss to the inside of her thigh. "You don't stop coming until you're crying from the pleasure."

Her breath hitched at my words, body stiffening beneath me. A moment later, she relaxed, giving in to the sensation as I teased her oversensitive clit.

I watched her face contort in a mixture of pleasure and pain as I skillfully manipulated her clit, my thumb grazing over the sensitive bud while my fingers delved into the slick warmth of her core. Her breath hitched as I added a second finger, stretching her further as I pumped them in and out.

"Fuck, fuck, fuck," she said, her face turning red and her legs twitching. The sight of her writhing beneath me spurred me on, stoking the flames of my own desire. I knew we were dancing on the edge of too much, but I didn't care. I wanted to see her unravel, wanted to hear her screams echo through the room as she came undone beneath my touch again.

"Jesus, fuck," she said, and when I looked at her face, I was sure her eyes were watering.

"Are you crying?" I asked, my voice rougher than I intended. "Are you crying from the pleasure? That's so fucking hot."

Her response was nothing more than a choked whimper, her body shaking as if on the brink. She was close; I could feel it in the tense way her body clung to me, in the desperate hitch of her breath.

"Crying yet?" I asked once more, my voice dripping with intent. Her reply was a gasp, a strangled sound that only spurred me on.

"Answer me," I commanded, feeling her tremble beneath me.

"Yes... yes," she stammered out, the tears glistening on her lashes proving her words true. The sight was beautiful — Jade Bentley, lost in the throes of forbidden pleasure, crying out because of me.

"Good girl," I praised her, my fingers slipping out only to plunge back against her sensitive bundle. I could feel her tightening around my fingers once again, the coil within her winding tighter. "Once you come for me again, I might give you my cock. You want my cock, don't you?"

"Yes...I want it," Jade whimpered in response. Her voice was hoarse and strained, evident of the pleasure that I had inflicted upon her. The mere thought of my hard length buried deep inside her elicited a shudder of anticipation within me—an anticipation mirrored in the tremble of her curvy frame beneath my touch.

"You'll have to earn it," I goaded, my tone dark and teasing yet laced with an unmistakable promise. My thumb began circling her clit again, eliciting a sharp gasp from her

"No more...I can't..." she pleaded, her fingers clutching at the sheets beneath us, knotted in an attempt to ground herself amidst the pleasure I was relentless in providing. It was marvelous—seeing her so undone, so beautifully wrecked, all because of me.

"But you will," I responded without mercy, increasing the pressure of my thumb on her clit. A renewed cry of pleasure erupted from her lips, her body quaking as she edged closer to another orgasm.

But I was done holding on. I was already very close to coming myself and the sight of her, so lost in desire, the feel of her slick walls clenching around my fingers, was driving me to the brink. I needed to be inside her, needed to feel her from the inside.

With a final flick of my thumb, Jade cried out again, climax washing over her with such force it left her shaking. As the waves subsided, she collapsed on the bed, chest heaving and body drenched in sweat.

"You're ready for me," I said, climbing up the bed, hovering above her.

My chest heaved with anticipation as Jade, with her eyes glazed over and her body still quivering from pleasure, gave a slight nod—the only permission I needed.

"Fucking hell," I hissed through gritted teeth, the sensation of being inside her nearly overwhelming in its intensity. From the grip she had on my shoulders, digging her nails into my skin, I could tell she was feeling the depth of me as well.

"Dante...too much," she whimpered, writhing in both pleasure and discomfort underneath me.

I thrust into her hard as I leaned down to whisper against her ear. "It's okay, beautiful," I said. "You're so wet. You'll get used to me soon."

The words were an assurance, an oath, a vow that I would take care of her. That I would reduce her to the same quivering mess as before but this time, with my cock buried deep inside her.

But also...there was no chance I could pace myself. Not after I had seen her come over and over again, not as I fucked her with the taste of her arousal on my lips.

She began to match my rhythm, her hips lifting with each of my thrusts. I felt a surge of triumph as she began to respond to me, to give herself over to the pleasure we were creating together.

"Shit," she whispered, her nails scraping down my back. Her voice was strained, and yet something sparked inside me at the sight of her beneath me, soft and wanton and all mine.

"Come on, darling," I murmured, dragging my lips down her neck. "You can take more." My voice was rough, filled with the desperate need that was spiraling tightly within me. Her body met each thrust with a delightful shudder, her satisfying groan a clear indication of her pleasure.

I fucked her hard, so hard, so relentlessly, that I could feel the tremors rippling through her body like electricity. Her gasps and cries echoed in my ears, spurring me on to heights that seemed unfathomable.

Each time I buried myself deep within her, a fresh wave of pleasure washed over me, pushing me closer and closer to the precipice. Her legs wrapped tightly around my waist, drawing me in deeper with each thrust.

"Dante, I can't—I can't—fuck, oh my God," she said.

I knotted my hands in her hair and pulled it softly, exposing the expanse of her neck to me, raking my teeth along her pulse.

"You can and you will," I growled back, our bodies slick with sweat as I pushed her further and further into the abyss of pleasure. The scent of our mixed arousal filled the air, a heady perfume that made my cock throb with each thrust.

"But Dante," she whimpered, a plea for mercy that I ignored.

"Just one more," I demanded, my voice so hoarse with desire that it was barely more than a growl. I shifted my angle, thrusting into her harder and faster until her body was shaking beneath mine.

I felt her walls tighten around me in response, her body trembling as she was sent over the edge once again. Her cries echoed in the room, lingering in the air as a powerful testament to our carnal union.

Feeling her body convulse around me, I let out a groan, my own climax tearing through me like a tornado. The world spun around me as I buried myself deep inside her one last time, my body shuddering as I emptied into her, my orgasm so overwhelming my other senses dulled into nothingness.

After our bodies stilled, I collapsed onto her, my weight pressing her into the soft mattress beneath us. Her breath came in pants as she struggled to catch her breath. I could feel her heartbeat against my chest, erratic but slowly returning to normal.

"Dante..." she whispered softly, her hands trembling as they ran through my hair. My name on her lips was laced with an intoxicating mix of satisfaction and exhaustion.

"Shhh..." I murmured back, brushing a stray lock from her forehead. "Just rest."

"Aren't you going to pull out?"

"Nah," I replied, kissing the tip of her nose. "Not yet."

She laughed. "Why not?"

"So that when I wake up," I said. "I can just fuck you again."

Chapter Thirty-Six:
Jade

I was so exhausted.

At some point, Dante had rolled off me.

Sunlight snuck in through the curtains, a traitor to the darkness of my thoughts. I blinked away the remnants of sleep, the soft cotton of my pajama shirt rumpled against my skin. A chill crept along my spine as last night's whispered horrors tangled with the morning's quiet.

Lying there, the afterglow of Dante's touch still lingered on my body, a deceitful comfort. He had drawn moan after moan from me, each one a veil over the sinister truths I'd stumbled upon. The words spoken behind the bathroom door clawed their way back into my consciousness, Dante's low voice a soundtrack to the nightmare.

Clipped.

That word hung in my mind, repeating like a broken record. The ache wasn't just from the betrayal; it was the confirmation, the solidification of the fears I'd danced around since meeting Dante. He belonged to a world painted in shades of blood and obedience, a world I'd pretended could be separated from the man who held me at night.

I sat up, pushing the sheets away, feeling the morning air kiss my skin. It was a stark reminder, a cold slap of reality against the tender flesh of ignorance. My heart thumped a heavy beat, acknowledging the truth I'd sidestepped for too long – Dante Moretti, lover, confidant... mafia.

I swung my legs out of bed, the room tilting slightly as I stood. I braced myself against the dresser, the reflection in the mirror a woman caught at the crossroads of her own conscience. Could I continue to turn a blind eye, pretend that the whispers of violence were just nightmares spun by my imagination?

Maybe I could. Maybe if I wasn't pregnant with his child.

No. I was Jade Bentley, a woman of science, of facts. And the fact was, Dante had never been just a businessman. He was a Moretti, through and through. The realization gnawed at my insides, a bitter pill coated in the intimacy we'd shared. And now, with daylight as my witness, I couldn't unhear or unsee the reality of his world – our world.

I steadied my breath, a practiced calm settling over my features as I sifted through my wardrobe. The soft silk of my pajama shirt clung to me, a tactile reminder of the night's restless sleep. Selecting a pair of jeans and a blouse that projected confidence, I dressed with deliberate care, each button fastened, each crease smoothed out, just as I arranged my thoughts.

With each measured pace toward the living room, the distance felt like miles, every step sinking into a morass of doubt and fear. My heart raced, a frenetic drumbeat drowning out the silence of the apartment. What would I say? How could I confront the man whose very presence twisted my insides with both dread and desire?

But confront him I must. There were no more excuses, no more ignorance to hide behind. Dante's world had bled into mine, staining the fabric of our relationship with secrets too dark to ignore. And somewhere between the love and the lies, I had to find the truth—for both of us.

No. For all three of us.

I left my bedroom and watched him move around my kitchen. This normalcy now seemed like such a farce.

The rich scent wrapped around me, a comforting lie that stood in stark contradiction to the chaos churning inside.

"Good morning, beautiful," he said, barely looking over his shoulder. I was sure this would have been easier if he was wearing more than just his boxers, but the sight of him - the delineated muscles beneath his skin, the crucifix tattoo on his chest, the dark ink lines wrapped around his biceps - it was all a stark reminder of the night before, of his touch, his taste. It was an alluring distraction that I fought to ignore.

"Dante," I began, my fingers worrying at the hem of my shirt. His dark gaze fell on me, a curious smile playing at the corner of his lips. My heart pounded in my chest as I met his eyes, as though every beat echoed my resolve, steeling me for what was to come.

"Yes?" His voice reverberated through the spacious room. The very air between us seemed to thrum with anticipation.

"We need to talk." My words hung in the air, heavy with so much unsaid. His expression flickered, a guarded look replacing his relaxed demeanor.

He put the carafe down. "Why?"

"It's important," I said, my voice barely above a whisper. I watched him closely, his expression unreadable as he turned fully to face me.

"Alright then." Dante slid a mug of coffee across the counter towards me - as if this was any normal morning. As if my world wasn't about to shatter the moment I opened my mouth.

I moved closer, ignoring the warmth emanating from the cup and focused on the man standing before me. His tousled hair, his relaxed posture, his piercing gaze... All seemingly out of place in the kitchen of a simple scientist like me.

I cleared my throat, every cell in my body screaming at me to retreat. To crawl back into bed and pretend none of this was real. But I couldn't cling to that blissful ignorance any longer. I had a child to protect...our child.

"Tell me I didn't hear what I think I did," I said, the words sharp, even as they trembled on the brink of something more vulnerable.

Dante turned, his expression unreadable, eyes locking onto mine. The silence stretched between us, thick enough to choke on. He played dumb. "Hear what?"

My pulse hammered, betraying the calm I fought so hard to maintain. "Last night. In the bathroom...talking about clipping someone." I hated how my voice cracked.

He smirked, a flicker of amusement crossing his face. "You shouldn't eavesdrop, Jade. It's rude, especially through a closed door."

Dante, all casual in his boxers, seemed unfazed by our standoff. His nonchalance was a slap in the face, the reality of who he was—and what he was capable of—suddenly undeniable.

This was Dante Moretti in the flesh: charming, lethal, and utterly indifferent to the turmoil he inflicted. And I, Dr. Jade Bentley, was caught in the crosshairs of a life I never signed up for, my heart warring with my head over a man who was both my haven and my hell.

I squared my shoulders as Dante leaned against the counter, his posture so relaxed you'd never guess our world was in free fall.

"I was working, Jade," he said.

"Working on what?" I asked him.

"My job is none of your business," he shot back, the words hitting me like a bucket of ice water.

"None of my business?" I echoed, the tremble in my voice betraying the storm within. "You were doing it in my house. It feels like my business."

"Jade," he began, his voice a velvet caress that contrasted sharply with the hard lines of his jaw. "You know I can't just—"

"Leave," I cut him off, my voice sharper than I intended, a scalpel to the heart. "I need you to leave." The words hung heavy between us, the air dense with the things left unsaid.

That's what I should have done last night...but the man was really, *really* good with his mouth.

Dante's gaze pinned me in place, as if he could see right through the façade I struggled to maintain. His eyes held mine, and for a moment, I saw the flicker of something vulnerable, something human, before it was quickly masked by the stoic exterior he wore like armor.

"Jade," he said again, softer this time, but I stood my ground.

"Please," I whispered, clutching the fabric of my shirt as if it could somehow fortify me against the ache in my chest. A single tear escaped, traitorous and hot against my cool cheek. "Get out of my apartment."

"I'm going to get dressed first," he said.

"Fine," I snapped back, retreating from the kitchen. The taste of coffee, usually so comforting, now tainted with bitterness. I could feel his gaze on me, burning holes into my back as I moved away. A part of me wanted to turn around, to run back and throw my arms around him. But the cold, hard truth was cutting through the fog of my emotions.

He emerged a few moments later, fully dressed in the suit he had worn the night before. I couldn't bring myself to look at him as he moved towards the exit, each step echoing in the chilling silence.

He left.

The click of the door closing sliced through the silence like a verdict, final and unappealing. I stood frozen in the kitchen, the chill of the tiles seeping into my bare feet. The space around me felt too vast suddenly, as if the apartment had grown, walls stretching with Dante's absence.

I moved mechanically to the sofa, my limbs heavy, drained from the tension that had cocooned us. Collapsing onto the cushions, I let out a breath I hadn't realized I was holding. Around me, the room was still, the only sound the soft hum of the refrigerator acting as the metronome to my rapid heartbeat.

My hands, shaking slightly, found their way to my stomach. There was nothing to see, no bump to betray the secret nestled inside me, but it was there—a life, an innocent tethered to a world it had no part in choosing. My mind raced with the possibilities, every one of them tinged with fear and what-ifs.

I needed to...do something else. Anything else.

I needed to stop worrying about Dante and start worrying about my own fucking life.

And about my child.

Chapter Thirty-Seven: Jade

I couldn't shake the unease that clawed at my insides as I approached the imposing glass façade of BioHQ. I was lost in my own thoughts until I saw all the police cruises parked outside. The flashing red and blue lights reflecting on the icy ground felt like a punch in my gut. I knew instantly that something had gone horribly wrong.

But the sirens weren't on, the lights weren't even flashing.

The officers were quietly conversing, their breath like smoke in the cold night air. The place was crawling with them, blue uniforms against the stark concrete. Their faces were grim, their eyes hiding secrets that I wasn't privy to. I felt my heart pound in my chest as I stepped out of the shadows and moved towards them.

The place I had devoted countless hours to was now a stage for something sinister. A charged hush hung over the clusters of my colleagues; their usual morning banter was now just anxious murmurs that skittered through the chilled autumn air like fallen leaves.

"Something's wrong," I whispered to myself, my breath clouding in front of me. I quickened my pace, the click of my heels on the pavement sharp and urgent. I hadn't slept well; images from last night's heated exchange with Dante kept replaying in my mind—his smoldering gaze, the hard lines of his jaw tensing as he spoke in that gravelly voice that always seemed to find its way under my skin.

The revolving doors spun me into the lobby, and I was hit by an atmosphere thick with anxiety. It wasn't the familiar hum of productivity but a discordant symphony of hushed voices and the clatter of security measures being ramped up. Detectives, with their keen eyes and notebooks at the ready, stood among our own security staff, who looked more on edge than I'd ever seen them.

"Dr. Bentley," one of the guards nodded curtly as I passed.

"Morning," I returned, my voice steadier than I felt. Each step I took resonated against the marble floor, mirroring the pounding in my chest. What had happened? My thoughts raced, trying to connect the dots, but coming up empty.

I let out a slow breath, determined not to let the chaos rattle me. Today, I needed to be the scientist they all knew—the one who solved problems, not the one drowning in them. But as I watched a detective photograph what looked like a broken lock near one of the labs, I couldn't help but feel I was walking straight into the storm.

"Jade, there's been a development." Dr. White's voice cut through the lobby's din, and I turned to find him striding toward me, his face etched with concern.

I followed him, my heart thudding in my chest, as we moved away from prying eyes. The nausea that had been an ever-present companion since my pregnancy began seemed to swell, but I swallowed it down. "What is it, Dr. White? What's happened?"

He took a deep breath, looking at me like he was about to shatter my world. "The security breach from a few weeks ago…" His voice trailed off, and he met my gaze squarely. "It's been traced back to your ID."

My blood ran cold, and I felt the color drain from my face. "That's impossible," I managed to choke out, the walls of the lobby suddenly too close.

"Where's your ID now, Jade?" he asked, his eyes scanning mine for any trace of deceit.

"I...I lost it, a while ago. I didn't think—it was just an ID card." Panicked, I tried to remember when I last saw it. I usually kept it in my bag, but God...I hadn't seen it for what I was sure was weeks. Maybe even a month or more.

Dr. White's brow furrowed. "How have you been getting into the building?"

"Well, I know the receptionist," I said, confusion lacing my words. "I don't understand your question." It was true; Sarah at the front desk would often wave me through with a smile. It never crossed my mind that this casual convenience could be twisted into something so damning.

"Okay, Jade. Okay." Dr. White's voice softened, but his expression remained grave. He glanced over his shoulder, assuring our isolation. "We need to keep this quiet. If word gets out to the other families, to the press... it could be catastrophic for BioHQ—and for you."

"I mean, it's just an ID card. Surely I can't be the linchpin of this whole operation..."

"Look, Jade," Dr. White cut in, his hushed tone urgent, "the stakes are higher than you realize. Your ID grants access to secure areas—areas that were compromised. We've got to get ahead of this."

My head spun. The implications were staggering. Someone out there was using my identity to infiltrate BioHQ's inner sanctum, and I was the perfect scapegoat. My dedication, my naivete—it all made me an easy target.

"Dr. White, I need you to believe me," I said, my voice barely above a whisper. "I haven't done anything wrong." My plea hung in the air, heavy with desperation. It was vital he understood—I was as much a victim in this charade as BioHQ itself.

He nodded, his eyes locked on mine. "I know you're not guilty, but the evidence suggests otherwise." His words landed like a punch to the gut. "The security footage, the missing prototypes, the breach—it's all tracing back to you, somehow."

I felt like I was drowning, each breath more laborious than the last. My mind raced desperately through every interaction, every misplaced trust. Who had I let too close? Who had seen my ID last?

"Jade, listen to me," Dr. White continued, seeing the panic in my eyes. "We'll get to the bottom of this. But until we do, you must be careful. Trust no one. Not even Ellie."

"Ellie?" I balked at the notion. Ellie was more than a colleague; she was my closest friend, my anchor. "She'd never—"

"Everyone is a suspect until proven otherwise," Dr. White interrupted sternly. "Remember that."

"But Dr. Harper would never..."

"Jade," Dr. White leaned in closer, urgency etching his features. "You need to understand the stakes. They're not just after a scapegoat; they want a confession. And they'll twist your words to get one."

His warnings echoed in my head as I entered the boardroom where several of my colleagues had already gathered. There was an unspoken understanding in their furtive glances—the kind that comes when fear is the only common language. The detectives moved like shadows among us, their questions sharp and probing.

Ellie wasn't there. I wondered where she was for a second, but before I could text her, I heard the sound of my name being called.

"Dr. Bentley?" One of them called out, and the room hushed instantly. It was my turn to face the music, no matter how discordant the tune.

"Ms. Bentley, please take a seat," one detective motioned to the chair opposite him. His eyes were hard, unreadable.

"It's Doctor. Dr. Bentley," I replied.

"Of course, Dr. Bentley," he corrected himself, a flicker of annoyance crossing his features. I felt a pang of satisfaction - at least I had control over something in this madness.

He folded his hands on the table, creating a barrier between us. "We have reason to believe that you are involved in the serious security breaches that have been occurring." His tone was flat, but there was an undercurrent of accusation that made me bristle.

"I didn't..." My voice trailed off, and I took a deep breath. "I didn't have anything to do with it. I lost my ID."

"Did you report that?"

"No," I said. I noticed Edward Rodriguez sitting next to the detective, scribbling his own notes. "I mean, what for? That seemed pointless, and I was busy with other things."

The detective's gaze narrowed, his lips forming a thin line. "Dr. Bentley, negligence in reporting lost items, especially ID cards that provide access to secure areas," he gestured towards the lab's entrance, "is taken very seriously here. It is tantamount to breaching security protocols."

"I understand that now," I replied, fighting the lump in my throat. "But it was an oversight on my part, not a deliberate act of sabotage."

"Dr. Bentley, your lost ID card could have potentially allowed unauthorized access to the building and its sensitive information," Rodriguez helpfully said.

I felt a lump forming in my throat. Sarah's face flashed before my eyes—the sweet receptionist who always let me in without a question. Tears pricked at the corners of my eyes as I thought about what she would think of me now.

"Explain your activities on the night of the breach. October 3rd," Rodriguez demanded, the hard edge in his voice slicing through the tense air like a scalpel.

Who was he to ask me for an explanation?

"Well, I don't know exactly, but I think I was at home," I replied. "Can I check my calendar?"

"Go ahead," the detective said, the corners of his mouth twitching ever so slightly. I could feel his gaze boring into me as I fumbled with my phone, pulling up my calendar.

"I was... at home," I affirmed, pointing to the date on the screen. "All night."

"And can anyone verify this?" He asked, his tone implying skepticism.

"No. I live alone," I confessed, feeling once again like a cornered animal.

His gaze lingered on me for a moment longer before jotting something down in his notepad. "Interesting," he muttered under his breath.

"Explain this to me. Why would I steal my own data?" I said, straightening my back.

"That's what we're trying to figure out, Dr. Bentley," Rodriguez replied, his tone devoid of any sympathy. His eyes never left mine, their icy blue stare probing for any hint of deceit.

"Well, I can assure you I wouldn't jeopardize my own research," I said, forcing myself to hold his gaze steadily.

"You'd be surprised what people are capable of when money's involved," he countered, his voice filled with derision. "A scientist like you could make a fortune selling the kind of information we keep in those labs."

"I'm not a corporate spy," I snapped, my patience wearing thin. "I haven't stolen anything and I haven't sold anything."

"If you tell us who you're working with—"

"I told you, I'm not—" My protest was cut short as the door to the boardroom swung open. "Do I need a lawyer?"

The detective cleared his throat. "I don't know, Dr. Bentley. Do you need a lawyer?"

I shook my head. "I have work to do. Can I leave?"

The detective considered that for a second.

"Yes. Dr. Bentley, you're free to go. But be aware that we're not done here," the detective finally said, closing his notebook with a snap that echoed off the sterile walls of the conference room. I blinked, the abrupt shift catching me off guard. My legs, numb from sitting too long, protested as I stood up.

I walked down the corridor, my shoes clicking on the linoleum in a steady rhythm. With each step, I felt a layer of suspicion peeling away, but it was like shedding one cloak only to find another, heavier one underneath. I knew how these things went; the questioning might be over, but the real scrutiny had just begun.

I remained in the crosshairs, and somewhere out there, hidden in the city's vast underbelly, the real culprit lurked, watching...waiting. And despite the detectives' grilling, I couldn't shake the feeling that the worst was yet to come.

Chapter Thirty-Eight: Dante

I flicked the dimmer switch, and the room darkened like a shroud settling over the dead. The Raven's Nest was Caruso territory, but tonight it was the stage for my play, and I had to nail every act. Unease crawled under my skin, an unwelcome guest at this gathering of wolves. This was a ballsy move. Maybe even a crazy one.

But I had to do something.

My men had killed Bruno, and that hadn't gone how I had hoped. He wasn't a capo, but he was well-liked by the rest of the men who worked for Caruso, and they were angry.

They needed someone to pin it on. They would find out it was a Moretti hit sooner or later. They wanted blood. I just needed to find a way to redirect their anger.

I took a deep breath and looked at all the faces around me. There, in the corner, Marco's silhouette was a fortress against my dread.

"We're making moves," I announced, my fingers dancing through the air, outlining invisible networks, alliances yet unformed. The table in front of me was littered with documents, the scent of fresh ink a sharp promise of wealth yet untapped. These papers could change everything, not just for us but for her—Jade. Her name was a prayer on my lips, a silent plea for strength.

Giovanni, with his granite-hard gaze, sat across from me, his doubt a living thing between us. He toyed with his scotch, the glass catching what little light was left. "Why should we trust you, Dante?" His voice was rough, like gravel tossed in a tin can.

He was a bit older than me, toughened by years on the streets and the scars of countless battles. Still, I stayed my ground, leaning forward, elbows on the table, a predator ready to strike.

Marco's lighter snapped open, its flame a beacon as smoke curled towards the heavens. I leaned in, so close I could taste the skepticism on Giovanni's breath. "Because the Caruso family is blinded by tradition. We're offering progress. Real money." My words were low, the truth in them ringing louder than any bell tower.

The hum of the neon sign outside bled through the walls, a ghostly soundtrack to our clandestine meeting. Here in the half-light, with the future hanging on a razor's edge, I played my hand, ready to bet it all to shield Jade from the darkness that threatened to swallow her whole.

Giovanni leaned back, his chair creaking under the weight of his decision. "But one of our men is dead. And we think you did it."

I met his accusation head-on, my resolve as unyielding as the city's concrete foundations. "You think I had your guy taken out?" I asked, the lie rolling off my tongue, smooth as silk. "Come on, Giovanni. If I could do that, don't you think I'd wipe out all of Caruso's pawns while I'm at it?"

Marco's steps punctuated my words. He circled like a hawk, eyes sharp and ready.

The mid-level goons from Caruso's side were harder to read, their expressions as closed off as a bank vault. But they were here, in their territory, sure, but listening to me.

"Look," I said, pushing the folder towards them. Its contents spilled slightly, revealing the shimmer of blueprints and numbers that spelled out our future. "We're not just talking about turf wars or gun running. This"—I paused, letting the gravity of the moment sink in—"this is biotech. Revolutionizing medicine. And getting filthy rich while we're at it."

Marco struck a match, lighting another cigarette. The smoke twisted and danced upward.

"Caruso is stuck in the past, but we…" I let the sentence hang, dangling the bait. "We will own the future. With these advancements, we leverage power in ways Caruso can't even imagine."

Their eyes flickered to the documents.

"Think about it," I urged. "Not just what you'll gain but what you'll escape. The shadow of Lorenzo Caruso is long, but we're offering a way out from under it."

The air was charged now, thick with thoughts of rebellion and the sweet scent of possibility. Marco closed his lighter with a snap–why he always carried a box of matches and a lighter around was beyond me–and the room went dark for a heartbeat before the lights flickered back to life.

"New York City," I said, sweeping a hand over the map, "is ripe for the taking. And with your help, we'll pluck it like an apple from a tree."

Giovanni's brow furrowed, but his eyes betrayed his interest. "And what's in it for you, Dante?" The question was pointed, a knife poised at my throat.

"Isn't it obvious?" I replied, my voice edged with the steel of conviction. "I'm securing my family's legacy—and offering you a piece of it."

There was that. That was part of it, certainly. But I couldn't lie to myself. Most of this was about protecting Jade.

Caruso had me in his crosshairs, which meant he had Jade in his crosshairs. I couldn't afford for that to happen.

Giovanni eyes darted between the heavy envelope and me, searching for any sign of deceit. His lips parted as if to argue, but nothing came out. The thud of the cash had spoken louder than any reassurance I could offer.

"This is just the beginning," I repeated, letting the promise settle over them like a mantle. They were street-smart, these men; they knew opportunity dressed in many guises, and tonight she wore the sharp cut of a Moretti suit.

"Come on," Marco said. "Would we be here if we weren't serious? Enzo can make this happen all by himself. But you're here, and we're both here..."

"He's right. My dad completely backs us up," I said, another lie. Our father would be furious if he knew we were here...but only if we failed.

Marco continued, his voice low and steady, weaving a tale of ambition and potential that knitted the room together in the web of our design. "The old ways are dying, boys. Get on board now, or get left behind."

The words hung in the air like gun smoke, their message clear: adapt or perish. Changing times called for changing alliances, and I could practically see the gears turning in Giovanni's head as he wrestled with the prospect.

"It's a dangerous play," Giovanni said. The rest of the men hadn't spoken at all. I assumed they were happy for Giovanni to speak for them.

"It's the only play," I replied, meeting his stare with equal intensity. "The truth is that the Moretti name has plenty of pull in this city and with the healthcare facilities that are popping up everywhere, transportation and logistics are going to be much easier for us."

"And what about the cops? You think they're going to turn a blind eye to all this?" One of the Caruso goons finally spoke up, his words slurred by the cheap whiskey that Marco had graciously provided.

"What are they going to do? Investigate the perfectly legitimate transporting of drugs between clinics?" I countered. "We're not talking about street level drugs here. We'll be able to transport anything. Anything. Without scrutiny."

The goon's brows furrowed, the gears in his head grinding slowly.

Giovanni spoke up. "They gonna look the other way if they know the Moretti's are involved?"

"We'll be operating under the radar," Marco chimed in, blowing a puff of smoke into the air. "Clean records, clean money. No need for them to ever know our involvement. And I'm serious—the clinics and labs are there to help people. But if we can make extra money on fentanyl, why not?"

Giovanni's gaze flickered to the cash, now pushed aside, forgotten amidst the grandeur of our vision. "And you have the resources for this? The equipment? The manpower?"

"Everything is already in motion," Marco said, his voice steady as a ticking clock. "We've been preparing for months."

"And Jade?" Giovanni turned his gaze back to me. His question was a punch straight to the gut. "The skip said you were getting serious with a girl. Is she going to be a problem?"

Jade. My distraction. My dilemma. My obsession.

"Dr. Bentley is not involved. Her research spurred this on, but she isn't part of this."

Giovanni's eyes bored into me, and I could tell he wasn't just asking about her involvement in our plans. He was digging deeper, prying into my personal matters. It was no secret that Jade had become dearer to me than I'd ever anticipated, and it was unsettling how quickly the Carusos had picked up on it.

"You sure, Moretti?"

"Yes," I said, my voice sharp enough to cut through lead. "She'll never be a problem."

Giovanni studied me with those cold, calculating eyes of his—long enough for my heart to beat a rapid tattoo against my chest, long enough for sweat to form a thin sheen over my brow.

"Alright," Giovanni finally said, breaking the tension. "We're in. But remember this, Dante: if anything goes sideways, if we so much as suspect that you're playing us..." He let the words hang in the air like a threat, unsaid but understood.

I nodded, acknowledging his warning. It was always the way with the Caruso family; they'd shake your hand with a smile while keeping a knife at your back. As long as everything went according to plan, we'd stay on their good side. But one wrong move...well, I'd seen what happened to those who crossed Giovanni Testa.

And if Caruso found out...I shuddered at the thought, my blood running cold at the mere idea of his wrath. I was playing a dangerous game, but I knew this was the only way. Every move from here on out had to be precise, calculated, flawless.

Marco leaned against the door frame, his hawk-like gaze intense as he watched the men around him, his hands casually tucked into his pockets. "We'll keep our end of the deal," he assured them, his tone unwavering.

I felt each man's eyes on me, their scrutiny like a furnace's heat. But I wore my poker face well; I'd been schooled in deception since childhood. A wrong look or a hesitant word could cost us everything now.

"So long as we all understand each other," Giovanni said, rising from his seat. He extended a hand towards me, and for a moment, time seemed to stand still.

"You're going to make so much money, Giovanni," I said. "You have no idea."

As he offered his hand, I reached out, clasping his gnarled fingers in a firm grip. His eyes met mine, two seasoned players acknowledging the high stakes of the game, and I could see the cautionary glimmer behind his hardened gaze. This wasn't trust – it was a fragile truce built on the promise of wealth and power. But it was a start.

"Let's hope so, Dante," Giovanni replied, releasing my hand. "For your sake. And for the sake of your lady doctor."

Chapter Thirty-Nine: Jade

My headaches were getting worse, not better.

I stumbled into the sanctuary of my apartment, a place now shadowed by the day's nightmares. I took to lighting up my scented candles around my apartment, the flickering flame lighting the space softly.

Lavender—the scent that once calmed my storms—could barely touch the pounding in my head.

The lab, my life's work, had turned into an interrogation room. My mind replayed every question, each insinuation they lobbed at me, trying to tie me to things far beyond my comprehension. A scientist, I could handle. A suspect? That was new territory.

I didn't like it at all.

And I already felt like I was carrying a terrible secret.

A shuffle from the hallway yanked me back to the present. My heart kicked against my chest like it wanted to break free.

"Jade?" The voice was deep, familiar—and absolutely not welcome here.

I squinted against the dim light spilling in from the corridor. Edward Rodriguez loomed there, his shadow sprawling across my floor, a dark omen. He wasn't supposed to be here. I could barely stand the sight of him at work.

"Open up, Dr. Bentley. We need to talk." His words were a low rumble, but I heard the urgency lacing each syllable.

"Why are you here?" I asked through the door.

"Look, I just want to talk." Edward's voice reverberated against the walls, too close for comfort.

"I don't want to talk to you."

He muttered something under his breath. He raised something—a badge, shiny and insistent. "Look. I'm Edward Rodriguez, tech security expert for the NYPD. I'm not just someone BioHQ hired. Can I come in?"

Fuck. He was a cop?

"Talk then," I said, my voice steadier than I felt as I opened the door just a bit.

He nodded, a silent thank you passing between us, and I stepped back, allowing him just enough room to slip past the threshold. The door whispered shut behind him, its click a punctuation in the quiet of my apartment. He was wearing a dark suit tailored perfectly to his muscular frame, the official NYPD badge clipped onto his jacket. The sight of him in uniform gave a formal reality to the situation and amplified the tremors unsettling my nerves.

"Are you okay, Dr. Bentley?" he asked, eyeing me with a concern that felt too intimate.

"I'm fine," I retorted, crossing my arms over my chest defensively. "What do you want?"

The warmth here, usually so welcoming, now felt like a liar as it enveloped him. He looked around, taking in the details—my escape from the lab's sterility: colorful throw pillows, photos of my family, and a bookshelf littered with biotech journals beside classic novels. But tonight, the candles that usually brought soft light and comfort seemed to mock me with their dance, their shadows playing tricks on my walls.

Edward stood there, solid and real, his badge catching the candle-light. His body language had shifted since the hallway; he was tired, sure—but there was something else. Regret? Fear? Both were bad news.

"I wanted to check in on you after today's interrogation. You don't look well. You looked very...uh, nauseous."

He didn't know anything about my pregnancy.

"And what's that to you? My health is hardly your concern, Officer Rodriguez." I shot back, my tone harsher than intended. His eyebrows knitted together, casting a shadow over his intense gaze.

"Given the circumstances, I think it might be."

I didn't like his insinuation. I was a respected scientist, a pillar of integrity in my field. I had nothing to do with the illicit activities they were suddenly so interested in.

"I've done nothing wrong," I said tersely, holding his gaze. "Do you have any more questions?"

"Yes." Unfazed by my standoffish demeanor, he cleared his throat. "Do you trust everyone at BioHQ?"

"Yes," I said. "With my life."

He sighed. "Can I have some water?"

"Sure," I muttered, leading him into the open kitchen. I grabbed a glass from the cabinet and turned on the faucet, the gentle rush of water filling the silence. Edward watched me carefully, his gaze never wavering.

"Thank you," he said as I handed him the water. He drank it slowly, his eyes closing briefly before they opened again, focusing on me with an intensity that left me feeling exposed.

There was a moment of silence as he lowered his glass onto the counter. "I have reason to believe that BioHQ has been targeted by a criminal organization. Their interest seems to be in your work."

My chest tightened at his words. "What...what are you saying?"

His steady gaze met my wide-eyed one. "Your life might be in danger, Dr. Bentley."

The fear that had been simmering under my skin bloomed into a full-blown dread at his declaration. A shaky breath escaped me as I braced myself against the counter.

Edward's expression softened, watching my reaction. "I know this is hard to take in," he murmured, grappling for the right words. "But it is in your best interest to make it look like you're not collaborating with the police. Unless..."

"I don't understand. Aren't you the police?"

"Yes," he said. "But I also want you to stay alive long enough to help."

"What the fuck does that mean?"

"It means you're in over your head," he said, breaking the silence that had settled between us. His voice was low, carrying a weight that made my stomach churn. "You don't know the kind of man you're dealing with by getting involved with Dante Moretti."

That name. That damn name sent a chill through me, colder than any draft this old building could conjure.

"Edward, you need to leave," I said, my voice steady despite the chaos that threatened to erupt within me. "I can handle my business. It's not your concern."

But Edward didn't move, his eyes searching mine as if looking for a crack in my defenses, a sign of the vulnerability I was desperate to hide. "Jade, just listen—"

"Enough!" My words sliced through the air, sharp and brittle. "Just stop. I don't need your protection."

He took a step back, hands raised in a gesture of surrender that somehow felt more invasive than comforting. "Okay, Jade. But this isn't over. The Morettis play a long game; they won't let go easily. Be careful."

With that, he turned away, his figure retreating as he made his way to the door. I watched him go, my breaths shallow. As the door clicked shut behind him, a profound silence filled the room, punctuated by the gentle flicker of candlelight.

The scent of lavender hung heavily in the air, once soothing, now a bitter reminder of the danger I had unwittingly invited into my life. Dante Moretti—the man with a smile that could cut through the darkness, now cast as the villain in my story. How had I been so blind?

He was so good in bed he'd stolen my ID out from under me and I couldn't fucking believe it. I had been so naive.

The realization settled in, heavy and undeniable. I had been a pawn in a much larger game—one where the stakes were higher than I'd ever imagined. And Dante, with all his charm and enigmatic allure, had been the one to maneuver me into place.

As the last traces of daylight vanished beyond my window, I was left with nothing but the echo of Edward's warning and the gnawing doubt that clawed at my conscience. What had I gotten myself into?

How could I have been so naive? My search for answers led me here, to the heart of darkness itself, and now it was clear—I was out of my depth. These weren't just petty criminals or corrupt officials; this was the mafia, an entirely different beast. They played by rules I couldn't begin to fathom.

"Focus, Jade," I breathed, forcing myself to stand. I needed a plan, something to cling to in the chaos. The walls of my apartment felt too close, each shadow a lurking threat. I paced, every step a sharp rap against the hardwood floor, as I tried to shake off the suffocating dread.

"Think," I urged myself. "You're a scientist. You solve problems." But science had logic, variables I could control. This—this was madness.

I stopped at the window, peering out into the evening. The city was alive, indifferent to the turmoil within me. Lights flickered on in buildings as people went about their lives, unaware of the sinister undercurrent that flowed just beneath the surface.

The solution was terrifying. It was also clear.

I needed to get away.

Chapter Forty: Jade

I wrestled with my phone, the damn thing slippery as if it knew I was about to dive into something dangerous. My chest tightened, each breath a battle as Edward's last words still echoed somewhere in the pit of my stomach. The screen flickered to life, throwing ghostly patterns across the walls of my cramped New York apartment.

"Come on, come on," I muttered under my breath, heart knocking against my ribs like it was trying to break free. Then the ringing stopped, and the void on the other end of the line sucked all the air out of the room.

"Jade?" he asked.

"Dante," I spat out, unable to keep the tremor from my voice, "did you have something to do with the stolen data from the lab? Did you swipe my ID card?" Anger flared up, raw and biting, mixing with the fear that had settled in my gut.

The other side of the call stayed quiet, and I could almost imagine him there, Dante Moretti, with his unnervingly calm demeanor, weighing his words like they were gold. Seconds stretched into an eternity, and my pulse pounded a frantic rhythm—I counted four. ..five...six thumps, each louder than the last in my ears.

"I need to speak to you in person." The words slithered through the phone, Dante's tone unreadable as a poker face. My fingers clenched around the device so hard it hurt.

"Absolutely not," I shot back, venom seeping into every syllable. I felt cornered, wild, the way animals must feel when they're about to get their throats cut. The silence that followed was a living thing, thick and suffocating.

"Stay put. I'll see you soon," he said, his voice a steel cable that tethered me to the spot. There was no mistaking the command, the iron will behind the words. The line went dead before I could argue, leaving the apartment drowning in a quiet so heavy I could almost feel it on my skin.

I stood there, phone still pressed to my ear, the echo of Dante's last words haunting the static air. My heart hammered against my ribcage, demanding attention, demanding action. Dante Moretti was coming, and every instinct screamed at me to run, hide, disappear. But where does one hide when the shadows themselves are out for your blood?

My heart was a drumbeat out of sync, the rhythm jagged and frantic as I yanked open the closet door. Getting away was still the plan. I just needed to make sure to do it...right now.

The suitcase—a plain black affair with scuffed corners from too many conferences—came off the top shelf and landed with a thud that matched the chaos in my chest. Hands shaking, I flipped it open and started tossing in clothes.

I didn't care about folding or sorting; it was a mad dash against the clock. Jeans, shirts, my favorite sweater—the one that felt like a hug on cold nights—all thrown in without a second thought. I snatched my toothbrush from the bathroom, a handful of undergarments, then my laptop—my lifeline to the work that had consumed my life until now. Until him.

"Think, Jade, think," I muttered to myself, the words a lifeline as I rifled through drawers for my passport and any cash I had stashed away. Hotels, motels, anywhere with a bed and a lock would do, just somewhere to clear my head, to figure out my next move. My mind raced—calculations, escape routes, contingency plans—anything to stay one step ahead of Dante Moretti and his relentless grip on my world.

The dread knotted up inside me, dense and heavy, threatening to drag me down into panic. But I couldn't afford to lose it—not now. So I focused on the essentials, on survival, because that's what scientists did: we adapted, we evolved, we survived. And right now, survival meant getting the hell out of dodge before Dante decided my time was up.

My hand stilled on the zipper of my overstuffed suitcase as a knock, sharp and insistent, shattered the chaotic rhythm of my packing. My breath hitched, heart slamming against my ribs like it was hell-bent on escape. Edward's smug face flashed in my mind, but the terror that gripped me now was colder, more visceral.

I crept to the door on legs that felt like they were made of lead, every step deliberate, as if walking through water. Another knock, louder, more demanding, cut through the silence that had reclaimed my apartment.

Peering through the peephole, my gaze collided with Dante's—a man who could command an army with a look. His eyes, dark pools in the corridor's dim light, gave nothing away. I knew that expression.

I didn't like it.

"Jade," his voice filtered through the door, a low rumble that had once made my stomach flutter. Now, it only tightened the knot of dread lodged firmly in my throat.

I told myself that my best bet was to remain quiet. That I could pretend I wasn't there, that would be easier.

I tried to take deep breaths, to still my hammering heartbeat in case he could hear it.

Unfortunately, my body had other plans. Before the logical part of my mind could stop it, my hand reached out, twisting the doorknob until it relinquished its hold and swung the door open just a fraction, the chain snapping as it did.

"Dante," I whispered through the small gap. His muscular frame filled the rest of my view, his intimidating presence seeming to absorb all of the light in the hallway. His eyes met mine, and for a moment, I was lost in their depths, a deer trapped in the headlights of an oncoming truck.

"Why are you here?" I demanded.

"I told you. I wanted to talk."

"I don't want to talk to you. Go away."

"Jade, open the door," Dante commanded from the other side, his voice a mix of velvet and iron—impossible to ignore. My fingers coiled around the cool brass knob, every instinct screaming at me to bolt, but where would I go? I couldn't exactly leave my apartment through the fire escape.

"Give me a reason," I shot back, defiance flaring up to keep the panic at bay. "Because right now, you just seem like a fucking asshole."

There was a beat of silence, and I could almost hear him weighing his next words. "We need to talk, Jade. It's not what you think."

"Talk," I scoffed, a bitter laugh escaping me. "That's rich, coming from you. Talk now?" But even as anger fueled my words, doubt gnawed at me.

"Please," he said, a single word laced with an urgency that tugged at the edges of my resolve. There it was—the crack in his armor, the sincerity that made it hard to keep hating him.

"No," I said. "I'm not doing this."

But as I tried to close the door on him, he put his foot in the crack and stopped me.

"Just give me five minutes," he said.

"No!" Struggling against the pressure he was putting on the door, my heart pounded in my chest like a war drum, my hands slick with perspiration as I pushed with all my might. "You're not coming in."

But it was too late. In one swift motion, Dante had taken the chain off the door and shoved it open, stepping inside. His towering figure blotted out the faint illumination from the hall

"Five minutes, Jade." His voice was low but firm, his gaze holding mine hostage.

My throat was dry as I looked at him. "Okay," I said. "Five minutes. Then you leave."

He nodded, closing the door behind him.

And I was trapped.

Chapter Forty-One: Dante

B ut Jade didn't want to give me five minutes.

   She ran, which made me feel like shit. The door slammed shut behind me, a sound that echoed like a verdict in the tiny living room of Jade's apartment. My heart was pounding, but I kept my voice even as ice. "Jade, I'm serious. We need to talk."

She wasn't there in front of me, probably holed up somewhere in this cramped excuse for a home. The place was a stark contrast to the grandeur and calculated opulence I was raised in. Here, the furniture seemed to absorb the weak light from the lamp, making the shadows stretch long and thin across the walls.

I shifted on my feet, my jacket protesting with a soft creak, and my gaze landed on the worn-out couch. It was then that I saw them—the books and that damn prenatal vitamin bottle that made my stomach drop. Pregnancy guides looking like they'd been read a dozen times over and prenatal vitamins carelessly left out in the open.

The realization settled deep in my stomach before I managed to speak.

"Are you pregnant?" The question shot out of me before I could reel it in, my voice betraying the shock that was slamming into me. It wasn't supposed to go this way. Nothing about this night was going as planned.

But there was no answer.

She emerged like a specter from the shadows, standing near the window with the city skyline painting her in light and darkness. The silhouette of her body was outlined against the glass, arms crossed over her chest—a fortress of one.

"Jade," I said, my gaze darting between her and the books. "Tell me the truth."

"Yes," Jade confirmed, her tone flat but with an undercurrent of something I couldn't quite place. Was it fear? Defiance? All I knew was that the sight of her standing there, poised to flee, ignited a fire inside me.

"Yes? You're pregnant?"

"I am," she said.

"Jade, look at me," I commanded, my voice low and dangerous. She turned slowly, her eyes meeting mine. There was a flicker there, an uncertainty that she tried to mask with a hard set to her jaw.

"Was that your plan?" I nodded toward the open suitcase teetering on the edge of the couch, stuffed with clothes that screamed of quick decisions and desperation. "Were you planning to tell me or just disappear?"

For a moment, she said nothing, letting the question hang heavy between us. Then a cold silence spread through the room, only broken by the distant hum of traffic filtering in from the streets below. It was a familiar sound, one that usually brought comfort, but tonight it was just a reminder of all the ways life could go wrong.

"Answer me, Jade," I demanded, my hands clenching into fists at my sides. I had to fight to keep my composure, to keep from shaking her until the truth came out. My world was spinning, the foundations cracking, and she stood there, the catalyst of it all.

"Would it have made a difference?" Her voice was barely above a whisper, but it hit me like a punch to the gut. Would it have? I didn't know, and that uncertainty was the most terrifying thing of all. "You have your life and I have mine."

"Of course," I snapped, feeling the raw edge of betrayal slice through me. "Of course it would have made a difference!"

My thoughts churned like the East River during a storm, dark and unrelenting. The idea of her leaving—without a word, without a trace—stung worse than any wound I'd taken in the streets.

Jade's defiant spark didn't waver as I scrutinized her, trying to decipher the enigma wrapped in that curvy frame. She was an open book when it came to her research, but outside the lab, she was a fortress. And right then, her walls were up, the drawbridge pulled tight.

"Well, I can raise this baby by myself—"

"Doesn't matter now," I grumbled, stepping back as if the distance could dull the sharpness of the situation. "Look at me."

Jade's shoulders squared, her body language shifting into something more combative. It was clear she was readying for a fight, perhaps the most important one she'd ever faced. And damn if that didn't make her even more compelling.

"And what is it to you?" she shot back, those words edged with a defiance that sent a ripple of both anger and admiration through me.

"Everything," I admitted, the weight of my own confession anchoring me to the spot. "It's everything to me, Jade."

For a moment, neither of us spoke, the tension strung between us like a high wire. Outside the window, the neon glow of the city painted everything in surreal hues.

"Then you shouldn't have fucking used me," she said, her voice slicing through the silence. Her eyes never left mine, challenging, demanding—seeking an answer I wasn't sure I had.

"It just happened," I replied, the harsh truth of it tasting bitter on my tongue. "It would have been so much easier if I had just been using you, but I wasn't just using you, Jade. I...fuck, I care about you, okay? I love you."

She tilted her head. "If you loved me, you wouldn't have jeopardized my life's work...for what? Money?"

"It isn't just money," I said. "You don't understand. Biotechnology is my legacy. It's a way to get the Moretti name legitimacy. It's a..."

"A way to steal my research and use it for what, exactly?" Jade said, venom creeping into her voice.

"To do good, Jade!" The words burst from me. "I've been trying to change the Morettis, trying to find a way out of this life for myself, for you and now...for our child." I threw my hands up in frustration, raking them back through my hair.

She scoffed at that, her laughter a bitter sound slicing through the room. "Good? You think dragging BioHQ into this is good?"

"Will it make things better? No. But it's a start," I said slowly. "We can use my family's resources to advance your research beyond anyone's expectations. We can build a life together."

Jade glared at me. "You lied to me, Dante. You pretended you were someone you weren't. And now you're acting like I want this—what if I don't want this?"

My heart pounded in my ears at her words, each one a stinging slap. We stood staring at each other, both of us wounded, lashing out from fear and confusion.

"It's not pretending if the feelings are real," I said quietly, the truth of that hitting me like a freight train. It was true - the lies were a front, but what I felt for Jade was achingly, confusingly real.

She let out a harsh laugh, shaking her head. "It's clear you've made all the decisions here, Dante. You decided to get involved with BioHQ, you decided to hide your true identity from me, and you decided to risk everything I've worked for. You don't get to play innocent now."

A flood of guilt washed over me at her words. She was right. I had made those decisions, not thinking about the potential fallout, only seeing the benefits they could bring. I'd gambled with her trust, using it as collateral without her knowing.

"But this is my body. This is my baby. I get to make this decision," she continued.

I shook my head as I looked at her. And in that charged space, I realized that regardless of her reasons, I couldn't let her slip through my fingers—not now, not ever. Because whatever Jade was running from, or to, it was my job to make sure she faced it with me by her side. Whether she liked it or not.

And this wasn't just her baby.

They were my baby, too.

I took a step closer, the hallway seeming to shrink with the intensity of my purpose. The door to her bedroom was ajar, revealing the hastily packed bags that betrayed her plans to run. "You're coming with me, now," I commanded, my voice as hard as the resolve setting in my bones.

"No, Dante." Her refusal was a whisper, but it might as well have been a shout for the way it stoked the fire in my chest. I reached out, my fingers curling around her wrist with an iron grip, and I pulled her toward me.

She tried to wriggle out of my grip.

"Don't make a scene," I said. "I can do this nicely or I can do it hard, but I need to keep you safe. You and our child."

"You're hurting me," she hissed, trying to pull her wrist back.

I loosened my grip but didn't let go. The last thing I wanted was to hurt her, but circumstances called for desperate measures.

I pulled her out of her apartment. "Where are you taking me?"

I only had a vague idea. I needed to hide her away from my own family, away from the Carusos. I needed to make sure she had this baby.

I needed to keep her safe.

And if that meant locking her up in one of my apartments so she couldn't leave until she had our baby...well, then that was exactly what I was going to fucking do.

KEEP READING IN IVORY CROWN

Made in United States
Orlando, FL
05 October 2024

52251548R00183